Steven Sherrill, an Assistant Professor of English at Penn State, Altoona, earned an MFA in Poetry from the Iowa Writers' Workshop and was the recipient of a National Endowment for the Arts Fellowship for Fiction in 2002. His work has appeared in *Best American Poetry*, *The Kenyon Review* and *The Georgia Review*. He is also the author of *The Minotaur Takes a Cigarette Break* (Canongate, 2003). He lives in Pennsylvania.

Visits From the Drowned Girl

Steven Sherrill

CANONGATE

Edinburgh · New York · Melbourne

First published in Great Britain in 2004 by
Canongate Books Ltd, 14 High Street,
Edinburgh EH1 1TE

This edition published in 2005

10 9 8 7 6 5 4 3 2 1

British Library Cataloguing-in-Publication Data
A catalogue record for this book is available on
request from the British Library

ISBN 1 84195 599 X

Typeset in Janson by Palimpsest Book Production Limited,
Polmont, Stirlingshire
Printed and bound by Nørhaven Paperback A/S, Denmark

Text design by James Hutcheson

www.canongate.net

To Maude, always.

Chapter 1

BENNY POTEAT HAS SEEN A LOT OF THINGS.

Benny PO-teat has seen a lot of things.

Benny Poteat has seen a LOT of things.

Almost NOTHING would surprise him.

Almost nothing would SURPRISE him.

ALMOST.

Emphasis is negotiable, and emphasis is everything.

Of the vast array of things Benny Poteat would claim to have *seen* in his life, the ones he'd consider formative, the handful, or less, of those experiences one tends to have while hurtling blindly through the banalities of day-to-day existence, moments that leap so suddenly, so forcefully into your path that you career off them two or three degrees into a different sort of future than before – for better or worse, who can say – most of *those* things he's witnessed from above. That day, as with countless days before it, from two hundred feet up, the Carolina Piedmont spread out 360° around him, county bleeding into county: dogwood, pitch pine and red dirt hills for mile after mile. It was Spring, wet and fecund. Benny Poteat had been climbing towers, legally, since he was fifteen years old, and fifteen years later he still loved the struggle between the late-March winds and the rigid metal framework he buckled himself to Monday through

Thursday, weather permitting, well into winter. So, while it's true that Benny Poteat had seen a lot of things from up there, mostly he just did his job, and bore witness to hour upon mundane hour, in, sometimes vertiginous, solitude. He was rarely prepared for the extraordinary. In fact, he'd be hard pressed to come up with anything that could have prepared him, truly prepared him, for what he saw that day.

Off in the distance, the perimeters of Buffalo Shoals were defined on one end by the harsh silver dome of the water tower Benny painted just last summer, and at the other by the tall rusting hoppers and conveyors at the defunct Purina factory. Goat, swine, and other small mammal foods. Counting the drivers, almost eighty jobs lost. Somewhere behind him, Benny knew that the pitted quartzite crags of Crowder's Mountain jutted skyward, in places, six hundred feet higher than the surrounding hills. It was a tired and crumbling relic of some ancient, grand range of mountains that made its tectonic march across the land long before any humans ever trod there. Now, Crowder's Mountain, with its token of a name, claimed its position of power in smaller, more provincial ways. At least three times a year some fool fell to his death. A cocky climber, too cool for ropes and other safety equipment. Drunken frat boys from Piedmont College. The occasional depressive. Mostly men; boys really. The worn out little mountain seemed to eat them. Depending on who you asked, Crowder's might or might not be the starting point of the Blue Ridge Foothills.

Between him and the town, maybe two miles away, Benny could see a gouge in the pine and poplar forests; the hills and gullies stripped of all usable wood for pulp. What remained was ravaged red clay earth, stripped limbs and the shattered trunks of the trees too small or gnarled to be of any value. Acres and acres of this wasteland, cut by dozer tracks and deep muddy ruts left by the logging trucks when they chuffed and chugged out for the last time. Like a war zone, Benny thought. Not that he'd ever seen one. But, because he was prone to lapses into fantasy, he kept thinking in that vein. War zone.

This would be a good vantage spot. He could see enemy movement for miles in every direction. Planes. Tanks. Ground troops. He'd radio headquarters. He'd stay in position as long as it took. Purple Heart. Medal of Honor. Taps. Every girl he ever fantasized over weeping at his graveside.

Boredom was one of the more benign hazards of the job.

It took an adamant gust of that March wind to bring Benny back to the task at hand, a gust that roared through the tower's metal frame with the pitch of a jet engine, and sung in the guy wires Benny was checking for Bard's Communications. Despite its anchoring guys, the tower succumbed, just a little, to the wind. It swayed. Despite his years of experience, and despite the leather harness and carabineers holding him in place, Benny nearly dropped a wrench as he grabbed for the rungs at his chest.

'Shit!'

On a guyed tower, *masts* they're called, the vertical structure is often less than two feet across. Square, or triangular, the entire apparatus, made of channel iron or tubing, is held erect by a series of woven metal guy wires equally spaced up each side of the tower and angling off down to the ground where they terminate in massive concrete pillars sunk deep in the earth. From tower to guy, to pillar, to earth. The number of guys depends on the height of the tower. There were mornings, rare and sweet, when he came to the job site early and saw the tower rising up out of a silent, reluctant fog; it looked for all the world like the guy wires and chunks of concrete were all that kept the towers from lifting, no, hurtling, skyward, rocket-like, through our own shallow atmosphere and beyond. Propelled by what? The sheer beauty of their construction.

Other mornings, less rare, Benny was acutely aware that the masts he perched on came to an impossibly small, triangulated point at the base; the precarious balance at the mercy of properly maintained guy wires.

More wind. Benny held to a rung with his gloved left hand, while the right hand checked the turnbuckles of the uppermost guy, north side, for correct tension. Each time the wrench clanked against the metal frame, the note rang up and down the tower and out through the sky for miles.

Benny Poteat had seen a lot of things. As a kid, mostly unsupervised, though not out of apathy or unconcern, he'd regularly climbed the water towers in Buffalo Shoals and the surrounding towns. By the time he was a teen, the communications industry had gained momentum, so the type and number of towers available for climbing was dizzying. Every time the police called him down off the towers, put him in the backseat of their cruisers, and took him back to his Uncle Nub's, Benny got the lecture about, the threat of, Jackson Training School.

Judging by the sun rolling doggedly overhead, it was almost lunchtime. Benny clipped the wrench to his tool belt then took a long gulping pull from the water bottle he kept holstered at his back. Benny was a lean but well-hydrated man. He took a minute to gage his hunger. He took another minute to gage the wind's direction before unzipping his jeans and wrestling his penis around the leg-strap of the harness. He pissed. East side. Sometimes he urinated out into the air, marveling at the fluid geometry that caught and toyed with sunlight as it fell earthward. That morning his pumpkin-colored van was parked just below, and Squat, his decrepit dachshund, was asleep in the shade of its wheels. The likelihood of his urine actually reaching the ground 200 feet immediately below him was, given the wind, slim at best. And, both the van and the dog would suffer little, possibly even benefit, from a bath of any kind. Nevertheless, Benny Poteat wasn't taking chances. He aimed his stream down the east side guy wire where, in the protective runnels of the taut woven wire, some of it would no doubt reach the terminus and pool at the top of the concrete pylon embedded near the bank of the Big Toe River.

This particular tower, the first and tallest of all Bard's towers, was Benny's favorite for a number of reasons. It was forty-five minutes from town, even with good traffic; the gravel access road snaked almost two miles into the woods, so while the tower was a popular drinking spot on Friday and Saturday nights, through the week Benny Poteat could work in peace; and he could take a leak without having to climb all the way down. But the thing he liked most was the water. The tower stood on the wide wedge of land at the confluence of the Big and Little Toe Rivers. Benny could hear the water, even from the top of the tower. The access road paralleled the straighter path of the Big Toe from just past the bridge on Plank Road, sweeping around the big willows that grew along the banks. Fifty yards beyond where the gravel road ended abruptly in an irregular circle that collared the tower's base and the sagging chain link fence that pretended to secure it, the Little Toe River spilled out of a stone-choked gully, slowed in a loblolly of pines and cattails before feeding into its sibling. It was spring, a very rainy one. The whole earth seemed soggy. The water in both rivers, swift and muddy, was so high that the banks seemed absent. Mere notions. The transition from land to water was seamless.

Benny Poteat shook himself off, then reconfigured his package behind the harness. Calculating the time it would take to finish the job, against the time it would take to climb down and eat his tomato sandwich, he decided to keep working. Using two hooked fingers, he whistled for Squat. When the old dog waddled from beneath the van Benny said 'Good dog,' though not loud enough for anything to hear. After a few minutes, Squat waddled back to the shade. Benny spat twice, but the dual tastes of line grease and urine lingered in his mouth.

Funny, how memory works. Benny recalled another spring day, the last year he attended high school. It was Mrs Dishman's English class, and they were studying mythology. He remembered some god impregnated a lady through a *shower of golden rain*. Benny said it aloud, because he liked the way it sounded. *A shower of golden rain*. Then Debbie Cranks rubbed her belly and said 'that's exactly what happened to me,' and everybody laughed. Even Mrs Dishman. Benny remembered it clearly, and he remembered that Debbie's baby was stillborn, but he couldn't remember the god's name. Maybe he'd stop by the library on the way home.

A lot of people would be surprised that Benny knew anything like this. Benny Poteat was a closet thinker. Sometimes, when he was in a thinking mood, he speculated that there were only a handful pure *things* that happened on the earth, sort of a distillate of experience, and over and over again, through generations and time, they get repeated in different variations. He tried to write the idea down one time but on paper it didn't make any sense. Up there, though, two, three, five, seven hundred feet in the air, with nothing but jute rope or a thin leather harness and couple carabineers to hold him in case of a slip, in case of a missed step at a steel rung while re-lamping a radio tower, or stretching just one inch too far for balance while painting the hot dome top of a water tank, up there you got a clarity of perspective unlike anything to be found at ground level.

Sometimes it took a lot to surprise Benny Poteat.

Just last week he was repositioning a satellite dish on a low tower across the Interstate from one of those strip malls that seem to be proliferating along every four-lane road in the country, particularly where the stink of money is high. *New South*, they call it. Benny could clearly see the backs of the stores: the dumpsters, the busted pallets, the Styrofoam packing peanuts strewn everywhere. He could see all this stuff so clearly because it was new to him. He didn't look at it every day. On the other hand, the people who came and went on the loading docks and through the back doors of the stores were so certain of the presence of the radio tower across the road that it became invisible. It and anybody clinging to the top of it. Benny Poteat watched two guys come out of the back of the Container Store. Both wore jeans, white shirts, and ridiculously colorful ties.

The men immediately began to fight, a fist fight with serious intent. He couldn't hear the men speaking, maybe they weren't, but he heard flesh and bone connect. Before long the smaller of the two men landed a solid two-punch to the chest and jaw of the other. And when the bigger, defeated man fell into a stack of cardboard boxes, gasping for breath, the little guy helped him stand then knelt down and fellated him. Right there, in front of God and everybody. Took about two minutes, and Benny watched as the big man's hands came around to cradle the giver's head as he finished. Then they both went back inside. But, while entertaining, none of that really surprised Benny.

'What a big old goofy world,' he said to no one.

Nor was Benny surprised, on this day, by the distant appearance, across the Big Toe River, of a person making his or her slow way out of the woods and down the opposite access road toward the water. Probably some yahoo coming to fish for channel catfish where the rivers meet. As long as Benny could remember, people have talked of 'catfish big as Volkswagens' cruising the riverbed there, lurking and stealthy in the muddy flow; waiting for cats, small dogs, or toddlers, but way too smart for ham hocks tied to meat hooks. Nobody he knew ever caught one. Probably some third-shift linthead from the Mill, coming to fish, but Benny couldn't see, and didn't care anyway.

Tower work is rife with horror stories. During construction, a snapped guy wire can send a tower crashing down, can wreak apocalyptic havoc on the jobsite and the crew. It doesn't happen often, not with professional crews anyway. Benny had only witnessed it once. But sometimes catastrophe is bound and determined to happen. A more likely occurrence is some tower jockey – hung over, distracted, or just plain stupid – doesn't pay attention to his safety harness. How messy the whole affair is depends on how many rungs and guy wires he bounces off on the way to the ground, and then, what he lands on. Benny had seen that happen a couple times too. He'd known at least one man to jump. It crosses everybody's mind, but not all of them would admit it.

Benny wouldn't want anybody to get the wrong idea, however; there's ample beauty in his line of work. He'd seen baptisms, outdoor weddings and dogfights. Sunsets and sunrises you couldn't beat. A partial eclipse. Once, he watched a red-winged hawk drop out of the top of a poplar tree, hit the ground a hundred yards away and come up with a field mouse in its talons. But before the hawk reached the safety of its perch, an audacious little mockingbird angled in and landed on its back, right between those powerful outstretched wings. Then the whole lot flew so close to Benny on the tower that he heard the mouse squealing in terror; saw its absurd pink feet clawing the sky; he felt the stir of wind whipped by the hawk's wings; and he saw the malice in the mockingbird's black eye.

A couple years ago, Benny watched a field of broomstraw catch fire. It was early Fall, still hot and dry. Benny was re-lamping a radio tower near the state line. On one side a hilly apple orchard rolled over the horizon; to the other, farther away and beyond a copse of pines, acres of waist-high broom straw, already yellowing into the season, genuflected to the slightest breeze. There was no visible road to the field. There were no people around. It was after noon and blue saturated the sky. Benny saw the smoke first, stuttering tentatively near the field's center. Then the conflagration leapt, more orange than anything had ever been, toward heaven. Benny watched the flame spread in an uneven circle through the grass. It's core grew, smoldering and black, to eventually consume most of the field. Benny felt real close to God then.

What does it mean to *see* a thing? Benny asked his friend

Jeeter that question once. Jeeter told him to shut up. One thing Benny couldn't do was see into the future, and he wouldn't want to. But he worked hard on his ability to look clearly at the past. That took more effort than most people realize.

Another time, Benny saw three girls sunbathing topless on the roof of an apartment building in town. He was too far away for any real satisfaction, but since then he'd started carrying a small pair of binoculars in a leather case clipped to his tool belt. The binoculars were in their case, on his back, that day up on Bard's tower. Down below, Squat barked at something off in the woods, but never bothered coming from under the van. When Benny looked again across the river, the walker had gotten closer. Close enough for him to tell that it was a woman, and she carried no fishing rod. She wore a long baggy tee shirt; Benny couldn't read what was written on the shirt, but he could tell it was a woman wearing it. She wore a backpack with straps, clipped in the middle, laying between and defining where her breasts ought to have been. Itty bitty titty club, Benny thought. And, there was something funny about her gait. She walked unsteadily, tired like. Not drunken, but it seemed that each step took more planning than it ought to.

Benny liked the thin, skeletal towers best of all, and liked them most when it's windy. When he was a kid, the fat water towers were exciting enough, with their heavy, enclosed ladders. Now, painting a tower, even the famous ones like the Gaffney Peach, which if you're honest about it looks like a 100-foot-wide ass with a silly leaf grafted at the top of the crack, bored him. Despite the fact that people drove for miles to see that thing, he hated water tower jobs. He reckoned it was the risk that drew him to the higher, open framed towers. But, he'd never consider himself foolhardy.

There are a few things Benny had experienced from up high that he never told another soul about. Sometimes, in late summer, storms come up quick. The distant threat of bad weather wasn't enough to keep him grounded, but nobody in their right mind wanted to be three hundred feet up a metal pole during a thunderstorm. *Right mind*, however, is awfully subjective. Benny just wanted to get done that day. Three summers ago, it was Friday, and he normally didn't do tower work on Friday because he worked for his uncle Nub on the weekends. But the flashing beacon and two other bulbs had burned out at the very top of a tower not too far from the county airport. Leaving the dead bulbs in place for the weekend was a dangerous proposition, because of all the weekend flying lessons. All Benny had to do was go up and change the bulbs. He knew the weather report called for something wicked, but even without the weather band radio harping away, or the little beep-beep-beep of the warning that scrolled across the bottom of the TV screen, Benny could've predicted an afternoon storm. It had been hot, sweltering hot for three days in a row, and no rain. They were due.

'Come on, Benny,' his boss said on the telephone. 'You're quicker than anybody else. Forty-five minutes minimum, hour and a half max. That's all it would take.'

Benny hesitated, just to hesitate. He knew he'd do the job.

'It can't wait till tomorrow. You know that, don't you?'

By the time Benny got to the site, he could see the storm clouds banking on the southern horizon. By the time he got in harness, all he could smell was ozone. The storm was a mile or more away, so the sky overhead was clear, but the color shift had already occurred; everything that could reflect light did so with a yellowish pall. Forty-five minutes; maybe an hour. The wind picked up when he was halfway to the top of the rungs. Benny hurried. Because he was in a hurry, he clipped himself to the tower at intervals of twenty-five feet, or more, instead of the usual ten feet. Besides, Benny never fell. He watched a wall of heavy rain overtake a small dairy farm a quarter of a mile from the tower. The cows got nervous when the thunder started; they trudged single file toward the barn. With one bulb changed, the mist that moved ahead of the rainfall cooled Benny's face.

He'd forgotten to roll up the windows in his van. Oh well. Benny let the second bulb, the burned one, drop to the ground. Even through the gut-rumbling thunder, he heard the bulb explode on impact with whatever it hit. Before Benny made it to the top bulb, the most important one, he was in the thick of the storm. All the towers are grounded, so Benny wasn't that afraid of the lightning. But Lord, the wind, and the thunder, and the heartless black of the clouds so thick he could no longer see the trees, the field, his van nor the ground below him. Benny went to reach for the last rung. He knew he'd clipped the carabineers in place. He remembered doing it. But he never expected such a gust of wind, such a thunderclap that seemed to have him at its core. Benny fell. It scared the hell out of him. Despite the carabineers. Despite his good common sense, and plenty experience. Benny felt himself lose grip, slip away from the tower and begin that most serious dance with gravity.

So why is Benny still climbing towers? What happened next was the thing he couldn't get a grip on.

Benny fell, two times the distance from the last

carabineer. All he saw was black cloud shot through by the steel tower. He felt the rush of wind swelling in his ears. He felt the surge of heart and belly. Then it stopped. He stopped. He wasn't falling any longer. There was no sudden gut-wrenching jerk. There should have been, but there wasn't. He didn't slam against the metal tower frame, didn't have his breath knocked out of his body. He should have slammed against the tower, but he didn't. He just stopped falling. Found himself holding on lower on the tower, as if he'd been placed there. Benny was clipped to the tower, sixty, maybe seventy feet from the top. He held on and cried until the storm passed. Benny considered himself as good a heathen as anybody else, but sometimes you have to consider the alternatives.

One time, when they were both drunk, Benny asked Jeeter if he believed in angels.

'Shut up, Benny.'

That was the closest Benny ever came to talking about it. All the other reasons he's still climbing towers is anybody's guess. For sure, the woman across the river wouldn't have the slightest idea, because she apparently didn't see Benny at the top of the tower. And his van was probably obscured by the fence and by the tower base itself.

Benny wanted to get done with the day's work. Doodle, one of the waitresses at Nub & Honey's, and Benny's neighbor, asked for help moving her fish tank. He didn't really want to, but he planned to do it right after work. To get it over with.

From so far away, and so high above, Benny couldn't discern much about the woman who'd laboriously walked all the way down the long dirt road and had stopped on the opposite bank of the river. She must have walked three, maybe four miles. To Benny's limited sight, each step seemed a chore. In addition to her pack, the woman carried something else slung over her back. Later, he might give himself time to wonder why. When Benny heard the sharp click click click of the tripod legs locking into place across the river, he figured the woman to be some arty type out to take pictures of the high water. It had rained all month. The water churned through the landscape, gorgeous in its ferocity.

If he wasn't in such a hurry, if he wasn't distracted, or if the woman had interested him more, Benny might have reached for his binoculars. As it was, he didn't go to the trouble. Not when she attached her camera. Not when she positioned then repositioned the tripod, leaned into the eyepiece to set the view. Benny realized then that it was a video camera she looked through. From his distant perspective, it seemed she was filming a random spot on the river. He didn't reach for the binoculars when she walked to the riverbank directly in front of the camera. Nor when she pulled the tee shirt over her head and dropped it beside the backpack, then did the same, less gracefully, with her pants and underwear. Understand, Benny would postpone most anything for a naked woman. But by the time he noticed the oddity of her leg – left? right? he was too befuddled to tell – something was wrong and before Benny could figure out what it was, she had walked into the water.

'Hey!' Benny thought this as loudly as possible. Stupid. It's stupid to swim when the water's so high. The important point is that she didn't swim. She didn't dive, but neither did she pronate and embrace the surface of the water. The woman simply walked into the water. With no apparent distress. And without hesitation. No hint of anguish. And, without hesitation, the water, swift and muddy, betraying no confidence, took her in. She just disappeared.

'Hey!' Benny may have said it aloud this time.

He reached around to fumble with the clasp on the binocular case. Realized it was pointless.

On the riverbank, the tripod stood dutifully. Beside it, a pile of clothing, absurdly empty now. And the backpack.

Benny Poteat had seen a lot of things. Almost nothing surprised him. But that day, that woman, that camera . . . What do you do after watching someone die? After watching someone kill themselves?

Benny finished what he had to do on the tower.

Chapter 2

What do you do after watching someone die?
Benny Poteat played the scene over and over in his head.
Over and over as he climbed down the tower.

She walked. She walked into the water. She walked into
the water and drowned.

'Hey!' he'd thought. A pre-conscious act, however
small, registering Benny's awareness that what happened
shouldn't have.

Benny made a list. It's a thing he did when he was
nervous: ball cap, cowboy hat, porkpie, bowler, top hat,
straw hat, hard hat, pillbox . . . he couldn't think of
any more.

She walked into the water. She walked into the water
and drowned.

'Good dog,' he said to Squat, who waddled from beneath
the van. Benny slid the side door open and lifted the dog in.
Squat jumped from Benny's arms into the passenger seat
and lay down, panting from the effort.

'Hey!' he'd said to the girl, but it made no difference.

Benny put his harness and tools in the wooden box that
slides out from under the bed at the van's back door.
What else do you do after watching a woman die? Benny
locked the gate to the tower's fence. It was really none
of his business, what that girl did. Besides, somebody else

probably saw it. Benny realized the absurdity of this, even before he finished the thought.

Another version: 'Hey!' he said to the girl, just as her foot touched the roiling surface of the water, and she paused. She paused. One insistent toe skimming the water. 'Hey!' he said, and she didn't look up, but she paused, mid-step, until Benny climbed and clanked down the tower, drove helter-skelter up one side of the riverbank, across the bridge at Plank Road, and down the other dirt road to where she stood before the tripod and camera. Naked. Balanced. Impossibly balanced. Until Benny realized, in that moment, it wasn't only her frozen in hesitation. Everything. Everything. Overhead, two juncos hung in mid-air before a backdrop of static clouds. The sun spun in place, tracking nowhere. Surely, the sap stopped rising in the trees. And the river itself ceased its flow: gape-mouthed minnows suspended in the non-current; turtles, driftwood, snake doctors and the cattails' sway, detritus of every sort, marked the stillest time. Inanimate, everything awaited Benny's arrival.

'Hey!' he said again, but in that version too, things had gone too far. Before he could reach out and touch her flesh, the juncos continued their swoop to catch the snake doctor in flight as it hovered over the cattails; the sun engaged its orbit, which in a roundabout way, drew the sap up through the trees; minnows dithered and flitted in river's spill; and she walked into the water and drowned. The lopsided moment, as they always do, rectified itself. Benny would swear he heard the cogs and gears meshing.

'Hey!' Benny said, in still another translation of the story. And the woman stopped her walk into the water. She turned, shielded her eyes from the midday sun, to look for Benny at the top of the tower. 'Wait!' he said.

'I'll be right there,' he said. She folded her muddy legs beneath her and sat on the bank, and was still there, naked and patiently waiting when he pulled up in the van. Benny helped her dress. They didn't talk much. Benny took her to her apartment, but they decided she'd be better off with him. Benny told her she didn't need to bring any of her own stuff. She said Ok. Benny got her a job at Nub & Honey's, waiting tables. She made good tips. Once a week they made love in the van, because it reminded them of that day.

What do you do? In the world as real as Benny could know it, when he got there, on the other side, those versions of what happened were far from true. The world and its messy business hadn't paused for this moment, significant or not. Hadn't even slowed. She wasn't sitting cross-legged on the bank, waiting for him. All that remained was a tripod and camera, some clothes, and a backpack.

Benny opened the side door of the van; Squat jumped out. The dog grunted as his low-slung belly hit the dirt.

'Good dog.'

For a fleeting instant, Benny wished for a cell phone. A lot of good it would do now. Maybe he shouldn't even have come. Maybe he should've just driven right on down Plank Road to Buffalo Shoals. But there he was. Once there, Benny didn't know what to do. He made another list: spit, shit, tit, kit, lit, pit, clit, wit, sit, slit, shit . . . If you repeat a word, you have to stop. Benny tripped, his fat work boot hanging in a rut in the dirt road. Almost fell on the dog. He flushed, hung his head, as if there might actually be somebody five miles out in the middle of nowhere waiting to laugh at him.

What do you do when you see such a thing? This death.

Benny looked around. For what, who knows. He walked to the riverbank. Stood right on the spot where she stepped off. He could tell by her footprints. Except that there was only one clear footprint: the right one. The other, her left, showed no delineation of toes. No lines on the sole or heel. Nevertheless, that ghost of a footprint too, led into the water.

'Hey!' Benny said. He yelled it that time. Out over the flowing river. There was no answer.

Benny picked up her clothes. Both hands. He smelled them, the whole bunch. The walk had made her sweat. Jesus! Benny loved the smell of a woman's sweat. He wished he could tell her that. Wondered if it would have made a difference. He felt a little pathetic.

Even before Benny got to the video camera on its tripod, he heard it running. Humming almost. One time, when he was little, Nub held him up to a plank wall of an old building. Told him to listen. Benny pressed his ear to the splintery gray wood. From within came the most beautiful, most mysterious sound he'd ever heard. 'Might be wood fairies,' Nub said. 'Or termites.'

That's what the camera sounded like. Benny felt his stomach pitch and yaw. He didn't want to touch the video camera, but he scowled at it long enough to find the *off* button. It's silence shrieked in Benny's ears. The only other thing there was the backpack. Was it wrong for Benny to root through this dead woman's possessions? Or, did she abdicate her right to privacy through her act? Or, did she have no need, possibly even disdain for the notions of privacy? At some point, Benny stopped trying to figure it out. He took everything over to the van, he emptied the contents of the backpack on its floor. Squat stood with his truncated legs up on the door channel.

One. Two. Three. Five. Six. Eight videotapes, labeled and dated. An extra camera battery and a business card:

> Claxton Looms Apartments
> 3 Shuttlecock Court
> Rebecca Hinkey, Resident Manager

Something was familiar about the card. Maybe the address. Maybe the name. Benny was in no state to figure things out. He put all the tapes back into the pack. On each shoulder strap, a small pin: one reading *potters do it on the wheel*; the other, *hung like a horse*. There was no wallet. No license or ID of any kind. No letter, no written note. No photos. No chapstick, keys, tampons, sunglasses. No aspirin bottles, no spare change. Only the business card. Benny folded the dead girl's clothes, neatly, and put them in the pack with the tapes. He lay the business card on the faux wood console sitting atop the engine cover between the van's front seats. Benny knew the address. Sort of. He lifted Squat back into the van.

CHAPTER 3

BENNY LAID THE OPTIONS OUT AS HE DROVE. THINK-ing, in the van, was difficult, particularly on warm days. Not long after he bought it, from Nub's cousin Sweeny – who always had something for sale in his front yard – Benny stripped the heater control knobs. So no matter how he configured the plastic grilles, hot air continually blew out at his feet and up through the defrost vents. A short time later, the on/off switch for the radio relinquished its power, and stuck *on*. 'She's got one helluva sound system,' Sweeny had said, and pointed to speakers in the doors and built into the paneled walls at several places in the back of the van. It was one of the selling points. Now, the din of the radio babble – almost, but not quite, out of earshot – filled the van whenever the ignition key was on. Benny usually kept it tuned to WSOL, *Your Light to Jesus*, for no other reason than it kept him a little edgy and mad. At least that's the only reason Benny would give you.

He could go by Nub & Honey's. Honey would know the 'decent' thing to do.

He could go straight to the address on the card: Claxton Looms Apartments.

He could go home, and try to think clearly about what to do.

Or, he could just drive out to the trash dump, throw

the backpack and everything else into the compactor, and forget about the whole ordeal. Eventually, calling the police occurred to him. Maybe he'd do just that. He'd stop at the next convenience store, get a snack, and call the police. It'd be good to get out of the van.

Sweeny gave him a sweet deal on the 1972 Dodge. The paint job, a high-gloss orange with black pinstripes, had lost some of its luster over time, and Benny liked the custom work, more than he'd admit: a moon roof and a tinted porthole window on each side; along the driver's side a long smoky mirror and two small cabinets hung over a sink, a broken refrigerator. The walls and doors in the van covered in button-and-tuck Naugahyde, a cheap vinyl upholstery fabric, red as new blood.

'Them's highway miles,' Sweeny said when Benny climbed up into the high bucket seat behind a steering wheel shaped like a miniature ship's helm. He looked in the rearview mirror, but couldn't see out the back because of the orange velvet curtains hung to provide privacy in the low bed at the rear of the van. 'No telling when you might have to lay down,' Sweeny said when he saw Benny looking in the rearview mirror. They had a little laugh together, each man making assumptions about the other. Benny gave Sweeny $350 that day, and paid him once a month until the van was his free and clear. The only real change he'd made was replacing the shag carpet with a piece of indoor/outdoor he cut to fit with scissors and glued down with Liquid Nails. And that he did because Squat peed several times on the floor between the two center seats. He'd like to get a CD player someday.

Benny reached over to Squat in the passenger seat. The dog rolled belly up for a scratch. Acutely aware of his cargo lying just out of reach in the back, Benny drove carefully. Much more carefully than usual. Like he was protecting something. Coming from the south, once you went under the by-pass, Plank Road was Buffalo Shoals' business corridor. Halfway to town, Benny thought his feet were going to melt inside his leather work boots. Those steel safety toes got hot as ovens beneath the van's heater. Benny pulled off the road at the first open business he passed. Squat sat up in the seat, panting expectantly, when Benny came to a stop against the concrete curb at Pandora's Back Door, Open 25 Hours a Day. He'd driven by the place countless times, but never stopped. Benny wrestled his boots off, socks too, then opened the door and hung his feet out to cool.

'You stay here,' he said to Squat.

Maybe this wasn't the best place to pull over. There was a 7-11 just a few more miles down the road. But maybe Benny saw it as a test, a penance of sorts, for not doing more to stop the girl. The mirrored windows promised that *all the best stuff happened in the extra hour. Adult novelties beyond belief. Largest selection of videos this side of the state line. More magazines than you could shake a stick at.* All in huge, white, grocery store font letters. Benny just hoped they had a telephone. Walking barefoot across the sun-baked asphalt, he dodged broken glass and cigarette butts to the front door. Before the yank was complete, the smells of soured mop-water and Clorox, made heavy and cool by the air conditioner he heard struggling away somewhere out of sight, those and the smells of cigarette smoke, musty paper, and general rank maleness hit him full force the second he stepped inside.

'Cain't come in without shoes!' The voice called, too fast, from the back of the store.

'You got a payphone?' Benny walked towards it's source,

which as far as he could tell, was an oversized, long sleeve flannel shirt.

'What?' It came from back near a cash register, through a maze of shelves and display racks whose goods Benny, for the moment, lacked the wherewithal to peruse.

'You got a payphone?' The tile floor was gummy, gritty, and cool.

'What?'

Benny finally picked out a head, large, and either bald or so blonde and cropped as to appear thus. When the clerk spoke again, the black gape of his mouth helped Benny get his bearings.

'Read that sign! Cain't come in without shoes.'

The problem was due in large part to the man's skin. He was huge, of indeterminate age, and the great mass of visible skin – his head and hands – was so pale that it, in the all-encompassing wash of light from the ample fluorescent bulbs and from the array of flashing marquees advertising this special or that delight, in all the busyness, his flesh just disappeared. Benny took a deep breath and spoke.

'You wouldn't believe what I just saw.'

'What!?'

'I saw something.'

'What?!'

By then he stood at the cash register facing the clerk. Each time the man barked 'what' he cocked his head toward Benny and leaned closer. Deaf, Benny thought for a brief moment. Thought it with some pity until he saw the quarter in the man's ear. A shiny new 25¢ piece, stood tucked behind the tragus, that little flap of skin at the front of the ear canal, and resting on the auricle. Heads. What could it mean? Something about the wages of sin? The cost of redemption? Benny decided he couldn't fight this battle. It was this ear the man turned to Benny's predicament.

'You got a payphone!?' he shouted, directly into George Washington's tiny ear.

'Outside!'

Benny hadn't seen it on the way in.

'Can I get change?'

'What!?'

Benny pulled the tight ball of a dollar bill from his pocket.

'No change!' The man pointed to the front of the cash register where a shop-worn index card bearing this scribbled message hung by a strip of duct tape: No change without purchase.

Benny looked closely at the man. He wondered about the kind of *things* this man had seen. Quality and quantity. At the register, haphazardly displayed, was a selection of unguents, salves, and potions, most working to death the -glide, or -lube, or -probe suffixes. Remembering his hunger, Benny grabbed the only edible products within easy reach: two sticks of turkey jerky, and a penis-shaped chocolate lollipop. Balls and all.

'You got any other shapes?' Benny asked, pointing the chocolate at the clerk.

'No.'

'You got anything to drink?'

'No'

Benny paid for his purchases.

'You cain't come in here without shoes.'

While the initial transition from the parking lot to the store had been harsh, the reverse, the stepping from the carnal artificiality of Pandora's Back Door into the parking lot, and the hot wet and sunlit world it was configured in, caused Benny to stagger. He stubbed his toe on one of the ankle-high concrete barriers, meant to prevent a person, in a fit of lusty exuberance, from driving through the storefront. Benny cursed and fell on the pavement, dropping the turkey jerky and chocolate penis. Gravel chewed his palm. Squat barked and fell off the van's driver seat. He was unhurt.

Embarrassing enough in a vacant parking lot, the cosmos timed Benny's humiliation to coincide with the passing of a State Patrol car. Which Benny didn't see, because he was lying on the ground. But he sat up when he heard the quick deceleration and the bite of rubber on pavement as the policeman whipped his car into Pandora's parking lot and pulled up beside Benny. For the longest time the policeman just sat in the car with his window up looking out at Benny. 'Looking out at' was an assumption. The praying-mantis-eyes quality of the officer's sunglasses made it impossible to tell.

This could have been – should have been, even – the solution to Benny's problem. He'd stopped with the explicit purpose of calling the police to report what he'd seen. And there, like a gift from God, a *deus ex machina*, swooping in to save the day, a cop. All Benny had to do was state the facts.

'What are you doing?' the officer asked. The best thing about conversations with police officers is that there's nothing superfluous.

'I stubbed my toe?'

With both hands, Benny sort of held his foot aloft.

'Have you been drinking?'

'Drinking? No, sir. I just went in to use the phone.'

There was a meaty pause. Benny noticed the officer's hair, so short and shellacked that it too could be a weapon.

'That yours?' the officer asked, pointing at the chocolate penis.

There was another meaty pause.

'Yes, sir.'

Benny put his foot down, and occupied himself with picking gravel out of the exposed derma at the tip of his big toe.

'Well?'

'Well what, sir?'

'You going to eat it?'

'What? Sir.'

'Littering is a crime, son.'

Benny picked up the two sticks of turkey jerky and the chocolate penis, clutched them bouquet-like, and remained sitting in the parking lot. The officer was, at best, five years older than Benny. With the window down, the temperature in his air-conditioned patrol car was, no doubt, at least 30°. The radio hissed and spit, but the officer seemed to understand something in its racket. Benny knew, then and there, that he couldn't report, couldn't confess, anything to this man, in this moment of humiliation.

'That your van?'

'Yes, sir.'

'That dog bite?'

Benny didn't realize that Squat had witnessed the whole sordid affair.

'No, sir.'

'You might want to clean that toe up.'

'Yes, sir.'

Satisfied of Benny's harmlessness, or redirected by some higher, colder power, the officer closed his window, reversed his car and sped away down Plank Road. By the time Benny stood up, the cop was completely out of sight. Benny considered himself quick on his feet. A problem solver. But the biggest problem in his recent life was still piled on the floor of his pumpkin-colored Dodge. Why couldn't he tell the policeman about the drowned girl? Why didn't he open the van and unburden himself of the horrible responsibility and its proof? Why did he buy a chocolate dick from a man with a quarter in his ear, then bust his toe wide open? Fear, maybe. Pray, not apathy. Perhaps, even in the best of circumstances, Benny wouldn't be able to rise to the occasion.

'No loitering!'

The command spat from a speaker hanging loose beneath a security camera at the corner eave, except that it came out 'No law-terin'!' Benny put his boots back on, figured, however half-assed that he ought to make one more attempt at reporting the death.

'Good dog,' he said to Squat then tossed his purchases onto the center console. Each step away from the van brought pain; the raw wound on Benny's toe raking the protective steel shell inside his boot. He hobbled around behind Pandora's looking for the payphone.

'Shit.'

'Fuck.'

'Shit.'

'Fuck.'

'Shit.'

There was, as promised, a battered but still blue Southern Bell phone booth at Pandora's side. It seemed to have shifted on its foundation. Seemed, even, to be listing a little to its right. Benny sort of half hopped, half limped up to the box and tugged at the folding door. Inside, on every possible surface, at every available height, and at every conceivable angle there were phone numbers, promises, propositions, assertions, dimensions, denials, even prayers of the more bestial sort, recorded using any available writing implement. What must have been the phonebook lay in a mildewed heap at Benny's feet. Too, there were the remains of umpteen Christian tracts. The pamphleteer brigade liked to target phone booths. One piece of propaganda, still intact enough to read, was a miniature hundred dollar bill on one side. On the other, a diatribe against Benny himself, in the form of moral do's and don'ts. Most disappointing however was the phone itself. More accurately, the absence. The coin box and dial were there. As was the cord. But it hung from the box, limp and flaccid. The receiver was nowhere to be seen.

'Fuck.'

'Shit.'

'Fuck.'

'Shit.'

'Fuck.'

By the time Benny got back to the van, Squat had eaten one of the sticks of turkey jerky and half of its plastic wrapper. He'd also chewed the tip off the chocolate penis, the entire glans, and was gnawing away at the shaft.

Dogs shouldn't eat chocolate, no matter what shape. Benny took it away from Squat and opened the remaining turkey jerky for himself. Half a mile down the road, he was still hungry. After the briefest hesitation, a check up the road and in the side mirrors, Benny went to work on the chocolate shaft, biting off chunk after chunk, swallowing them down, until all that was left was one bittersweet testis, which he gave himself license to suck.

'Dogs shouldn't eat chocolate,' he said to Squat. Squat belched.

'What the hell am I going to do?' Benny asked, paused, then asked further. 'What about all this stuff?' He gave a nod to the backpack and camera equipment. Squat's chocolate smeared tongue lolled. 'I ain't going to the police station. Not unless . . .' He couldn't finish the sentence.

Benny had a culturally, if not genetically, ingrained aversion to uniformed authority of any kind. The brief encounter with the cop in the parking lot had been terrifying enough. To imagine himself walking into a police station, full of cops and Authority, was beyond Benny.

Talking to his dog in times of crisis brought Benny some small comfort. He'd been talking to Squat since finding him one day, seven years ago, beneath the Welcome to Gastonia water tower. Benny had returned that morning to complete the lettering on the newly painted tower. *Welcome to Gas* greeted the interstate travelers throughout the night; Benny expected to have *tonia* done by lunchtime. He hadn't counted on finding the dog carcass at the foot of the ladder. A beautiful, red dachshund bitch. Beautiful despite the condition of her poor dead body. Someone, some malicious asshole, had thrown her from the top of the water tower. And, as if that wasn't enough, the dog was pregnant, fully pregnant, at the time. Clearly, she had ruptured upon impact, her sweet taut gut gave way; blood, viscera, and half a dozen pups the size of small rats ejected from within, splayed out blossom-like on the concrete pad. The dog was dead; no room for debate. But it stood to reason that if the dog was dead, its belly shouldn't be moving. Not regular, like breath, but something compelled the mass of intestines, shattered bone, and blood-matted fur to twitch. Benny knelt close and poked around in the organs with a stick. Whatever had moved was hidden inside. Benny reached, with his thumb and forefinger, into the body cavity of the dachshund bitch and plucked a living pup free. Wet. Struggling with breath. As pliable as an overripe fig, and about the same color. 'Good dog,' Benny said, taking off his tee shirt to wrap the orphaned puppy in. 'You're okay.'

Benny went to the vet straight away. Came back later to bury the bitch. He tucked the lifeless pups into the hollow glove of their lifeless mother, wrapped them in a clean work-rag, and lay them in a shallow hole dug near the tower's base. Benny sang a little song, but he couldn't muster up what it took to pray. Namely, belief.

He made a list that day too: fucker, chicken shit, candy ass, pencil dick, cowardly lion, mountain lion, panther, bobcat, tiger, tiger-striped, pinstriped, horse whipped.

In his time and place, worldly speaking, meanness reared its glorious head regularly; some pissed-off boy run amuck, killing and hurting with beautiful, perfect fury. Benny could think of at least a dozen idiots capable of such a thing, and those were only the ones he knew personally. None of this surprised him. He buried the dog. He finished painting the tower. He went back to the vet's office, half expecting bad news.

'Good dog,' he said to Squat. Old now, obese, arthritic, and an olfactory barrage, Squat as a confidant was unbeatable. Benny took him everywhere. What do you do after watching someone die? With the possessions of someone recently drowned? The logical option of going to the address on the business card escaped him. Benny's old van sagged under the burden of those questions, the engine backfired and sputtered. Driving toward Buffalo Shoals seemed as good an idea as any. It's where his friends were. It's where he lived. There were telephones there, in Buffalo Shoals, but neither buffalo, nor shoals to speak of. Only an abundance of feral cats and the pitiful Dye Creek that ran through the mill district. But nobody seemed to question the discrepancy. One time, before Benny dropped out of school, his class went to the Buffalo Shoals Public Library for a lecture on 'The Founding and History of Buffalo Shoals, as told by Myrtle Sperling: President & Oldest Living Member of the Buffalo Shoals Historical Society'; Lord, even the name of the program threatened to put Benny to sleep. He did, in fact, nod off, sitting on the back row in a creaking straight-back chair, his head resting against the entire Dewy Decimal collection numbers 835.41–876.11. Went right to sleep the moment Myrtle opened her mouth and began rattling on about cotton mills and turpentine camps. She hadn't said anything about buffalo by the time Benny went to sleep; he woke with the over-emphatic applause, just in time for peanut butter crackers and tea, and to this day felt like he might have missed some important information. Many times when Benny was little, riding in his uncle Nub's pickup at night, the old man would slam hard on the brakes and swerve, claiming he narrowly missed a buffalo crossing the road.

'Big as a damn house!' he'd say. 'Did you see it?'

'I didn't see it! I swear I didn't.'

'Lord-a-mighty! That was the biggest one yet.'

'Let's go back, uncle Nub! Let's go find it!'

'Noooooo,' he'd say, shaking his head. 'Too dangerous.'

It was years before Benny figured out the joke.

CHAPTER 4

THE FURTHER BENNY GOT FROM WHAT HAPPENED AT
Bard's Tower, the further he drove from the Big Toe
River, that no doubt carried the body, a stranger's body
Benny felt all too connected with, farther away from him,
the less inclined he became to get involved with any kind of
hasty resolution. What, really, was the hurry? His toe hurt.
His feet were hot. He didn't want to be implicated in this
girl's death. Benny took the tapes and the camera; that much
was sure. It's the dubious *why* nonsense that confused him.

He needed to look through the backpack one more time.
To get some feeling for what it was all about. The tapes,
the camera, everything. If he pulled off onto the shoulder
of the road, he'd run the risk of attracting another Trooper.
They had uncanny tendencies for showing up in the midst
of a person's private ordeals, and stomping around in those
big black boots. He could go to Dinks Clean 'em Up:
Carwash & Launderette, and pull into a stall, but Little
Dink was sure to be there. Benny didn't want to explain
anything to him. Benny blew the horn as he drove by;
people constantly blew their horns at Dinks. Little Dink,
standing, hunching really, by the vacuum machine at the
third stall, waved.

Benny didn't want to go home. Not with the tapes.
Not yet.

Plank Road led into the heart of Buffalo Shoals, a grid of half-a-dozen streets, some named for the farmers who'd pastured and tilled the rock-choked fields years ago, others named after the got-rocks who, with no small sleight of hand, pulled the cotton mills up out of the dust and commanded them to turn profits: the owners. Nearly one hundred years later, the mills had all but closed, and Benny Poteat had washed the windows of all three newer buildings that qualified as modest skyscrapers in the center of the city – there were four if you counted the brick behemoth put up by Duke Power, but it was practically windowless. He hated that job; hated the things he had to see through the windows. Nevertheless, in Benny's opinion, Buffalo Shoals wasn't a bad place to live.

Once you went through the center of the city proper, southbound, with all the banks, fancy restaurants, the condos, and the too-cool-for-you stores, things got edgier. And more affordable. Benny lived in that direction but he was avoiding home. Benny turned north, towards Jeeter's. It was an instinctive move.

Throwing the tapes away was out of the question. Driving by the police station and leaving the box, orphan-like on the steps, didn't seem right either. Claxton Looms? The address on the business card. Maybe later. For the time being, Benny thought it best to get some advice. Expert, or otherwise.

Jeeter claimed, regularly, that he wouldn't live in the city for 'all the pee in China'. No doubt, his lifestyle and habitat would be an eternal boil on the ass of any zoning ordinances. The five miles of Hager's Creek Road between the city and Jeeter's empire seemed a workable buffer zone. He was far enough from any businesses to avoid complaints and his few distant neighbors probably shared his aesthetic, so Jeeter was left alone. Left to rule the ebb and flow of a rag-tag entrepreneurial domain, a hodgepodge of businesses he built on the site of what was the first turpentine camp in the county, in peace.

'Nice panties,' Benny said. Followed it by a slow wolf whistle.

'Screw you,' said Jeeter, but he didn't move.

'Why do you bother with them skinny little Speedos?'

When Benny saw the stepladder at the back of the dump truck, he knew he'd find Jeeter already tanned but still tanning, slathered in oil, lying on a webbed folding aluminum lounge chair up in the bed of the truck. Benny climbed the ladder, and the heat and the stench of chemical coconut almost knocked him back down. Jeeter lay belly up.

'You might as well be naked,' Benny said.

'Too many buzzards,' Jeeter said. He picked up a squirt bottle, misted quickly from head to toe.

'What?'

'Buzzards. I'd hate one to fly overhead and look down, see me laying naked here and think he was gonna' have hisself a big old snake for dinner.'

If Benny was a thinker, then Jeeter was a doer. Driving the dump truck was one of the things he does. Dozers and backhoes, too, when he's hired to do so. But the dump truck, he bought with hard earned money. Unlike Benny, Jeeter sought his answers inside the earth, through the intimacy of hydraulics. They differ. In more ways than one.

'Or a robin? Looking for the early worm.'

'I didn't hear you drive up,' Jeeter said, taking his sunglasses off and sitting up. 'You want a glass of tea?'

Benny, lean and stealthy, stood exactly one inch taller

than Jeeter's five foot seven inches, but unless they were side by side Jeeter, because of his fullness, not fat just full in his skin, looked bigger. Both men were tired of the tattoos on their arms; picked and endured drunkenly from Slim Deals Tattoo Palace when Benny was seventeen and Jeeter was sixteen.

'Yeah,' Benny said. 'I want a glass of tea.'

After pulling off Hager's Creek Road onto the long rutted dirt track that was Jeeter's drive, which comes up quick once you go through the corrugated steel underpass beneath the railroad tracks, a road flanked by deep ditches filled with mosquitoes and muddy spring run-off, and would be easily missed if not for the cast-iron mailbox shaped like a humongous blue-gill – which Jeeter made himself in a welding class he took at Piedmont College – Benny stopped the van and hid the tapes, backpack, camera, tripod, and clothes in the cabinets under the sink. Sneaking up on Jeeter was always possible. He was liable to be occupied anywhere in the acre-and-a-half patch of earth – ringed by pines and sweetgums, the one anomalous mimosa; a hardscrabble piece of property, its center bare of flora, but occupied by a mobile home way beyond any hope of mobility; three wheel-less school buses in different mutations to which he pirated electricity, a dump truck, several piles of assorted junk (some in recognizably motorcycle form), and one shed in haphazard orbit around it – a prize of real estate he called his compound. Benny liked coming to Jeeter's.

'What's the matter with your foot?' Jeeter asked, noticing Benny's limp.

Squat followed behind, wheezing.

'Nothing,' Benny said. 'You got a band aid?'

They sat on the trailer's plywood porch, where Jeeter

had bolted bus seats, drinking sweet tea from colored aluminum cups, while Benny doctored his toe with rubbing alcohol and mercurochrome.

'You stink,' Benny said. 'Like a coconut cake. Put some clothes on.'

Jeeter faced the sun. 'Oh, but I'm purty,' he replied. 'All the girls think so.'

Red dust from the bed of the truck clung to his oiled feet, darkened and clotted.

'All of 'em?'

'Yup.'

Jeeter claimed to have inherited the land, the remnants of this turpentine camp. Not everybody believed him. In fact, there were many uncertainties surrounding his existence. Jeeter was an educated man. When not hauling fill-dirt, or operating the dozer or other heavy equipment for Crew's Brother's Logging and Landscape, he was either servicing a growing list of clients for his (successful despite the abundance of naysayers) aquarium set-up and maintenance business: Tanks-a-Lot; or he was at Piedmont College working toward another Associates degree. To date he'd studied welding, horticulture, funeral science and culinary arts, and while he hadn't actually completed any of the degrees, Jeeter was rounding himself out rather nicely.

With an acetylene torch, Jeeter had cut the steel roof from one of the old school buses and replaced it with a glass-paneled structure, rigged a fan and heater system, fashioning a very functional greenhouse in which he nurtured an amazing array of plants. At the rear of the bus, blocking the door, were more varieties of cacti than Benny knew existed. Some were tall, thick and intimidating; others tiny with impossibly delicate flowers. Jeeter liked

the succulents best. Jades, rubber plants. At the other end
of the bus, on a series of shelves built around what was
the driver's seat and console, sat the bonsai trees that
Jeeter pruned, tended and cared for with no less love
than he would give a child. The Japanese black pine:
nearly fifty years old and no more than ten inches tall
in its upright pose; the cascading fichus; a miniature grove
of maples. A dozen trees, or more, displayed in various
stages of manipulation, at the mercy of binding wire
and the insistent pruning shears. For the more tenuous
specimens, Jeeter rigged a water drip system to prevent
them from dying of thirst.

The other buses were closer to the trailer. There, Jeeter
housed the livestock and supplies for his aquarium maintenance business. In one, another feat of engineering genius,
another manifestation of his need for small controllable
worlds, Jeeter built the hatchery where he raised the
discus and the corydoras catfish that he specialized in,
as well as the supply of fish species that he stocked
his clients' tanks with. The inside of the bus was lined
with ten- and twenty-gallon aquariums, floor to roof, three
high. A fifty-gallon tank, long and wide, stretched across
the back of the bus beneath four bright fluorescent bulbs.
In it, Jeeter kept the aquatic plants. A submerged garden.
To walk into the bus was like entering a deep lake in the
dry confines of a glass bubble. Except for the lights over
the plants, the bus was dim, and all around the sounds
of water surging through filters and splashing back into
itself, sound buoyed into view by the schooling, dithering
fish, and the lush and fluid green of the plants. Jeeter had
clients all over the county. Businesses mostly, wanting the
tanks in the reception rooms to make a good impression.
He had a few private clients as well.

On top of the third bus, two satellite dishes mooned heavenward; but Benny had never seen a television inside Jeeter's trailer.

'I'm thinking about branching out, Benny,' Jeeter said, leaning close to look at Benny's toe. He scratched the dog's head.

Benny didn't reply right away; sometimes Jeeter's roller coaster of obsessions was exhausting.

'Ponds,' Jeeter said. 'Fish ponds are hot now. Everybody wants one.'

'I don't,' said Benny.

'I'd need some help. Digging. Stocking. And maintaining.'

'I don't want to dig holes, Jeeter.' Benny said. The ongoing catastrophes were easy to imagine.

'You better take care of that toe.'

Benny had known Jeeter for as long as he'd known. They weren't always friends, but the nature of their world was such that things overlap, and, consciously or subconsciously, sometimes you just go with the flow. Jeeter was Nub's nephew. Benny wasn't. But, in familial matters, as in nearly everything else, Jeeter existed on the fringe. Benny grew up with Nub and Honey, in their house. In the fish camp, where his father and mother had worked.

Down the road from Nub's was the catfish pond owned by Jeeter's grandfather. The old man kept it well stocked; he ran a little concession stand under the pond's only tree, selling nightcrawlers, canned corn, grubs, homegrown boiled peanuts, and coke. Cost you $2 to fish, all night. Out by the road a plastercast fish, big as a horse, leapt skyward; the hours of operation painted in red on its sickly green flesh. Even after the old man died, after the pond dried up and became a bed of scales and fish bones, spines like tiny ladders climbing nowhere, Benny continued to have dreams about that plaster fish; it swam nightly through the skies of his dreams, its big trout mouth chewing up stars that spewed as clouds from its gills. The dreams lay somewhere between nightmare and sheer ecstasy.

Benny put his boot back on. Jeeter went into the trailer, came out a moment later with an open pack of hot dogs. He took one out, bit off one half and handed the other to Squat. He offered the pack to Benny. Benny shook his head. What do you do after watching someone die? After busting up your toe, then eating chocolate testicles? Benny had a hard time deciding.

'I want to ask you something, Jeeter.'

Jeeter ate another hot dog, started to reach a second one to Squat.

'Don't give him no more of them,' Benny said.

For a few minutes it was quiet but for Jeeter's chewing and Squat's hopeful panting.

'You ever see anybody die?' Benny asked.

'Yep.'

Benny stared at his friend, who offered no more. Neither did Benny.

'You acting awfully damn spooky, big boy,' Jeeter said.

At that moment Benny realized what he had. He had a secret. It was his. His possession. He'd never owned a thing so important. A thing so much his and his alone.

'Never mind,' Benny said.

They drank their iced tea, Benny and Jeeter, while the sun inched toward red, and the gibbous moon crept up over the shoulder of the pines along Hager's Creek Road.

'There's a race tonight, at Shuffletown Dragstrip. I'm going on my motorcycle, me and a couple other guys. Want to come?' Jeeter asked.

'I'm cooking at Nub's tonight.'

'This ain't Friday.'

In fact, it was a lie. Benny had no plans for the evening.

'Well, if you come don't bring Dink.'

'Come on, dog,' Benny said.

The way back to town was blocked. A battered and rusty pickup truck sat at the end, in the middle of Jeeter's drive. Benny pulled up behind the driverless truck and considered his options. He could try driving around the truck, but there wasn't enough room. He could put the truck into neutral and just push it out of the way. That seemed risky. Or, he could just blow the horn and see what happened. That's when he heard the commotion in the side ditch. There, a scrawny, shirtless man stood bent, almost squatting in the muddy water; his hands struggling with something beneath the surface. You're liable to see anything that far out in the country, so Benny was unfazed. But the small pistol that jutted out of the back pocket of the man's cut-off jeans could prove problematic. Benny heard him curse when he slipped; wet now to the crotch. Benny tried to come to terms with the man's struggle. It wasn't as if he, the man, was holding a thing down. Rather, he pulled against something, a thing he was trying to get out of the water, and that something pulled back with considerable force. Just as Benny was about to get out of the van, to offer either assistance or interference, the man reached a momentary place of balance. A skinny arm held tight to whatever was beneath the surface of the water; the other reached back for the pistol grip.

One shot.

Another.

Two cap-like reports from the small-caliber gun, and the struggle ended. The man pocketed his gun then reached under the water and lifted. Benny heard the man grunt as he lifted the big turtle's body into the air. A terrapin. A cooter. It's shell, as wide as the lid of a garbage can, a web of blood catching sunlight.

'Dinner time,' the man said, his snaggle-toothed grin as wide and mean as a carpet knife. He threw the terrapin's heavy carcass into the bed of the truck, with no ceremony. He climbed behind the wheel, turned the ignition, and drove away.

CHAPTER 5

BENNY POTEAT WENT HOME. FINALLY.

Where else could he go?

He stepped out of the van and before his foot hit the dirt there was an all too familiar call.

'Hey! Benny Poteat! I got something to show ya.'

'Hey, Doodle.'

Doodle was Benny's neighbor. Doodle liked to flirt with Benny, and because the duplex they occupied shared bathroom and bedroom walls, as well as the concrete slab that was the back patio, and because Doodle waited tables at Nub & Honey's Fishcamp where Benny cooked on Friday and Saturday nights, he sometimes felt married to her. Sometimes, Benny flirted back.

That day she came out and sat on her front stoop.

'Hey. How about my fish tank? You were supposed to be here earlier.'

The duplex – a clapboard rectangle chopped in half by that thin mutual wall that made it possible for Benny to hear Doodle, a voracious reader of paperbacks, turn the pages every night, made possible an unasked for aural intimacy: Doodle's regular and restrained crying, Doodle at her toilet, Doodle on the telephone by her bed, Doodle's whispered, guilt-heavy, *no no no* on those rare nights of self-pleasure – this duplex designed by economics, not aesthetics, a front door and a driveway at either end, set back from the street by a thin patch of Johnson grass that Benny mowed infrequently, on a lot with only the merest pretense of yard, halfway down a block of similar rental properties, in a tight neighborhood of the same, making up one of the once numerous, never prosperous Mill Hill districts of Buffalo Shoals – this duplex Benny had shared with Doodle for the past seven years.

'Aw, Doodle. I'm sorry. I just forgot.'

Benny opened the door for Squat, who immediately ran to Doodle. The tapes, of course, the secret, stayed in the van. Doodle, who wasn't nearly as dumb as her name might imply, was more forgiving than believing.

'Can we do it tomorrow?'

'Yeah. We can. Did you eat?' Doodle asked. She fingered the pages of a fat, dog-eared book resting by her thigh; there was no front cover, which meant she got it out of the 10¢-each box at the flea market.

She was pretty, in a mature woman sort of way. Forty maybe, or forty-two. Doodle was several years older than Benny, and two inches taller. Benny liked her mouth; it was big and she smiled a lot. For six of the seven years they'd been neighbors, Doodle and Benny worked together on weekends. Sometimes he cut lemons for her; she brought him iced tea when things were really busy. And for five of those years Doodle had greeted Benny with the same phrase. 'Hey, Benny Poteat, I got something to show ya.' Benny knew what it was that Doodle wanted to show him, he just wasn't ready to see it. Most of the time he pretended not to understand.

'I made some white beans. And cornbread,' she said. 'Got fresh tomatoes at the farmer's market.'

'I already ate.'

That was another lie.

'What's wrong with your foot?' Doodle asks.

'Nothing,' Benny said. 'Come on, Squat.'

He thought to go back and lock the van, decided against it. That act would certainly arouse suspicion. If not from Doodle, then from any number of neighbors who were, blatantly or covertly, sitting on the front porches or fingering the window blinds, watching their exchange. Under normal circumstances Benny didn't mind the scrutiny. It was familiar and safe in a way. Warm days, everybody in a two-house radius knew that T.C. Hewit awoke at 6.00 a.m., to WROC *Sunrise With Stanky*, and that he left for work at Brother's Tire somewhere between 7.00 and 7.15. In high summer the whole block heard Mr Trivett's window unit struggling to cool the air in his bedroom. Lawn mowers. Dogs barking from within bare circles of earth where they were chained. The couple, whose name Benny didn't know, that fought drunkenly almost every Friday night, and made raucous love on Wednesday mornings. At the end of his street, a long-distance truck driver regularly parked his rig; its diesel engine sometimes running all night, rattling like a box of bones. And then there was Clyde directly across the street who sat on his front porch all day, everyday, waving at passersby. Weather be damned, Clyde intended to wave at every single person that drove or walked past his house. Last Christmas he wore a Santa suit.

Not everybody shared Benny's welcoming acceptance however. Periodically some poor soul would crack under the tension of the communal intimacy and hurl obscenities out into the night.

'SHUT THAT GODDAMN DOG UP!'

'Who the *fuck* are you looking at!'

For some, existing in that Petri dish of virulent curiosity became unbearable. Case in point: Benny's previous neighbor. Before Doodle, Benny shared the unit with a lady whose full name he never knew. For two years Benny heard but rarely saw Missus Younts. There was no evidence of a Mister Younts. No friends called or visited. One morning Benny heard her front screen door slam shut then watched her walk out of the door, down the center of the driveway, the sound of gravel crunching beneath her sensible pumps, nod deliberately to the Terry's Taxi driver, climb into the back seat and disappear into the day. Terry's Taxi took her away and never brought her back. When Benny asked the landlord, he mentioned something about nosy neighbors.

Then Doodle moved in, and Benny – although he couldn't tell you why – sheepishly, under the cover of darkness, took a razor blade and scraped the *If this van's a rockin', don't bother knockin'* sticker off his truck. It was on the van's rear bumper when Benny bought it from Sweeny, but hadn't bothered him until then. Over the past few years, he'd come to know Doodle through the thin walls, and through their conversation, both at home and at work, as intimately as he had ever known anyone, and he assumed that she knew things about him as well. Predictably and Janus-like, that intimacy brought its inverse; as the newness wore off it grew increasingly difficult to open up to her in any emotional sense. Not that he would have ever been labeled 'forthcoming', but even Benny recognized that it was much easier to bare your soul to perfect strangers. (There was a trial and – mostly – error period of obscene phone calls, Benny picking sexy, or at least interesting, sounding names out of the telephone book, Benny dialing furtively, shamefully, and trying out various lines – *What color panties are you wearing?* – in hopes of making an erotic connection.) And the more you got to know someone, the more opportunities arose for deceit, denial, and avoidance, or just plain apathy. Some days he wished he lived in a more isolated, less transparent world. But never, until that day, had Benny possessed a secret so worthy of protection.

Benny sat in the one truly comfortable chair he owned – the upholstered rocker, the one with thin looping swan's necks supporting the frayed armrests, the chair Benny had hauled, with its attendant ottoman, throughout his adult life because . . . well, because it seemed the right thing to do, the chair sitting now by the window overlooking the front yard and driveways – and took his boots off immediately; his poor toe oozed pus from beneath the band-aid he'd gotten from Jeeter. If it had been a normal day, Benny might've turned the news on, had himself a cold beer. But what could he possibly find in the news of the day to provide ballast? What, in that flickering shadow box with its heartless circuitry, its cabled analogue IV drip, could provide guidance or explanation for the things he saw out by the river? Even more pressing, how to reconcile the apparent, possibly growing, lack of concern for the *person* of the drowned girl? Benny watched her die. She walked into the water. She didn't resurface. Benny did little to stop her. But what could he have done? She just walked right off the solid earth and was gone before Benny had time to react. There was no hesitation. No ceremony. No pomp and circumstance. In fact, her death was quite unremarkable. If not for the video camera, the whole thing could easily be dismissed as a daydream. Or, relegated into that vault of unattended memories that eventually shrivel into dust motes, to be blown willy-nilly, and forever lost in the craggy deserts of the cerebral cortex. There ought to be, Benny thought, some acknowledgement of the event. Of the moment. Of the loss. If we, each and every one of us, are as invaluable to this world as we so adamantly profess to be, doesn't it stand to reason that, for each human that dies, the entire natural world should stop in its tracks and bemoan the passing? Wouldn't the grackles bow, wings over beak, and lament? Trees – sycamore, oak, all of them – lower their branches, leaves curled in on themselves? Shouldn't the waves acquiesce to gravity and lay flat? Fishes roll belly up in sorrow? Ought not the constellations to reconfigure for a moment of silence? The girl was dead; Benny was the only living soul that knew it. And for now she was just a dead girl, with the emphasis on *dead*.

'Squat,' Benny said, shifting his foot slightly, 'Quit it.'

But the dog kept licking Benny's toe. Truth be known, Benny only half wanted Squat to cease and desist; he'd grown up hearing, thus believing, that there was something curative about a dog licking your wounds.

Even with the windows open, the neighborhood seemed quiet to Benny. Doodle blew her nose. Laughed out loud at something. Opened, then closed, her silverware drawer. Because it stood by her bed, against the wall they shared, Benny could hear the incessant trickle of water through her fish tank filter. Jeeter was the one that talked Doodle into setting up the tank; he ought to be the one to help her move it.

Benny looked out the window at his van. He looked back at the clock, an Eiffel Tower made of wire with a clock face lodged at its midpoint, hanging over his sink. He should've been hungry by then. Benny sat and thought about lots of things: macaroni and cheese, the re-lamping job he had to do tomorrow, how to get the tapes out of the van without being seen, Ramen noodles, his throbbing toe, what to do with the tapes if and when he did get them inside. Benny didn't have a VCR. It was an unclear point of pride for him.

Laundry. Benny had a load of dirty laundry in the two plastic milk crates beneath his bed, a good reason to go to his truck. Sometimes Benny did his washing at Dink's, but usually he took it to Nub and Honey's house. Neither he nor Doodle had a washer or dryer, but Doodle regularly filled the clothesline that stretched from the back of the house out to the power pole in the corner of the yard with hand-washed socks, pantyhose, shirts and underwear. Benny stood, working hard over the decision of whether to go to the refrigerator for food, or to drag the dirty laundry from beneath his bed and take it out to the van. Then, as if by telepathic coincidence, the phone rang.

'Whatcha doin?'

It was Little Dink.

'Eating supper,' Benny lied.

'Let's go to Shuffletown.' Dink didn't have a car, only a moped. 'They're racing tonight.'

'Can't,' Benny said. 'I have to help Doodle.'

'You gonna poke that poon this evenin'?'

'She wants me to move her fish tank.'

'That's what I'm saying! You gonna' *move* her *fish-tank*?'

'I got to go Dink.'

'You ever lick her butthole?'

'Goodbye, Dink.'

'I wouldn't lick that thang. Too dang old for me!'

'I'm hanging up the phone now Dink.'

'I'd look at it tho . . .'

Benny hung up. From through the wall Doodle farted,

which surprisingly, she didn't do, audibly, often. A different day, a different mood, and Benny would try to work up a sympathy fart. Little Dink was, at worst, an annoyance. At best, he was a harmless, in many ways helpless, friend to Benny. Benny knew that Little Dink had a shunt. Had it since he was a kid. Benny'd known it forever, but he really wasn't sure what the shunt did. It – the shunt, as well as the musky odor and nocturnal-animal-like quality with which Dink carried himself – were the kinds of thing that made people both suspicious and strangely tolerant. Of Dink's incessant, obsessive, crude-to-the-point-of-infuriating sexual comments, Benny chalked them up to the shunt. As for those other, more covert, behaviors, who knew? When Dink was a kid, they all played in the red-dirt gullies back in the woods behind the mill. Someone had tied a thick jute rope to the top of a massive poplar tree whose branches hung out over the eroded gouge in the earth. All the kids took turns swinging. Back and forth. Back and forth. For years. Little Dink just happened to be on the rope when it finally broke. Happenstance. Any other possibility was denied. Dink had always been a little odd; even among the everyday oddity of mill-hill life he stood out. But after his month as a shut-in, convalescing from the fall, Little Dink was stranger than ever. And that's when the non-stop sex talk started.

Little Dink ran his folks' business. Which is to say, he maintained the laundry and carwash equipment. His father was dead, and his mother was resisting mightily any suggestion that she go to The Brian Center, where the old and infirm came from miles around to while away their last days strapped wheezing to wheelchairs or gurneys. Dink never got a driver's license, and everybody who knew him was sure that he'd be killed one day on the puttering, smoke-belching little moped he constantly rode around town. Most likely, he'd be run down by a semi out on the by-pass where, every Saturday, Dink went to the Kroger's Super-Supermarket at lunchtime for the abundance of free samples. At the end of nearly every aisle somebody was giving away something spread on a cracker or impaled on a toothpick. Lordy, how Dink's eyes rolled, his tongue flicked, when he talked about Kroger's.

Doodle's phone rang. Benny heard her go out the back door where she often sat on the patio, in one of those ubiquitous molded plastic chairs, and talked. He usually tried not to listen. A car door slammed down the block and Benny jumped. He fingered the Venetian blinds, peered out to make sure no kids were playing around his van. His van. And the terrible secret locked up in its cabinets. What exactly was the secret? That someone died? No. More than that. Don't get the impression that Benny was a stranger to death. In many ways, tragedy had been his boon companion since childhood. Here's a story, informed by memory and its attendant mythomania.

Shooks. That's all the sign said. *Shooks* – routed out of plywood, painted olive green; hung from two fat posts over, and sometimes obscured by, a thicket of nandina bushes. It could've been anything. No punctuation. No symbol or image to suggest a clue. If you didn't know that the sign referred to the seven mobile homes, most without skirting or foundation, at the far end of the one-lane gravel road that snaked behind the old white house, a peeling two-story farmhouse, built too close to the macadam for comfort, whose front lawn and nandina bushes garnished the sign, owned by one Mr Shooks, trailers laid out around the horseshoe loop (an historic design pattern found throughout the South) of the drive in what used to be, when old man Shooks was a boy, a goat pasture, at the center of which, then, sat a barn – nothing left by the time Benny was born but the stone foundation with a gnarled black walnut tree reaching up and out from its center – if you didn't know about Shooks trailer park, then you had no business there.

Benny had business there. Briefly. It's where his parents lived. Past tense.

Shooks lay at the far end, the worst end, of an unincorporated community called Thankyalord. However, most of the hundred and fifty-odd residents had long since given up the ghost on gratitude, and spent their time waiting for their government checks, furiously spending that pittance, or conniving and planning ways to get injured so that they might start receiving disability checks themselves.

Pete Shooks had standards though. If you wanted to live in his trailer park, you had to have a job. Of the six trailers Shooks rented out – he kept the one closest to his house empty for personal reasons – all the residents of working age did so in some capacity or another.

Pete Shooks, sitting up in the back bedroom of his house lording beneficently over his domain, saw it all coming that day. It was hot. After noon. And so oppressively humid that no one would've been surprised to step out in the back yard and find the grass alive with minnows, silver and belly flopping, and more, having swum heavenward from the creek down the road, falling out of the sky. Pete Shooks saw it all coming. What he couldn't see, he intuited. Because it was Sunday he saw that the young Crews brothers were not at work logging for pulpwood. JC, the youngest, slept beneath a circulating fan on the couch in their trailer. DW and AJ, sweating profusely, pitched horseshoes in the regulation size pit laid out within the barn foundation. A motley flock of guineas wandered the grounds, wandered occasionally into the path of a flying horseshoe.

Ralph White, the sometime garbage collector, planned to join the Crews brothers at horseshoes after he finished sanding the rust from an old wrought iron bed he found earlier in the week. Ralph liked to work in the back yard for the off-chance look at Myrtle Plowman in the next trailer over, for whom he'd silently carried a torch since she moved in. Myrtle worked at the cotton mill. Heavy in the rump, with an amazing blade-like nose, she was everything the scrawny, nearly pickled Ralph dreamt about. Beautiful without vanity. Devout without sanctimony. Prone to singing hymns, unselfconsciously and with rapture, throughout the day. And married to a complete buffoon. Mr Plowman was never at home. He was a loom fixer at the mill, with a puffed-up sense of self-worth, and preferred the company of grease and wrenches to the woman he wedded. This indifference was sunshine and rain for the seeds of Ralph White's desire. He never missed an opportunity to help Myrtle with one household task or another that needed the male influence. Myrtle suffered her husband's absence with dignity. Whether or not she knew the effect it had on Ralph when, on warm evenings, she'd sit on her back porch in a housedress of muted floral print, sit in a straightback chair with a dishpan cradled in her lap shelling peas – pinching back the stem and string, easing open the thin shell at the seam with both thumbs, pulling one deft digit, a thumb tip, through the verdant membranous trough, raking the peas out in a soft rain – and singing or humming softly to herself: 'A Closer Walk With Thee', 'The Old Rugged Cross', 'I'll Fly Away'; whether Myrtle had even the vaguest notion of the powerful stirrings these simple domestic acts generated in the industrious but skittish trash collector living next door was open to debate. She was a woman, no doubt, young enough, of this earth and therefore fecund. But you could not, in good faith, accuse her of either dalliance or coquettishness.

That day, it was too hot to shell peas on the back porch. Pete Shooks had a feeling, and when the rogue breeze pushed aside the curtains of her bathroom window the briefest shadowy glimpse, that Myrtle was engaged in her only decadence, the long bath. Ralph, in his own back yard, rubbed at the rusty bars of the old bed with a steel wool pad clutched in his sweaty palm. Myrtle sang through the window; Ralph struggled to keep time to her singing with his strokes, and to position himself so that the erection pushing so desperately against his overalls would not be immediately obvious to anyone who happened to look his way. Everybody at Shooks, except for, maybe, Myrtle, knew how Ralph felt; there were contradictory opinions about Myrtle's position. Nevertheless, it was too hot that day for her to be anywhere out of doors. Had Ralph known, had Pete told him, that Myrtle was lying, naked but for the damp rag on her forehead, in a bathtub full of cool water, just beyond the window closest to him, Ralph's poor rummaging heart may not have been able to stand it. Had Ralph known, or Pete suspected, that Myrtle had sang herself almost to sleep, had slipped into that sort of semi-conscious place wherein the mind lets down its guard and makes itself available to forces both inside and out, a warp in everyday reality where the keening of a cicada can mutate into love songs, where the flick of a housecat's tail brushing one's wrist as it walks by becomes a tongue, both welcome and feared, had the two men known this about Myrtle, and more, had they understood that despite her moral fortitude, she had succumbed, there in the raw wet moment, to the dream state, had in fact taken the aural gift of Ralph's rhythmic sanding to heart and was at that moment thoroughly engorged *down there*, the two tight buds of her nipples blossoming above the water's surface, had they known . . . well . . . it's best that it didn't happen that way.

Pete Shooks knew most everything that went on in his trailer park. He felt it was his right and his obligation. You cannot protect and manage from a place of ignorance. He was well aware that Old Lady Dishman, the most reclusive resident of them all, was holed up in her trailer with the blinds drawn and the doors closed. He knew she was alive because of the weekly delivery of snuff, groceries, and tablets of lined writing paper from the store. Pete made sure her bills got paid.

Pete knew the mimosa trees and the lilac bushes. He knew the yellow jacket's nest in the rock wall. He knew the toad that lived inside the door of the well house. He knew of the hatred between Shooks' neighbors Ed Pinch and Ed Sault, one an erstwhile preacher, the other a dedicated heathen. A hatred, shared by their wives, that manifest most often in bitter silence and spiteful petty acts. A hatred not embraced by their children, the three Pinch boys and the Sault brother and sister, who were that day gathering bugs: beetles, roly-polies, caterpillars, anything slow enough to be captured; and dropping them one by one into a small bonfire made of a pair old work boots doused in gasoline, built next to the stone barn foundation.

Pete knew that in the farthest trailer, a two-tone thing with sleeping berth at one end that made it look somewhat ship-like, a young couple, tired but proud, and in love, was easing into their first act of intimacy after bringing their newborn son from the hospital not two weeks before. Mayree Poteat had endured a hard hard labor, but she was a dutiful wife, and eager in those matters. Nevertheless, when, as they lay naked for comfort from the heat on the narrow bed they shared with their infant, when Maynard's hand slipped from its resting place on Mayree's loose paunch, that sweet space where Benny had taken root and grew, when the hand eased on down to the tender portico of her sex, not selfishly, but unthinkingly, he was gently rebuffed.

Benny lay peacefully, sucking a sugar-tit, on a folded-up quilt tucked into a peach crate beside the bed. Maynard moved on to a more tolerable expression of his love, putting his fingertip to Mayree's nipples again and again, transferring tiny beads of the watery milk that seeped out to his mouth. It was Sunday. The next day Maynard would go back to work as chief fry cook at Nub & Honey's. In a few weeks, Mayree expected to go back as well, cashiering for a while until she felt strong enough to waitress again.

But while Pete knew most everything about Shooks, its politics and shenanigans, its hopes and shortcomings, its hothouse-like qualities, and could, sometimes wisely, often less so, muck about in the lives and livelihoods of his renters, he was powerless against many things. Weather for instance.

Pete saw the sky change. Saw it go from the bleached impenetrable gray to a luminous green, the color of an angry sea. He saw the leaves on the sugar maple trees along the paved road furl and present their undersides. He witnessed the already nervous guineas cower and tremble. A black presence grew and loomed on the western horizon. Massive and wicked looking, the presence was ushered in by a moment of immaculate silence. The mockingbird shushed. The cicadas and crickets stilled their tegmans. Snapping turtles wouldn't snap. Even the burning boots stopped their sizzle and pop. The kids didn't laugh. Ralph White stopped sanding in mid-stroke. Myrtle held her dreaming tongue; the cool tub water refused to splash around her nakedness.

Everyone else was standing still, expectant, when DW Crews flung his horseshoe, flung it mostly because he was already in mid-pitch when the silence descended. The iron U cut the quiet air in a high graceful arc and it rung the post with a thunderous clink. Round and round the horseshoe spun, bringing with it the biggest tornado to hit Thankyalord in a century.

Thunder. Lightning. Hail. Rain. And wind.

Lord have mercy, the noise.

Most things in life seem to be about aftermath. About dealing with consequences.

Shooks trailer park was decimated. All but the empty trailer were ripped from their foundations and tossed helter-skelter up and down the road. Furniture, household items, kitchenware, personal belongings, displaced, became a grand spectacle of incongruity. Pete's house withstood the storm, but he was killed by a thin stalk of broomstraw that flew in the window, pierced his closed eye, and penetrated his brain. The children, the Saults and the Pinches, huddled behind the stone foundation, were, in a moment of temporary grace, spared. Ralph White was killed, but not before being stripped of his overalls and shirt, and deposited in the back of his own garbage truck. It became clear, months later, that he must have been still quite alive when Myrtle, naked, wet, and ready was dropped on top of him, and/or he was thrown into her. Myrtle conceived, but had been rendered a vegetable by the act. Jeeter Plowman was born nine months later, after gestating in the womb of his drooling catatonic mother. And Mr Plowman surprised everyone by doting on the boy until he died when Jeeter was twelve.

Havoc does funny things to the mind, and often originates there. Over the years the rumors grew into myths and legends. Sometimes it was hard to differentiate the real from the misremembered. It's a fact that one of the guineas was blown through the keyhole of Pete Shooks' front door. And that the rest were unharmed. It's a fact that JC Crews was left lying on his couch while the mobile home, yanked up and away, made unexpected advances in its claimed mobility. JC slept through the whole thing.

'What happened?' he asked of DW and AJ when they, pale and shaking but unharmed, shook him awake.

'Everthang got blowed to hell.'

Just who made the other claims isn't clear. But existence carries with it a degree of validity, however specious. It might be truth that a family bible was slung clear into the other county, through the window of a fish camp, landing in a deep-fat fryer full of sizzling hushpuppies. It's possible, isn't it, that a sheaf of hand-scribbled poems from a snuff-dipping old recluse fluttered into the windows of a train passing miles away, settling in the lap of a high-powered literati who'd proclaim them genius and spend the rest of his life looking for the author. Or, a favorite, that a tart green apple could be ripped from the branch of the gnarled tree at the head of Shooks drive, and hurled three-quarters of a mile away straight up the ass of a preacher, ruminating over a successful sermon and bending over to wipe a smudge from his boot.

Is there harm in believing these things?

People choose what they want to believe. The choice

based often on what provides the strongest sense of security. Erroneous. I *know* this, therefore it cannot hurt me. I know *this*, therefore it will protect me. Benny believed it all. He'd heard the stories for years. It wasn't a conscious choice though. He'd arrived at gullibility by default. They never found the bodies of Maynard and Mayree Poteat. Benny, although he wouldn't eagerly claim to be a Christian, believed they were taken up to Heaven. Capital H. And that grace had deposited him, peach crate and all, into the top of one of the sugar maple trees. Impossible as it seemed, Benny was sure he remembered looking up at the sweet expanse of sky, clear and blue not moments after the storm passed. And looking down into the worried faces of Nub and Honey Goodwell, and all the other folks gathered at the scene of the tragedy. It was Nub himself that climbed up into the maple tree and plucked Benny from its branches.

Sometimes, when Benny drives by where Shooks used to be, he pulls over to look and think. Nothing's there now except the old foundation. And some nandina bushes. It was a quiet place to think. For making plans. For figuring things out. Like what to do with the backpack full of the drowned girl's videotapes.

Several hours had passed since her death; Benny wondered if she was missed by anyone. Without a VCR, he obviously couldn't watch the tapes. Sometimes, on Thursday nights, he and Jeeter would watch pornos on Jeeter's VCR. But Benny wasn't about to take the drowned girl's tapes over there. Benny wandered aimlessly through his tiny apartment for a long time, chuckling to himself when he remembered the WWJD bracelets the waitress at Big Pig BBQ had on her wrists last week. What Would Jesus Do? Benny asked her if she wore two bracelets so that she could get a second opinion if she didn't like the first answer. The girl didn't think it was funny. Benny knelt by the foot of his bed to pull one of the make-shift laundry baskets from beneath it.

Nub or Honey Goodwell would know the decent thing to do. Nub would probably tell him to go straight to the police. Honey, she was always praying about something. And it seemed to work. Benny left the milk crate beneath the bed, but he didn't stand. He'd never, not in almost thirty years, prayed on his knees. He had seen a few pictures though. What the hell? Benny assumed the position he thought most conducive, on his knees, feet aligned, hands palm to palm in front of his heart, and bowed his head. Nothing happened. No special feeling simply from kneeling.

'Dear G . . .'

Benny stopped when he realized he'd spoken aloud. What if Doodle heard him? When a car passed on the next block, it occurred to Benny that his windows were open and the lights were on. Anybody looking could see him there on his knees. The smell of sour laundry filled his nose. Squat snorted, huffed at the screen door to go out and pee for the last time of the night. Benny's face burned with shame. His ears stung. He took the dog out. He went to bed. Fits and starts. Fits and starts. Benny slept in fits and starts.

CHAPTER 6

TIME PASSED. WHICH IS ONLY TO SAY THAT THE EIFFEL Tower clock on Benny's kitchen wall kept at its mannered dervish for nearly a week. His mind hung in a snag five days old. For the past few nights Benny had dreamt of Jeeter's big plaster-cast fish, only this time the drowned girl sat perched on its back. Smiling and waving at Benny as they floated overhead, she appeared sometimes naked, other times in what must've been a prom dress. Once, he could swear, she wore a ribbon reading Buena Vista Pork Princess.

Benny's toe took a turn toward infection. He bought hydrogen peroxide and ointments. Distracted, he worked, high above the earth. Looked down as little as possible.

It was almost inconceivable that the videotapes, the camera, and all the drowned girl's other possessions remained hidden in his van the whole time. Remained locked away through no sense of resolve or iron will on Benny's part. And forgetfulness was out of the question. Not a day, not an hour went by, during that first week after she killed herself, that Benny didn't watch it happen in his mind. Her decisive exit. Her possessions stayed hidden because he simply could not bring himself to touch them again. Transmutation. Transmogrification. Transubstantiation. Benny hoped that if he left the tapes alone long enough things would change into something, anything, more palpable.

He'd decided against asking Honey for advice. Or Doodle. Or Jeeter. And certainly not Little Dink. He just needed to think for a while. The girl was dead, for godsakes. Drowned. No amount of urgency on Benny's part could resuscitate her. For a few days, he read the *Buffalo Shoals Observer*, but saw nothing about either a missing girl, or a discovered body. As time passed, the tapes, the backpack, the clothing did seem to change; they took on a corpse-in-the-basement quality. As if the very stench of secrecy, emanating from his van, would incriminate Benny. For what crime? Inertia? Cowardice? Benny himself could not explain the hem and haw of his heart. Why hadn't Benny watched the tapes already? Certainly not through self-control. The tapes he took out of the van on Thursday night. Late. He'd helped Doodle move her fish tank to the opposite wall where it would get less natural sunlight, therefore, less algae. Distracted all the while, Benny couldn't remember what they'd talked about. He pulled away when she tried to give him a goodnight kiss on the cheek, which she often did, and he occasionally allowed. Through the walls he listened to her get ready for bed, then, finally, quiet. Benny gave Squat a can of dog food to keep him engaged, then crept out to the van with a milk crate full of dirty clothes. Benny brought the dead girl's stuff into his apartment covered in a beach towel bearing the faded image of several NASCAR heroes and smelling of mildew. Unable to bring himself to look through the things, Benny shoved them under the bed and waded ankle-deep into sleep where he thrashed about until the sun came up.

Because he didn't want to be watched, even by a dog,

Benny chained Squat to a tree beside the back patio. The fifteen feet of chain, little more than pretense; all the old dog ever did back there was crawl beneath the one folding lounge chair and go to sleep. Benny closed all the blinds in the house and sat on his bedroom floor. He pulled the laundry crate from beneath the bed, but left its contents covered by the towel. It was Friday. He'd be expected at Nub & Honey's around two. The morning loomed.

Step by step. Address the moment at hand. By default, Benny had learned to bumble his way through difficulty. Through loneliness. Through isolation. To look back from any given moment inevitably brought guilt and shame. To peer into the future, as near as the next hour or as far as eternity, meant fear and doubt. It wasn't an easy thing, nor even always possible, but when push came to shove way down in the deepest most conniving hollows and gullies of Benny's psyche, he was occasionally able to find the present moment and cleave unto it. To remain in the unfolding now, however briefly, brought clarity and insight. Benny peeled back the NASCAR towel.

Egg Rock Pentecostal. Shinn Presbyterian. Holy Ghost Deliverance Tabernacle. Epworth United Methodist. Rod of God Ministries. Hoop Leaf Baptist Church. Mt. Nebo Chapel. Benny made a list to settle his mind then lay the inventory from the crate neatly on the floor.

The tripod, insect-like, with its telescoping legs and wing nuts.

Her tee shirt which Benny, without thinking, pressed to his nose, then folded.

The drowned girl's underwear. Not the cleanest. Folded, with both embarrassment and a momentary but quickly withering semi-erection. Her black pants. Same.

Eight videotapes, dated and titled. He arranged them

chronologically without reading the titles.

The camera itself. He remembered the tape in the camera. *The* tape. With great trepidation Benny pushed at the eject button, missing the first time, his fingers fat with culpability. He put the unlabeled tape, in order, with the rest.

Aside from the two button pins – *potters do it on the wheel*; *hung like a horse* – there was nothing else remarkable about the backpack. Benny unzipped each pocket numerous times, hoping for small miracles. The only thing, except for what might be contained on the videotapes, offering any semblance of tell-tale was the business card and its troublesome sense of familiarity:

> Claxton Looms Apartments
> 3 Shuttlecock Court
> Rebecca Hinkey, Resident Manager

Benny ran a finger along the upper edge of the card, then, as if there were some secret to be revealed only through a Braille reading, he brushed his fingertip over the printed surface. Could this be the drowned girl's name? Her address? Benny hoped not. These details were too real. She didn't seem like an apartment complex manager. Not from a high distance anyway. Just before the telephone rang, Benny realized what bothered him so about the card. That name. Hinkey.

'Hey, Sugar.'

It was Honey Goodwell. She called everybody Sugar.

'Hey, Honey.'

Benny covered the drowned girl's stuff with the towel.

'What time you coming in today?' she asked.

'Two,' Benny said. 'Unless you need me earlier.'

'Nub says that tub of tartar sauce went bad. Says we'll need another before we open tonight.'

'We got enough pickles to make another batch?'

'Let me ask Nub.'

Benny heard the muffled repetition of his own question. 'Yep.'

'I'll be there after lunch,' Benny said.

Almost immediately after hanging up the phone, Benny heard Doodle's ring through the wall. Honey, no doubt. Benny put the drowned girl's things back into the laundry basket, covered them, and pushed it under his bed. Benny raised his blinds. A school bus stalled and backfired at the corner stop sign. Its levered maw gaped and a writhing chorus of children scurried bug-like up the steps out of sight. Already, the humidity pressed against Benny's chest. He brought Squat inside, gave him a bowl of water.

'What am I going to do, Squat?'

Squat kept his opinions to himself. Benny wasted the rest of the morning then readied for work.

Clyde, no surprise, was sitting on his front porch across the street when Benny walked out of the door. Somewhat surprising was the rain that must've come and gone in the night, leaving as its only clue the saturated driver's seat in Benny's van; he'd left both the window and the sunroof cracked open. He only noticed the musty smell after his pants had become soaked. The most surprising thing about the morning, by far, was Doodle's tits. Benny had already cranked the van, and opened the windows against the incessant heater. The rainwater had just seeped through Benny's workpants and briefs, and he was settling into the discomfort when he heard Doodle call out from behind her screen door.

'Hey, Benny Poteat! I got something to show you.'

He looked. She lifted her shirt. An old Nub & Honey's Fishcamp tee shirt with the image of a fishing rod bent double against the strain of its barbed hook embedded in the lip of a grinning catfish. *Best hushpuppies in town.* Benny had seen the shirt thousands of times before. All the waitresses wore them. He'd seen Doodle's breasts, bared and most often divided by a small gold cross on a chain, for various reasons, probably half a dozen times. They always took him by surprise.

'You better cover them things up, Doodle.'

With the door screen between them and the soft shadows cast by the morning sun, Benny could just make out the pale elliptical flesh. He couldn't see Doodle's face, but he knew she was grinning at him.

'Can you give me a ride to the store?' she asked, rolling her shoulders to settling the shirt down into place and pushing the screen door open. 'My gas tank's empty and I won't have any cash until after work.'

'Not this morning,' he said, searching for an easy lie. 'I got to take Dink to the doctor. I can loan you ten bucks though.'

Benny reached for his wallet, confident in the slight deception. All he really wanted to do was drive by Claxton Looms on his way to work. Just to look. Doodle would've asked too many questions.

'You sure you got it to spare?' she asked, pinching the folded bill between two fingers and pulling it away.

'Yup.'

'You charging me any interest?' Doodle grinned. 'I'll pay.'

Benny smiled back. He liked her. But she made him nervous.

'One day Doodle, when you least expect it . . .' Benny paused.

'Yeah?'

'I might just collect on all them promises you've been making.'

'Lordy lordy. Talk like that makes my thighs all tingly.'

'Well I better leave before things get messy . . .'

Benny cupped his palm and waved as he drove off. As an afterthought, he gave a tap on the horn for Clyde. Claxton Looms and its neighborhood lay in the opposite direction from the fishcamp. Benny had no plan for what he would do once he got there, but he was determined to go. Benny didn't know exactly where the apartment complex was but he knew from the address on the business card it had to be just north of the center of Buffalo Shoals. With a hoity-toity name like Claxton Looms, Benny suspected the old mill district that succumbed to moneyed northerners when the Buffalo Shoals economy, clinging to some techno-coattails, made an effort to turn around nearly a decade ago. Beyond attitude, he didn't know what he would find, but the deeper he drove into the belly of gentrification, the less confident Benny became.

As predicted, in the space of two, maybe three blocks, things changed. In what was once a small hub of textile mill life and industry: blue collar shops, chicken and rib joints, shitty apartments, Benny witnessed the miracle of transformation. Dollar stores and pawnshops gave way to futon emporiums and specialty boutiques. The free coupon paper racks were replaced with *Creative Loafing* racks, the free artsy-fartsy weekly. In the window of what used to be a cheap tire store and garage Benny saw the irrefutable evidence of a coffeehouse-cum-bookstore. Tiny cramped tables ringed with mismatched chairs. Shelves and shelves and shelves. He saw the sign. *Retreads.* The sidewalks were cleaner there, better lit. And everything smelled of Ethnic restaurants. Capital E. As a nod to the fringe, to danger, a wide alley, dubbed Grub Street, led to the tattoo and body piercing salons and a retro pool hall. Benny saw posters advertising an art gallery's monthly 'crawl', but couldn't read the address. By the time he stopped at the second traffic light Benny became acutely aware of how much his van – ugly, loud and dirty – stood out among the sleek imported sedans parked along the street. Looking in the window of a store called Vortex, where a larger-than-life bronzed Buddha sat in full lotus position, his hands in the cosmic mudra, surrounded by geodes, crystals, trickling fountains and all the other contemporary trappings of the salvation industry, where in the awakened one's hammered and polished lap a propped sign read *Gifts For The Discriminating Lover*, in that window Benny could make out the diffused reflection of himself, the roosting chicken tattoo on his left forearm he'd long since stopped thinking of as funny, and his vehicle, and he felt ashamed.

A horn blared from behind, the sense of urgency conveyed through duration. The light had changed while Benny wallowed in self-doubt, and the Audi driver showed no mercy. Flustered, Benny drove right past the entrance to 3 Shuttlecock Court. Claxton Looms Luxury Apartments, however, was impossible to miss. The massive brick edifice, a three-story refurbished textile mill spanning nearly a full block, had been gussied-up to enhance both its luxury and industry qualities. The sign fashioned from an antique loom, and long narrow banners of dungaree and gingham hung, undulating, from every other window, projected just the right tone to passersby. You'd love to live here. Are you good enough to live here? Benny kept driving. Reconnaissance, he thought to himself. He'd gather his feral wits and come back a different day.

Chapter 7

'YOU LOOK TIRED, BENNY,' HONEY SAID. 'YOU BEEN sleeping OK?'

'Yeah,' Benny answered. A lie. 'Where's Nub?'

'Gone to the bank, I think. You need him?' Honey worked as she talked, wrapping tinny forks and dulled knives in paper napkins. Three folds and a roll. She loved that task for its meditative quality.

'No, just wondering. Who's here?' Benny asked, turning so that Honey could tie his apron in the back.

'Me and Scotty. What's wrong with your foot?'

The toe was improving, but slowly. Benny limped.

Scotty was the dishwasher. Honey, more mother than boss to most of the employees of the restaurant but especially to Benny, ran the cash register and greeted folks as they came in the door. Nub & Honey's Fishcamp, Est. 1961, sat in a clearing hacked out of a pine grove, at the end of a dirt road somewhere in Buncombe County. For the first twenty years of its existence the single-story clapboard building operated as a liquor and gambling house that just happened to have a deep-fat fryer because the proprietors eventually figured out that their customers would drink longer and more if they occasionally got some other form of nourishment, preferably salty. Secluded, but not really secret, the business ran successfully until the third, reported, homicide, or was it suicide, forced the county, caving in to ample Baptist protest, to close it down. Nub got the building for a song (and more work than he cared to remember trying to get the various stains out of the floors, walls, and ceilings).

'Hey, Scotty.'

'Hey, Benny.'

'Did you get them shrimp peeled?'

'Yep.'

Scotty was learning his way around the kitchen, much like Benny had. He, Benny, had been underfoot at the restaurant since his first toddling steps. Before that, Honey kept him in a bassinet near the register. By the age of ten Benny swept floors and refilled iced tea glasses on busy nights; at thirteen he filleted flounders as well as any man. Scotty, a pimply kid struggling to pass driver's ed., had a ways to go before he could be trusted with any serious kitchen task, but Benny was patient.

'What're you doing now?' Benny asked.

'Got to mop the Buoys and Gulls,' he answered, almost giggling. Scotty hadn't been there long enough for the bathroom signs to loose their humor. Or maybe he was just slow on the up-take.

'Did Nub ask you to feed the fish?'

'Yep.'

Benny never minded coming to work early. Usually, he liked the semi-quiet time before the other cooks and the waitresses got there. Liked the way the pitch increased incrementally, predictably, as the afternoon progressed. Sometimes he sat and watched the angelfish in the 55-gallon tank Jeeter installed a few years ago: Nub was his first official client. The fish were beautiful. Exotic even, with names like Gold Marble, Black Lace, and Smoky Blue

Blushing, their veiled fins trailing behind as they glided effortlessly among the driftwood and amazon swordplants. A small foyer, lined with Naugahyde-covered benches, opened into the main dining area of Nub & Honey's, where the mural of the sea floor covering the length of the back wall had begun to peel, and where in each corner of the ceiling hung a fishing net filled with plastic lobsters and shells, and that room was flanked on either side by smaller rooms, one of which could be rented for private parties and anniversaries. Sometimes, particularly weekends when the wait for an open table could be up to half an hour, things got a little tense and edgy in the foyer. Honey doled out mints and platitudes from the cash register, but often that wasn't enough. Jeeter convinced Nub that a fish tank in the foyer would bring a sense of calm. By god, he was right. The kids loved it. And even the adults usually chose to watch the angelfish, prolific and diligent parents, rather than complain to Honey.

Benny was too distracted that day to pay attention to the fish. His secret gnawed at him from within, and pressed him from the outside. Despite its intangibility, the thing got in the way in a very physical sense. Benny could not think clearly, therefore he did not act clearly. At three o'clock the other cooks would come in: Spalding, who helped with the fryers, and Rob, who took care of every-thing else. Nub & Honey's menu – a complicated affair of platters and combinations, (perch, flounder, catfish, trout, oysters, shrimp [popcorn or jumbo] scallops, stuffed crab, crab legs) fried (salt and pepper, cornmeal, or traditional breading) or broiled, not both unless you pay extra, bowl after bowl of hushpuppies on every table, and the choice of onion rings, salad, baked potato, fries, or coleslaw –

required a good bit of precision work if things were to flow smoothly.

By 4.00 p.m., two of the waitresses, usually Doodle and Audrey, would be there making tea and refilling the tartar sauce squeeze bottles. Then, at 4.30, Ruth and Jonette, both career girls at Nub & Honey's, arrived. When the doors opened for business at 4.45, the swelling crowd of fish-eaters, the sounds of clinking glass and chatter and fork tines against knives and ice and pouring water and tea and laughing and the cash register and dishes would build and build in orchestra-like fashion until the crescendo at around eight o'clock when things would just fizzle out. That vacuum, that space left by retreating sound, brought solace to all who worked in it. All but Nub, probably. His office filled to overflowing what used to be a closet at the back of the kitchen. He'd hacked a window to the outside, made a gravel drive-up lane, where he sat the night filling take-out orders and watching televangelists on an eight-inch TV screen, getting more pissed off at them as the night went by.

'Hey, Scotty?' Benny called as the boy dumped his mop water into the drain. 'I need you to peel and quarter these onions for me.'

'Sure thing, boss man.'

Benny pulled a case of lemons from the walk-in, a knife and cutting board from the dish racks, and went about the business of slicing. Halved. Quartered. Into eighths, if the lemon was big enough. Benny tucked a wedge into his mouth, bit down, and sucked. Hoping for something in the tart shock, some way of understanding revealed. Why? Why hadn't he reported the drowned girl's death? Why had he kept her possessions? Why hadn't he, at least, watched the tapes? Benny spat the lemon wedge into the trash, slipped another in its place. Bitter and pithy. Nub came in the back door with a cloth sack full of change.

'Hey, Benny.'

'Hey, Nub.'

Nub, a gentle and sweet man despite that televangelist nonsense, was by some accounts oblivious to the day-to-day workings of his business.

That Friday night, as with countless Friday nights before it, while the bats whipped up the dusky Carolina sky, most of the fish-eating population in a thirty-mile radius would return to Nub's restaurant and grease their chins around his tables.

Once, for a whole summer, Benny wrote down on the grainy white expanse of a take-out bag the names of those who came to Nub & Honey's Fishcamp. Benny headed and dated the list – The (Mostly) Regulars: July–August, 1985, penciled beneath the Rite-White Bags label – and tacked it on the corkboard by the employee bathroom where over time it became faded, spattered with ketchup and tartar sauce, and scribbled on, but remained nonetheless an impressive tribute to Buncombe County's potentate of hushpuppies and popcorn shrimp.

From Buncombe, then, came the Chuck Crouches and the Plevels, and a man named Edsell who Benny knew from the Ford place, and Superintendent Haw Mayhew who lapsed into a coma at a tractor pull last summer up in Virginia. And the Ridenhours and the Dew Belks, and a small herd named Diggs, who always took up several tables in the big room and snorted through bared teeth when they laughed. And the Whitlows and the Masseys (or rather Lem Bolick and Mr Massey's wife), and Trow Ketchie, whose body hair, they say, fell off one winter morning for no good reason at all.

Bill Raby was from Buncombe County, if Benny remembered correctly. He only came one time, on an old Norton motorcycle and wearing leather chaps, and got blessed out in the parking lot by a Mary Kay representative. From out near the rivers came the Ingles and the G.G. Huffmans, and the Isaac Myerses from somewhere up north, and the Jimperts and the Big Penson Skeens. Penson came three nights in a row before being born again during an impromptu parking-lot homily. So slain-in-the-spirit was Penson that, one by one, he picked up the back ends of nearly every car in the lot. The Rinehardts came, too, and Mrs Eula who was believed to be a hundred and three, and Jim John McKinzie, and the Ruckers, and Spivy who owned the first Jiffy Lube in town, and Spivy's dirty sons.

From Alamance County came the Byers and the Awlreadys and Ed Sault and Ed Pinch, who remained neighbors, Shumake the erstwhile mayor and one Mr Honeycutt, who ran the Triple X drive-in and adult novelty stores just beyond the town line, and Mullis and Strom Craven and Lloyd T. Downers (Junior) and Shaw Spanks, all engaged in the burgeoning vice industry in one way or another. And the Eeberns and the Yates and Connie Trivett, sister to that Trivett who cut off his wife's toe to pay a gambling debt. Rev Chambers the tent revivalist came there, and Mitch Hambright and Maynard ('Pup') Suggs and the Tousignants and Andy Auten – they came to eat crab legs, and when Pup Suggs staggered into the bathroom it meant he had overeaten and the tattooed and multi-pierced girls who worked with him, third shift, on the box and tape line at Draymore Shirt Factory would have to cover for him that night.

A man named Settlemeyer was there so often and so

long that he occasionally pitched in to bus tables when things got hectic – Benny seriously doubted that Nub paid him for the service. Of the entertainment types there were Eve Sinclair and Salina Tweens, exotic dancers, Shoshana Wingate who was rumored to have appeared in some network TV commercials as a girl (Benny believed it; she was beautiful), and Yates Bumgarner the wrestler. Also from Alamance County were the Brawleys and the Novernes and Fran Kistler and the Tubroses and the Witherspoons and the Culbertsons and the now divorced Curtises whose open hatred towards each other made shopping in their Hallmark franchise painful, but irresistible.

Dexter Brackett always arrived with two other guys. One claimed to have a fifteen-inch penis; the other was said to be a hermaphrodite. You couldn't tell from looking at them if either was true, or which was which. There was one girl whose name Benny refused to speak; she lost her virginity, at least once every summer, draped over the life-size plastic cow on the roof of the Dairy Barn. And then there were all the sad daughters of the great NASCAR drivers, who came and went together, a tight pack jockeying for vague positions of power; flashy and too loud for such a small restaurant.

In addition to all these Benny remembered, from time to time, other folks who frequented the restaurant. Humpy Wheeler came there at least once and the Fish sisters and G.I. Cockrell who returned from Vietnam with a plate in his head and not a lick of sense, and Ms Rummage and Mr Lawler, her significant other, and Chiquita Arnot-Smith and Mr D. Dauber, once famous all over the state for his motivational speeches, and Widow Tucker with a man reputed to be her plastic surgeon, and, believe it or not, the best damn country music star ever to pick a tune whose name, it goes without saying, didn't even need to be called.

These were the people that dined at Nub & Honey's Fishcamp.

'Here's your onions, Benny.' Scotty clanked the metal bowl down on the table in front of Benny, whose eyes began to sting immediately.

'Thanks, Scotty.'

Benny took the bowl of quartered onions, put them in the buffalo chopper with the pickles and capers. He turned away while the chopper worked, but the action didn't prevent the burning tears. It happened every time Benny handled onions.

'Why don't you let me do that?' Scotty asked. 'If it hurts you so damn much.'

'I don't mind,' Benny said.

He seasoned the mixture. Put it in the Hobart with the mayonnaise and lemon juice. All measured by sight. Making tartar sauce was about derivation. Sometimes subtle, sometimes extreme. As long as the concept of a thing, tartar sauce for instance, was met, who cared if it tasted a little saltier or had more sweet relish than the last time? Everything, really, was about derivations. There were no new experiences, or ideas, or sauces. Just revisions.

'Hey, Benny Poteat.'

Benny looked around, half expecting Doodle's bare breasts. The lemon wedge a yellow beacon behind his lips.

'Sexy dentures,' she said, tucking an order pad into her apron pocket.

'You look tired,' she said. 'How is Dink?'

'Waah,' Benny spat the lemon wedge into the garbage. 'What?'

'Dink? Didn't you take him to the doctor.'

'Oh. Yeah. He's pitiful as ever, but healthy.' Benny's

lies seemed to come easier. He lifted the dish rack full of clear, clean squirt bottles onto the counter. 'Will you do something for me?'

'What you got in mind, big boy?' Doodle winked. 'Got some fresh sauce for me?'

'Can you get Audrey to fill these?' Benny asked.

'No, sour puss. I'll do them myself. Audrey's liable to pitch a conniption fit if I ask her.'

'Ask me what?' Audrey stood behind Doodle curling her hair into a bun.

And so the night began. Benny, behind schedule. Audrey in a tiff. Rob came in late because his wife had blood in her stools that morning, which he repeated to everyone in the kitchen at least a dozen times before Nub took him in the office and closed the door. Ruth decided she couldn't walk another step with the corn on her big toe, so she leapt full force into a multi-stage home remedy process that left her sitting on an upturned pickle bucket shoe-less for a good hour. Honey couldn't find the mints to replenish the bowl by the cash register. And nobody knew if the dirt track race out at the fairgrounds had been cancelled. But by six the customers were stacked at the door and a modicum of order had been restored.

'What's the worst thing you ever saw, Doodle?' Benny sidled up to her by the ice machine.

'What do you mean? Like a car crash or something?' She lined up glasses for a four top then clipped an order to the wheel.

'A car crash. Or anything.' Benny took the order, called it to Rob and Spaulding. 'Something that really fucked with you.'

'Let me think about it,' Doodle said on her way out into the dining room.

The night progressed. Scotty only broke three plates. And that was because he and Benny were having a long complicated discussion about climbing towers. Things began to slow down around seven thirty. Doodle pulled a pecan pie from the reach-in cooler and called Benny over.

'One time out at the lake, at a party, I saw these guys pull a chain with this really drunk girl.'

'Pull a what?' Benny asked. He held the pie in place as she sliced it.

'Pull a chain,' she said. 'You know . . .' and when it was apparent that Benny didn't know, she offered, 'they gang banged her. For hours.' Doodle raked the knife blade with her finger, then stuck the finger in her mouth.

'How come nobody stopped them?'

'Everybody that was there took part. She was a mess.'

'Did you know them?' Benny asked.

'I did.'

Audrey came into the kitchen to make a fresh pot of coffee. They stopped talking until she left.

'Did you know her?'

Nub shrieked at the television.

'Why are you asking this stuff, Benny?'

'Did you ever see anybody die?'

'Well, yeah. Sure . . . a couple times. But dying is the easy part.'

Later, much later, after the customers had gone home to their antacids and dual Lazy-boys, after the noise, after the tubs of cocktail and tartar sauce were put in the walk-in, after the grease in the deep-fat fryers had begun to congeal and the odor of bleach subsided and Nub & Honey's fell into a brief torpor, Doodle and Benny sat on their shared back patio after work, smelling of fish and grease and sweat, and split a beer. Benny fed Squat some leftover shrimp from a styrofoam box.

'So?' Doodle asked.

'So what?'

'What's the worse thing you've ever seen?'

'I'm still trying to figure that out.'

CHAPTER 8

THE FIRST THING BENNY NOTICED UPON PULLING
into the Claxton Looms Apartments parking lot the next
day was the placard:

Employee of the Month
Rebecca Hinkey

It hung from, and partly obscured, a sign reading:

Reserved for Resident Manager
Rebecca Hinkey

A car sat in the parking space, a clean car. Benny
figured two things. If she'd been gone from work for
more than a week, Rebecca Hinkey probably wouldn't
still be Employee of the Month. And, the car wouldn't
be so clean. Evidence thus far indicated that the drowned
girl was not Rebecca Hinkey. Evidence. By now he'd begun
to think of the drowned girl as his own personal mystery.
Benny maneuvered his cumbersome van into a tiny spot
allocated for visitors.

He hadn't planned on going there. In fact, had actually headed toward Jeeter's then, with him, planned
to go to the flea market to look for a CD player for

the van. And he needed some milk and cereal from the grocery store. Twenty minutes later found him parked by the mirrored doors of Claxton Looms Apartments. Twenty-three minutes found him opening those same doors and walking inside. Twenty-four? He stood in the marble foyer, transfixed by the vision before him. Benny had seen plenty of fish tanks in his day. Lord knows, there were enough fish, dead and alive, in his life that it seemed like thematic overkill even to Benny. As if fate were hammering home some point that he was always just a little too dense to get. But the tank in the foyer of Claxton Looms housed a creature he'd never, ever, seen before. It was big, the tank. A hundred, maybe a hundred and fifty gallons, saltwater, and contained within the interior wall of the room so that it was the first, and only, thing you saw upon entering. Benny deduced that it was a saltwater tank by the artful arrangement of bleached coral and delicate, beautiful, but lifeless sponges, gorgonia, and sea fans rising from a substrate of crushed oyster shells, by the brilliant lighting, and by the livestock: tangs the color of lemons, a pair of animated clownfish, wrasses and something called a dog-faced puffer he'd only seen pictures of. Nowhere, however, not in pictures, nor encyclopedias, not in real life, nor even in his dreams, had Benny seen a thing like the one sitting atop the stepladder that rose from the substrate, through the depths of the aquarium, towards the surface. It was a woman. A tiny woman, in tiny woman clothes, perched on the ladder, her shoe-clad feet crossed on the second rung. She held a small jar in one hand, reached out with the other, and seemed to be negotiating a conflict between a moray eel, a snowflake moray whose gaping, beakish mouth could swallow her whole, and a lionfish with elaborate, venomous fins. Steady she sat, in the current that worked the gills and fins of these fishes that were held captive by her presence, and fearlessly decreed in miniature. And when she finished, the little woman climbed, with exaggerated care, down the stepladder and walked across the substrate, out of sight.

'Oh!' she said, coming around the corner startled. 'I didn't know anyone was here.'

'Sorry,' Benny said, trying, but unable, not to stare. He realized his mistake. A victim of visual chicanery, hoodwinked by physics, Benny had been looking through the aquarium to the other side. And through the trickery of refraction, light, therefore his perception, was bent. Altered. She was not a miniature woman who lived among the fishes, nor amphibious, comfortable both on land and in water. No. Before him stood an air-breathing creature of the earth. But, and this was the focus of Benny's stare, she was not a *real* woman . . . or not a *whole* woman . . . or at the very least not a full-sized woman. It was as if, in the transition from the shrunken illusion atop the submerged stepladder to the startled person rounding the corner, she had lost something. Some part of herself. She was a midget, no two ways about it.

'Are you delivering something?' she asked, looking Benny up and down.

Benny shook his head *no*, becoming more and more self-conscious about his tattered jeans and tee shirt from a tower company called Goliath Erections, and most self-conscious about his Ripley's Believe It Or Not hat. He crossed his arms in an attempt to hide the tattoo.

'This is Claxton Looms . . .' she paused, almost gesturing with the can of fish food in her hand, 'Luxury Apartments. May I help you?' There was a subtle inflection to the *you*.

– *Yes, in fact. You may be able to help me.* –

It occurred to Benny that he had never seen a midget up close before. Not a pretty one anyway.

– *Do you know the drowned girl?* –

'Apartment,' he said, his head bobbing in a way that indicated absolutely nothing.

– *Can you tell me who she was? Can you tell me why she did that terrible thing? To me?* –

'Ok?' she said, expecting more from him.

'You're Rebecca Hinkey?' Benny asked.

– *What could I have done to stop her?* –

'Have we met?' she asked. Judging from her demeanor, Rebecca Hinkey saw herself as the first line of defense for Claxton Looms. For maintaining their standards. The warmth or chill of her greeting certainly depended on your perceived potential as a resident. Benny, it was plain to see, held little promise.

'Employee of the month,' he said, thumbing towards the door.

'Most people ring the bell,' she said, pointing in the same direction.

Standing just a head above Benny's waist, he guessed the midget, Rebecca, to be four feet tall. He tried to remember whether it was dwarves or midgets that had disproportionate limbs; decided it must be dwarves. Rebecca's short arms and little legs that led all the way up to what Benny perceived as a cute, solid butt, while far from normal, seemed to fit well her diminutive trunk and its equally diminutive breasts. Nor did she have a grotesque head with those pitiable features that come to mind at the mention of dwarf. Rebecca Hinkey was pretty. Off-kilter, but stunning even, in a compacted sort of way. She filled her tiny figure almost to the point of breaking.

'Staring is rude,' Rebecca said, making clear that she'd

said the same thing thousands of times in her life, and expected to say it thousands more.

Benny expected none of this. Not the midget. Not the lust. However, his own ignorance rarely surprised him. Benny barely knew how to act with normal women. Not only did he categorize incessantly, but the boundaries of his categories were usually vague, overlapping, and based in nothing but momentary (flawed) cognition. Black, white. Woman, girl. Normal, abnormal. Pretty, ugly. Stupid . . . These terms and more he threw about like loose change, rarely clued in to where they were spent. And Rebecca Hinkey was . . . well, different.

'Sorry . . . um, I'm looking for an apartment. One bedroom, an efficiency maybe.'

'There are no *efficiency* apartments at Claxton Looms. And, our one bedrooms start at $750 per month.' Rebecca offered this information without moving from the foyer. And with some certainty that it would be prohibitively expensive for Benny. Which it was, but he had his poker face on.

'Ok.'

Rebecca sighed after coming to terms with the silence that followed his response. 'Come with me,' she said, and Benny followed her around the wall housing the fish tank to the office where her desk sat. Followed her and tried hard to concentrate on why he had come, and not to form opinions about her or her anatomy. Followed her and looked for signs that would link her to the drowned girl. There were none readily apparent. She wasn't dressed in black. In fact, her skirt and blouse were almost cheery. There were no official-looking papers. No indications of worry or concern, although could Benny recognize them if they were present? Maybe midgets can't be read in that way. From so high up, the drowned girl had looked of normal height. As for her features, her hair and eyes, the way her nose might have angled from her face, the lips and their fullness or lack of, Benny had no clue. So what was her connection with this abbreviated person? Blood kin? Friends? Enemies?

Rebecca showed him the apartment. Not to do so would have been discrimination. She didn't have to put her heart into the act, though. Benny got the standard spiel, sans oomph. Sans emphasis. Sans anything but breath and pared down syllables. Every time Rebecca stood near a wall or a doorjamb, Benny had to fight the urge to place his hand palm down on top of her head and mark her height.

'Claxton Looms was founded . . .' she said. 'Blah blah blah . . .' she said . . .' units facing the courtyard . . . a secure building,' Rebecca eyed Benny, then the door before continuing, '. . . blah blah blah . . . all the best amenities . . . pool, sauna, clubhouse . . . two parking spots . . . blah blah blah blah . . .'

Benny didn't care what she said.

'I need you to fill these out,' she said, handing Benny a clipboard with a Claxton Looms pen dangling by a chain from the corner. The forms were the truest filter for Claxton Looms. With questions about current residence, salary, and information necessary for a credit check, this was where the unsavory types usually went away humbled. Benny took the forms, sat in a squeaky couch right by Rebecca's desk, and tried his best to fill them out. He took his hat off, tucked it between his thigh and the couch.

'Where do you work?' she asked, just as he was getting to the question on the application.

'Uh, I'm a chef,' he said, not too far from the truth. 'Downtown. At Shaw's Crabhouse.'

A big, big lie. Shaw's was probably the finest seafood restaurant in the state.

'Oh . . . ?'

The phone rang. The handset filled her diminutive palm. He told her nothing about climbing towers. Nothing about the fishcamp.

'Claxton Looms Luxury Apartments. This is Rebecca, may I help you?'

Conjecturally, the call provided time and opportunity for Benny to redirect towards the truth. For him to realize the absurdity of his actions. He should just go home. Excuse himself and leave. Rebecca obviously recognized the name of Shaw's. Anyone would have. The lie seemed to buy Benny a little respect, so he wrote it on the form. Her easy acceptance of the lie fueled the rest. Rebecca sat up straighter, in her full-size desk chair, watching Benny write while she spoke on the phone.

'Sorry, Mr Setzer,' she said, transferring the phone from one hand to the other; the act took all of her fingers. 'I didn't realize it was an internal call.'

Benny lied about everything on the forms. About his salary, where he lived, where he used to live, his references – two long-dead relatives and Gene Whoey, his imaginary childhood friend – everything. Even his social security number, which she would use for the credit report. Benny lied while Rebecca struggled to maintain her role of authority for Benny, and concerned servility to the man on the phone.

'Yes, sir, I put in a work order for it yesterday. But . . .'

Aside from the stepladder for feeding the fish, Benny saw no evidence that Claxton Looms made accommodations for their Employee of the Month's diminished stature. She seemed almost lost behind the big desk. Benny would've dropped his pen as a ploy to look under the desk to see if her little feet rested on a stool, or dangled above the floor, but it was chained to the clipboard, and dropping the clipboard was too stupid even for him. A tableau of ornately framed photographs formed an arc in the center of the desk. The angle was wrong so Benny couldn't see the pictures clearly. Couldn't make out the faces, the bodies, the contexts.

'No, sir, I didn't have . . .'

Benny finished the forms long before Rebecca Hinkey finished making promises and serving up apologies to the disgruntled Mr Setzer. Benny's own ragged sense of decorum, tempered by a streak of impudence that tended to flare whenever anyone was being told what to do, urged him to move away from Rebecca's desk. To find some distraction until she was off the phone.

With faux-Art, capital A, on the walls, spotless carpeting, décor straight out of Pier One Imports, Crate & Barrel, or some other such place, and idyllic pictures of ideal residents frolicking in the pool, working out – and sweating beautifully – in the exercise room, and gathered for an evening of perfect socializing in the clubhouse, Benny, for reasons both phobic and real, couldn't even begin to imagine himself living here.

On a low table, at the other end of the couch, a stack of magazines drew his attention. The top magazine lay open, its cover folded beneath, with an uncapped Claxton Looms pen crossing the page. Benny picked up the magazine, only to find that the second magazine was folded open too. As was the third and fourth. They were all *Cosmopolitan* magazines, and all open to something called *Cosmo* Wants To Know. Quizzes. Surveys. Personal tests. And all completed. A nearly empty bottle of some fancy fizzy water sat by the stack on a Claxton Looms coaster warped by condensation. Benny intuited the impression of a small body in the couch seat and back. Rebecca had been sitting there.

Build Your Perfect Man
A chance to build a guy who's got it all.

Confess Your Career Crimes
Share your story with *Cosmo*.

Need Beauty Advice?
We have the answers.

What's Your Vagina Attitude?
Cosmo wants to know how you feel about 'down there'.

So did Benny. Who wouldn't? There were other magazines, and other tests, about love and relationships, about work, about desires and dreams, all the boxes X'd in Rebecca's careful script. The scores tallied and averaged, then evaluated by the omniscient and anonymous wisdom of the editorial board. Benny was saddened, somehow, by the implications of these tests, but not enough to keep him from sliding the bottom magazine from the stack to find out how she'd answered those very personal quesitons.

'Ahem . . .' Rebecca cleared her throat once, her hand over the phone's mouthpiece, then again a little louder before Benny got the point.

'Sorry,' he mouthed, closing the page on her innermost secrets. He registered the flush of anger and embarrassment on her face.

Benny went to the aquarium to watch the fish. He

wondered various things about this midget he was lying to. Did she have a boyfriend? He saw no ring, although he didn't look closely. Where did she shop for those small clothes? How did she feel about 'down there'? Why was her business card in the drowned girl's stuff? And what the hell did he plan to do when she found out he was lying?

'I'll call them right away, Mr Setzer. Absolutely. Yes, sir. Have a good day.'

Rebecca hung up the phone. Benny heard the handset land in its cradle, but he didn't turn around. He waited for her to speak. When she didn't, he filled the silence.

'Your tang's got a serious case of hole-in-the-head disease.'

'What?' she asked.

'It's actually called lateral line erosion. Pretty contagious.'

'Do you know about fish?'

'A little,' he said, the truest things he'd said to her yet. He knew enough to be certain that the gaping holes in the yellow fish's head would kill it if left untreated.

Rebecca came from behind the desk and stood beside Benny at the aquarium.

'One died already,' she said. 'I don't know what to do about it.'

She held the clipboard full of lies in her hands. Funny, how deceit can seem at once weightless and crushing.

'When were you thinking about moving?' she asked.

'What?' Benny asked, forgetting momentarily the ruse.

'Once your references are checked and the credit report is run, when would you be able to move in?'

'Oh,' he said. 'As soon as possible.'

Before leaving, Benny reached tentatively with his hand to shake hers, unsure of what she would give back. On the way down the road he spent little time pondering the after-math of his lies, but he looked periodically at his hand. *I touched a midget*, he thought, and marveled at the normalcy of her hand, which, despite his apprehensions, was not oily or scaly, not fin-like at all. Was quite human.

Enough of this shit. What am I afraid of?

Benny decided then and there, at a stop sign on Plank Road actually, to watch the drowned girl's videotapes. It was stupid of him to wait. Benny didn't even know why he waited. But, the lack of a VCR presented a small problem. Maybe he could borrow one from Jeeter. No sooner did he arrive at this point of resolved determination, a moment of quiet clarity, than disturbance and confusion, in the form of a squealing-tired, high-revving, barely muffled Harley Davidson, jarred him back into a fuzzier reality.

'Where've you been, man?' Jeeter asked, leaning the bike to stick his head too far in the van's driver's side window for Benny's comfort. 'I thought we were going to the flea market. It's past noon and you know all the good stuff is going to be gone.'

'What I know, Jeeter, is that you smell like dirt *and* that there was never any good stuff to begin with at the flea market. It's all shit all the time. We just convince ourselves that there's something more exciting about unknown shit than our own familiar shit.'

'Wow. You're deep.'

'Fuck you,' Benny said. 'Get out of my window. How'd you get so filthy?'

'Ponds, my friend-without-vision. I told you I was expanding. I've been out in Meyer's Park digging holes for the monied and dumb. If you had any sense you'd get in on the ground floor of this enterprise.'

'I guess you won't find many people bragging about my over-abundance of good sense.'

Jeeter filled Benny in on his day. It occurred to Benny that borrowing a VCR from Jeeter would require too much explaining. Doodle. He'd ask Doodle.

'Hey, is there a cure for hole-in-the-head disease?' Benny asked.

'You mean lateral line erosion? Like in fish?'

'No, like in Dink. Of course in fish. Is there?'

'Yeah. Sure,' Jeeter said. 'Why?'

'You got a tank out at Claxton Looms? That apartment building in the old mill?'

'No.'

Jeeter told Benny how to cure lateral line erosion.

'I passed him this morning,' Jeeter said, putting his helmet on.

'Who?'

'Dink, riding that damn moped out on the by-pass. I almost ran over him myself, just to spare some trucker the inevitable misery.'

Benny ignored him.

'Let's go to the flea market tomorrow. First thing in the morning,' Benny said.

'I might have to go to church first.'

'Fuck you. I'll pick you up at eight.'

'I got a hot date tonight. Planning on doing a lot of sinning.'

'Bye, Jeeter.'

When Benny pulled into his driveway, Doodle, with her back to him, stood bent over at her front stoop. Benny tooted the van's horn and she wiggled her ass at him. She was planting tomatoes in five-gallon pickle buckets. The paperback she'd been reading all week lay on the concrete stoop by a Mr Pibb can, the bookmark only a few pages from the end.

'Hey, sexy,' Benny said, 'How'd you know it was me?' he asked, feeling playful. And genuinely appreciating the sight of Doodle's behind. Doodle answered without turning around.

'Radar,' she said, wiggling again. 'When are you gonna do more than just whistle at this thing?'

Benny walked up behind her, and pinched.

'There,' he said. 'What're you doing?'

'Careful now,' Doodle said. 'Don't let your passion get the best of you.' She turned and sat on the stoop facing Benny. 'I'm planting tomatoes, like I do every year. And I'm sure, after the rabbits and the raccoons eat their fill, I'll harvest three pitiful little wormy tomatoes, like I do every year.'

Benny sat on the stoop.

'I admire your spunk,' Benny said. 'They say trying is what counts.'

'Do they? I always found counting the tomatoes a more reliable conclusion.'

'Me and Jeeter are going to the flea market tomorrow. You want to go?' Benny asked.

'Can't,' she answered.

'I'll get you some more dirty books,' he said.

'Ooo! You do know how to satisfy a woman, Benny Poteat.'

'Hey, Doodle, you got a VCR?'

'Yeah. I do, but it's busted. Why?'

'Just wondering. How much did it cost?' Benny stood up.

'Didn't cost me anything.' Doodle stood up, brushed the hair from her eyes, leaving behind a smudge of black dirt on her forehead. 'By the way, you never told me the worst thing *you* ever saw.'

'You never told me if you knew the girl at the lake,' Benny answered, licking his fingertip and wiping the smudge from Doodle's head.

Benny picked up the Mr Pibb can, shook it, found it empty and crushed it.

'I'm going to the recycle center today. Want me to take yours?' he asked, walking towards his door.

'Sure. Thanks. Hey . . .' she said.

Benny turned, half expecting to see her tits.

'You can rent one at the video store,' she said.

'Oh,' Benny replied, a little disappointed by the lack flesh, and a little apprehensive over the new information. A VCR would put him one step closer to knowing. One step closer to doing something, anything, about the situation. Benny wasn't convinced of his own readiness for such a big step. He took it anyway.

CHAPTER 9

BENNY THOUGHT SATURDAY NIGHT AT NUB & HONEY'S
Fishcamp would never end. But it did. Like all things, even
the most unbearable, its time simply ran out. He made
excuses until Doodle, Scotty, and everyone else had left
the restaurant before him. Benny didn't want anybody
following when he went to the video store. He passed
Buffalo Video, adjacent to the 7-11, several times a week,
on his way to work and back, never noticing the *We Rent
VCRs* sign until Doodle mentioned the option. He hoped
they would still be open. And he hoped he'd have the balls
to actually go inside.

Benny made a list: Channel catfish. Banjo cat. Corydoras.
Talking catfish. Bullhead cat. Bristle-nosed cat. Plecostomos.
Blue-eyed plec. Whiptailed cat. Upside down cat. Ghost
catfish. He ran out of road before he ran out of fish. Killing
the engine and lights, Benny eased into the parking lot
with as much stealth as the old van allowed. Judging by
the marquee, lights flashing manically, Buffalo Video was
open for business with only two other cars in the lot. In
the hope that he wouldn't have to deal with them, Benny
said a little prayer that those customers would be skittish
old perverts, skulking around in the adult room.

One apparently wasn't. They were a couple actually, new
in love, holding hands and no doubt looking for something

to mirror, even bellows, their stoked-up feelings. Something that'd make them want to kiss even more than they already did. Speculation on Benny's part, but pretty clear. It occurred to him that if he owned a video store, he'd arrange the movies according to the customers' moods or emotions, rather than by vague genres. Sometimes all a guy wanted was to pick a movie from the 'plights worse than your own' aisle and go home to brood. Sometimes a girl just needed a good cry, even when nothing specific in her life warranted it. More speculations, from a guy who didn't even own a VCR. Benny wandered the aisles, picking up and reading boxes at random, until the couple left.

'Can I help you?' the clerk, a pimpled kid with nice hair covering half his face, asked when Benny, nearly skulking himself, approached the counter.

'You rent VCRs?'

'What?' the clerk asked, cocking his head at Benny.

Goddamnit! A quarter! Just like that lunatic at Pandora's. Benny's heart did a double step. This kid couldn't be related, and he actually seemed friendly. There are times when it seems that life is trying to teach a lesson, or at least get one to pay close attention. Benny had no idea why he was meeting this odd twin, or what he could learn from the recurrence, but he couldn't help thinking of conspiracy. Maybe he'd stumbled upon a secret society.

'VCRs? Do you rent video machines?'

'Yep. Fifteen bucks a day. Want one?'

The kid took Benny's only credit card and gave him some forms to fill out. Benny did so truthfully. When Benny handed back the finished paperwork the clerk knelt behind the counter, mumbled and grunted, then heaved a thick plastic briefcase looking thing onto the countertop.

'Let me show you how this works,' he said.

Benny listened patiently until the lesson was finished, then picked up the VCR and started to leave.

'Don't you want a movie?' the clerk asked.

'What?' The question confused Benny. 'Oh . . . yeah. I guess I do.'

Benny didn't move from the counter though.

'Our adult selection is in the back. Behind the green door.' The kid pointed with both index fingers.

'I . . . uh . . . I'm not looking for an adult movie,' Benny said. Situationally true. He liked porn movies as much as the next guy, but even if he'd had a VCR, Benny would be too ashamed to actually rent one.

'Ok,' the clerk said. 'The signs will tell you where everything's at.'

Benny wandered down the closest aisle, comedies, and picked the first asexual normal-seeming video he came to.

'I hated this movie,' the clerk offered, scrutinizing the box for who knows what. Benny shrugged, for lack of any better response.

'That'll be three-seventy-five.'

Benny handed him a five-dollar bill. The clerk took a dollar from the register and, with all the flourish of a magic trick, plucked the quarter from his own ear and held it out to Benny.

'One-twenty-five's your change,' he said. Grinning. 'Due back tomorrow before midnight.'

The exchange shook Benny up so that he tripped over the curb as he walked out of the door. He struggled, and did not drop the VCR, but the rented cassette fell victim to his stumble and skated two spaces away across the lot. Lo and behold, his tripping coincided with the passing of a State Patrol car. Benny felt the spray of gravel when the officer pulled to a stop two spaces away from

Benny, in front of the 7-11, over top of the dropped videocassette.

History repeats. Momentarily as well as millennially. *Déjà vu* implies subtlety. What do you call it when the past knees you in the groin? Opportunity, once again, presented itself. Opportunity to make things right. Opportunity for redemption. Opportunity to report the drowning. All Benny had to do was open his mouth and tell the truth. Much to his surprise, the officer – the same officer from Pandora's, sans sunglasses – paid only perfunctory attention to Benny when he got out of the patrol car, engine running, window down. Nodding once, as if completing an assessment of the situation, the officer put his hat on and went into the convenience store, giving no indication that he recognized Benny. Benny, of course, said nothing.

Benny opened the passenger door of the van, put the VCR inside. He figured he'd just stand there until the cop left then get his tape. But the cop didn't come back out right away. And after ten minutes, Benny realized that he didn't go to the bathroom after work, after a night of iced tea, and he really had to pee. To worry, to obsess, only exacerbates any situation. Benny probably didn't need to urinate nearly as bad as he convinced himself he did, but within a few minutes he stood, thighs clenched, stepping in place. Inching close enough to look into the window of the store, Benny saw the cop leaning against the slurpee machine, sipping leisurely and laughing at something. This called for decisive action. Benny, hands and knees on the pavement, knelt by the driver's side of the patrol car. A wave of air-conditioned cool spilled out of the car and over Benny's head. He saw the tape, dead center beneath the car. He stuck his arm under, first on his belly, then on his back, as far as possible, but the tape lay just out of reach. He inched his torso beneath the undercarriage, grabbed the tape, held it tight.

'What the hell are you doing?' the officer asked. As if there might be a plausible answer.

Benny held the tape from beneath the car, but remained hidden.

'Dropped my video,' he said.

'I would've moved if you had asked,' the officer said. 'Are you finished?'

Benny pulled himself out, then stood. 'Sorry,' he said.

They stood face to face for an insufferable moment, Benny smelling the chemically enhanced hyper-strawberry in the cop's mouth and feeling like he didn't have the authority to end the situation, before the officer spoke again.

'How's your toe?'

Benny looked at his sneaker, hoping it would by some miracle provide the answer.

'Better,' he finally answered, then sheepishly climbed into his van.

Back in the duplex, Squat paced by the back door, whimpering, while Benny peed in the bathroom sink. It made him feel like a rebel. A trouble-maker. Anyway, the sink, wide and just the right height, made the perfect hurry-up receptacle when the toilet lid was down.

'I'm coming,' Benny said, shaking himself off and rinsing the sink. 'Good dog.'

Benny stood in the yard while Squat ambled around to do his old-dog business. No sense in rushing him. Benny stood there thinking about the disgusting nature of males. Jeeter, Benny himself, Dink, especially Dink, every guy he knew displayed publicly one or more repulsive habits, and what they did privately was better left unknown.

He wondered about women. He often wondered about women. Lots of things. But that night in the dark, in his back yard, he mostly wondered if women were actually higher on the evolutionary scale of cleanliness, or if their dirty little secrets were just better kept. He hoped, if and when he ever got married, that he'd discover the truth. Benny knew, also, that all this wondering was little more than avoidance of what he planned to do. No lights shone in Doodle's windows.

Benny called Squat inside, gave him a few dog biscuits to keep him quiet, then set about moving the television, his rocking chair, and ottoman to the far end of the duplex. Afraid that Doodle may hear something, he'd rather hunch in the corner, ears straining, eyes too close to the screen. By flashlight, which Benny held in his mouth, he struggled to connect the VCR cables. Standing at the refrigerator, debating the need for a beer – his last act of procrastination – it was Benny who heard something. Doodle, calling out in her sleep. A mumble of words, full of slurred urgency. Benny couldn't tell if the urgency was fearful, or playful.

'G'night, Doodle,' he said softly, trying to project comfort through the wall.

When Benny pulled the milk crate containing the drowned girl's tapes and possessions from beneath the bed, his heart picked up its pace. When he folded back the NASCAR towel, a flood of images stormed his mind.

She walked into the water.

She drowned.

Herself. She drowned herself.

Again and again, that moment of disappearance played like a tape loop in Benny's head.

Two weeks and three days since the suicide, two weeks and three days that Benny had held tight to her secret. His secret. In that brief time, he'd tried to imagine the circumstances of her life, those events, collusions or collisions of things done, undone, and words said, heard, or denied, that made it necessary for her to walk forever into the Toe River. Anything other than necessity seemed absurd. Try as he might, though, Benny's imagination wasn't up to the task. He couldn't get beyond his own memories, his own face. Watching the tapes became *his* necessity.

The clothing, her clothing, Benny stacked neatly on the floor. The business card, Rebecca Hinkey's, he placed on top of the clothing. He figured then and there, he could never go back to Claxton Looms. Benny left the camera equipment alone. All that remained were the tapes. Nine, altogether. Scotch. Maxell. Kodak. Tapes that could be purchased at any drugstore. Each in its thin cardboard sheath. Benign in stasis, their secrets codified by magnetization, perfectly defended, useless even, without the appropriate tools: VCR, electricity, desire. One by one, Benny traced each hand-written label with his fingertip.

Triptych: Psalms, The Gospel of Crows, Revelations. Fall 1997
Winter Solstice. April/May 1998
Prophets, Etc. Summer 1998
Epiphanies. September 15, 1998
Lillith Kickin' Ass. Winter 1999
Homemade Bible Stories. Fall 1999
March 3, 2000
Duplex. Winter 2000–2001
Untitled. April 3, 2001

Heavy stuff. Heavy handed, even. Even to Benny. The first tape was almost four years old. He tried to put himself back four years, to imagine the changes, however small, in that passage of time. The things he'd done, and seen. Nothing, really. Nothing to warrant recording. Not his habits. Not dreams. Not his secrets which, until recently, seemed banal and unremarkable. But Benny knew that even the most banal secrets took their toll.

Which tape to watch first? Was there some cosmic order or logic he could employ to help with the decision? Ultimately, what it boiled down to was fear. He feared the drowned girl at the moment of her death, and wanted to begin this portentous voyage as far from that moment, that girl, as possible. The decision to watch them over a period of time was made at a subconscious level. Was non-negotiable.

Benny pulled the first tape from its sleeve. Triptych. His hands shook, his mouth went suddenly dry. Benny thought he might vomit. He pushed the tape into the slot on the VCR, stabbing at the stop button before the machine had completed its mechanical swallowing of the cassette. Benny closed his eyes and took some deep breaths, holding the last when he fingered the remote.

Finally, with trepidation, Benny pushed play.

August 7, 1997   **• • • Rec**
10:40 a.m.

Psalms.

No tricky fade-in. No dissolve. No credit list or text, other than a momentary shot of the title, written on cardboard in magic marker, in the same script as that of the labels. *Psalms.* The camera sits at ground level, in the middle of what must be a macadam road. The angle of the lens is wide; beyond the few feet of pavement just in front of the camera, in which every stone and fissure is crystal clear, things blur. After a while, the camera remaining stationary, the focus begins to narrow. To sharpen, following the safety-yellow stripe. With deliberate, incremental slowness, the field of vision creeps forward. At some point a form takes shape at the center of the picture. There, where black macadam, yellow paint, and the slate gray of the sky converge, something swells into sight. A blooming almost. Its shape irregular, ovoid if anything. As clarity develops, the mind, uncomfortable in confusion and eager for recognition, begins to assume. A crushed box? No. Fallen tree? No. The mind initially resisting anything painful or awkward. Pile of garbage? An old coat? A child's toy? No. No. No. Benny recognizes the true form of the dead cat before the camera officially allows it. A ragged carcass, several days into death, the animal had no doubt been hit by a car. Several by now. The camera begins to move, to pivot, first around, then above the dead cat. Painstakingly slow. And when its position is finally fixed directly overhead, the exquisite beauty of the decaying carcass is revealed. It is, in fact, a blooming, as organic and purely natural as any flowering bud. The camera begins a slow, steady zoom. Down, down, down into the body cavity. Beneath fur and flesh. Beneath bone. Into darkness.

What the fuck? Benny thought.

Cut to another wide focus, another macadam road. Another plodding zoom into roadkill. This time, an opossum. After that, some sort of bird. There were two, after the bird, before, mercifully, The End.

What is this nonsense? Benny thought.

Where is she? Benny wondered. He desperately wanted to fast-forward, but couldn't. Again, fear.

The drowned girl never appeared in the tape Benny watched that night. Not in the second portion of the *Triptych*, *The Gospel of Crows*, which was nothing more, or less, than the repeated scene of three crows taking turns ribboning the viscera from the split belly of a dead turtle somewhere in a patch of Johnson grass. Repeated, and repeated, and repeated, for the better part of ten minutes.

Nor did the face of the drowned girl come to light in *Revelations*, which starred? featured? contained? bore witness to, maybe, a thin man in a chef's coat, the picture cropped at his neck and by the table at which he stood. Before him, on the table, a cutting board with a filleting knife and sharpening steel forming an X in its center. Flanking the cutting board to the man's right, a case of whole chickens. To his left, one huge stockpot and a stack of hotel-pans. At some signal, known only to the man on screen, he began de-boning the chickens. Quickly. Expertly. Incessantly. One after another, he sat the chickens, backs to him, ran the thin blade down either side of the spines, then began to peel the flesh away from the ribs. Traced the thigh and leg bones with the knife tip, and within three minutes, he'd removed all the meat, intact, from the bones. He tossed each skeleton into the stockpot, without ceremony, or even pause. But the flesh of each de-boned chicken he folded into a corpse-like pose and placed delicately in neat rows in the pans.

Benny Poteat, utterly exhausted by the night's apprehension, utterly disappointed by what he'd seen so far, utterly bored by the same, fell asleep halfway through the case of chickens, halfway through Revelations, hunched in the rocking chair.

CHAPTER 10

BENNY POTEAT AWOKE BEFORE DAWN. JUST. AWOKE certain of a few things. First of his discomfort. His back, his shoulders, nearly every muscle of his body had something to say about sleeping doubled over in a rocking chair all night. Too, he awoke certain that he knew nothing more about the drowned girl that morning than he did the morning before. And, he awoke fairly certain that something horrible must have happened in the night. The evidence being that the sun, which normally eased egg-yolk yellow through his kitchen window every clear morning, now a luminous blue, streamed in from the opposite side of the house. Only after the square of his television screen, less than two feet away, came into focus, did Benny realize what he saw. Empty of image. Empty of movement. Empty of sound. And blue. In fact, the sun wouldn't be up for another twenty minutes.

At Benny's feet Squat sat at attention, concern wrinkling his dog brow. The change in sleeping arrangements no doubt confusing.

'Good dog,' Benny said, scratching Squat's head. Benny stood to stretch his back, but instead fell to his knees on the floor, almost knocking the television over in the process. Both feet numb and cumbersome as blocks of wood, from lack of circulation. Squat licked his face, whimpered with even more concern. By the time Benny massaged his feet back to life, hid the evidence of last night's activities and ate breakfast, the sun beamed in all its regular yellow glory through his windows.

Benny, hiding the tapes, in his kitchen, in the bathroom, moved as quietly as possible; Doodle liked to sleep late on Sunday mornings.

At quarter till nine, Benny pulled to a stop in Jeeter's driveway. Tapped a rhythm on the horn. Jeeter came from the greenhouse bus, wiggling both middle fingers at Benny.

'What in god's name are you wearing?' Benny asked, although he'd seen Jeeter in the red kimono numerous times before.

'Been working on my little trees,' Jeeter said. 'This is my bonsai uniform. Sexy, ain't it?'

'You got any coffee?' Benny asked, climbing out of the van, with obvious difficulty from his sore muscles.

'Damn!' Jeeter said. 'You look like you've been up all night. Rode hard and put up wet, as they say.'

'Who?'

'Who, what?' Jeeter said.

'Who says that?'

'Ours is not to question why, my pencil-dick comrade.'

After coffee, Jeeter and Benny went to the flea market, held every weekend on the grounds of Honeycutts Triple-X Drive-In out off the by-pass. Every Saturday and Sunday, hundreds of people from Buffalo Shoals and surrounding counties milled about the tables of useless goods set up among the speaker poles standing like grave-markers, spooky in both their orderliness and silence, milled about in the detritus of the previous night's meager decadence – cigarette butts, old french fries, broken beer bottles, the occasional condom – milled about near the mosquito-thick slough from which rose long, leggy reeds and cattails, upon whose stalks those brilliant damselflies the color of fine silk panties flitted, milled about in a numbed and desperate search for *the* bargain.

Both men avoided the tables specializing in wood-burning arts. And the hooked rugs. And the plaster Jesus and Last Supper tableaux. Jeeter fingered the tools, both new and (often over-) used, as if they were delicate porcelains. Benny picked up every car stereo he found, turned them over in his hands, tugged at the umbilical-like wires. He did the same thing every time he went to the flea market.

'You want a corndog?' Jeeter asked.

'It's not even ten o'clock yet,' Benny said.

'I didn't ask you what time it was, I asked if you wanted a corndog.'

'Sure,' Benny said.

While they stood in line, Benny noticed a man selling books from the trunk of an old Ford Pinto hatchback. The exploding model, Benny recognized. Half expecting pornography, Benny wandered over after laying a precise stripe of mustard along the length of his corndog from a gallon pump-bottle bolted with its red sibling to the side of the concession stand.

'Howdy,' Benny said to the sunken-eyed man who perched so intently at the edge of a straight-back chair that rested against the Pinto's rear bumper that he probably scared away most of his potential customers.

The man nodded in return.

No pornography, which disappointed Benny a little. Mostly the man had college textbooks, boxed by category, each category named and/or misspelled in marker on all sides of the boxes: science stuff, math, history, litature. Benny flipped through the box of history texts. He opened a volume of earth science, drawn by the photograph of an erupting volcano. When he picked up a book from the misspelled category, the man finally spoke.

'You can have that thang for a dollar.'

Benny didn't recognize the title, nor the author.

'This one of them sci-fi books?' he asked, skeptical.

'I couldn't make any sense of it,' the man confessed. 'Kinda stupid if you ask me.'

'You got any paperbacks?' Benny asked, returning the book he held to its box, whereupon the lackadaisical bookseller extracted a secret stash, a stuffed-to-overflowing plastic grocery bag, from the backseat. Most were coverless, fat, epic romances, set in a past as unreal as the characters and their actions. Benny picked three, based solely on their level of discoloration, and paid the man.

'What'd you get?' Jeeter asked, returning with a set of three pipe wrenches in his hand.

'Books for Doodle.'

'Ya'll set a date yet?'

'Fuck you,' Benny said.

'It's her you ought to be sweet talking, not me.'

On the way out, Benny scanned the remaining tables for a decent looking VCR, with no luck. He couldn't have bought one anyway; Jeeter would ask too many questions. At the last table, by the entrance gate, something caught Benny's eye. For as long as he could remember, Dink had been collecting Avon chess pieces, those six-inch-high bottles of Wild Country Aftershave. Dink had nearly a full set, thanks to the help of friends, and once a few years ago Benny made a list of the pieces he lacked. But Benny lost the list shortly after making it, so he usually just bought any piece that crossed his path. There were two variations: amber bottles with silver-flaked plastic tops, or the reverse, silver-flaked bottles with brown plastic tops. A knight caught Benny's eye as he and Jeeter left the flea market. The complicated, tripartite eques. A dark horse with a silver head. Dink didn't play chess. But the inherent beauty of the game, as manifest through Avon, and possibly even the smell of Wild Country, captivated him. Benny plucked the horse from its encampment between a Pee Wee Herman lunchbox and a deck of playing cards spread out to reveal a dozen or more Playboy centerfolds, and paid for his purchase.

He dropped Jeeter off at home.

He went to Dinks Clean 'em Up: Carwash & Launderette.

Dink often paid himself in quarters, paid himself for the time spent cleaning the lint traps in the dryers and the cement trough running through the center of the Laundromat into which the washers drained their sudsy waste, and replenishing the soaps and buffing towels in the car wash stalls, so it came as no surprise when Benny pulled into the business to see Dink standing there with his pockets bulging, so heavy that the waistband of his jeans peeled away from his belly.

Benny pulled to the fully-automated 'Touch-less' bay, and fed it money. He tapped at the horn to get Dink's attention, then held up a five dollar bill, pinched at either end with forefinger and thumb. Dink climbed into the van, tucked the bill into his shirt pocket.

'Hey, Benny,' he said, as the big door rolled open.

'Hey, Dink,' Benny said, easing the van forward until the red light flashed. Before the door had fully closed, Benny had his pants unzipped. Before the rinse cycle climbed over the van's hood, his penis stood out and hard. And by the time the high pressure sudsing began, Dink's mouth worked away at that penis.

Dink, guileless therefore regularly beguiled by life, had been giving five-dollar blowjobs for years. Most everybody knew it. And most folks kept the secret respectfully. From time to time, some drunken redneck, feeling guilty about his role, or perhaps unable, due to age or circumstance, to place the moment of intimacy in its true perspective, communicated that confusion with his fists. Dink got the shit beat out of him about once a year. But overall, it was a welcome convenience. The Super-Deluxe option, complete with undercarriage wash, wheel soak, and vortex dry, took four and a half minutes. Dink rarely needed that much time.

And what did Benny think about with Dink's head busy in his lap? Benny often thought of Mary Steenburgen, the actress. Sometimes, though not through conscious choice, Doodle came to mind. That day, surprise surprise, the image of Rebecca Hinkey, her hands in particular, cradling the telephone, pushed Benny over the ejaculatory precipice. At the moment, just when the hot wax cycle began, he gripped tight the steering wheel of his van, mostly to keep from stroking Dink's head. For a whole lot of reasons. Benny didn't want to touch the shunt, which lay visible through the skin and Dink's short lint-flecked hair. Anyway, the action seemed too tender, too affectionate. Borderline queer. Dink finished the job, retched, but kept the semen down. Retched again as the mechanical door climbed its track.

Benny crept through the pivoting mouths of the vortex dryer, then pulled to a stop by a vacuum machine that was still running, sucking away at nothing. He reached under the seat for the chess piece, which Dink took with a flash in his eye, all that Benny would get for gratitude.

'You go to the flea market with Jeeter?'

'Yeah,' Benny said.

'I seen Doodle this morning,' Dink said, then opened the door and spit on the cement.

'Where?'

'At the Krogers buying groceries. Man, I'd like to suck them titties!'

Benny knew better than to encourage him.

'You think she's got a lot of hair on her pussy?'

'I wouldn't know, Dink.' Partly true.

'I bet she does. Might even have hair on her dookie-hole.'

'Hey, Dink,' Benny changed the subject. 'You ever see anybody die?'

'Yeah. My daddy died.'

'And you saw it?'

'Yeah.'

'What was it like?' Benny asked.

'I cried some.'

Doodle, grateful for the paperbacks, made a lunch of fresh tomato sandwiches on white bread with mayonnaise and lots of salt and pepper. She and Benny ate sitting on their shared back patio and talked of familiar, comforting banalities. As the afternoon temperature crept toward 90°, Benny suggested they go to the Dairy Queen. Doodle suggested they do laundry – across town; she couldn't deal with Dink – after the ice cream, and while their combined whites and colors churned, spun, and fluffed, they played game after game of pinball on the old low-tech machine wedged between the soap dispenser and the unisex bathroom. Doodle won, five out of seven. Thus the day passed.

Thus the day passed, and Benny attended to the passage of time as best he could. He remembered a film from high school. Earth Science class. A huge spool of old film about erosion and the things that shape the earth. He remembered three tiny pebbles trapped in a shallow dip where one stone lay against another. He remembered their tick tick ticking as they danced in an unremitting wind, and how, over time, the pebbles had milled out a hollow the size of a mouth and polished smooth as marble. Benny, even then, felt the rightness of that far more than he could ever articulate. Later, much later, after Benny determined that Doodle had to be asleep, he once again moved the rocking chair and television. Connecting the rented VCR came easier the second time around. Even handling the tapes seemed less traumatic, albeit no less hopeful. Without hesitation, Benny selected the second tape in the sequence: Winter Solstice. April/May 1998.

Discrepancy in season and date duly noted, Benny pushed *play*.

April 15, 1998   **• • • Rec**
12:00 p.m.

Blur.

The camera is so close to its object of attention that detail is indiscernible. Colors? Yellow oxide browns. Eggshell. Sound? There is a soundtrack, its tune unclear. Something disconcerting about the music. And the camera begins to pull back, slowly. Steadily. Not changing in level or angle. A wall becomes some sort of wooden box, takes further shape as . . . what? . . . is it an altar?

No panning from side to side. No sweep of the lens, up or down. The growing awareness is confined to, restricted by, only what can be seen as the camera backs away from its original source of focus. Backs. Backs. Backs away to reveal the full altar. Further the aisle and empty pews. Backs right out the door, which becomes a dark portal in the sun-bleached façade of Egg Rock Pentecostal Church. The soundtrack, vaguely familiar in certain turns of the notes, but something is wrong. The ear, the mind is kept off-balance.

The camera, and one assumes the camera's operator – although nothing human, or living, has been seen – continues to reverse. Away from the house of worship into, what must be, a car. The view defined by the back glass and the shallow plane of the trunk. The car begins to move down the road. And you know the car moves forward, but you are looking backwards. By the time the car reaches its destination, after several empty miles, a realization occurs about the accompanying soundtrack. The song. The song is 'Amazing Grace'. Everybody knows the tune. But here, it, too, is played backwards.

The camera shifts from the back seat of the car smoothly, without giving away anything, takes in the car itself. Tight focus. The focus widens as the camera pulls back, through a yard: a clothesline, lilting; three dogwood trees in bloom; a shed. Mostly through intuition, it is clear that the camera is backing up a series of low steps. One. Two. Three. A doorframe constricts the view. When the door closes, the frame is filled with color. Then goes black.

Benny paused the tape. Sat back in the rocker. Sighed. He didn't think he could stand another night of pretentious nonsense. Benny needed some sense of progress, of forward motion. He got a beer from the refrigerator. He pushed play.

Benny closed his eyes through parts of the second viewing in hopes of checking the imbalance in his equilibrium.

May 3, 1998   **• • • Rec**
12:00 a.m.

Mouth.

The camera opens on a mouth. A girl's mouth. A woman's mouth. Only the mouth. Small but well-defined lips fill the frame. The tip of a tongue slips out and back. Preparation for speech. The lips part, a sliver of tooth suspended from the thin inverted parentheses of space.

My name is not Esther.

My name is not Esther.

My name is not Esther.

A girl's voice? A woman's voice? It belonged to the mouth. Seemed right coming out of it.

Jump-cut to the eyes. So green they are almost gray. The eyes lack the confidence implied by the voice. The eyes struggle to remain steady.

My name is Jenna.

My name is Jenna.

My name is Jenna.

Jump-cut to a face split vertically: the forehead; her right eye; a small blade of a nose, halved, its nostril a near perfect circle; the fine cheekbone receding back to the tragus and visible rim of her ear; that mouth, split twice now; and the chin. This is half of a pretty face. Boyish, but definitely the face of a young woman.

I was not Esther.

I was not Esther.

I have never been Esther.

Cut, again. This time the other side of her face. Asymmetry? Yes. A small dimple in the left cheek. A slight, barely perceptible crook at the tip of her nose. The left eye, offset slightly.

I am Jenna.

I am Jenna.

I have always been Jenna.

And now the camera offers the face, whole. She is beautiful. Whether or not she is the drowned girl is hard to say. But her beauty stands without question. The head shot, backlit in soft yellow. Ample defiance in her voice.

My name . . . is Jenna . . . Hinkey.

My name is . . . Jenna . . . Hinkey.

My name is Jenna Hinkey.

Benny dropped his beer on the floor and rewound that moment of tape as it spilled.

My name . . . is Jenna . . . Hinkey.

My name is . . . Jenna . . . Hinkey.

My name is Jenna Hinkey.

What did this mean? This girl on the tape, who may or may not be the drowned girl, is related to Rebecca Hinkey. Rebecca Hinkey, the resident manager and employee of the month at Claxton Looms. Rebecca Hinkey, who Benny blatantly lied to three days prior. Benny stopped the tape.

He gathered his wits, and pressed play again.

May 5, 1998   **• • • Rec**
5:55 p.m.

Dinner.

A dinner table to be precise. The camera, an intrusion no doubt, is mounted on a tripod looking over the shoulder of Jenna Hinkey, her lean face occasionally in profile as she speaks to the person on her right. That person? Diminutive. Childlike, even, in stature. Not at eye level with Jenna. It was the midget. Rebecca Hinkey. Compact. Fuller in her small body than Jenna, but there is a resemblance in the face. The camera looks down onto the remains of a modest dinner. Looks down into the faces, the averted eyes, of the three people – Rebecca, an older, stern, man, an older, resigned, woman – all distinctly familial: the posture, the cut of the jaws, set of the eyes. The dinner is cold.

Jenna Hinkey speaks.

'I'd like to introduce myself,' she says, and after a pause, 'my family.'

There is less cockiness in the voice now. But an edge of determination prevails.

'My name is J . . . Jenna Hinkey. This is my sister, Rebecca Hinkey. I call her Beck.'

Rebecca Hinkey smiles; it takes effort. She is plainly uncomfortable in front of the camera.

What could Benny determine about the house? Much. Even from the limited view offered by the solipsistic eye of Jenna's camera, Benny recognized mill-hill architecture.

'That's my mom beside her. Our mom. Her name is Hazel.'

Hazel Hinkey demures. A woman so defined by self-doubt, masked as modesty, that it has shaped her physical presence.

'And that,' Jenna starts, but isn't allowed to finish.

'Why'd you bring that thing in my house?' the man asks. 'To my table?'

'It's an assignment, Daddy,' Rebecca says. 'Jenna told us all about the assignment.'

Jenna Hinkey chews on her bottom lip, then speaks.

'It's a family history, Daddy,' she says. 'I'm supposed to document my family.'

Benny, having spent much of his life in and out of mill-hill houses, could tell you the lay of the three tiny bedrooms of the Hinkey household. Could probably tell you which wall the single beds were pushed against. He knew, without doubt, which corner of the kitchen the washing machine occupied. Benny intuited, with quick accuracy, not only the layout of the small house, its weedy yard, but the architecture of the family relationships as well.

When her father doesn't respond, she continues.

'You know, for *film* class . . . In *college*, you know . . . where *you* insisted I go, then decided you weren't gonna' help with tuition . . . I . . .'

'You know damn well I didn't have any of that foolishness in mind when I told you I'd pay for your education!'

'Fooli . . . I . . . I finally find something I actually like to do, something I'd really like to learn about, and you decide it's foolishness!'

'And what have they taught you so far, Esther? Arrogance? Disrespect? I'll tell you this much, you can waste your time, but you're, by God, not wasting my money!'

'Esther, honey . . .' her mother starts.

'No!' Jenna shouts, reaches into her back pocket, pulls out her driver's license. Reaches her thin arm across the table. 'Look, Mama. What does this say? It says Jenna! That's what it says. Jenna.'

'I'm ... I'm sorry. Jenna, I mean. Jenna, honey ... you ... you were Esther when I nursed you. You were Esther at all the church services and all the birthday parties, and every Christmas. You've been Esther to me and your Daddy, to all of us for more than twenty years. We can't just change overnight. This isn't going to be easy for any of us.'

'It'll damn well be easy for me,' the man says, his fist to the table one solid time. 'If and when I speak, I'll speak to Esther.'

'That,' Jenna turns to the camera, 'is my father. *The* Deacon Hinkey.'

May 5, 1998   ● ● ● **Stop**
6:25 p.m.

End of tape. End of family history.

CHAPTER 11

DEACON HINKEY. OF COURSE! THAT'S WHY THE business card seemed so familiar. Benny had known the Hinkey name for most of his life. The drowned girl must be Jenna Hinkey, though he couldn't be sure until he watched the final tape. Benny dreamed about it all night. Dreamed, too, of Jeeter's big plastercast fish, with the drowned girl on its back. Closer and closer it came, swimming through the night sky. But, every time, just as her face was about to come into clear focus, the big fish turned, its rigid tail nearly sweeping the earth.

From high above, on the tower, weeks ago, Benny could discern little about the girl's true features or stature. He recalled something odd about her gait as she walked out of the distance down the long dirt road; and something unusual about one of her legs after she stripped. Weeks later, time had conspired with distance to alter his perspective even more radically. Foreshortened? Elongated? Warped, for sure.

Two realizations struck Benny Poteat that night.

First, that he was watching Rebecca and Jenna Hinkey as they were three years ago. Before what? Before Rebecca's job at Claxton Looms, maybe. Before everything that was filmed in the remaining videotapes. Before, long before, Jenna Hinkey had decided to walk into the Toe Rivers.

Secondly, Benny was sure that he would have to go see Rebecca Hinkey again. That he would have to do so the coming day. That the once insurmountable issue of his ridiculous lies could be, must be, overcome. How? Through the strength of his knowledge. Benny's secret. If, in fact, the drowned girl and Jenna Hinkey were one and the same, Benny held, in a tenuously figurative grasp, a powerful tidbit of truth. Its potential for destruction didn't go unrecognized.

All Benny had scheduled for Monday morning was a re-lamping job on a 200-foot cable-TV tower standing in the fringe of pine trees at the back of the Triple-X Drive-In property. The trees served as a, mostly theoretical, visual block for the folks driving on the by-pass who might not want to see a thirteen-foot vagina, and as a deterrent along with a shoddy two-strand barbed wire fence, again mostly theoretical, to the residents of the trailer park sharing the property line on the north side who might actually want to see a thirteen-foot vagina, but weren't willing to pay for the privilege. Benny remembered the tower from when he was in high school, and already doing tower work on weekends. For a small fee, he'd take his friends up on the tower, after dark, after the concessions vendor-cum-projectionist had flipped the switch and that wicked wedge of light sliced open the night sky, swallowing up moths, fireflies and spastic bats, before colliding with the painted plywood screen and filling it with somebody's idea of pleasure. Benny clipped the carabineers in place, snugged the harnesses, and they watched from above. How much he charged depended on several things: how long they wanted to stay up, the quality of the film, and whether or not they intended to jack off. It goes without saying that most of his clients were boys. But not all.

In fact, what brought Benny's fairly successful business venture to a sudden halt was the time he convinced Gwen Sloop to go up the tower with him. No charge, of course. Benny had nurtured a crush on Gwen all through junior high. Gwen was a 'good' girl; not prone to lapses in moral judgment, nor readily swayed by the general stupidity of boys. But for reasons still unclear (Benny relegated it to the category of miracle) she agreed, one Friday night, to climb that 200-foot tower with Benny for a private screening of *Insatiable*. Benny had to promise beforehand that he wouldn't 'try anything'. But he hoped the bottle of Wild Irish Rose he'd stolen from the 7-11 would open things up for negotiation. The ease with which Gwen agreed to take a few sips of the fortified wine urged Benny on. So eager was he to get to the negotiation phase that he didn't pace the sips of wine. The bottle was empty before the star of the film was good and naked. Benny and Gwen were drunk. The next morning the police, two hundred feet below, shouting and banging the tower with nightsticks, woke them up. They'd dangled there, cinched in place, all night. Benny, as well as he remembered, never even got a kiss.

Despite the lack of any tangible success with Gwen that night long ago, Benny smiled every time he pulled up to the tower. Smiled, this day years later, all the way to the top of the tower, the fresh bulb, its 300 watts mere promise, tucked away in a pouch at his side. Clipped to the other side of the harness were his binoculars, luckily so because as soon as Benny had climbed above the tops of the trees he saw a commotion at the entrance to the drive-in.

While the north side of these nocturnally carnal grounds

bordered the trailer park – whose inhabitants, their lost souls, were most likely too far gone for salvation anyway – on the south side, as providence would have it, one being the very necessary reagent for the other, the properties of the Triple-X Drive-In and Egg Rock Pentecostal Church abut. The sagging strands of Honeycutt's barbed wire fence shored up by an eight-foot-tall privacy fence.

Benny pulled the binoculars from their pouch, but even before he put the rubber-cushioned lenses to his eyes, he knew it was Deacon Hinkey, and the congregants of Egg Rock Pentecostal, protesting the presence of sin and iniquity in their town. Their frequent protests used to make the local papers, sometimes a three-minute spot on the six o'clock news. Now, though, except for the occasional wave of piety sweeping the county churning up righteous indignation, the Deacon and his flock are all but ignored. Given the location of the drive-in, off the by-pass, on a much less traveled road, much of their time was idle. But when the occasional car passed, the whole motley crowd of ten or so whipped themselves into a momentary righteous frenzy.

Benny watched for a few minutes, watched Deacon Hinkey mostly, looking for signs of grief, or at least worry. None found. Odd, Benny thought, and disconcerting, this recent proliferation of the Hinkey name in his life. It was like learning a new word, then hearing it everywhere. Or, like buying a car then it seeming as if every other driver on the road has the same model. For the briefest moment, Benny considered climbing down the tower, going over to the pious man, and telling him the whole story of the drowned girl and what was witnessed out by the rivers. Considered, even, giving him the tapes. Reality, of course, proved different. Benny did no such thing. Instead, he slipped the binoculars back into their pouch, and unscrewed the light bulb at the very top of the tower.

From that far up, Benny could make out some of the geological history of Buffalo Shoals. The remnants of a volcano, millions of years past, littered the town and surrounding county with granite boulders. Some, massive, the size of barns or cadillacs. Others, smaller, more forgiving, cropped up in yards and roadsides. Once, on Benny's first and only helicopter ride, at a 4th of July picnic hosted by Bard's Communications, from high above, he saw a vague outline of the volcano's circular rim and its inward slopes; you could see a ragged pattern of stones and boulders, spat from the hot belly of the past. Benny had learned the details in school, but had played all his life on the rock shaped like a whale in Nub's back yard. Too, he'd known about Egg Rock his whole life, picnicked nearby as a kid. Less than a quarter of a mile into the woods from where the drive-in and the church stood side by side, at the crest of a series of hills, were some of the area's largest granite boulders. Some standing, some lying. Others stacked with frightening imprecision, one serving as fulcrum for another. Some were all but buried, generations of trees and plant life having grown and died in and among them. Each rock formation striking in its poise, or lack of. By far the most dramatic balancing act was Egg Rock. True to its name, the ovoid piece of granite stood nearly three stories high, stood on its smaller end, stood balanced atop a flat stone plateau, free and clear of any visible support.

Benny could see Egg Rock easily from where he was.

Benny could see the members of Egg Rock Pentecostal Church with their cardboard signs and posters. The church had been built decades ago, and the Egg Rock congregation – with Deacon Hinkey at the helm – quickly earned themselves a well-deserved reputation as politically conservative bulldogs in Buffalo Shoals. Over the years, Benny himself had seen them protesting movies, abortion clinics, and, once, the school when one of the teachers dared suggest an idea that countered their own beliefs. Benny had seen it all before. Never cared though. Not until he had a personal connection to the good Deacon. Most folks in town knew things about the Egg Rock Pentecostal Church and its beliefs. Knew for instance, that the congregation as a whole seemed to believe that, come judgment day, Egg Rock, the granite stone, would fall. And somehow, in the wake of its fall, the lives of many sinners would be lost. Benny didn't spend much time considering the questionable logistics; judgment day as an idea, as a thing to be feared, hung like an out-of-focus backdrop in the recesses of his day-to-day existence. Like the loss of his parents. Nagging things. Things to be avoided. It hung in the place he hoped to finally deposit all the memories of the drowned girl. Benny just hoped nothing happened, in the way of divine judgment, until he found out who the drowned girl really was and why she walked into the Toe.

Benny changed the bulb and climbed down the tower, taking care not to get too dirty. On the way to Claxton Looms, he stopped at a gas station to wash his hands. As he pulled out of the parking lot Benny noticed, across the street, a wrecking crew gathered at an old apartment building. A two-story rectangle of dark red brick, the building had obviously been worn out from use. Already three of the men had taken the panes and sashes from several of the windows on the upper floor, and were pushing and tugging with a long pry-bar on another when Benny drove past. He heard the hollow ring of a piece of brick falling into the metal dumpster.

Benny didn't know what to expect from Rebecca Hinkey. The chances of her just not remembering him were nil. But he didn't know if she would react out of anger, or what. He had at the ready his gambit, the chemicals and apparatus necessary to cure the yellow tangs of hole-in-the-head disease, all carried in a five-gallon aquarium that would serve as the hospital tank. Wisely, Benny pushed the doorbell before walking in. Rebecca didn't come to the door. No one came to answer the bell. Instead, Benny got a buzzer in reply. He opened the door and went inside.

'Hi Ro . . .' she began, stopping as soon as Benny rounded the corner. The moment Rebecca Hinkey saw him, the mistake of not checking the door registered on her face. Fear. Fear no doubt hinged on Benny's blatant lies on the application earlier, his willingness to reappear, and what dangers might lie behind such behavior.

'I am calling the police,' she said, trying to sound confident. 'Right now!'

Benny watched her hand reach for and take the phone. Wished he could rewind the scene.

'Please,' he said. 'Please wait.'

And she did. Less convinced by his plea than by the strange assortment of things he held out to her.

'What are you doing here?' she demanded, but didn't give him a chance to answer. 'No! I don't care why you're here. You need to leave.'

'Can I just explain . . .' Benny said, nodding his head toward the huge aquarium hoping the act would be a sufficient answer. Rebecca Hinkey seemed to pause; the initial surge of anger, of fear, receded a little. Benny sat the supplies down on the coffee table, by the stack of *Cosmopolitan* magazines.

'Who the hell are you?' Rebecca asked.

'Benny,' he said. 'My name's Benny Poteat.'

'Yeah, right,' she said.

'No, it is,' Benny said, holding up both hands, palms out, as if displaying a stigmata or some other verification of genuineness. 'Everything else was bullshit, but that's really my name. Benny. Benny Poteat.'

Rebecca Hinkey looked at him from behind her desk. Benny looked at her, searching her face for similarities with the drowned girl.

'I could show you my driver's license,' he said.

'Ok.'

He didn't expect her to actually want to see it, but he couldn't refuse. Rebecca scrutinized the license, looking up from it several times to compare the facts of the man before her with the proclamations made on the laminated card. Then Rebecca eyed the things Benny put on the table, but said nothing about them. She asked the more pressing question.

'Why did you lie to me?'

Benny sat down on the same couch he sat on and lied the first time. Took a breath. But before he jumped into deceit again, with both feet, somebody came through the front door. Rebecca looked up, then at Benny, and back at the door. She clearly expected someone. And when the tall, lean man in work-out attire – the spandex shorts and sleeveless tee shirt version – the look that crossed Rebecca's face wasn't the fearful one she'd given Benny. No. Not fear. Benny knew this look. Knew not only that it rose out of the murky cesspool of desire, but that the look, and everything bearing it up for all to see, was whetted by the fact that her desire was, and would always be, unrequited.

Midget tits.

Benny couldn't stop the thought, even though it embarrassed him. Rebecca sat up, tall as she ever could in the big chair, and stuck her chest out. Benny imagined her feet dangling.

'Hey, Roger,' she said. 'Going to the gym?'

'Hi, Becky,' the man answered, looking at Benny. 'Listen,' he added, turning to face the aquarium, and with his middle finger, scratching his groin. 'We need some towels in the locker room.'

'Oh,' Rebecca said, jotting the information down with a painful degree of enthusiasm. 'I'll see if housekeeping has some clean. I'll get on it ASAP.'

'Thanks, babe,' Roger said, finally looking at her. He winked, but either Rebecca or Benny could've been the target. 'You gonna come spot me later?'

Rebecca laughed. A lot.

'I'm thinking about the stationary bike,' she said. 'Maybe I'll do half an hou . . .'

'See you,' Roger said, leaving.

Benny closed his eyes, hoping it would black out the image of Rebecca Hinkey and her stubby legs pumping away madly at the exercise bike, sweating, drooling all the while as that arrogant bastard does rep after obscene rep of squats, or leg curls, or flies . . .

'That's Roger,' she said, her voice verily oozing.

'So I heard,' Benny said.

Rebecca called housekeeping; chided whoever answered the phone for their inattention to the towels in the locker room.

'He teaches out at Piedmont College.'

'Who?' Benny had hoped the conversation about Roger was over.

'Roger.'

'Oh. Yeah? What's he teach,' Benny asked, assuming from the look of the guy, Phys-Ed. Reserve Officers' Training Corps, maybe.

'Andy Griffith,' Rebecca said, and nothing else.

'What?'

'Andy Griffith. He teaches a course about the Andy Griffith show. Sociology, I think. Something about values and ethics.'

'Oh,' Benny said, truly not knowing how else to respond.

'So,' Rebecca said, after coming to terms with Roger's departure. 'You were about to tell me why you lied.'

'My family used to work here,' he said. 'When Claxton Mills was making the best towels in the country.'

The lies came easy, and seemed too plausible for Rebecca to doubt. Benny took her silence to heart. He hadn't planned the story, but knew true versions of it well enough that, once he got started, filling in the details was effortless.

'My grandpa was a doffer,' Benny said. 'Second shift. I used to come with my mom and grandma to bring him supper. We'd come to the back gate at seven o'clock, with tomato biscuits and sometimes a bowl of beans, sometimes salmon patties.'

Benny paused. Rebecca mindlessly arranged and re-arranged the pictures on her desk.

'He died a while ago.'

Benny let this pause hang. Before long, Rebecca Hinkey filled the silence.

'My daddy worked here too. Before he became a preacher; then he preached in the mill church.'

'I bet they knew each other,' Benny said.

'Yeah,' she said, weighing the complex ramifications of this, and how it impacted what she would say or do next. 'They prob'ly did.'

'But . . .' she said. 'Why did you lie on the application?'

'I drive by here all the time,' he said. 'On the way to work . . .'

'Which is?' she interrupted, doubt once again flashing across her face. It was a look he'd seen before, on her sister's face in one of the tapes.

'I do cook. That part is true. On the weekends I cook at a fishcamp north of town. Nub & Honey's.'

'I've been there,' she said.

– Not when I was working. I'd remember. –

'Through the week, I do tower work, painting and changing bulbs and stuff. Anyway, I've always thought it'd be cool to live here, in the place where the old man spent so much of his life. So, the other day, I just stopped in. I hadn't planned it or anything, but once I got inside, and sa . . . and met you, I couldn't turn back. Then, I found out how much it costs, and . . . well, I was too embarrassed to leave.'

Rebecca swallowed the story hook line and sinker. Benny explained that, by way of making amends, he'd brought the things necessary to cure her sick fish. She eyed the hospital tank, the chemicals, and the long net – they both understood that she'd never be able to reach in and catch the sick fish from the deep tank, not even with her stepladder – she agreed, almost eagerly.

Benny talked as he worked, tried hard to make her relax.

'Have you been here for a while?' he asked.

'Almost a year,' Rebecca answered. 'I got a degree in

Hospitality Management from Piedmont. This was the first job I applied for.'

'Congrats.'

Benny stood at the top of the ladder. With his sleeve rolled up, net in hand, he chased the diseased fish around the tank, his arm going in almost to the shoulder; the crescent moon scar on his biceps grinning wetly each time it surfaces.

Rebecca relaxed. She talked to Benny about her job, about living there at the old mill.

'So,' she said, almost grinning. 'Who the hell is Gene Whoey?'

'What?' Benny had forgotten the reference names he'd given on the application.

'There *is* no Gene Whoey.'

'Oh, yes, there is,' Benny said. 'That's what I named my imaginary friend when I was a kid.'

Rebecca laughed. A genuine, natural, pretty laugh. While Benny was arranging the heater and putting the chemicals in the hospital tank, the telephone rang on Rebecca's desk.

'Be back in a minute,' she said.

Benny positioned himself so that he could hear the conversation without looking as if he was trying to.

'Claxton Looms Luxury Apartments. This is Rebec . . . oh, hi mom.'

Benny wished he could watch her with the phone.

'No. No. Not yet. She hasn't called or anything?'

Benny knew right away the context of the call. The mother's, Hazel's, concern was palpable even filtered through Rebecca.

'Well, it wouldn't be the first time she . . . I know but . . . I know. Ok. Yeah, me too.'

Rebecca hung up the phone. When she finally got up from the desk, she had lost any trace of exuberance or interest in either Benny or the sick fish. Benny, not wanting to press his luck, told her he'd be back tomorrow to check on the tang.

'Bye,' he said.

Rebecca gave a half-wave as the door closed.

Some people would find it easy to dismiss Benny's actions, his secrecy, as cruel. At the very least, selfish and thoughtless. He wouldn't argue the accusations, but he truly couldn't see, not yet anyway, the kindness or compassion in delivering his version of the truth. Rebecca didn't know her sister was dead. Neither did Hazel or the Deacon. They might, at some point. Then again . . . Benny Poteat couldn't tell you anything wise or insightful about the nature and purpose of secrets. Nor could he define the sweet qualities of secrecy that compelled him to cling so to his own secret. Nevertheless, as time stacked its incremental log pile between the drowning and the present moment, Benny grew more and more sure of his lessening desire to come clean.

Squat's nails needed trimming. Had for weeks; the poor old dog clicked his way across the linoleum to sit at Benny's feet.

'Good dog,' Benny said, taking a forepaw into his hands. The nails were thick, and black through and through, making it nearly impossible to know how deep to cut before reaching the quick. Out of eight nails, ten counting the dewclaws, Benny only made three bleed though. And Squat didn't protest those.

Benny watched the clock. He ate dinner. He cleaned up

a little. He watched the clock some more. The certainty of the drowned girl's identity gnawed away at his normally high sense of caution. Urgency grew, with viral-like fervor. By dark, Benny could stand it no longer. He didn't care if Doodle overheard. He moved his rocking chair and television into place, pulled the milk crate from under the bed, and retrieved the third tape. The one called Prophets.

Doodle started her bathwater; Benny heard it through the wall. He got a beer from the refrigerator and, with his socked foot, wiped a thin blood trail from the floor. Then he sat and pushed play.

July 9, 1998   **• • • Rec**
7:00 a.m.

Prophets.

There is a title board. Some clumsy attempts at stylization: light coming up slowly to reveal each letter of the title, then cut to black.

P   r   o   p

Doodle cursed, loud enough for Benny to hear her, then turned off the water. Benny stopped the tape, muted the television, and waited. He heard a closet door open and close, then several cabinets. She must've found what she was looking for because the noises stopped. After a few minutes, Benny started the tape again.

p   h   e   t   s

Daylight. Bright. So bright that, outside the context of

camera and film, it would be painful. The scene is washed of color. A park, maybe. A picnic table in the distance. Someone sitting there.

The knock on the door startled Benny. He fumbled with the remote, dropped it. In his haste to pick it up, the little black miracle worker got kicked under the chair.

'Shit!' Benny said. 'Just a minute.'

'Benny,' Doodle said. 'It's me.'

In the half-light of the room, he found the button on the television that turned the screen blue.

Doodle stood at the door, barefoot, wearing an extra large Bisons tee shirt – the local double-A baseball team – and probably nothing else. When Benny opened the door, she tried to stick her head inside.

'Hey, Doodle,' Benny said, stepping in front of her. 'Whatcha' need?'

'You, sweetie,' she said, less playfully than usual. 'What're you doing in there?'

'Nothing,' he said quickly, trying to maneuver his body to block her view. 'What do you need me to do?'

'You watching dirty movies, Benny Poteat?'

'No, Doodle. Do you really need something, or are you just trying to bug me?'

'I'm sort of embarrassed to tell you.'

'What in God's name could you do or say in front of me that you haven't done before?'

'You don't have to be mean,' she said, genuinely hurt.

'I'm sorry, Doodle. I didn't mean that like it sounded.'

Benny followed Doodle into her side of the duplex. Squat hobbled along behind. Benny liked the moonlight on the skin of Doodle's legs, but couldn't bring himself to tell her.

'Promise you won't be disgusted?' she asked, as they stood in the doorway to her bathroom.

'Sure,' Benny said, and meant it. 'We all shit, Doodle. I'll still love you in the morning.'

'It's not that,' Doodle said. 'My cross. My necklace fell in the toilet.'

'That's it? That's what you're embarrassed about?'

'Yeah, well . . . it sank way down. You can't even see it.'

'No big deal,' Benny said. 'We'll just get it out.'

Benny followed her into the bathroom, a reversed image of his own architecturally. A shallow tub beneath a window, whose glass was as obscured by hard water deposits as by the waves molded into it, filled the back wall. Crammed into the remaining space along the wall, the one they shared, a sink in a cheap pressboard and laminate cabinet, the rectangular medicine chest/mirror hanging over it – its door sprung so that it never quite closed – and a plain white toilet, lid down. Doodle found room for a wicker corner shelf, full of salves, unguents, lotions and soaps, and further defined the bathroom as hers by the accents: a clear shower curtain with large vibrant fish and ocean plant life swimming its surface, a waste can made from a hand-painted pickle bucket, stacks of colorful towels and washcloths, and several bras and panties hanging, at eye level, to dry.

'I love what you've done with the place,' Benny said, blowing at the hanger of underwear closest to him. Which caused them all to sway.

'Smart ass,' Doodle said, backhanding him on the rump.

'I'll be back in a minute,' he said.

'What's that,' Doodle asked when he returned.

Benny held in both hands a flexible metal tube, three feet

long, a quarter inch in diameter. At one end, something akin to a syringe: two arched braces for the fingers, and a loop of rigid plastic at the top of the plunger for the thumb. From the other end emerged three angled claws that came to a pinch-point. When the plunger was depressed, the claws reach open; when it was extracted, they pulled to a close.

'I call it a nut-grabber,' he said. 'Don't know if it has another name.'

After several attempts, with some maneuvering and delicate tugging, Benny actually pulled the cross from the toilet, it's dripping chain wound around the grabber's claws.

'Thanks,' Doodle said, following Benny to the door.

'You know,' she said. 'If you asked nice I'd watch one of those dirty movies with you.'

'Goodnight, Doodle.'

By the time Benny got back to his side of the duplex, the thought of starting the tape again seemed daunting. He shoved the milk crate back in its hiding place, moved the rocker and ottoman, disconnected the VCR and sat it on the kitchen table. What he didn't do was eject the tape named *Prophets*.

CHAPTER 12

ON THE WAY TO JEETER'S THE NEXT MORNING BENNY reached over to the passenger seat and tucked the dangling cords beneath the rented VCR. Although Buffalo Video was in the opposite direction from Jeeter's, Benny wanted to return the machine first to avoid the inevitable interrogation.

He didn't see the Back In 5 Minutes sign, hand-scrawled on a piece of receipt paper, taped at eye level to the locked door, until he stood in front of it. After seven minutes of standing, the door to the adjacent convenience store swung open to a crisp electronic *ding-dong*, and the video clerk emerged with a huge bottle of neon-green Sun-Drop clutched in her skinny hand.

'Thawy,' she said, unlocking the door, not bothering to hold it open for Benny.

She spoke again when he lifted the VCR onto the counter.

'I wath sthowing my fwiendth my new thounge wring,' she said, then produced said tongue for Benny. The gold ball glinted in the dead center of her speech organ, pimply flesh swollen and red where the stud penetrated and disappeared. Benny couldn't tell if she kept her mouth open, tongue shoved between lips, out of pain or pride.

'Ou wreturning at?'

'What?' Benny said.

'Ah ou bwining dith back?' she asked, placing her free hand on the VCR.

'Yeth,' Benny said, unable to resist the opportunity.

While the girl processed his credit card, she told him all about getting her tongue pierced the night before. Told him that her boyfriend thought it was 'thexy,' but her mom would probably throw her out of the 'houth' when she found out. Benny listened, his concentration as impeded by the recent events of his life as her speech was by the previous night's aesthetic modification in her mouth. What choice did he have?

'Holy thit,' Benny said, when he saw the total charge for the rental. He'd forgotten the daily fee.

'Sthe ou yater,' the girl said, following Benny out of Buffalo Video and locking the door behind her.

Never good at budgeting anyway, Benny realized he'd have to wait until payday at Nub's before buying a VCR. Wait three days before he could watch another tape.

Benny didn't expect Jeeter to be at home. Expected him, it being a Tuesday, to be out with his dozer, or digging a pond with his backhoe. Benny's plan was to go into the greenhouse bus, pick out a present for Rebecca – a sort of *forgive me for the lies, I'm really an Ok guy* offering –, and just leave some money on the table for Jeeter. He'd done that kind of thing before; Jeeter wouldn't mind. But Benny smelled the evidence of Jeeter's presence as soon as he stepped out of the van. Hops. And boiling malted grain. The ever-industrious Jeeter was making homebrew, a thing he did every couple months. Benny walked into the trailer without knocking.

'Hey brew-meister,' Benny said. 'Whatcha' making?'

Jeeter, at the stove, with one hand, stirred the ingredients, called the wort, in a large stainless steel pot; the other hand holding the recipe book, he extended to Benny.

'Goat Scrotum Ale,' Benny read aloud. 'Mmmmmm.'

The trailer smelled wonderful. Sweet caramel-scented malt, infused with the oily perfume from the hop flowers, filled the air. Benny knew that Jeeter would ask him to help with bottling the beer in a few weeks, after it fermented, then they'd both get to enjoy the fruits of their efforts.

'How come you aren't out milking some Meyer's Park resident out of his hard earned cash?'

'Priorities, my friend,' Jeeter said, dropping a floating thermometer into the wort.

'Hey,' Benny said. 'Can I get something out of your greenhouse?'

'The door's open,' Jeeter said. 'What do you want?'

'I don't know. Maybe one of them little trees.'

'You ain't got enough sense to take care of a bonsai, Benny.'

'Fuck you,' Benny said, flipping an unused bottle-cap at Jeeter's head. 'It's not for me.'

'Ohhhhhh,' Jeeter said, his eyebrows roller-coastering. 'You pitching a little woo?'

'Can I have a tree, Jeeter?'

'In the service of friendship and fornication, my world is at your disposal.'

Jeeter didn't push the issue, and Benny offered no more information.

In the old bus-cum-greenhouse, air thick with humidity and the smell of damp earth, Benny sized up his choices. Shunning the more showy plants and flowers, what he held up for final inspection barely filled his palm. A bonsai, a juniper with bright green needles, being trained in the slanting style, its rough-barked trunk angling out of the small clay pot, limbs spare and reaching downward. The tree stood no more than six inches high, but may have been five years old. Beautiful. Beautiful in spite of, or because of, the strand of thick copper wire wrapped from its base to the tip of its stretched limbs, forcing the tree to hold its hard shape. Pinching back each new bud, each attempt at growth, kept the juniper squat; not allowed to grow up, the tree fattened and strained against the molding wires. Bonsai is an art. Several arts. The art of force. The art of insistence. The art of patience. Who is to judge the by-products of a man's attempt to define his world? Other men and women? God? What, then, of God's own lapses? It all confused Benny. He left ten dollars on the table in the greenhouse, and tapped the van's horn as he backed out of Jeeter's drive.

The second time he passed by the old apartment building on the way to Claxton Looms, all the window casings in the front of the building had been removed, and the roof was gone. Completely. Through the gaping square spaces on the top floor, blue sky hung.

Benny left the bonsai tree in the van when he went back to see Rebecca Hinkey. Wanting to gauge her frame of mind before risking the gift.

'Hey, Rebecca,' he said. 'How are you?'

'Hi.'

'How's the patient?' Benny asked.

Rebecca, distracted by something, didn't understand.

'Oh,' she said. 'The fish. It's Ok, I think. Still swimming anyway.'

While Benny changed the water in the hospital tank, and re-medicated the tang, Rebecca sat at the big desk doing paperwork. She didn't have much to say to Benny, nor to the few callers that phoned in the time Benny was there.

'I got something for you,' Benny said. 'I'll be back in a minute.'

He brought the little tree in behind his back, and had he known Rebecca any better would've asked her to close her eyes.

'For your desk,' he said, bringing it into view.

Reading her initial reaction with any accuracy was beyond Benny. It definitely contained surprise. It may have held embarrassment. Too, there may have been an instant of perverse recognition. A cross-species bonding of sorts. Whatever it was came and went quickly. A flash. Rebecca, apparently, had mastered the art of the masking smile. And probably, correctly, understood that Benny gave the gift without malice.

Benny sat the juniper on the edge of Rebecca's desk.

She eyed it from a distance, at first. Then stroked the base of its trunk where the wire wrapping rose from the shallow soil. Finally, she spoke.

'That's sweet,' she said.

'You probably ought to water that thing at least once a day.'

Benny put away the fish-doctoring supplies.

'I'll see you tomorrow, Rebecca,' he said.

'You know,' she said as Benny opened the door to leave. 'You can call me Becky.'

'Fuck!'

Benny said it aloud once, then again.

'Fuck! Fuck! Fuck!'

He pulled up to his house and was looking for some change that had fallen between the van's seats earlier, at the Dairy Queen drive-thru, when his fingers raked the plastic spine of the videotape he'd rented – how many days ago? – along with the VCR. He'd simply forgotten about it. This led to another, more critical, realization.

'Fuck! Fuck! Fuck! Fuck!'

Benny remembered the tape left in the VCR when he returned it. A flood of *What if*'s swept over him. What if . . . the video clerk watches the tape? What if . . . something on that tape implicates him in some way? What if . . . what if . . . what if, compounded and magnified through the irrational lens of fear. Fear, boiled up, boiled over. Benny grew certain that the young woman at Buffalo Video, through the first of what would become a career of divinations, had already solved the great mystery of the drowned girl and Benny's connection to her, and had already called the police who, at any minute, would bust down Benny's door and haul him away.

'Fuck! Fuck! Fuck!' became Benny's mantra all the way back to Buffalo Video.

He pushed the old van to its limited capacity, nearly squealing to a stop in front of the store. Thank god the Back In 5 Minutes sign was gone. Benny wondered if the same clerk was still on duty. He opened the door with more force than he'd intended. All of the half dozen customers in the store turned to look at him.

'Sorry,' Benny said, to anyone who could hear him, holding out the late video as an explanation.

She was still there, talking to the guy with the, very visible, quarter in his ear. Both of them looked at Benny. Both of them smiled.

'Ou looking for thith?' the girl asked, holding up the videotape labeled *Prophets*.

'Oh,' Benny said, quick on his feet. 'No, I was returning this.'

He held out the rented tape, hoping, praying that the exchange would be quick and easy.

'Thith wath in the V-ThC-aR ou wreturnthd.'

'Was it?' Benny said, with as much incredulity as he could muster. He reached for the tape, extended the one he held for the guy to take.

'What?' the guy said, although it was unclear to whom. 'I hated this movie,' he said, scowling at the box.

Benny took some deep breaths. While the two video clerks clearly were engaged in some unspoken dialogue, much to Benny's relief, it didn't look like the police would be involved. He got through the exchange of the videotapes, struggling alongside as the girl wrestled with each word, and, with minimal reluctance, repeating things when necessary, for the guy, to get them through his aural tollgate. 'Fuck,' Benny whispered to himself as he left the store, this time over the amount of the late fee.

'You can call me Becky,' she had said.

And so he did. The next time he went to Claxton Looms, and the next, and the next. Benny went, after working on the towers, every day that week. Benny involved himself in Becky's life so much so that he almost forgot about the tapes under his bed. Almost. Each day he passed the abandoned apartment building, demolition had progressed. One day, most of the exterior front wall was gone. A day later, the demolition crew started in on the interior walls.

Benny and Becky talked a lot, but not about the fact that their relationship had gone beyond the fish-care pretense. Got comfortable with one another. She moved the bonsai tree to the front edge of her desk. He asked her about Roger, and more about the Andy Griffith class. Becky admitted to having a crush on Roger, no surprise to Benny. He'd seen them interact a couple more times, and watched as Becky's face flushed and her pupils dilated. Benny began to tease her about it. Becky, playfully, accepted. In the same way that she accepted Benny's growing attention.

When he felt Becky was ready, he asked about the photographs on her desk.

'That's my mom,' she said. 'That's my dad. Me. And that's my sister, E . . . Jenna. We can't seem to find her.'

'She's . . .' Benny paused.

'Normal?'

'I was going to say pretty.'

'Like I said, normal.' Becky picked up the frame and traced its edge with her finger. 'Where are you?' she asked softly.

'I didn't mean that you're not pretty, Becky,' Benny said. 'You are. To me. I mean, you just are.'

Becky smiled at Benny. A sad, appreciative smile.

'What do you mean you can't find her?' he asked.

'She changed her name,' Becky said. 'Esther. Her name was Esther, like in the bible. Like Rebecca. Then she went to college and got all arty.'

'You can't find her because she changed her name?'

'No, that's not it.'

'Because she's *arty*? I don't know what that means.' But he did.

'That's not it either. Well, I guess that's part of it. Both. But Jenna was different long before she changed her name.'

'So she ran away?' Benny asked, pushing the issue.

'I don't . . . we don't know. I mean, she's been gone before, and she is an adult, but . . . we usually, after a while, find out somehow where she's at. It's been too long this time.'

Becky placed her sister's picture back on the desk.

'My folks are really worried,' Becky said. 'I've got to go potty,' she said, and the confession, its tone, content and attendant implications, given how determined she usually seemed to convey herself as *adult*, took Benny by surprise. Becky disappeared behind a door Benny hadn't seen used. He heard the water tap turned on and, without hesitation, opened Becky's top desk drawer. There, among the pencils, pens, scissors, and paperclips, an old child's block caught Benny's eye. Not too far from square, the hand-carved block bore out-of-sequence letters on three of its side: E, R and G. The other three sides were vaguely recognizable bas-reliefs of Jesus, the cross, and (presumably) a dove. Benny plucked it from its rest, stuck it in his pocket. He was sitting on the couch flipping through a *Cosmopolitan* magazine when Becky came out of the bathroom.

'Sorry,' she said.

'I was just building my perfect man,' Benny said, splaying the magazine open.

'Give me that,' Becky said, and snatched it playfully from his hands. She regained her composure.

On the way home from Claxton Looms, Benny saw that the interior walls on the second floor of the old building he passed earlier had been removed. All that remained were the back and side walls. Stopped by a traffic light, Benny studied the structure. Something was disconcerting about the standing wall. No. Not disconcerting. But Benny couldn't find the precise word to describe the effect of what he saw. The remaining wall had obviously been the kitchen walls of all the apartments. Five equally sized rooms, with small windows in their centers, demarcated by the only surviving evidence of their past occupants' humanity: wallpaper and paint. Alternating, as if by grand design. In one corner a dingy beige paint-job confessed years of unhappiness. Beside it, a stern striped wallpaper peeled away from where there was once a ceiling. Another, brighter paint. Benny convinced himself that he could almost make out some childish crayon scribblings near floor level. The next room, no doubt the happiest in the house, was the most audacious. Two wallpaper patterns: a bold black and white check from the chair rail down, and a floral print spiraled and snaked toward the absent ceiling. The room on the end, stark and white. Benny thought about the lives that had passed through those kitchens. He sat imagining the dinners, imagining families playing or fighting, laughing or weeping, year after year. He sat imagining folks cooking and eating, some alone, others blessed or cursed by companionship. Benny sat imagining right through the change of the traffic light, and jumped when the horn of the car behind him sounded.

When he passed again the next day, after eight hours of painting a water tower in the next town over, his hair, arms, and clothes spattered battleship gray, Benny saw that the building was completely demolished. Even the pile of rubble had been bulldozed away. The lot was vacant. Impermanence. Sometimes the fact hit Benny with enough force to take his breath away. Nothing lasts. Benny realized, too, that the yellow tang's lateral line disease had been successfully reversed. The fish was gaining back some of its striking beauty. And Benny had no further, official, reason to go visit Becky every day.

Becky helped him transfer the fish from the hospital tank back into the large aquarium.

'So it looks like this guy is going to be Ok,' he said, trying to sound leading.

'I guess so,' she said. 'Thanks a lot for all your help.'

She sat on the edge of the low couch and watched him pack up the supplies. Her feet just touched the floor.

'No problem,' he said. 'It was not only my pleasure, but my penance for all those lies I told you.'

'Oh, you paid for those a long time ago,' she said. 'I feel like I owe you something now.'

This was the moment. The door had opened. Could Benny actually bring himself to ask the midget for a date? He wanted to, for more reasons than he could articulate.

'Well,' he said. 'You could come and eat some fish with me. At Nub & Honey's. I mean, I'm not a professor of Andy Griffith or anything but . . .'

Becky smiled. She nodded, slowly.

'Let me think about it,' she said.

Benny gave her his phone number and left.

'Best salt and pepper catfish in town,' he said on the way out.

CHAPTER 13

TWO DAYS LATER REBECCA HINKEY CALLED BENNY Poteat. As fate would have it, the phone rang the second Benny knelt beside his bed to look at the tapes trying to figure out how he could afford to buy a new VCR.

'Hello.'

'Hi, Benny.'

'Hey, Becky,' he said, sliding the milk crate out of sight.

'What're you doing?' she asked.

'Vacuuming,' he said.

'Ha!' Becky said, laughing. 'I'll bet you don't even own a vacuum cleaner. You're probably watching wrestling or something on TV.'

'Ok. You caught me. I confess,' Benny said, pleasantly surprised at her playfulness. 'How are you?'

'Good,' she said. 'But I'll be even better after a fine fish dinner.'

Benny had picked up the stolen toy block from where it sat on his dresser. He ran its polished surface over his upper lip, smelled the faint scents of pine and varnish. He wanted to ask about Jenna. Had they found her? Had they given up?

'You'll go?' he asked.

'Yep, unless you've changed your mind.'

They decided on day after next. A Monday.

'I'll pick you up,' he said.

Affordable or not, Benny realized he had to have a VCR because he lacked the willpower to go another day without watching at least part of the Prophets tape. He counted his cash. He called Jeeter, but Jeeter was busy. He called Dink, and they went to the flea market.

Some days, the flea market felt good. Like you're part of a big and vibrant cycle of living: buy, sell, give, get. A transferring of energies. Some days, you found exactly what you came looking for. Or, better still, that perfect bargain you didn't even realize you needed.

Other days, nothing is more destitute, more empty and pathetic, than the endless tables of detritus, worthless junk dredged from the black and hopeless bowels of people's lives. The day Benny and Dink went fell somewhere in between. The biggest problem was the heat and humidity. One of those days that insisted on your misery. Just inside the gate sat a pickup truck with a sign propped in its bed. Lots of folks gathered around it. Dink read the sign aloud, slowly.

'Cock-a-docks and peek-a-poos.'

'They're dogs,' Benny said. 'Mixed breeds. Cocker Spaniels mixed with dachshunds, and Pekingese mixed with poodle.'

'Lets go pet 'em,' Dink said.

Benny pulled him away after about ten minutes.

'It's hot, Dink. Come on.'

'We used to call them mutts,' Dink said. 'Dogs mixed up like that. My mama had a dog one time, funniest-looking dog I ever seen. It was a thing called a Shih Tzu mixed with a beagle. Them dogs in that truck was two hundred dollars each. If we'd a called that dog of my mama's a shit-eagle, we could've made some good money off it!'

Benny laughed.

Dink laughed harder.

After they found a VCR for the right price, still in the box so most likely stolen, Benny treated them both to corndogs, which they ate on the way home.

'You gonna watch titty movies on that thing?'

'Probably not, Dink.'

'Shoot, I would. Ever day. I like them kind where the ladies look regular.'

Despite his better judgment Benny asked, 'What do you mean, regular?'

'Just regular ladies. You know. Where they ain't got them big plastic titties and no hair on their cooters. I just like regular titties, big or small, and hairy pussies.'

'Oh,' Benny said, wishing he'd just intuited the answer.

'Regular,' Dink said.

Benny handed Dink a napkin, told him to wipe the mustard off his chin.

'I seen one, one time . . .' Dink said, and Benny tuned him out when he heard the word 'emena'. Benny wasn't about to correct him. After a while Dink just stopped talking, but as they pulled into the Laundromat parking lot, he had one final question.

'I wonder what that feels like?'

'What?' Benny asked, truly having forgotten the earlier conversation. Dink spoke as he climbed out of the van.

'To have all that old water squirted up your butt?'

'Goodbye, Dink,' Benny said, putting the van in reverse.

'Then it's got to come back out.'

'Bye, Dink.'

'I might like it, pendin' on who did the squirting.'

He was still talking when Benny drove off.

Doodle didn't come home after the shift at the fishcamp. Which was ok with Benny. She probably stayed with Jean, one of the other waitresses, who had air-conditioning in her trailer. That'd be Benny's guess. Or hope. He pulled the box fan out of the bedroom window, and angled it in the doorway so the air, warm but moving at least, flowed over him. Squat shuffled over and lay in the path of the breeze.

'Good dog,' Benny said, and pressed play.

The tape had been rewound.

July 9, 1998   ● ● ● Rec
7:00 a.m.

Prophets.

The title board. The clumsy stylization: light coming up slowly to reveal each letter of the title, then cut to black.

P r o p h e t s

The scene bleached of color. Hot bright daylight. The park. The picnic table in the distance. The camera, handheld, approaches, each rhythmic jolting step recorded. A man sits at the table, with his head down. He jerks up at the sound of the camera-bearer. The man's hand goes out to grasp the push-bar of a grocery cart parked against the table. The cart is, more or less, half full, and the camera perspective pivots for a better view.

'Hnnnnh.' The man speaks.

Shoes. The shopping cart contains shoes. The camera

pivots again. Gets closer. Shoes. Old shoes. Mismatched. Worn out. Loafers, athletic shoes, pumps, a black-and-white wingtip. Others. The focus widens to contain the man's hand, knuckles white, gripping the bar. There is movement. Sudden movement. The camera swings, off balance, and blurs. Quickly refocuses on the man running away, pushing the cart of shoes, one misaligned front wheel whipping madly back and forth. And the dissolving squeak, squeak, squeak, squeak, sque . . . sq . . .

The camera watches until the man is out of sight, then turns downward. A wedge, the camera-bearer's legs foreshortened, seeming to rise out of the field of vision, a fringe of denim shorts, and stub out in a pair of black canvas sneakers. One foot lifts, its toe rakes the heel of the other. Strips it of the shoe. The naked toes, with more grace, repeat the action on the remaining shoe. With her feet, the camera-bearer arranges the pair of shoes neatly, side by side on a patch of dirt by the picnic table. Long, still, shot. Fade to black.

Hot. Hot. Very hot. Benny stopped the tape to get a beer. Resumed play.

July 11, 1998   **• • • Rec**
12:00 p.m.

'My name is Jen . . . No, do it again . . .'
Jenna Hinkey stands before the camera, holding a microphone. Her lean body outfitted for contrast: red bandana tied as a skullcap, an undersized strapped tee shirt with 'wife beater' stenciled across the meager slopes of her breasts, lycra shorts, and thick soled boots with a crisscross maze of laces.

'This is Jenna Hinkey . . . Nope. Again . . .'

She stands on a busy street corner, a corner ripe with the sounds of traffic, of passers-by.

Jump cut to the same street corner. The same day. Same hour. The same Jenna Hinkey, sans microphone. Her arms are crossed.

Jenna looks directly at the camera. Elbows tucked, she opens her right arm, hinge-like. Displays her palm. Written on it, in black marker, *Prophets*. Folds back her right arm. Opens the left. *Part II*. Jenna crosses her arms again, tucks her fingers under the hem of the tee shirt, lifts it slowly. On the flat plane of her stomach, just above the lycra shorts, in red marker: *Film as Concept*. A little higher, the momentary (intentional?) peek at two thin sickles of flesh, the undersides of her breasts: *Assignment 4*. She lowers her shirt. Pauses. Hooks her thumbs behind the waistband of her shorts at the apex of her hipbones. Eases the fabric down. There, on the sweetest part of her belly, the words *Prof. Good*, borne up by a mere trace of her pubis.

Benny paused the tape. He rewound it and watched that moment again. Then again. Then again. He paused the tape, first at the fleeting instance of her breasts, then at the (unfulfilled) promise of her sex. He spent half an hour, maybe more, watching and re-watching Jenna's introduction of the tape. During that time Benny Poteat got a hard on. During that time Benny Poteat – he'd swear it – fell in love.

Jenna Hinkey steps out of the camera's line of sight. A hot dog stand fills the view, the vendor animated, in constant motion. And although you can't hear what he says, the man is talking nonstop. The camera begins to move in . . .

Benny Poteat resisted the urge to fast-forward as long as possible, resisted in part out of embarrassment. All he really wanted was to see more of Jenna Hinkey's naked flesh. But Benny would never be known for his great will power. He ran the tape ahead, through the hot dog vendor, through a segment about a lady who worked at Jiffy Lube. Watched, with growing disinterest, as the players trotted herky-jerky back and forth across the screen, their very existence made comic by the technology. When the tape moved into the next Prophet segment, the opening shot a four-burner Bunn coffee maker, one pot in the process of filling, two others warming, Benny Poteat actually got up to go pee and left the tape running on fast forward. When he settled back in his chair, things had changed.

'Ballsy stuff,' the man says. He is tall, lean. His face cut from some ancient stone, then polished. He talks directly to the camera. 'You've got potential. But . . .'

And it's Jenna Hinkey's voice – cocky, excited, sexy – that responds.

'But? But? But what?'

Benny rewound the tape. Stopped it where the camera panned left, from the coffee maker to a restaurant counter, and the half-dozen booths beyond it. Two waitresses hustled, resignedly, to attend to the customers, a motley assortment of what had to be students. In the far booth Benny could see the tall lean man in profile, talking, his long long hair, gathered in a tight ponytail, sweeping the back of the booth each time his head turns. Benny watched the man stand and say something to his friends. They laughed, and watched him approach the camera, carefully folding a napkin in half as he came.

'I know you,' he says.

The man is beautiful. Anyone can see that.

'Oh, yeah, how's that?'

Jenna must be nervous. She fidgets and jostles the camera.

'Your name is Jenna. I've seen your work around campus.' The man's face and torso, his black tee shirt, fill the screen. Raptor-like eyes scan the room then lock in just right of the camera's focus. On Jenna. Prey. The man brings something dangerous to the moment. Anyone can see that. 'Do you know who I am?'

'Ye . . . ,' she starts, then hesitates. 'Should I?'

He smiles.

'Ballsy stuff. You've got potential,' he says. 'But . . .'

'But? But? But what?' Jenna asks. 'Anyway, you graduated last year.'

'Got to keep my finger in the pie,' he says, and winks.

'So . . .' she says. 'Potential, but . . . ?'

There is the clink of cheap silverware against glass. He smiles. Nods.

'But you're still holding back. You're afraid of something.'

Jenna sucks her teeth. There is no other explanation for the sound.

'You've got to cut the fucking heart out of every piece you do,' he says. 'Cut it out and eat it.'

Jenna does not respond. This man's presence overpowers her. Consumes her. He holds the napkin out in his open palm, as if it is a heart to be eaten. Jenna reaches for it.

'Come see my studio,' he says. 'I'll show you what it means to be fearless.'

'Maybe I will,' she says. As he walks out she unfolds the napkin. Whispers, 'Yessss!'

Jenna opens the napkin for the camera. The automatic focus struggles with the sudden change in depth of field. Eventually, out of the blur, a sketch arises. It is Jenna. Clearly. With a few simple lines, the man captured the essence of her face: the cut of her cheekbones, the slope of lips, the counterintuitive fall of her hair. Beyond the face, his imagination played freely. In the sketch Jenna is naked. In the sketch Jenna's eyes express rapture. In the sketch Jenna kneels, as if in prayer, her hands lifted palms up, receiving. In her hands, the exquisitely detailed shaft and scrotum of a fat long penis. In the bottom corner, an address, and a name in cryptic, cuneiform fashion: MAX.

'Fucker!' Benny said, too loudly. 'What an asshole.'

The word pretentious wouldn't come naturally to Benny, but its meaning he intuited.

'Twisted fucking prick,' Benny said.

Squat scratched on the door, needing to go out. Benny stopped the tape. Turned off the television. He sat for a minute, staring at two of the three framed things in his house that he thought might pass for art. The first, an idealized landscape in greens and browns, hung on the living room wall exactly where it was hanging when Benny moved in. The warp in its frame hurried along no doubt by the accumulation of dust. The second piece of art Benny bought at a yard sale. A lady on a couch, so horribly done that it still made Benny laugh. He proudly displayed it over his kitchen table. The third probably didn't count as real art, but his primordial lust for Farrah

Fawcett kept him from getting rid of the poster in his bedroom.

'Bastard,' Benny said.

He let Squat out then went to bed. The oppressive heat infected his sleep.

CHAPTER 14

REBECCA HINKEY CLIMBED UP INTO BENNY'S VAN with noticeable effort. She had hesitated when Benny offered to pick her up, then agreed. She was standing by the door to Claxton Looms when he arrived, and opened the door to get in before Benny had a chance to turn the ignition off. Benny took note of her sexy little legs, the way her knee-length skirt translated their shape, the way her calf grew taut, swelled, when she made the high step into the truck.

'You hungry?' Benny asked.

'A little.'

Rebecca offered a forced smile. Benny was having second thoughts about his date with Becky, for several reasons. He'd really rather be watching the tapes of her sister Jenna. And he hoped against all hope that Jenna's obvious interest in Max the artist had fizzled. Benny had the gnawing suspicion that the next tape would include more of that sorry excuse for a man.

Too, Benny doubted his own logic at suggesting Nub & Honey's for the dinner date with Rebecca. Everybody would be watching them. Everybody would talk. Benny couldn't remember the last time he'd brought a 'date' to the restaurant.

'How about we go to Red Lobster,' Benny said, already

turning off the road to the fishcamp. 'This is shrimp night, and I got a hankering.'

'Awww,' Becky said. 'Wasn't it you who bragged so much about Nub & Honey's?'

'Yeah, yeah, yeah, but the choices are so limited there.'

'What do you mean?' Becky asked.

'Fried? Fried? Or fried?'

'Oh. I see. Well, . . . Ok.'

Benny cringed at the notion that Rebecca had sensed his embarrassment.

'We can go to Nub & Honeys if . . .' he let the offer dissolve.

'No,' she said. 'Red Lobster sounds great to me.'

They rode in silence for a while. Becky finally broke it.

'It's hot in here,' she said.

'My heater's busted,' he said.

More silence.

Despite the open windows, Benny felt sure the oppressive heat heightened whatever trace was left of the few dabs of cologne – from a green bottle left in the medicine cabinet of the duplex by some previous renter – he'd put on earlier then immediately washed off. He wished now that he'd changed out of the crisp new denim shirt.

On the short trip Benny became acutely aware of how little of the passenger seat Rebecca filled, and how, despite being of just average size, he felt bulky and cumbersome. After they pulled to a stop in the parking lot, Benny ran his hand over his hair several times, although he kept it cut so short that it never really had many options as to how it lay.

Fortunately for them Red Lobster was a popular spot; even on a Monday night, the place was bustling, and the busyness made that awkward transition out of unfamiliarity less painful.

'I love these cheese biscuits,' Becky said, once ensconced at a two-top, beneath a shellacked marlin. Benny didn't doubt the wisdom of not going to Nub & Honey's. At Red Lobster everyone clearly took note of Benny and Becky's entrance, and throughout the meal Benny caught several furtive glances in process. Even though Doodle had Mondays off, dinner at the fishcamp would've been worse. When the Red Lobster waitress placed their food on the table, Rebecca bowed her head and prayed silently. Benny looked to see if anyone was watching.

'Sorry,' she said, catching Benny's embarrassment. 'It's something I grew up doing.'

'You know what they say about the preacher's daughter,' Benny joked.

They talked for a while, skimming various surfaces, seeking common ground. During a lull, Becky took a chance.

'I feel like I've been sort of a dud all night,' she said, then continued before Benny had a chance to disagree. 'It's my sister.'

'Did you find her?' Benny asked, putting the tea glass to his mouth to hide his eagerness.

'No,' she said. 'No. Nothing. There's absolutely no trace of where she went.'

'How about New York?' Benny said. 'Lots of artsy types go to New York. Don't they?'

An assumption on Benny's part. Most of the very little he knew about the art scene, he gleaned from occasionally skimming through the weekly *Creative Loafing* newspaper.

Becky looked at him. He knew she was trying to remember when, or if, she'd told Benny about her sister's interest in the arts. Again, Benny thought about *opportunity*. Here, in the moment, an opportunity opened up for Benny to let go of trouble. He thought of telling Becky the truth. While Benny had always considered Truth a relative thing, open to compromise, and quite possibly empty at its core, this current degree of dishonesty was new territory for him. Suppose he told Rebecca the truth about her sister. That she didn't go to New York, or California, or even to the grocery store. That instead she walked, big as day, into the Toe River and drowned herself. And was so proud of the act that she documented the whole thing on film. What would happen? Outrage, most certainly. Fear, yes. Confusion, yes. The police, maybe. And what did Benny gain by keeping the secret? A most delicious power. So succulent that it hurt. Barring the discovery of Jenna's body, Benny had a secret that no one else in the entire world knew. How long could he hold it?

'She didn't go to New York,' Becky said. 'Esther was afraid of big cities.'

'Esther?' Benny said, to see what would happen.

'Yeah. Remember I told you she changed her name. She thought Esther was a hick name. She thought Jenna sounded more cosmopolitan.'

'She changed it on paper? Through the courts and everything?'

'Not at first. At first she just stopped answering to Esther. She did, finally, go through all the legal stuff.'

'What did your folks say?'

'Daddy got real mad. Mama, she just tried to keep the peace.'

'I still think she went to New York,' Benny said.

'No . . . They finally called the police.'

'Who? Your folks?'

'Yeah. Mama's been crying for a week.'

At that, Rebecca herself began to cry. Not loudly, not even very obviously. Tears welled up in her eyes, but only fell from the left. One, two, three, and that was all. Benny understood in that moment that Rebecca Hinkey had wept many many times in her life, and expected to weep many more. She caught the tears with her napkin as they traced the sweep of her cheek. When she put her hands on the table, opposite Benny's crossed hands, he wished he could reach out and offer some kind of comforting touch. He couldn't. His calloused, banged-up knuckles, hands aged from sun and work, lay still and in stark contrast to Becky's doll-like hands. The light glinted in the gloss of her manicure.

'Sorry,' she said. 'So . . . you weren't a church-goer?'

'Not too much. Nub didn't like to go, but sometimes Honey made me go with her. Mostly revivals and vacation bible school.'

'Why'd you go with Honey?'

It was than that Benny remembered the lie he'd told Becky about his mother and grandfather. Benny dredged a shrimp through a pool of cocktail sauce on his plate. The horseradish stung his eyes.

'My Grandpa . . . ,' he said, stalling. 'He got mad at something the preacher said, and wouldn't let me or my mama go.'

'Think it was my daddy he got mad at?'

'No. They stopped going to the mill church a long time before then.'

Becky looked across the dining room without focusing on any one thing or person. With her finger at its tip she navigated the plastic straw emerging from the iced tea around and around the rim of the glass. Mindlessly, she puffed her cheeks full of air, once, twice, and again.

Benny had seen her do that before while listening on the telephone. Distress veiled Rebecca Hinkey's face, and Benny knew it had little or nothing to do with him.

They sat, again, with silence. Benny, without knowing exactly why, decided to tell her a little bit of truth.

'You know, I got *saved* one time, when I was about ten, maybe eleven. At a tent revival.'

Rebecca's dark eyebrows revealed interest.

'I guess I got saved,' Benny continued. 'I went home and told everybody I was 'borned again' and they thought the way I said it was funny as hell. So I kept saying it that way. Borned again.'

'How long did it last?' Rebecca asked, seeming to know from experience that salvation was short-lived.

'I don't know exactly. But after that, I got it in my head that I wanted to be a preacher. So, I'd go out to . . . we used to have this old tool shed in the back yard. Just a tin building with a dirt floor and no windows. I'd take the bible I got for Christmas when I was nine out in the tool shed and pretend to preach.'

Benny paused while the waitress put the dessert down on the table, then filled their tea glasses. Rebecca paid attention.

'Did you actually write sermons?'

'Hell no. I just talked off the top of my head. And I always closed the door so nobody could see me, or hear me. It was almost pitch black in there. And hot. Really hot. I'd stay shut up in that shed, with the jugs of gasoline and motor oil until I'd be so dizzy from the heat and the fumes when I came out that I couldn't walk a straight line. For years I thought it was the spirit of the Lord that made me feel that way.'

'Oh my. Did you ever get caught?' she asked.

'Yeah, sort of,' Benny said. 'One afternoon I got all worked up, stomping around and praying, laying my hands on everything I could, healing the blind and the lame. Everything was going Ok until I knocked a mattock over into a wasps nest that I didn't know hung in the corner. A huge nest.'

'Oh my god, Benny. What happened?' Becky dabbed at her lips, pursed in concern, with a napkin.

'Well, I don't really remember much about it. I got stung. And stung. And stung. All over my face and my arms. My neck. Through my shirt. And I couldn't see them. One minute I was preaching and the next minute I felt like I was in a lake of fire.'

'You're lucky you didn't die. How'd you find your way out?'

'I didn't. I mean, I must've been screaming really loud, 'cause uncle Nub came out and opened the door. I'd passed out by the time he found me. And my eyes were swollen shut. My whole body swelled. I didn't wake up for three days, and I didn't feel completely right for months.'

'Oh, Benny . . . poor thing.'

Benny took Rebecca Hinkey home. He would have opened the passenger door of the van for her, but she jumped out, literally, before he had the chance. Benny heard a barely audible grunt when her feet hit the ground.

'Looks like we might get a storm,' he said.

'All this heat,' she said.

'Try not to worry too much about your sister,' Benny said, and then before he could stop himself, 'I'm sure she's Ok.'

'That's real sweet of you. Goodnight, Benny.'

Benny levered the van into reverse.

'Hey,' Rebecca said, tapping on the window. 'Next time we'll take my car.'

Benny Poteat, exhausted by the effort to bear and conceal his secret, went to bed.

How could he know? There was no hesitation. No surface disturbance. From 200 feet up, her disappearance seemed almost insignificant. How could he know what she thought? What she felt? Whether her resolve broke down at the last minute, as the river closed in over her head. Whether she thrashed and fought against the current. In his bed, in the sticky humid night, Benny Poteat dreamed the possibilities.

Jenna Hinkey walks into the water, smiling. Jenna Hinkey presses her bare toes into the muddy riverbed, seeks footing, as the water rages around her. And what of the breath? That twin parcel she smuggled down from the surface. Jenna Hinkey holds it tight. Once, maybe twice, a small bubble escapes from her nostril, immediately consumed by the river. Jenna leans against the flow of water. The river supports her. For an instant Jenna, her heart – her physical heart – making its frantic call for fresh air, wants to run. To rise. For an instant Jenna, her heart – that organ of emotion – surging with notions of loss and desire, wants not to be at the bottom of the Toe River.

Then comes the itch. A slight tickle somewhere deep inside her neck, where the jawbone ends, the earlobe hangs. An itch, a faint genetic memory that turns to a burn along her jaw line. Jenna, submerged, begins to rub, first one side then the other. Jenna scratches, raking at the sore spots on her neck. Jenna's manic heart is about to jump ship. Jenna's lungs, two stoked furnaces, flame.

Jenna's eyes roll madly in their sockets. Jenna believes, and why shouldn't she, that death approaches.

Then the skin of her neck opens. Two thin slits gape and suck water. Jenna convulses from that first shock to her lungs. Convulses again as the spent air is forced out, and river water is drawn in. After that, praise be, death turns away from Jenna Hinkey. After that her newly formed gills discover their purpose. After that, Jenna gathers her saturated wits and begins to walk along the river bottom. She walks and walks and walks, and soon enough she meets other drowned folks in their waters, their rivers. Together they all walk, all the drowned, toward the ocean, greeting others as they go. Their gills pumping. A roaring in their ears. They walk the river bottoms, the lake beds, toward the stinging salty water. Toward what? A reunion of the drowned. Toward the storming tide. And toward the waves, deafening waves that pound and pound and pound and pound and pound.

The roaring. The pounding. The pounding, pounding, pounding on Benny's door that will not stop. Loud, loud, pounding.

'Benny!' someone yelled. 'Benny Poteat!'

'Hummh,' he called out into the night.

'Benny? Are you in there?' More knocking at his door.

Benny, dazed and still half asleep, thought he recognized the voice. But it came accompanied by other sounds, rendering the voice muted and fuzzy.

'Who is it?' he asked. What is that sound, he thought.

Benny staggered to the door.

'Who is it?' he asked again.

'Open the door Benny! It's me, Doodle.'

The instant he unlocked the door, Doodle burst in, her

own urgency bolstered by a raging wind, and spraying rain.

'Jesus! Don't you hear that?'

'Hear what?' Benny asked, working harder than he expected to close the door. He rubbed his face with both hands, wiping away sleep and rain. Doodle went, in the dark, to the kitchen table and sat down.

'A tornado I think. I don't know what else it could've been.'

Doodle shivered, mostly from fear, but she had gotten wet standing in the rain, in her nightgown, waiting for Benny to wake up. Benny shuffled into the bedroom, got a flannel shirt for Doodle.

'Power must be out,' he said. 'Are you okay?'

'Yeah. Scared shitless, but Ok. Thanks,' she said, putting the shirt on.

Benny lay one hand on the table, put his weight against it, and struggled to keep his eyes open. He listened as Doodle told him about the storm.

'The worst of it's passed. Sounded like a train coming through the wall,' she said. 'I can't believe you didn't wake up.'

'Tired,' he said.

Doodle talked, in the dark, until she was relaxed. She talked until the wind subsided. After a while the electricity returned, and the duplex began to hum and click. Doodle kept talking. She did that when she was scared. She talked until Benny was nearly asleep, standing there leaning on his kitchen table. Too tired to sit down. His eyes must've closed for a minute, because he certainly didn't see Doodle reach up with two fingers and give a little tug on the tip of his very flaccid, sleepy penis as it peeked out of his briefs.

'Early bird gets the worm,' she said. And just as she spoke, just as she tugged, one final thunderclap ruptured the night.

'Goddamn it, Doodle!'

'Goddamn it, Benny!'

'You have to quit doing that!'

Benny twitched and twisted until he was situated and hidden.

Doodle rubbed at a spot between her eyes.

Benny came back wearing pants.

'You really have to quit that.'

'Quit what?' Doodle asked, recovered enough to still be playful.

'All that stuff.'

'Why, Benny, I have no idea what you mean.'

'You know damn well what I mean. Flashing your titties. Wiggling your ass. And pinching my dick. Doodle, you can't just touch my dick like that!'

Doodle was hurt. And embarrassed. Benny saw it clearly, and any other time, he may have retracted his comments. Or at least softened them.

'It's not all me, Benny.'

Benny didn't respond.

'It takes two to dance,' she said. 'You have to admit that you flirt with me, too. You know that, don't you, Benny?'

Benny got them both a beer. They drank in silence. After a while, Doodle spoke.

'Think we ought to call and make sure everyone is Ok?'

'Prob'ly,' Benny said. So they did. They called mutual friends and people from the fishcamp. Everybody seemed to have weathered the storm, everybody except for Jeeter.

'. . . the number you have dialed is not in service at this time . . .'

'I hope he's Ok,' Doodle said.

'I'll go out there as soon as it's light.'

'Want me to come with you?'

'That's Ok,' Benny said. 'He probably just forgot to pay his bill.'

'Want your shirt back?' Doodle asked, standing to leave.

'Keep it for now.'

'I heard a rumor about you, Benny Poteat.' She paused. 'I heard you were two-timing me.'

Benny smiled, both at Doodle's unstoppable playfulness, and at the speed with which news and gossip traveled in his world. He didn't, however, answer the charge.

'I'm sorry I touched your dick,' she said.

'I'm sorry I cussed at you.'

They hugged. What else could they do? Doodle went back to her side of the duplex. Benny waited for daybreak.

CHAPTER 15

WHAT TO DO? THREE MORE HOURS OF DARKNESS loomed before Benny could go out and check on Jeeter. It didn't occur to him to check on Rebecca. And sleep, at that point, wasn't an option for him. Benny thought of the tapes, of Jenna. Jenna in his dream and Jenna in the various realities she roamed through.

Benny stuck the *Prophets* tape into the VCR and rewound it to where Jenna offered up her stenciled belly for the camera. He paused the tape at the exact moment where the two thin swaths of her breast flesh became visible, fully intending to jack off to the scene. As fate would have it, a fate shaped by Benny's stingy nature and the cheap purchases that nature dictated, the pause function on his VCR left a fat band of static across the screen, right across Jenna's breasts.

'Fuck,' Benny said, his penis falling limp in his hand.

He fast-forwarded just a bit to where *Prof. Good*, writ large across her abdominal plane, gave way to dark tufts of pubic hair. The band of static no longer an obstacle, Benny's penis rallied. Briefly . . . But each time he reached the moment of truth, the turning point, a precise instant in the masturbatory process before which all thoughts and energies focus, hasten, and build toward – this body part, that movement, this pose, that reaction – and after which

there are no thoughts and nothing, save death, could stop
the spermatic outcome, each time he got close some dark
door opened in his mind and filled it with unwanted
images. Becky crying. Doodle embarrassed. Becky naked,
with Doodle's head. Doodle's body and Becky's head.
Monsters. Disgust and revulsion, projected outward. Disgust and revulsion, directed inward. Who's more monstrous than this man able to masturbate to the videotapes
made by the drowned girl, then in the presence of her
sister conceal or deny or transfer those feelings. Once,
twice, three times Benny whipped his raw dick toward
the finish line, to no avail.

'Fuck,' Benny said, wincing as he tucked his sore shriveled organ inside his briefs.

'Fuck,' Benny said, pulling off Hager's Creek Road onto
Jeeter's drive. He had to stop thirty feet in because of the
haphazard crisscross of pine trees, toppled by the storm,
blocking the gravel road. Benny was anxious about his
friend at the end of the road, but he never claimed to be
adept at dealing with crisis. As a tactic, delay, sometimes
outright avoidance, had worked well for Benny in the past.
He took his time crawling over or going around the trees
that lay across Jeeter's drive. It took Benny nearly half an
hour to walk the rest of the way to the trailer compound.
He made a list on the way, to calm his nerves: cherry
bomb, firecracker, bottle rocket, Roman candle, pinwheel,
whiz-bang, and before Benny could finish the list he heard
the chainsaw fire up. Jeeter was, at least, alive.

'Hey!'

Benny had to shout over the whine of the chainsaw.
Jeeter's back was turned.

'HEY!!! JEETER!!!'

The saw bit deep and stalled in a knot within the trunk of the tree that Jeeter stood over, an oak that lay itself down on top of what used to be Jeeter's greenhouse. Benny loved those smells: hot sawdust, the oily exhaust from a two-stroke engine.

'Jeeter!' he called again. Jeeter turned.

'Hey, Benny.'

Jeeter had been crying.

'What a mess,' Benny said.

'Yeah.'

Jeeter looked around at the damage.

'My fish are dead . . .' he said. 'A bunch of them anyway. And my plants . . .'

They cleaned up, as best they could. Benny helped Jeeter clear the driveway. They didn't talk much.

'You can stay with me,' Benny said. 'Until you get your power back.'

'I'll be Ok,' Jeeter said. 'Thanks, anyway. Did you happen to notice whether my mailbox was still standing?' Jeeter asked.

Benny hadn't paid attention to the big fish-shaped metal sculpture, but he lied to Jeeter to make him feel better.

'Yep. It is.'

Things were a mess all over Buffalo Shoals. By the time Benny pulled up at Claxton Looms, it was afternoon. He was filthy. Sweaty, oil-streaked, and covered with sawdust, but he wore his filth as a badge of honor. Irrefutable proof of his worth in times of duress.

Benny, somehow emboldened by the grace that seemed to have spared him, twice now, from a tornado, walked into the apartment building without knocking, or even ringing the bell. Walked in as if he brought that very grace with him. *Here comes help. Here comes good news. Here comes salvation.*

Becky sobbed. He heard her as soon as the door closed. And his confidence withered.

'Rebecca?'

He insinuated himself into the room.

She sat at her big desk, crying big tears. The telephone and a half-eaten sandwich vying for control in the middle of the desk.

'What's the matter?' he asked, not knowing what to expect.

'Oh, Benny . . .' she said, putting her head down on her foreshortened arms, crossed on the desk. She wept.

He wanted to reach out. He wanted to touch her, to lay his hand on her head, and comfort her. Benny lacked the courage. He sat in the chair in front of her desk. She spoke again, muffled and stuttered.

'. . . oh, Benny . . . Mama called . . . mama called this morning. They . . . they found . . .'

Uncontrollable sobs.

'What, Becky? Who found what?'

Expectation reared its head; Benny feared the answer. He looked at the door. He considered running. He looked at the huge aquarium, felt as trapped as the fish inside it.

'They found a body.'

'Who!?'

'I don't know. The police . . . somebody. They think it might be . . .'

She didn't need to finish.

'Oh, Becky, I'm so sorry,' Benny said, truthfully, but for a host of reasons. He wanted to hug Rebecca, to comfort her, but was afraid she'd feel his terrified heart storming against his ribcage. He wanted to speak, to say something helpful, but was afraid of saying too much. Of giving away his secret. He was about to ask *where* they found the body, but the telephone rang. Benny jumped. Rebecca jumped. She composed herself as best she could between rings. Swiped a hand across her nose. Benny saw the light glint in the thin trail of snot.

'Claxton Looms,' she said, bravely.

Benny held his breath. If this call was to identify the body as that of Jenna Hinkey, it could be the beginning of a whole lot of trouble. But why the sudden anxiety? It's not like he killed the girl. He couldn't have stopped her from walking into the Toe River, even if he'd tried. There were no witnesses, was no real evidence implicating Benny. Her stuff in his possession could be problematic, but was there a crime? Benny didn't do anything. Indeed. He didn't *do* anything.

'How can I help you, Mr Ray?' Rebecca asked, bravery giving way to professionalism.

Benny exhaled and learned from one side of a conversation that the storm caused the roof to leak directly over Mr Ray's brand new Barco-lounger.

'I'll get maintenance right over there,' Rebecca said. 'Yes, sir. I'm sure the water stains will come out. Yes. Ok. Have a good day, Mr Ray.'

The distraction seemed to have calmed her some, but did little to calm Benny. It meant that another telephone call was still to come, identifying the body the police had found. Benny could just confess, then and there. Could try and explain to Becky what he'd seen, and all that he'd found, and why he hadn't reported the incident, or told anyone until now, and about all the tapes and how he was watching them in order, and how he'd sort of fallen in love with Jenna through the tapes, but now he'd grown so fond of her, of Becky, through Jenna, not really as a surrogate or anything, and maybe even she, Becky, would like to watch one of the tapes with him. Then Benny realized the absurdity of his thinking. It had been too long; he was in too deep. But if the body was, in fact Jenna's . . .

'Did you hear about that family out on Berea Road?' she asked Benny.

'No. What happened?'

'Tornado picked up their car and dropped it through the roof. The father was passed out in the car. The mama and two kids were sleeping in the same bed . . .'

'Did it . . . are they?'

'Killed all three of them.'

Benny whistled. He told her about Jeeter and all that he lost.

'Daddy called me early this morning to see if I was alright. He told me that that X-rated drive-in was completely destroyed.'

Benny wondered what would become of the flea market. Of the vendors who needed that income.

'He said it was a victory for the Lord,' Rebecca said.

Benny wanted to ask if that dead lady and her dead kids were part of the Lord's booty, but he held back.

'Then he asked me to pray.'

Rebecca prayed often. Benny sensed it even more than he knew it. He grew momentarily fearful that she'd ask him to pray with her, so he changed the subject.

'Where?' Benny asked. He had to know.

'Where what?'

'Where did they find the body?'

And what of the look that fell across her face. A sort of hunger. A hunger for answers. For anything true. And what is hunger? The heart's curmudgeonly, inconsolable docent, shuffling from chamber to dark chamber making its feeble pitch. Benny had no answers. None he was capable of giving. When the phone rang again they both just stared at it.

'Claxt . . . what? Are you sure? Are *they* sure?'

Benny watched Rebecca's face. He knew the news was good. He knew, too, that he'd never tell Rebecca what he'd seen at the river.

Rebecca hung up the phone. She cried, again, but it meant a wholly different thing.

'That was mama,' she said. 'She just heard from the police. It's not Esther. I mean . . . it's not Jenna.'

Rebecca got up. Or rather, she climbed down from her seat, and came around the desk. She opened her short arms to Benny, sawdust, sweat, and all, and he took her in. They hugged for quite a while, with Becky crying. She seemed not to register his still-frantic heartbeat. Benny picked a tiny chip of wood from her hair. Then they kissed.

They kissed. Becky on her toes. Benny hunched in his chair. They kissed.

And when they kissed, that first time – who kissed who, and does it matter – when they kissed the little black devil that was Benny's secret did not fly from his mouth into Rebecca's, its sooty wings tangling in her larynx, seizing her breath. His wicked selfish falsehood didn't batter its way through her small trusting teeth like a ramrod. His lie did not pour itself down her throat, displacing everything – her organs, her hope, her gullibility, filling her gut to the point of rupture. No, Benny's secret did not leave his body for hers, to render him empty and culpable, and her decimated.

Neither was it, from Benny's perspective anyway, like

kissing a monster. The lips and tongue of that strange head, at once childlike and woman-like, were as human as any he'd kissed. Not shriveled, nor fetid. Not scalded, nor cankerous, nor overly phlegmy. Not veiny and ribbed with cartilage, or barbed. No foul, squatty spirit lodged itself in his nose. Benny tasted nothing of her fused misshapen spine, of her limbs bound hard and tight by some genetic buffoonery. Nothing of her life-long sense of aloneness, of rootlessness, that threatened daily to keep her spirit as battered down and diminutive as her body.

Nor did, during that first kiss, heaven itself open up its gilded doors for true love to spill out and wash them both clean. Him of deceit, her of credulity. Nor was Benny's skullcap peeled back and a hot nugget of desire dropped in the cavity; that ceaseless, burning want, want, want he'd felt in the past. It was not a kiss of sunsets or sunrises. Nothing stellar nor lunar about it. No flower petals the color of blood or peaches. No blooming of wings. No choirs or heavenly hosts. Not a vertiginous swirl of lights and sounds. Nothing that reeked of clichéd passion, nor heart-thumping freshness.

No. It was a plain, artless kiss. In fact, Benny's single tentative sortie with his tongue brought back the most tangible aspect of the kiss: a small flake of tuna, and with it, bound by mayonnaise and masticate, a few crumbs of bread and a grain of black pepper. Nevertheless, it was a kiss that propelled them forward.

'Oh, my,' Becky said.

CHAPTER 16

NO ONE WAS MORE SURPRISED THAN BENNY POTEAT to find himself sitting at the supper table with Rebecca and her family, and Deacon Hinkey asking him to bless the food.

'Would you ask the Lord's blessing for this meal, young man.'

Very little *question* in the tone.

Benny looked over the table. The big milk glass bowl of converted rice, drawing in the butter pats, each grain taking on a yellow sheen. Pork chops, pan-fried; Benny could smell the oil in the air. Biscuits. Over-cooked green beans and stewed corn. Good eats. Worthy of blessing, if one were so inclined. Benny hadn't blessed a meal in twenty years.

Benny hesitated. The silence spanned impossible distances.

He played in his mind all the various prayers he'd like to offer. He could pray for Jenna to resurrect. To walk smiling into the room and say it was all a joke. Or, even, to storm into the dining room thoroughly pissed off and ready for answers. Either would be fine. He could pray that, in good cliché form, he'd jerk himself awake and find the whole ordeal nothing more than a nightmare. He could, couldn't he? Isn't that what prayer is most often about?

The impossible? For a while, as a young man, Benny had this theory. He'd pray only for things that he already had. It minimized disappointment.

Deacon Hinkey cleared his throat.

Deacon Hinkey was a man of God. No doubt about it. Benny Poteat suspected that God even had something to do with the patches of black hair sprouting on the good Deacon's knuckles, and the small but noticeable conflagration of hair and snot in his nose. Surely, Deacon Hinkey's vanity came out in other ways. His suit, for instance. Hard and black as a beetle, and somber as a pall-bearer, Benny imagined him always in that coat and tie.

Benny could pray that Deacon Hinkey be struck blind and mute, just long enough for him to escape. Or, better, that he would have a mini-stroke and forget the request altogether. Half an hour ago, when Rebecca said 'Daddy, this is Benny Poteat,' Benny Poteat felt a hard, mean piety in the old man's scrutinizing once-over.

So, there Benny sat, at the dinner table with Deacon Hinkey, Mrs Hinkey, and Rebecca Hinkey. The family of the drowned girl. In some respects, it would've been a good time to come clean, but Benny wasn't willing to give any-thing to these people. Not to the Deacon anyway. It would be almost like betraying Jenna, except . . . except that she'd documented her act. Jenna had wanted people to know. Now, Benny was in control of that knowledge. While he'd been powerless to stop her suicide, the power, the control over how and when her death impacted all these people intoxicated Benny, more than he knew. How did things get to that point? Not two days earlier he'd been with Mrs Hinkey and Becky, moving Jenna's belongings out of an apartment the missing daughter had rented in town.

*   *   *

The elation over the body found earlier in the week not being Jenna fizzled in short order, simply because they still had no idea where she actually might be. Shortly after that first kiss between Benny and Becky, and a couple others, she confessed to him that the good Deacon, while he loved his missing daughter more than he'd ever say, wasn't about to pay rent on an empty apartment. Becky asked Benny if they could use his van. He told her that the van came complete with muscle.

'Benny, you think you could . . .' Mrs Hinkey said.

Mrs Hinkey lacked. What? Hard to say exactly, but something was missing. As if she'd been beaten down by the year-after-year tag team of God and her godly husband. She just looked tired. Gray. Formless.

'I just don't believe that we can . . .' Mrs Hinkey said.

Surely God provided Mrs Hinkey with complete thoughts at some point in her life.

'You reckon all this stuff is . . .' Mrs Hinkey said.

It took Benny a while to realize that Mrs Hinkey never finished her sentences. She always spoke in transit, as she moved from one room to the next, or even from one place to another in the same room. She got going full throttle with an idea, then just chopped it off, or let it fizzle out.

'Rebecca, I think we ought to . . .'

Most of Jenna's stuff was in paper bags or cardboard boxes already. After Benny got the futon disassembled and down in the van, he helped with the smaller items. He and Mrs Hinkey passed close in the narrow hall that led from the combined kitchen and living room, him coming from the bath and her from the bedroom. They both turned sideways with their loads, but when they bumped it was Mrs Hinkey's bag that started making noise. That started to whir.

'What in the world . . .'

Benny followed her into the living room where she sat the grocery bag, with its top rolled shut, down on a table. They both waited for Becky to come back upstairs. She was slow on the stairs. Mrs Hinkey and Benny waited patiently.

Rebecca came in, out of breath.

'Becky, honey, don't you strain . . .'

'What's that noise?' Rebecca asked.

'Something in that bag,' Benny said, pointing at the table.

'What is it?' Becky asked. She grinned at Benny, and he couldn't tell if the grin was nervous or playful. They all stared at the bag, listening to the faint, droning whir of a small motor, and watching a barely perceptible movement within the paper walls of the bag.

'For heaven's sake . . .' Rebecca said, then unrolled and opened the mouth of the bag.

It was Benny who lifted out the top layer of neatly folded socks.

What they expected to see, if they had expectations at all, surely differed with each of them. But, for certain, none of the three were quite prepared for the size, shape, or color of the battery-operated dildo doing its silicone hootchie kootchie before their very eyes.

'Oh, Lord . . .' Mrs Hinkey said. 'Oh, Lord . . . oh, Lord . . .'

Benny knew he'd never seen a nearly see-through neon green dildo before. Not a small one, not a medium sized one, and certainly not one the size of his forearm, like the one wiggling in the bag.

Becky sucked in a sharp breath and left the room.

'Lord have mercy . . . Lord have mercy . . . Lord . . .'

Despite the surge of embarrassment, Benny forced himself to look closer so he could figure out what it was that rose from the near the thick base of the vibrator. And it took him far too long to figure out what the little bunny-shaped appendage was for.

Benny tried to drop the socks back down onto the dildo, to cover it, to hide it from view and therefore deny its existence, but only one sock fell in place. It draped across the dildo and the sex toy brought the sock to life in a feat of obscene animation. Mrs Hinkey went from ashen gray to a grayish red. Benny, summoning all his courage, reached in and found the off switch. He rolled the top closed. Becky came through with another bag and went out the door without mentioning what happened.

'Let me see if that other . . .' Mrs Hinkey said, walking away too quickly.

And so they loaded the rest of the drowned girl's possessions into Benny's van. Only two other items of note: a small ceramic bowl full of origami frogs made, apparently, from the pages of the pilfered Gideon New Testament lying nearby, and a videotape in a white sleeve with Jenna's handwriting on the label. The former, inexplicably, filled Benny with a surge of tenderness towards Jenna, maybe even love; the latter, a surge as well, a churning mix of disquiet and yearning, with a fear thrown in for good measure. Benny tried to pluck the tape from its resting place, with the intention of hiding it in the waistband of his pants. But Rebecca walked into the room and picked up the box.

'Hmmm,' she said.

'One of your sister's films?' Benny asked.

'Did I tell you she made movies?'

Funny, how much literal space something as insubstantial and incorporeal as a sentence can fill. Benny misspoke and time ground to a halt. His gut, the room, the building, filled with anxiety.

Benny extricated himself from the situation by pointing to a framed certificate on Jenna's dresser; a Piedmont College Cinéma Vérité Society award for a film called *Lillith Kickin' Ass*. Becky winced at the sight of the certificate. But he didn't intend to mention the tape again. And neither Rebecca nor Mrs Hinkey mentioned the dildo at supper that night.

Benny also didn't plan to mention what he had seen the night before on the tape called *Prophets, Etc.*, in part for all the obvious reasons, but mostly because thinking about the tape made him seethe.

July 15, 1998   ● ● ● Rec
4:00 p.m.

MAX, the only word on the title board, fades out and what is left is his face. Max, the painter.

'Hey, Max,' Jenna says. 'Thanks for agreeing to the interview.'

Max lights a long brown cigarette in answer. The camera pans, wide right. Takes in the studio. Max is in his element. Large canvases, in soft focus, line the walls in the distance. A hard driving music throbs from a paint-spattered stereo stacked in a far corner.

'You seem to have made some progress on that piece,' Jenna says. 'What's it called?'

'*Need*,' Max says. 'It's called *Need*.'

Then for ten minutes he describes the painting, down to every brushstroke. Benny sat with his finger on the fast forward button. Benny knew some arrogant men, but never in his life had he heard someone go on at length about themselves like this Max guy. '*My work* . . .' this, and '*My work* . . .' that. Benny couldn't understand why and – he yet did not doubt – that Jenna was interested in him.

'You graduated from Piedmont less than a year ago, and already you're causing trouble in the art community.'

Jenna lets the statement hang. The camera hangs as well, on Max's face.

'I am the art community in this town,' he says.

'I'm talking about your current show, *Blood*, at the Firehouse Gallery.'

'I know what you mean, girly. Do you?'

'Why do you think the show caused so much contro- versy?' A leading, obvious question.

'You tell me.'

Jenna, as camera, pans the studio, taking it all in.

'What are you after?' he asks. 'What do you want from this interview?'

'. . . You,' she says. 'I want to know about you.'

'You want to know me . . . about me . . . come pose for me.'

Jenna is silent. Clearly thinking. Forgotten, the camera tilts toward the floor.

'For another *Blood* painting?' she asks.

'*Blood* is past tense. I've moved on to other things.'

'Another series?'

'Yes, as a matter of fact.'

'What's the theme?' Jenna asks. 'What's it about?'

'That's always a bad question, but since I like you so much, I'll answer it. It's *about* politics. It's *about* perception and hypocrisy. It's *about* body and flesh. And it's *about* desire and the absence of desire.'

'Do you have a working title?' she asks.

'I don't fuck around with *working titles*,' he says with a sneer. 'I name my work what it is.'

'So . . . what is it then?'

'It's called *Beautiful Women Shitting*.'

Benny stopped the tape. He'd had enough for one night. He couldn't listen to any more of Max's nonsense, and he all but prayed that Jenna would tell him to fuck off. That, when he started the tape again, there'd be no more Max. But Benny was doubtful of both, prayer and Jenna's decision-making skills.

He could pray for Rebecca's legs to straighten and stretch and grow, her spine to unfurl, her blocky face to sharpen. Benny supposed, rightly or wrongly, that these were tired old prayers, worn out from overuse.

Deacon Hinkey shifted in his chair, a ladder-back beast of burden with a cane seat, at least as old as Benny. The chair moaned beneath its charge, each joint straining against itself. In true call-and-response fashion, Mrs Hinkey and Rebecca shifted subtly as well, and their own seats cried out. Benny had no choice; he said the only prayer he remembered.

'God is great, God is good. Let us thank him . . .'

'Benny,' Mrs Hinkey said, after the *amen*. 'Help yourself to some . . .'

A child's prayer. Was that the best Benny could do? He knew he'd botched it by the way Deacon Hinkey snorted and reached for the biscuits. A botched prayer is a dangerous thing.

CHAPTER 17

BENNY HADN'T PRAYED OUTRIGHT FOR BECKY TO sleep with him. He wasn't even sure he wanted such a thing to happen. But eventually she did. The night of the dinner, the night after moving Jenna's things – dildo and all – into a musty old garage beside the Hinkey's house, that night the good Deacon closed the occasion with a guarded, almost accusatory prayer for Esther to return home safe, sound and penitent. They all held hands around the table, Benny between Becky and Mrs Hinkey. Becky's hand feeling much less like a doll's and much more paw-like than before; Mrs Hinkey's, stiff and damp.

'That wasn't so bad,' Rebecca asked. 'Was it?'

Benny didn't know whether she was asking about the dinner, or the kiss he'd just given her. They stood out by his van, it between them and the house. Lord only knew what Deacon Hinkey would do to the man that kissed his odd daughter. Benny was worried, but not enough to not kiss her again.

After the prayer Benny excused himself, saying he had a busy, busy day tomorrow. Needed to get home and sleep. He shook the Deacon's hand. Mrs Hinkey started a few sentences by way of goodbye. And Rebecca followed him out the door.

'Thank you so much,' she said. 'For helping move Jenna's stuff and everything.'

'I'll send you a bill,' he said.

'Sorry about that one thing,' she said, looking Benny straight in the eye.

'I'll send you a big bill,' he said, blushing in the dark.

There in the driveway, she came up to his chest. They stood close, her looking up, him looking down.

'Hope I can afford it,' she said.

'Everything's negotiable,' he said.

Then they kissed. He knew it was going to happen when she started coming up on her tiptoes.

Benny met her halfway.

'That wasn't so bad, was it?'

The dinner? Or the kiss?

Both, in their own ways, were excruciating *and* exquisite.

On the way home in the van, windows down to suck out the incessant heat, Benny realized something. In the Hinkey household, as at Claxton Looms, other than one step stool that he saw tucked in a corner, there were no obvious concessions to Rebecca's diminished stature. Benny stewed over this for some time. So engrossed that he almost forgot the *Prophets* tape, and *Beautiful Women Shitting*.

He couldn't bear to finish watching the tape that night, but his dreams were scatological in nature, and terrifying. Two hard days passed before Benny saw Becky again. Only one before he watched the tape.

'Wow,' Jenna says, the tone genuflectory. 'That's bold.'

'Fearless is the word, girl.'

Max, followed by the camera, gives a tour of the pieces in progress. Max works from photos this time; his studio walls are filled with Polaroid pictures, of various girls, from various angles and various distances, all squatting. Some, not all, reveal, in fact, the act.

'Jesus!' Jenna says.

'I told you,' Max answers. 'Beautiful women shitting.'

'I wasn't expecting it to be so literal.'

'Subterfuge is for cowards.'

The camera takes it all in. There are three paintings on easels around the studio; each painting a composite of one of the women in the photos. Big canvases, on which a dozen hyper-close cropped pictures – a thigh or hip, a profile, the folds of some fabric, indecipherable shapes and things – surround the predominate image: a woman squatting, clothed but uncovered, with her legs spread over a pile of excrement. There were women on toilets, women outside. A woman shitting on a fully made bed, and a woman shitting on a baseball diamond: home plate. There was a woman squatting on a dining room table, over a dinner plate. A wedding dress, hiked up. Behind the pews of a church. On an office desk.

'So . . .' Max says.

'So . . . what?' Jenna asks.

'You going to pose for me?'

Jenna laughs.

'I can't do *that*,' she says and the camera spins once around the room.

'You're saying you don't *want* to,' Max says, now just a voice off camera.

'No, not exactly . . .'

'You're saying you choose not to.'

'No, not that either.'

'Then I'll see you tomorrow.'

Jenna laughs again.

'I don't know about that.'

'Tell me this,' Max says, commanding more than asking. 'What time of day do you normally shit?'

'Max!'

'Call me before you come so I'll know you're ready.'

Benny had to turn the tape off again. He'd known some really fucked up men in his life, men whose taste and proclivities would, and did, get attention from assorted authorities and concerned citizens. But this Max guy, he was more blatant than anyone Benny had ever encountered.

Benny took a shower. He had a beer. He had half of another before he found the guts to finish watching the *Prophets* tape.

July 19, 1998   ● ● ● **Rec**
10:00 a.m.

Disciples

The title board is obviously edited in after the fact.

The camera focuses on a well-lit but bare model stand. Max moves in and out of view. Jenna talks.

'I don't think I can do this, Max.'

'You're here. That means you can and will. Take your underwear off but leave your skirt on.'

'Is this how you did all those others? Here, in your studio?'

'I do things all different ways.'

There is the sound of fabric against skin.

'Ok, what do I do now?' Jenna asks.

'Step up on the platform. And just stand there.'

Jenna moves into view. Takes the high step, faces the camera with her hands in the deep pockets of a floral print, rayon skirt.

'I'm embarrassed,' she says.

'Good,' he says. 'You're even more beautiful when you're embarrassed.'

Jenna smiles.

'Lift your skirt and turn around,' Max says. 'I want to see your ass.'

Jenna blows her bangs out of her eyes, gets a look of determination, then does as Max asks.

'Cute,' Max says, no doubt of the scarlet birthmark roughly in the shape of a fish on her right buttock.

Jesus! Benny thought. Maybe he even said it aloud. Jenna's behind is quite sexy. Despite what Benny thinks she's about to do he couldn't help but continue watching.

'Arch your back,' Max says.

She does.

'Take your hands and hold your cheeks apart.'

She does.

Max circles, like a raptor. His camera shoots rapid fire.

'You're beautiful,' he says. 'Now squat down.'

She does.

'Ok. I want you to shit for me.'

She does.

'Wow,' Becky said, entering the door of Benny's duplex for the first time. 'This your bachelor's pad?'

'I reckon so,' Benny answered. He'd gone through the place again and again that morning, making sure nothing of Jenna's was visible, even so Becky's presence made him twitchy and nervous. 'Would you like a beer? I've got Coors, and some homebrew my friend Jeeter made. Or would you like some iced tea?'

'Tea would be good,' Becky said, wandering around and exploring the tight confines of Benny's world.

'Sorry the place is such a pigsty.'

Becky didn't answer. She looked through Benny's stack of magazines – deftly avoiding the copy of *T&A Extreme* tucked among the issues of *Newsweek*, *People*, and *Trucker* – and fiddling with his few knick-knacks. The date was her idea; they were going to play miniature golf at The Dangling Anchor Putt Putt, where all the holes and hazards had some nautical theme.

'I've never been there before,' she said when she asked him over the phone earlier that day.

'Me either.'

Benny, ashamed that he felt it, hoped no one he knew would be there.

Becky came, promptly at 6.45, just as she promised. Benny had just showered and dressed, and was brushing his teeth when she knocked.

'Here you go,' he said, handing Becky the glass of tea. 'I'll be ready in a minute. You can sit there if you like.'

Benny pointed at his rocker. Becky accepted the offer, pulling the ottoman close to keep her feet from dangling.

'Comfy,' she said.

Benny couldn't remember the last time any woman, besides Doodle, sat in his chair. Or set foot in his apartment, for that matter. He worried, for a moment, that, given her lower point of view, Becky might be able to see under his bed. But all she'd really see was the milk crate.

'I got to get my dog in,' Benny said. 'Are you Ok with dogs?'

'Sure,' Becky said, but Benny could see apprehension cross her face.

'He's little and old,' Benny said, hoping to calm her fears. 'But he stinks to high heaven.'

When Benny opened the door and Squat lumbered

inside, having to pause a moment after putting his stubby front legs up on the stoop, his belly resting there, before hauling his equally stubby back legs into the house.

'Oh,' Becky said. 'A dachshund.'

Squat waddled in and went directly to Becky, despite the fact that his freshly filled food dish sat in its place by the kitchen sink. Squat, often hesitant around strangers, sniffed at Becky's block-like feet hidden away in their block-like black shoes. He sniffed at her calf, and when she put her hand out, palm up, he sniffed that too. Affinity? The dachshund, like the bonsai, like the fancy goldfish, are mutations. Created by, and for the pleasure of, humans. Maybe, in the limited confines of his old dog brain, Squat toyed with the idea that he'd finally found his human equivalent.

'Hi, boy,' she said.

'Ready to go?' Benny asked. He worried that Doodle may come home soon.

'Let's take my car,' Becky said, climbing out of the rocking chair.

Squat followed her to the door. Benny tried not to notice the similarities in their labored gaits.

Benny, happy to let Becky drive, climbed into the passenger seat of her car, his attention turning immediately to the mechanical contraption – a pivoting lever and some pushrods – that allowed her to drive.

'Some people use pedal extensions,' Becky said. 'My legs aren't quite long enough.'

Benny, fascinated, watched her work the controls all the way to The Dangling Anchor, where despite the fact that the only handicap space by the door was blatantly empty, Rebecca parked across the lot.

'How many?' the kid behind the counter said, as if he didn't see Becky. His buck-toothed pout and acne scars emphasizing his irritation over being pulled away from the guitar magazine spread out by the cash register. Benny recognized the boy from somewhere, some other miniature golf course, or maybe from Nub & Honey's.

Benny paid for the game; insisted on paying, in part so that he wouldn't have to watch Becky choose her putter from the children's rack. However, anyone playing the course that day couldn't help but notice the short shaft, thick grip, and fat plastic putter head.

'What color ball do you want?' Benny asked.

'Orange,' Becky said. 'That's my lucky color.'

Which seemed to be true. Becky scored a hole in one on the first hole, then again on the third, each followed by a little whoop that attracted more attention than Benny liked. Becky, it stood to reason, was far more comfortable with her status as a midget than Benny.

The giddy and rambunctious church group playing in front of them held things up at hole five, where the object was to negotiate a gangplank and a swinging pirate's cutlass – a staticy, feebly sinister laugh accompanying each sweep – which more often than not sent each player's ball into a shallow moat. Benny and Becky waited. They sat on a bench shaped like an open treasure chest and talked.

'I just wish she'd call, or send a card or something,' Becky said.

'Me, too,' Benny said, and the impossibility of their mutual wish pierced him deeply. Not so many hours ago, he'd watched Becky's sister defecate on videotape. He couldn't tell Becky about the horrible scene and how it had both disgusted and aroused him. He couldn't tell Becky how excruciating it was, the whole fucked-up situation. How as he got to know Becky more and more, and cared more and more about her, he was also discovering more about Jenna, becoming more invested in her life through the tapes that would soon lead him, without doubt or hope, to the end of that life. Soon enough he'd watch Jenna die, again, on videotape, no matter how much he and Becky wished for something different, and the scene would probably disgust and arouse him.

To lighten the mood, one of them made a joke, an oblique reference comparing the size of a plaster pirate's nose to the size of the lime green dildo found at Jenna's apartment.

Becky won, finishing the game at three over par. Her only trouble came at the final hole where two monstrous, plaster-cast, and clearly dwarfish sailors guarded the steep ramp up to where the balls dropped out of sight and clunked through the short pipe that led to a cardboard box behind the surly clerk. After the game, when they returned the clubs, the kid didn't even look up from his magazine.

'That was . . .'

'. . . fun.'

They spoke at the same time.

With little effort, Benny talked her into stopping at the Dairy Queen on the way home. Then, at home, noting Doodle's absence, and with not much more effort, he convinced her to come in.

'Just for a while,' he said.

Sex, better yet seduction, filled the air. Both of them felt it. They'd kissed several times by then. But Benny wanted to see Becky naked, no use in kidding anyone. He wanted to see for himself, to touch for himself, to find out, for himself, how her odd body differed from others he'd known.

As apartments went, Benny's lacked much in the way of

comfort, accoutrement, and design for wooing or entertaining of any sort. Becky, as before, sat in Benny's rocker
with her feet propped on the ottoman. Benny pulled up a
kitchen chair.

'You got any pictures?' Becky asked. 'Any pictures of
your grandpa that worked in the mill.'

Benny had to think quick.

'No . . .' he said. 'They all burned up in a fire when I
was a kid.'

'Oh my . . .'

'We lost everything,' Benny said.

Becky leaned forward and put her hand on his knee.

'You've known your share of tragedy, Benny Poteat.'

Benny leaned forward and put his mouth on hers. And
they kissed like that for a while, both pitched and off
balance. Both tasting of Heath Bar Blizzards. When Benny
ventured his hand out and placed it on her left breast,
Becky took her feet from the ottoman and leaned into him
even more, so much so that she almost fell off the chair.
If not for Benny supporting her by the breast and mouth,
she would have. With her desire clear and full against him,
Benny wanted to touch her more, but with her weight
full against him, Benny's caress was limited to rhythmic
squeezes of the single breast. Becky moaned softly at each.

'We can go in the . . .' Benny said, trusting that Becky's
skills at intuiting the ends of incomplete sentences had
been honed by interacting with her mother.

'Ok,' Becky said, and followed Benny and Squat into the
bedroom.

'Can we turn out the light?' she asked.

Benny did, but opened the blinds. The moon, full and low,
molting, cast its yellow feathers of light over the bed and
Benny and the naked midget. And naked, lying on the bed,

washed in moonlight, smelling of sex, and urging Benny on, there was nothing at all monstrous about Rebecca Hinkey.

In fact, considering that the videotape of Jenna Hinkey's death, the only certain answer to the question of her absence, the thing Rebecca and her parents ached to know, considering that the fact of the drowned sister lay draped by a NASCAR towel under the very bed upon which Benny penetrated and probed the unwitting and still living sister, the true monster wore the taut skin and elongated bones of a tower climber.

Afterwards, Benny lay propped on his arm, absent-mindedly circling Becky's nipples with his fingertip, each borne up by a sparse ring of unruly black hairs, each a dark beetle leaping out from the center of her breast.

'What's that noise?' Becky asks.

'What noise?'

'That noise.'

And in the mostly quiet, Benny could make out a sound he knew almost too well to hear.

Squat, licking. Licking something disgusting, no doubt.

'Where'd you put your panties?' he asked.

'On the floor,' she said.

'Squat!' Benny yelped, sitting up. 'Cut it out!'

Oblivious to the fact that he should offer to wash the garment for Becky, Benny returned to the bed confident that having put Squat out of the bedroom and closed the door, he'd proven himself a caring lover.

'So,' Benny said, curling into and around Becky, ready to ask the question he'd been wondering for a long time. 'You're a midget right? Not a dwarf?'

It was the first time either of them had uttered the words in each other's presence.

'They're the same, really,' Becky answered, after a pause.

No doubt, she'd heard the question before. She told him a little about her condition, mostly because she knew little about it.

'I only ever went to our family doctor,' she said. 'He attended daddy's church. I could tell he didn't know what to say to me, or to do about me. But he was kind.'

'What do your folks call you?' Benny asked, not intending the question to sound as cold as it came out.

'They call me Rebecca.'

Becky said she'd learned from reading books in the library that her condition was called achondroplasia.

'Used to be called fetal rickets,' she said.

Benny kissed her again, and eased his hands over the swell of her belly and down between those bowed legs where he found a most normal thing.

'I had this book one time,' Becky said. 'When I was a kid. I used to read it every day, sometimes more than once.'

'What kind of book?'

'It was a picture book, about this little acrobat who got sick and tired of the circus and decided to become a monk. Except that, he couldn't cook, or sing, or garden, or do any of the things the other monks living in the monastery did. He tried hard. He tried to do everything right, but he couldn't. He couldn't do anything right.'

Benny pulled his fingers from between Becky's legs. She continued the story, moving in and out of the words she'd read so often.

'One day, after the acrobat had accidentally trampled the tomato plants in the garden then spilled the watering can, the other monks got really really mad and told him to leave. The little acrobat went to his room in the basement of the monastery and packed up all his stuff. On the way out, he stopped in front of a statue of the Virgin Mary.

He put his bag down at her feet, stepped back, and began doing headstands and tricks for the stone saint.'

Benny thought she might cry, any minute.

'When he didn't come back out of the monastery, after an hour, maybe more, the other monks went in to get him. There, inside, in the basement, they found the little acrobat walking back and forth on his hands in front of the statue. He was sweating and trembling and crying. The monks were about to cry out 'Blasphemy!' and 'Sacrilege!' when the little man fell to the ground, exhausted. Before they could rush to him and pitch him out the door for good, something happened . . .'

Rebecca paused, closed her eyes.

'What?' Benny asked. 'What happened?'

'She . . . the Virgin, stepped down from her stone pedestal and tenderly, so tenderly, wiped the sweat and tears from the little acrobat's face with the hem of her own garment . . .'

After a long silence, Benny spoke.

'What a great story.'

'My daddy threw the book away,' she said.

'Why?'

'Because it was Catholic.'

Later, before sleep, they lay in bed, in the dark, with the windows open, sharing a beer.

'Hear the peepers?' she asked.

'Umm hmm.'

'I love that sound, don't you?'

'Umm hmm.'

Then Benny asked a question.

'Rebecca?'

'Hmmm?'

'You ever see anybody die?'

Chapter 18

THE NEXT DAY ON THE TOWER, BENNY THOUGHT about her answer.

I dreamed I saw Jenna die.

She had thought about it for a long time before answering. He didn't know why he'd asked. He didn't want to hear about her dream. He feigned sleep, only mumbling when she nudged him. He was thinking about that so intently that he didn't hear the car drive up to the tower.

'Benny Poteat!' a voice called. 'You're under arrest!'

Benny recognized the voice before the second phrase.

'Fuck you, Jeeter.'

'Watch your mouth, son. I'll shake you right off that tower.'

'What do you want, Jeeter?'

'Let's go to the ball game tomorrow night.'

Jeeter picked up a stick and whacked the steel struts, once, twice.

His friend looked small and bug-like down there. As if Benny could step on him.

'Jeeter!!!'

'Sorry.'

'Who's playing?' Benny asked.

'The daring, the beautiful, the damn-near-good, Mill Hill Lady Bombers!'

Benny, and all his friends, liked women's softball.

'Can't do it tonight,' Benny called down. 'When are they playing again?'

'Next weekend.'

'I'll go then.'

After Jeeter left, and the dust had settled, as Benny unhooked the safety belt, about to climb down for lunch, he heard a ruckus in the canebrake below. Seconds later the ruckus spilled out into the clearing in the form of a pack of dogs. Three, four, maybe five differing breeds of mutt, all chasing another dog, a skinny setter-looking thing with mud in its yellow fur. The dog being chased stopped in the middle of the clearing, and as soon as she stopped one of the pack mounted her.

The coupling lasted only a few brief, mechanical moments, and separation seemed painful; Benny heard the yelping. But no sooner than one dog finished, another climbed aboard. Benny clipped himself back to the tower and hung there for a good forty-five minutes watching the dogs fuck. He couldn't tell if the bitch's meager protests were merely for show or if she was just too fatigued to fight back. Benny watched until the largest dog in the pack, a shepherd, took his turn. When it came time to pull apart, they couldn't. The more effort the shepherd made to separate, the more the yellow bitch howled in pain. Moments later, having spun themselves so that their ass ends seemed glued together, the bigger dog began to run, an awkward splay-legged trot, and dragged the other into the weeds and out of sight.

That morning, when Benny had sleepily walked Becky out to her car, dew cool against his bare feet, and the sun rising over the peak of the neighbor's roof, he hadn't known Doodle was watching from her window.

Benny closed Becky's car door, waved as she pulled out of the drive. She gave a quick rhythmic toot of her horn before rounding the corner. Then Benny turned to go back inside.

'Mornin', Benny Poteat.'

'You spying on me, Doodle?' Benny said, playfully, but embarrassed nonetheless.

'I knew it was true,' Doodle said, leaning into the screen so that Benny could see her face.

'What? You knew what was true?'

'That you're two-timing me.'

Benny, surprising even himself, grabbed his crotch and said, 'There's plenty of this to go round.'

On his way home from working the towers that day, late and tired, the sun already collapsing behind the tree line so that everything to the west became sharp black silhouettes, Benny drove past Chick's Sales & Service, a business he had passed by countless times in his life. Chick was the only man in town who sold and repaired bucket trucks: mid-sized cranes holding at boom's end a hip-deep enclosure big enough for a man, or two. Some folks called them cherry pickers. They're most often used by the utilities companies and arborists. Benny, having driven by Chick's umpteen thousand times, rarely acknowledged it in passing. But that night, he did pay attention. Chick kept his trucks lined up across the gravel lot, facing the macadam. That evening, as soon as Benny rounded the curve that preceded the stretch of straight road along which Chick's enterprise lay, he saw a most amazing thing. The buckets. All the booms of all the trucks – different colors, different heights, all empty – all of them reached, fully extended, skyward. As if in praise of the coming night. Benny was so moved by the image that he decided he'd bring Becky out to see it later.

Their sex, more and more frequent (the state of desire in either or both of them communicated through a barely coded signal of raised eyebrows and kissy lips), became no less tentative at its beginnings and endings, bookended as it was by awkwardness, but during the act both Benny and Becky gave themselves freely. Becky, whatever else life had given her in the way of experience, seemed to know the mechanics of sex as well as anyone else Benny had slept with. Benny, rooting around, animal-like in her armpits and between her legs, turning her this way and that, appreciated her willingness. Becky, bucking and mewling to beat the band, appreciated his attention. They hadn't encountered Doodle yet, in the flesh, but once she gave a few taps on the wall following a particularly raucous headboard banging session.

'We've never done it at your place,' Benny said.

Becky deflected the statement.

'I thought you were going to take me to the ball game,' she said.

Benny had blown off Jeeter the week before; in fact he'd avoided all his friends. Even called in sick at Nub & Honey's once, although Doodle knew better and gave him shit about it for days afterwards. Benny didn't really care where they did it, as long as they did it. Doing it helped to keep his gnawing, increasing, guilt at bay. He liked her. He really did. But only when she lay naked on his bed, belly down with the full mounds of her rump up in the air, or straddling him with her midget titties bouncing, only then could Benny be fairly certain that she wouldn't talk about, or he wouldn't think about, the dead sister.

'Mama's thinking about making up a bunch of posters,' Becky said. 'With Jenna's picture on them. Will you help me put them up?'

'Sure,' Benny said. 'Sure. Hey. You ready?'

'For what?' Becky asked.

'Aren't we going to the ball game?'

It didn't surprise Benny to find Dink's moped parked beside the concession stand at the ball park. Dink went to every game – the ticket takers usually looked the other way and let him in for free. Between innings he'd scrounge in the trash cans and under the bleachers for 5¢-back bottles, then cash them in for candy at the concession stand.

By the time Becky and Benny arrived, the Lady Bombers were down by two runs and at bat with one out in the top of the third inning. Benny was surprised to find Jeeter sitting with Dink in the bleachers. Doodle sat one row back with another waitress from Nub & Honey's.

'This is a regular family reunion, ain't it?' Benny says.

'Hey, Benny.'

'Howdy, Benny.'

Somehow Doodle must've prepared them because neither Dink nor Jeeter registered any surprise when Benny showed up at the softball game with Becky – a midget? a dwarf? – in tow.

'This is Becky,' Benny said, and that was all.

'Hey.'

'Hey.'

'Hey.'

Not until they were settled up in the stands – Benny between his date and Jeeter, who sat beside Dink – did

Benny realize how uncomfortable bleacher seating probably was for Becky, her legs dangling over the gaping
spaces between the benches and the footboards.

'Do you want to sit down lower?' he asked.

'I'm Ok,' she said. 'Thanks for asking.'

Jeeter jumped right into conversation.

'What you doing with this fool?' he asked, playfully
indicating his friend.

She told him she was a preacher's daughter.

'Oh,' Jeeter said, with exaggerated surprise. 'That explains
everything.'

Becky pretended to swat at him. She asked what church
he went to.

'Church?' he said. 'My dear, I am a devout apathostic.'

'A what?'

Benny had heard it all before. Apathostic was Jeeter's
favorite made-up word.

'About church,' Jeeter said. 'Who cares.'

Dink split his time between watching the game, shouting
random insults at the umpire, and craning his neck behind
or in front of Jeeter to get a look at Becky. When Benny
said 'I'm hungry. You want a corndog, Becky?' and got up
to go to the concession stand, Dink was on his heels. And
the barrage started before they were off the steps and out
of earshot.

'Benny! She's a got-damn mee-jit, Benny! You fuckin'
that thang? Huh? What's she look like nekid? You suckin'
them mee-jit titties? Tonguin' that furry little pisshole?'

And Dink kept talking the whole time Benny was placing
his order at the counter, despite the fact that folks were
listening. When the clerk, no doubt a volunteer from one
of the churches, slid the flimsy cardboard tray holding
two corndogs, two Pepsis, and two bags of chips across

the worn formica countertop, sneering at Benny for his choice of friends, Dink said loud enough for everyone in line and everyone working the stand to hear, 'I bet she got a pussy like a snappin' turtle . . .'

Benny hit him. He couldn't take anymore, so he busted Dink's lip. And Dink fell. No sooner did Dink hit the ground than a strong arm came around Benny's neck from behind and his punching arm was twisted and bent up his back.

'Ungghh,' Benny said, from both pain and anger.

'What's the problem here, son?'

He'd heard the voice before. The pressure lessened, and Benny was allowed to turn and face a man at once familiar and not so. Not until Benny caught sight of his own reflection in the man's dark glasses did he recognize the cop – off duty and out of uniform, but for the glasses and the bulge at his side that was most certainly his weapon – from the parking lots of both Pandora's and the video store. He'd been standing in line behind Benny at the concession stand.

Benny convinced the off-duty cop that there'd be no more fighting. And Dink, of course, having been smacked around all his life, wouldn't push the issue. Benny bought him a cup of ice for his swollen lip, and Dink pouted and sulked all the way back to the bleachers.

'What happened to you?' Jeeter asked him.

'Nothing,' Dink said into his cup.

'Somebody hit him?' Doodle asked, her maternal instincts rising.

'Nothing happened, Doodle,' Benny said, with too much emphasis. 'Just leave it alone.'

'Why you acting so damn weird, Benny?' Jeeter asked.

No answer. Fortunately, Dink was incapable of remaining subdued for long. Within the half hour he was cajoling the umpire again. Shortly after that, Dink, fully himself once more, turned his attention, inevitably and finally, to the team.

'Them Lady Bombers sure is hot, ain't they? I wish one of 'em would come up here and swing my bat. Lord god, I bet them cooters is all sweaty. Mercy, what I wouldn't give to sniff 'em all.'

'Please shut up, Dink,' Doodle said, worried more about Becky's reaction than anything else.

But Dink was on a roll.

'I'd like to sop me a biscuit in that pussy stew. Hey, Benny? Know what I want for my birthday?'

'What, Dink?' Benny asked, against his better judgment.

'A wash tub.'

'A what?' It was Jeeter that followed up.

'A big old galvanized tin tub. I want to lay in it nekid. Then I want all them ball gals to hang their asses over the edges, with their butt cheeks squushed up against each other, and when I count to three I want them to pee all over me.'

'Dink! For godsakes, shut up!'

'Head to toe,' Dink added in closing.

'Sorry about Dink,' Benny said as he drove Becky home.

'Oh, I didn't pay him much attention,' she said. 'I've known worse.'

Benny doubted it, but she was kind to say so.

'At least we won,' Becky added.

The Lady Bombers rallied in the ninth inning with a home run, knocked over the *Jesus Saves And So Can You At Keepers Bank & Trust* sign, to win by two points.

Benny was sorry, truly sorry about the fight with Dink.

And even sorrier that Becky had to hear Dink's foul mouth.

When Benny pulled into the lot at Claxton Looms, Roger, the Andy Griffith professor, was walking into the lobby, gym bag in hand.

'There goes your boyfriend,' Benny teased, and remained in the van.

'Watch it, smarty pants,' Becky said, coming around to the driver's side, standing on her tiptoes for a kiss. 'I might just put the moves on him if you keep talking like that.'

'You got any interest in the County 4-H show next weekend? Out at the fairgrounds?'

'Giant tomatoes and homemade fudge?' she asked.

'Giant chickens and homemade pigs,' Benny answered.

'Yep,' she said. 'I'll go with you.'

'We still haven't done it at your place.'

Could it be that emotions are planetary in nature? That at birth the various orbs of feeling that wreck and wreak us are set in motion around the thump-thumping black hole of our frantic hearts, and gravitate and gravitate, bound not by action or event – although prone to excruciating coincidence – bound, rather, by nothing more than egg-shaped whim? Orbit. Benny, in the periastron moment, was overcome with black, black guilt. Back at the duplex, almost in tears (although skilled at holding them in) he pulled the laundry crate of incriminating evidence, of proof that he, Benny Poteat, was a bad man, from under the bed. Without uncovering the tapes, Benny took the basket out to his van. He didn't care that Doodle, clinking and clanking at the sink one thin wall away, might see. Might ask, 'What you doing, Benny Poteat?' How would he answer?

'Come on, Squat,' he said. The old dog being the only living thing to know Benny's secret, had a right to see it come to an end. He'd dreamed of Jenna regularly since witnessing her death, but his dreams had taken a frightening twist since Becky started sleeping over. In the dreams, Jenna talked to Benny. Mocked him. Chided him for his awful dishonesty. Benny's plan was to destroy the tapes. He wanted to get rid of the secret, without telling it, and to stop lying to Becky. He hoped that in flinging them one by one into the Toe River, near where he found them, that somehow the tapes would find their way to the drowned girl and rest in peace with her. That's what Benny hoped.

Not hope but bile churned inside Benny when he pulled to a stop on the dirt road along the river, just opposite from the Bard's Communication tower he'd climbed so many times. He parked the van so that the headlights shone out over the water; a sickly, and quickly disappearing, bipartite swath of light all but useless for the task at hand. Benny knew himself well enough to understand that, for him, hesitation was the death of action. Rather than getting out of the van by way of the driver's side door and walking all the way around for the laundry basket, he stepped over Squat who lay between the two front seats, knelt to open the hinged side doors, and climbed out clutching the basket in both hands. What he should've done was watched where he put his foot. Even then he may not have seen the bottle – Blue Nun liebfraumilch, someone's idea of romance, now partly filled with mud and silt from a trip down the river – lying on its side in the exact spot Benny intended to, or by karmic default was instructed to, place his own booted right foot. When he came down, the bottle didn't break. Rather, it rolled to one side, taking his foot with it, leaving his ankle behind.

'Fuck! Fuck!!!! Fucking shit fuck fuck shit fuck!'

Squat, too arthritic to make the two-foot leap from the floor of the van down to the ground, howled his own doggy curses from his place of abandonment. Benny fell, his leading foot taking that quick and unexpected jaunt in a direction other than that which his body expected, and when he fell, river-wards, the basket of tapes went up, and fell back down like dense anti-confetti. The basket itself, kept in a one-handed knuckled grip, inverted and came to rest over Benny's head, but the tapes, one, two, three, four, five-six, seven, eight . . . Benny listened for the thuds. One landed on is chest. Several more along the riverbank. But Benny heard one, at least one, splash.

'Goddamnit!!!!'

Lying on his back, in the dark – made extra-dark because he lay outside of the weak beams of light cast by the van's headlights – along the muddy riverbank, with a basket over his head so that all he saw he saw through the basket's mesh – a world parceled out in perfect plastic rectangles – lying there with his ankle – not broken, thank the Lord – already swelling inside his boot, Benny realized the error of his plan. Realized it the moment he heard the videotape splash in the moving water. A realization more visceral than intellectual; his gut seized, his heart stormed. Getting rid of the tapes would not eliminate the secret, or its damage done. Getting rid of the tapes might, in fact, cause the already raw presence of what he knew to fester and grow cancerous. And then there was Becky. Sweet, dwarfish Becky. It may just be that the secret had something to do with Benny's attraction to Becky.

'Owww!' Benny screamed into the upturned basket, then

flung said basket from over his head. Sitting up, Benny loosened the lace of his boot, pulled the tabs wide and let the tongue loll over the crisscrossing leather strand. Squat whimpered, wanting out of the van, wanting to comfort his master. Benny got to his knees and, using the running board of the van for support, tried to stand. Quickly toppled.

'Fuck!'

With no other recourse, he flipped the basket upright, and began crawling along the bank, stopping every few feet to drag the container up along side, gathering the videotapes. With most lying in an irregular arc around where Benny fell, he found all but one, the one the river took. Because it was dark, and because the pain shooting up his leg made thinking clearly all but impossible, Benny had no way of knowing which tape he'd lost. He'd have to wait until later. It took him a full forty-five minutes of crawling in the mud and grass and mosquitoes to collect all the tapes, place the basket in the van, then climb up and drag himself into the driver's seat. Figuring, correctly, that his right foot couldn't bear the pressure of working the gas and brake pedals, Benny twisted so that the injured foot extended into the passenger side, against the engine cover, and he could drive with his left foot: a thing he did from time to time anyway on long trips.

Benny turned the key without turning off the headlights. Mistake. The aging vehicle, its aging engine, and most especially its tired old battery didn't have the gumption necessary to crank under the added stress. One sluggish revolution of the crankshaft, one grunted exhalation, was all the engine mustered, and in its refusal to turn over again, dimmed the headlight beams even more.

'Shit shit shit. Fuck fuck fuck,' Benny articulated his frustration clearly.

What the hell was he going to do, stuck miles from anywhere, with an ankle so swollen he couldn't stand on it, much less walk. Benny thought through his options. Once, on a TV show, probably *Gilligan's Island*, he'd seen someone spell out SOS in burning coconuts on the beach. He wondered what he had to spell SOS with; what he had for fuel; and who was liable to fly over and pay any attention to the message anyway.

Sending Squat, with a note tied to his collar, up the road to find help was out of the question. The dog was too old and too stupid.

Benny himself crawling several miles for help seemed ill advised, too.

Benny wondered how long he'd have to stay there until his ankle healed enough for him to walk. He'd probably starve first. Of course he could crawl along the riverbank catching small fish and crawdads with his bare hands ... emerging finally from the wilderness months later as some hairy and feral creature a few steps back from man.

Or, he could turn off the headlights and try cranking the van one more time.

He did.

Without the added burden of powering the headlamps, the single half turn of the leaky V-8 sucked just enough fuel through the line and held sufficient oomph to fire all the cylinders. The van shuddered and stuttered to life. Benny, and even Squat, sighed in relief. The drive home, wet and muddy, ankle throbbing and swelling, the crushing millstone of secrecy still pressing mightily, was uncomfortable, but at least possible. Benny stopped three times on the way back to his duplex.

The first time was to remove the boot completely from his right foot and, using his hands, return the foot up onto the van's engine cover. The second time, Benny stopped at the drive-up window of Eckerds Rx, where normal transaction involved the pick-up and drop-off of drug prescriptions.

'I need one of them Ace bandages,' Benny said to the assistant pharmacist manning the window, a skinny, effete man peering over, around, and through the tiny eyeglasses pinching his nose.

'What?' he said, and Benny immediately looked for a quarter in the man's ear.

'One of them Ace bandages, and the strongest pain pills you got over the counter.'

'You'll have to come inside for those items sir,' the man said, seeming not so much power-mongering and defiant, rather more suspicious of Benny's bedraggled state.

'I can't walk,' Benny said. 'It's my foot.'

And Benny saw a shift take place, a movement from doubt to pity on the pharmacist's face.

'Just a sec, hon.'

Hon? Lord god, Benny thought, why? Why? Why does everything have to be so complicated?

'Here you go, sweetie, and I put you a tube of analgesic cream in there for good measure.'

Benny made one last stop on his way home, an unplanned stop. As he passed Dinks Clean 'em Up he steered the van into the parking lot, past the huge canister vacuums and the dispensers for Armor-All, polishes, towels, and air fresheners, past the wash bays, to where he knew a drive-up payphone stood in the back corner of the lot.

Benny, as if on autopilot, eased the van up as close as possible to the phone, lowered his window, and leaned out to retrieve the plastic covered phonebook dangling from a thick wire beneath the coin return. No one comes to a payphone without some sense of urgency or desperation or need, and that fact is borne out most clearly by the condition of the phonebooks. Often they are missing altogether, and when present, they are always battered and worn from misuse. That particular phonebook, many of its pages wrinkled and yellowed from rain – at least Benny hoped rain was the damaging liquid – whole chunks and passages of information ripped out – half of the E section of the yellow pages, all the maps in the front of the book, various sections of residents' names – and the remains scribbled over with doodles and notes and pleas, that phonebook served its purpose for Benny. He found, with very little trouble, midway through the Hs, the Hinkeys' telephone number. And, still acting without complete control or cognition, Benny slipped his quarter into the slot, listened to it clink home, and then fingered the numbers on the keypad.

By then it was nearly 2 a.m., and Benny didn't expect a quick answer. He expected enough time to figure out what he planned to say. So when Mrs Hinkey crackled her feeble hello halfway through the first ring Benny said the first thing that came to mind.

'Shit,' he said, although midway through he made an attempt to disguise his voice, so it came out more like 'sheet'.

'Hello?' Mrs Hinkey said again, not quite believing anyone would call her up to say *sheet* at two in the morning.

Benny's mind went blank. His foot hurt. A bitter back-wash of guilt rose in his throat. What could he say to this old woman whose daughter he'd watched die? He could tell her that Jenna was dead, and never coming back, but what good would that do?

'Who is . . .' she said, true to form in her incompletion.

In the background he heard the good Deacon snort 'Who in God's name are you talking to?'

Benny, never good in a moment of crisis, took the surest way out. He hung up.

Back at the duplex, Benny, after noting the presence of the white pickup truck parked beside Doodle's car, and after hopping the short distance from the drive to the front door, pharmacy purchase in hand, crawled into his bedroom and into his bed, muddy clothes and all, where he wrapped his ankle as tightly as he could stand with the stretchy bandage, swallowed four or five extra-strength Advil, then slept.

'Honey,' he said over the phone the next morning. 'Would you tell Nub I hurt my foot. I can't come in tonight.'

'You Ok, sugar? Can I bring you anything?'

'No,' Benny said. 'I'm fine.'

And in fact his ankle wasn't as damaged as he'd expected. After a fitful night's sleep, with the foot propped on the only pillow Benny owned, the swelling had subsided and the pain reduced to a dull throb, unless he tried swiveling his ankle.

Despite the discomfort, Benny had slept later than normal. He didn't wake up until he heard Doodle saying goodbye to someone and then, what must've been the white truck cranking and driving away. When Benny got up and hobbled into the kitchen, sure enough, Doodle's car sat alone in the drive.

Slut, Benny thought playfully. If he wasn't so filthy and miserable, he'd call her up and give her shit about it. Instead, he made himself a plate of sandwiches, some peanut butter, some baloney, and one banana sandwich with mayo, enough to last the day. He took the banana sandwich and a glass of milk into the bathroom and ate sitting on the toilet while the tub filled. Not until he was immersed and almost comfortable did Benny remember the lost tape.

Drying quickly proved painful until Benny realized that haste wasn't necessary. The lost tape would still be lost whether he went out to his van in ten minutes or two days. Nevertheless, he needed to know which tape the river claimed. The time it took Benny to dry and dress, make sure Doodle had left, then make the crippled orbit out to the van and back with the laundry basket was more than enough to insure raging, stomach churning anxiety. He sat back on the bed, the basket of tapes in his lap, Benny used the NASCAR towel to wipe dirt from the cardboard sleeves, then arranged the tapes chronologically.

Duplex. The missing tape was the one called *Duplex*, dated *Winter 2000–2001*. Given his status, for years now, as a duplex resident, Benny had anticipated that video. Had hoped that Jenna, with her insightful analog eye, truly captured the nuances of duplex living. The agonies. The intimacies. Had hoped that she – and through her some larger audience – recognized worth amid the banal and mundane. Would elevate his existence, his struggles, to epic levels. Jekyll & Hyde. Janus. Eng & Chang. And the like.

Given how close he'd come to losing all the tapes, Benny took some small solace in losing only one. He shoved the remaining tapes, all but *Epiphanies*, back into the milk crate and back under the bed. A lesser man might watch all the videos in a single sitting. This pacing, this delayed gratification, this denial, seemed to be the only self-control Benny had.

Avoiding telephone calls and sitting still as much as possible, Benny nursed his injured ankle for the entire day. Fortunately, Doodle left early, so she wouldn't be bothering him. Out of sheer boredom, and the desperation that often accompanies it, he scrounged around in the duplex's only storage closet, situated in the short hall between the kitchen and bathroom, its confines mostly consumed by the furnace and water heater; there he found what he sought, a birthday gift from Honey, several years back. A paint-by-number crucifixion scene. Golgotha. Place of skulls. A color-fragmented representation of the *father why hast thou forsaken me* moment.

Benny opened the box and laid its contents on the kitchen table. One plastic-handled brush. Two little bottles: one turpentine, one linseed oil. The canvas itself, a stiff board; Jesus' passion diminished somehow when rendered in thick blue lines against the white gesso. And then the paint: seven small vials, numbered, the colors not even named. Benny twisted open the bottle of linseed oil, just to smell it. He loved the odor. He opened the paint and found that all but a couple of the colors (numbers 1 & 4) had dried to the point of being useless. *Shit.* To amuse himself, Benny gave the colors names that seemed appropriate. Agony red. Suffering yellow. Misery brown. Damnation orange. Torment black. Etcetera.

No sooner did Benny get settled in to watch *Epiphanies* than the phone rang.

'What are you doing home?'

'Hey, Becky,' Benny said. 'I hurt my ankle yesterday. Thought I should stay off it for a while.'

'Oh, dear,' she said. 'Want me to come over and tend to you?'

'No, no,' Benny said, a little too quickly. 'I mean, I wouldn't mind but . . .'

'Men,' Becky said, and left it at that.

Benny wondered just how much experience she'd had with the species.

'So who's driving this weekend?' Becky asked. 'To the 4-H show?'

'You should, I guess. If you don't mind.'

They arranged a time for Becky to pick him up. Benny had to work a little harder to convince her not to come over that afternoon, and still half expected her to show up at his door. He was so unsure of her promise that, during *Epiphanies*, he spent as much time looking out the window and jumping at the sound of every passing car as he did watching the television. No great loss though; *Epiphanies* was nothing more than forty-five minutes of Jenna being filmed as she walked up behind various unsuspecting people, in assorted public settings, and without them knowing what was happening, displayed one of several handmade signs: hung like a horse; farts loudly when alone; pees sitting down.

'Hey, Gimpy,' Jeeter said. 'What's wrong with your foot?'

Benny's ankle had healed enough by the next day that he could, if willing to limp around awkwardly, at least get out of the house. He went to Jeeter's, to help bottle homebrew.

'I tripped,' Benny said, then felt the need to embellish and distract. 'Running from all those gorgeous women who can't keep their hands off me.'

'What women would those be, my crippled comrade?'

Benny thought. And he thought. Never as quick as Jeeter in this kind of banter, he usually fell short of success.

'The daring, the beautiful, the damn-near-fabulous Lady Bombers.'

'Ha!' Jeeter said. 'In your dreams. In your pitiful, no-pussy-gettin' dreams. About the only place you're liable to get chased is down at the VFW bingo hall, where the ladies have so many cobwebs in their cooters that nothing can get in or out.'

'You've been around Dink too long,' Benny said.

'Point taken,' Jeeter replied. 'Sorry.'

'What are you doing?' Benny asked.

Benny never knew where he'd find Jeeter, or what he'd be doing around the compound. Since the storm, Jeeter spent most of his time cleaning and rebuilding his various structures. That day, though, Jeeter wasn't hard to locate. He sat on his motorcycle, which sat on his front porch, across which was strewn the contents of a toolbox. Most baffling to Benny was the strange dance Jeeter seemed to be doing on the motorcycle. He'd scoot way forward on the seat then reach one or both hands back under his buttocks. Then he'd slide back to where a passenger would sit – should anyone be foolish enough to climb on with him – and slip one or both hands between his legs under his crotch, all the while craning to look at a magazine open on an upturned pickle bucket. Pressed against the screen of one of the trailer's front windows, a boom box spat the lyrics of what Benny knew to be one of Jeeter's favorite songs.

'Goin' up north babe, to get my hambone boiled. Gonna stay around up there, 'til my hambone's good and spoiled . . .'

'What the fuck are you doing?' Benny asked again.

Instead of answering, Jeeter climbed off the bike and removed its seat, which he flipped upside down across a layer of newspaper spread at the edge of the porch. He reached for a pair of pliers, then for a fat Philips-head screwdriver. Benny didn't speak again until Jeeter had removed the plastic plate under the motorcycle seat and had begun to peel back the black vinyl to reveal its foam core.

'Jeeter?'

Still no answer. Rather, Benny's mysterious friend pointed at the open magazine, his finger making quick circles in the air. Benny looked, but on the pages of classifieds advertising trips and products, Benny couldn't tell which one had so captivated Jeeter. Benny sat, with something closer to resignation than patience, while Jeeter went into one of his buses, coming back a few minutes later with a box of electrical items. Tape, resistors, wire, etc. When Jeeter marked out a small rectangle on the foam of his motorcycle seat with a felt pen, then opened a safety razor and began cutting a hole within the lines, Benny's pretence of patience dissolved.

'If you don't tell me what you're doing, I'm gonna leave.'

'I told you,' Jeeter said, stopping his work long enough to place an index finger directly on the advertisement to which he kept referring.

'Vibe-Rider,' Benny read. 'You have to be shitting me.'

The ad described a device that gets embedded in one's motorcycle seat at the precise spot where the carefully chosen female passenger's crotch rests against said seat. When activated by the driver, the oblong thingamajig vibrates – the intensity of those vibrations at the mercy of the driver's thumb – the goal being to twitch and wiggle the unwitting pudendal prisoner into a state of orgasmic ecstasy, and, by extension, availability.

'You didn't really buy one of those did you?' Benny asked.

'Nope,' Jeeter said. 'I'm making one.'

Benny listened as Jeeter explained the plan, and watched as he placed something beneath the seat fabric and wired it to the motorcycle battery.

'This seems ill-advised, Jeeter.'

'Spoken like a true coward.'

'I thought you wanted help bottling your beer.'

'I'm all done here,' Jeeter said, snapping the side cover back into place. 'Just let me give her a test.'

But when Jeeter pushed the starter, the motorcycle engine turned and turned over without cranking. He opened the gas cap and threw the bike from side to side between his legs.

'Shitsky,' he said. 'Benny, I'll make you vice president of the Jeeter empire for a whole week if you'll siphon some gas out of that backhoe for me.'

Benny flipped him off, on the way to the shed for a gas can and a hose. Ever since they were kids, Jeeter had an aversion to siphoning gasoline. The fumes made him sick to his stomach. Usually, Benny didn't mind doing the favor. Usually, he paid attention when he sucked at the hose. But he was so distracted that day his mouth filled with stinging orange fuel after one hard cheek-sucking pull, because he forgot to check the level of gas in the can.

He spat. Coughed twice. Retched and heaved.

He borrowed Jeeter's toothbrush. Didn't tell him.

At Nub & Honey's, later in the afternoon, Benny leaned against the worktable watching Scotty peel shrimp. Doodle came and went through the door to the dining room, winking at Benny each time. Benny wanted to talk to her, to see how things were going, but she seemed too busy.

'Where'd you say Nub went?' he asked Honey as she walked past with a five-pound bag of mints clutched to her bosom.

'Big Lots,' she said. 'Went to get some Red Devil Lye for the toilets.'

'Tell him I ought to be back at work by Saturday.'

Benny drove away from the restaurant, surprised. Surprised at how much, after really only one weekend's absence, he actually missed the place, its routines, its busyness. Surprised at how well the restaurant ran without him.

CHAPTER 19

'ARE YOUR FRIENDS GOING TO BE HERE?' BECKY asked, as Benny pulled to a stop at the County Fairgrounds front gate, where on either side geriatric sentinels stood with their hands grubbing around in the change-heavy pockets of their 84 Lumber aprons.

'At'll be one dolla,' the man on the driver's side said, poking his head far enough in the window for Benny to smell the coffee and tobacco-thick breath.

'I got some quarters,' Becky said, fishing in her purse. While she was distracted, the other old man, the one who stood on her side, took the opportunity to gawk. When Becky pulled the coins out, held tight in her stubby fingers, the old man stepped back, as if her condition were communicable.

'I think they are,' Benny said when they pulled away from the gate. 'Jeeter's coming anyway. I don't know about Dink.'

Benny, conscious of Becky's struggle with walking long distances and of his own still-tender ankle, circled the haphazard rows and rows of cars in the makeshift parking lot – a rutted, grassy field – until he spotted a rusty Mercury Grand Marquis full of kids pulling out of a space near the entrance. Even before the van came to a full stop, Jeeter, as prophesied, roared up beside them on his motorcycle, a skinny woman clinging to his back. Benny looked at the woman then Jeeter, who looked at Benny, then Becky, then Benny again. Then Benny, again, looked at the woman, who'd just taken her helmet off. No flush rose from up her neck; no obvious dilation of her pupils. The woman looked at Benny and Becky, then at the back of Jeeter's head. Benny looked at Jeeter who seemed to be fumbling with a switch on the motorcycle handlebar, then, as subtly as possible, looked at the woman's crotch. Nothing. No damp spot. No throbbing contractions. Jeeter's passenger was definitely not a woman in the throes of orgasm. Finally, Jeeter looked at Benny, shrugged his shoulders, palms up.

'Hey, ya'll,' Jeeter said. 'This is Angie.'

'Hey,' Angie said. She must've been forewarned because when Becky hopped out of the van no surprise registered. Jeeter, however, raised an eyebrow at Becky's short plaid skirt.

The group said their hellos then wandered into the fracas of the 4-H show.

'Let's get some cotton candy.'

'I want to see them big hogs.'

'Who's gonna win me a stuffed animal?'

So they roamed, a freakish lot in their own small and individual ways, through the stands of homemade fudge and fried pies, past the lemonade vendor and his swarm of yellow jackets, through Bldg. 3, the exhibitor's hall where they were, as a group and singularly, urged, entreated, beseeched, wooed and besieged to bone up on their watershed conservation knowledge, hone their turkey calling skills, test the qualities of buck urine, practice using a blowgun, and take a cool drink of water for Jesus, all in the same aisle. Becky refused to enter the taxidermist's booth, for several reasons, the main of which hinged on the practical joke of a creature hanging over his table. At one time, the creature was a rooster. And groundhog, maybe, or gopher. Had she looked hard enough, Becky would've seen the raccoon tail hanging from a hole cut in the bib-overalls the thing wore. Through grafting, shape shifting, form altering, and sheer determination, Ed, of Ed's Taxidermy Arts, had cobbled together a little monster to serve as his mascot. Benny clearly saw Becky go pale.

Angie, seduced by the flourish of his hands and his collar microphone, had to be pulled away from the man who alternately cut tin cans then vegetables with an assortment of serrated knives.

'Let's go,' Jeeter said. 'They'll be starting soon.'

'What?' Angie said.

'What?' Benny said.

Becky sat on a low bench taking deep breaths.

'Hill climbs,' Jeeter said. 'Regional championships of the American Hill Climbers Association. Motorcycles and fools of every size trying to ride to the top of that hill at the back of the fairgrounds.'

'Aha,' Benny said, feigning seriousness.

The four of them stopped at a pavilion sagging over half-a-dozen picnic tables; there they shared a heaping plate each of chili fries and nachos deluxe. Then Jeeter started telling Becky about his uncle, Reverend Small Smalley, who lost an eyeball in a baling-wire accident as a boy.

'He used to say that Jesus took that eye, and when medical science filled up the hole with a worthless glass bauble, Jesus came back and blessed him with special sight.'

'What do you mean?' Angie asked.

'He held tent revivals all over the state. And let me tell you those tents filled to busting. Small'd be up on the platform stage, stomping around and hollering; half the back-sliders hunched in their chairs like they'd just eked out a church poot. The other half whooping and praising the Lord like there was no tomorrow.'

Jeeter held the moment; a contrived dramatic pause.

'Yes . . . ?' Becky said. 'Then?'

'Then he'd pluck it right out.'

'What?!'

'What do you think? That glass eyeball. And the church-honeys would swoon so. Anyway, when he gave the altar call, all them sinners spilled out into the aisles ready for miracles. Even pitiful little ones. They brought up their grocery lists, their driver's licenses, prayer requests, letters and bills. Small took 'em, every one, held them up to that empty socket and read every word.'

Jeeter left it there. Let the story resonate.

'You're so full of shit, Jeeter,' Benny said.

Jeeter laughed, but neither denied nor accepted the charge.

'Well, look what the cat drug in,' Jeeter said, and everyone turned as Dink stepped up to the picnic table.

'What ya'll eatin?' Dink asked. 'Can I have some of them corn chips?'

'Nice to see you too, Dink,' Benny said.

'Angie, this is Dink,' Jeeter said. 'Dink, this is . . . Dink . . . where in God's name did you get them ugly-ass shoes?'

'Wha . . . ?' Dink asked, shoving a thick pinch of nachos into his mouth.

'Them boats? Jesus fucking Christ, those shoes are big enough to strap an Evinrude to!'

Dink reached into the plate again.

'Big *and* ugly. They look like something you get free

with the purchase of an ottoman down at Pug's Bargain Furniture. Made from the leftover Naugahyde.'

Dink ignored him. Watched Benny carry the paper plates to the trash can.

'What's matter with your foot, Benny?' Dink asked.

'Got hit by a truck,' Benny said.

Dink, sweet, stupid Dink, believed him.

'Let's go see some hill climbing,' Jeeter said.

Becky whispered something in Benny's ear.

'We'll be along in a little bit,' he said.

Dink, Angie and Jeeter headed toward the back of the fairgrounds.

Becky, debating between joining the lines formed at a row of Porta-Johns at the back of Bldg. 3 or braving the dank, spider-infested, cement-block facilities in one of the other buildings, chose the former, more because she knew the seat height was Ok.

'Want to feed the donkeys in the petting zoo?' Benny asked when she returned.

The donkeys, several chickens, a llama, and some sheep and goats were corralled in a dusty, straw-strewn lot between the two show barns. Kids with their nervous and/or bored parents waited their turns by the gate; the gate's attendant – a pimpled boy in pointy-toed cowboy boots – frazzled to the point of exhaustion by the Sisyphian task of keeping the lot free of animal feces, admonishing the older trouble-making boys not to chase the animals or feed them cigarette butts or rubber bands, and reimbursing for the quarters that regularly jammed in the food-pellet dispenser, that boy paid little attention to who came and went through the gate, and even less attention to the animals themselves.

'I'll get us some donkey food,' Benny said, digging in his

pocket for change. Finding none he asked Becky if she had change for a dollar.

'No,' she said. 'Maybe you can get change at the snow cone booth.'

'Be back in a minute,' Benny said.

And truly, he was only gone five minutes at the most. In that brief span of time, Becky had entered the petting corral. When Benny came around the show barn, it took him a moment to spot her – given her stature – among the busy swarm of children and the animals, all at about the same height. Benny almost called out Becky's name, then he saw her. Part of her anyway. Just the top of her head. The rest of Becky was blocked from view by three goats who had her pinned in one corner of the wooden fence. She wasn't struggling. She didn't cry out for help. But Benny knew she couldn't get away from the goats.

There was a parcel of time, calculable however fleeting, during which Benny could have acted. Ought to have acted. Should have. Should have dropped everything and rushed to aid his friend. But he didn't. Benny stopped to watch what happened.

That he stopped to bear witness, a sour little nugget of wickedness in and of itself, was bad enough, then another parcel of time – as brief as the first in the chronological march, but vast in its implications – unfolded. Something tectonic, something seismic shifted deep inside Benny Poteat. Transference? Reversal? Who knew. The important point is the change occurred without struggle in Benny. One instant he was watching a terrible thing – realized it was a terrible thing; realized he was just watching – and the next instant he took pleasure in the spectacle. Benny claimed his inaction, his passivity, and wanted more. He found palpable power in doing absolutely nothing.

Maybe the goats came to her out of curiosity, drawn by her dwarfishness. That as a human, she was more unusual than most they dealt with. But that theory gives too much credit to the animals. Perhaps their drive was less cerebral and more biological. Rut. Estrus. Becky's. The goats, like most male creatures, were attracted by smell. Benny watched as the smaller of the goats nuzzled and pushed against Becky, working to get its snout under her skirt. She slapped the goat on its nose, which slowed it down only briefly. Benny saw her mouth moving; he knew she was talking. He knew, by the look on her face, that Becky was afraid. He watched another of the goats actually nip at the hem of her skirt and begin to tug. The third goat insinuated itself behind Becky, between her and the fence, and began to push at her heavy rump.

Becky screamed, a tentative, embarrassed cry, but the gate attendant had his hands full with a little boy who'd been kicked in the shin by the llama; no one, it seemed, but Benny heard her call out. No one, it seemed, but Benny, saw the biggest goat push Becky forward, down onto her knees. Saw all three goats butting against her backside and against each other, jockeying for position. Saw the biggest goat step over Becky, who struggled but could not move the beast. The goat straddled the midget, one knobby goat leg on either side of, and pressing into, her ribcage. No sooner did the goat mount her than it began that most ancient of dances; the mechanical, the maniacal, hump hump hump of sex.

'Benny!!!'

That time everyone heard.

Benny scrambled into action, as if he'd just returned. His need to see how far the goats, the situation, would go, overridden by something closer to shame than chivalry.

Using his hands on the top rail, he vaulted the fence, but misjudged and fell to his knees in the dirt.

'Fuck!' Benny said.

'Benny!!!' Becky shouted.

Everyone in the petting zoo had turned to see, and by that time one of the other goats had climbed onto Becky from the side. Benny, and he was sure everyone else, couldn't help but noticing their goaty penises, erect and glistening, leaving wet tracks on Becky's clothes.

Benny and the pimpled gate boy reached Becky at the same time. The smaller goat, the one pumping futilely away at Becky's kidney, bleated in protest when the boy yanked it away. With the larger goat, Benny was less gentle. Benny punched it, first in the jaw, then in the ribs. But the old goat was so focused that it didn't stop its hump until Benny punched it in the temple.

After it was over, after they'd gotten away from the staring crowd, Becky began to sob.

'Why didn't you do something?'

Benny, terrified, wondered if she'd seem him watching from the fence.

'Why didn't you stop them?'

'I did, Becky. I did.'

Benny got her a lemonade, and a handful of paper towels to clean up with as best she could, and when Becky had calmed down enough, they headed towards the hill climb event. The closer they got, the more the sound of revving engines drowned out everything else.

As sporting events go, motorcycle hill climbs draw an edgier, more churlish group of both participants and spectators than most. All you need is a clear path several hundred feet up a mountain (defoliated and stripped of roots and rocks, ridiculously close to vertical), a specific date and some targeted advertisement, and throngs of boneheads towing, or hauling in vans, unmuffled motor-cycles with modified gears, stretched wheelbases, and tires with bolts screwed in for traction (along with their wives, children, coolers of beer and bologna sandwiches, gallons of gasoline, quarts of motor oil, all the necessary – and dozens of unnecessary – tools, several dilapidated lawn chairs, extra chains, very few bandaids and even less com-mon sense), will arrive ready at your command to charge like hell up that hill, knowing full well that nine times out of ten they'll topple backwards before they reach the top. And it's that guaranteed topple that draws the other half of the uncouth equation. Those who choose – not out of wisdom or an overall healthier sense of self-worth and preservation, more likely out of fear and doubt, and out of the driving need to watch others fuck up that tends to fester and grow amid that negative energy – to sit on weed-choked sidelines, in their own lawn chairs, with their own coolers of provisions, and watch. And hoot. And shout. And pray, quietly, to themselves, that the next guy falls too. Luckily, the falls rarely hurt anyone.

'Look at that,' Benny said, hoping to distract Becky, to take the mood in a different direction.

She couldn't help but see what Benny referred to. A battered and muddied Kawasaki sat on an upturned milk crate so that its rear wheel could spin freely as its owner fiddled with the clutch. The man wore stiff knee-high boots and racing leathers that were unzipped nearly to his crotch, revealing an expanse of hairy white flesh that made Benny wince. Screwdriver in one hand, pliers in the other, the man would squat and tinker, then stand and rev the engine until it screamed. What caught Benny's attention, what he called to Becky's attention, wasn't the motorcyclist's obscene belly. No. It was his kids. Two of them. Boys. Shirtless and tanned. Already at work on bellies of their own. Both the boys stood behind their father's bike, a foot, maybe less, from the exhaust pipe. Every time the man revved the engine, a billowing mushroom of blue smoke washed over and surrounded his sons. Every time the cloud hit the boys, they laughed and danced in its intoxicating warmth until it dissipated. Their mother, or at least the woman with the group, lay asleep on a blanket in the shade of the van.

'Them boys ought to quit that,' Becky said.

When they found Dink and the others, Jeeter was reading aloud from a slip of paper held up with both hands.

'One free breakfast, eat-in-only; one fish dinner, eat-in-only; woodcraft item; afghan; bucket of balls; flashlight; oil filter and change; beauty care package; spinal exam; one-gallon cleaner.'

Dink saw them first, and spoke directly to Becky.

'Dang girl! You been calf-roping or something?'

He must've been referring to the straw and dirt on her clothes.

'Dink!' Benny warned, his forefinger aimed between Dink's eyes. 'Don't start.'

Dink, remembering his busted lip, said no more. But Jeeter kept reading.

'Electric toothbrush; ceramic item; wreath; Smith & Wesson model 686 .357 Magnum!; choice of sandwich and fries; nautical picture, mug, and apron; hair-care package; steering-wheel cover.'

'What the hell is that, Jeeter?' Benny asked.

'Raffle ticket my man. One hundred and nine prizes.

One dollar per ticket. Small wood carving item; furnace cleaning; one case of oil; cast iron griddle . . .'

Becky wanted to leave. She never recovered enough from the goat incident to enjoy the hill climb.

'See you guys later,' Benny said.

The perfunctory kiss on his cheek when he dropped Becky off let Benny know clearly that he'd not be spending the night, nor any portion of it, at Claxton Looms Luxury Apartments. Becky walked toward then through the door and out of sight, without looking back at Benny.

Over and over again, images of those goats climbing onto Becky flooded Benny's mind. He drove home with them.

Dec. 11, 1999   • • • **Rec**
10:00 a.m.

Lilith Kickin' Ass

This is the tape that won the award. Jenna stands before the camera. She wears a white tee shirt. The only other thing in view is a table at her side, and on it a small bowl of something. Jenna dips a fingertip into the bowl, and begins to write red letters on the shirt, across her breasts. *Lilith*, just beneath her collarbones. *Kickin'*, the apostrophe marks her left nipple. *Ass*, at the base of her ribs.

Then Jenna lifts her shirt and the word *before* is written on her flesh.

What follows is a series of shots with Jenna lifting different shirts or wearing different bras or bathing suits, all with the word *before* written on her belly. Jenna is giddy; overly so. A wide manic grin accompanies each scene. It's hard to tell if she's alone, shooting everything herself, or if she has help.

The next scene is the table alone, and in place of the bowl, a book lies open. The camera circles at a dizzying pace, then stops and begins to zoom in. It's a telephone book. It's opened to the yellow pages. The camera tightens focus to the heading PHYSICIANS & SURGEONS (MD): PLASTIC and RECONSTRUCTIVE, and circled in red, the same red with which Jenna wrote on herself, *Body by Burk. As seen on TV!*

Even Benny knew what was about to happen. The camera had paused long enough for him to read the entire ad. Benny had no clue what botox injections were, nor endermologie. He was intrigued by nose reshaping and lip enhancement. And in true male form, blind and limited, thoroughly intrigued by breast augmentation. Finally, he thought, a good tape. Voyeurism at its most base. But those dreamy, premasturbatory musings gave way to shock as Jenna, god knows how she arranged clearance, showed the entire procedure on videotape. Benny, fully prepared with a washcloth to wipe up the ejaculate, never got more than semi-erect throughout the whole operation. Even during the series of *after* shots, written on her belly as before, exposed when she lifted the same shirts as before – obviously taken over time since the shock to her breasts, the redness and swelling gradually abated – even then Benny couldn't muster a full-fledged hard on.

By the time the scene changed, opening on the Hinkey's dinner table again, the camera positioned so that Jenna and her father, the Deacon, were in full view, Rebecca and their mother visible but more in profile, Benny felt certain the erotic quality of the video wasn't going to increase. And when Jenna and Deacon Hinkey came to loggerheads, her shrieking about what he paid for Becky's college and the things he refused to do for her, him spilling out one pious diatribe after another, both claiming disrespect, her a whore and tool of Satan, him a self-righteous holier-than-thou hypocrite, and Jenna, finally, in an act so planned Benny could imagine the storyboard, Jenna lifted her shirt to bare her new, and unfettered, breasts to her father and shrieked over and over 'How do you think Jesus would like these?' Benny had to turn off the tape.

Becky answered on the fourth ring, just as Benny was about to hang up.

'Hey,' he said.

'Hey.'

He wanted to ask her about all he'd just seen in the video. To say he was sorry, even.

'You Ok?'

'Yeah. I reckon.'

'I'm really sorry about what happened.'

'I don't want to talk about it.'

'Ok.'

A dirty, nasty silence oozed from one plastic mouthpiece to the other, filled the distance between them.

'Next weekend there's a 4th of July picnic out at Gnogg's Farm. Want to go?'

Becky didn't answer.

'There'll be lots of good music,' Benny added. 'And a tanker truck of beer.'

'Let me think about it,' Becky said.

'Call me,' Benny said. 'There won't be any animals there,' he said.

CHAPTER 20

BECKY CALLED. THE VERY NEXT DAY. SHE APOLOGIZED for 'pouting,' and said she'd love to go to the picnic.

'Want to come over tonight?' Benny asked, more horny than in need of companionship.

'The fish died,' Becky answered.

'What?'

'The fish. The tang with the hole in its head.'

'Shit. Sorry about that.'

'I can't get him out,' Becky said. 'He sunk to the bottom in the corner, and I can't reach him.'

Benny offered help.

Becky accepted.

'Poor little fucker,' Benny said, tossing the carcass into the trash two hours later. 'Let's go get a hot dog.'

Before Becky could answer, the phone rang.

'Claxton Looms Ap . . . oh, hi mom.'

While Becky talked on the phone, Benny moved around the room looking at her breasts from various angles. He was comparing them, in size and placement, to her dead sister's implants. Benny, like most men, was prone to lapses in judgment, was prone to fixating at the drop of a hat on one inappropriate thing or another, then acting out of that flawed moment. Sometimes, though not often, he had an acute awareness of the stupidity of his impending action. Even then, he rarely possessed the wherewithal to stop himself. Tits, Benny thought. Nice. Nice tits. Jenna had nice tits. Becky has nice tits. Benny felt the need of a titty in his hand. He circled behind Becky as she sat, legs crossed, at her desk talking to her mother. Benny paid no attention to the conversation as he stepped up, reached both hands over to cup both Becky's breasts in his palms, and give them one, two little bounces before she snorted, put her feet against the desk drawer, and pushed the chair backwards into Benny's shins.

'Shhttt!' Benny said, nearly falling.

'Quit it!' Becky said, her stubby fingers wrapped over the telephone mouthpiece.

After hanging up, it took a while to calm her down.

'I'm sorry,' Benny said. 'I wasn't thinking. I didn't mean it. I won't do it again.'

'Daddy's mad,' she finally said after some uncertain silence.

'At me?' Benny asked.

'No,' Becky said, although her tone didn't rule that out as a possibility sometime in the future. 'He's mad at Piedmont College, where Jenna goes to school . . . went . . . where Jenna went to school.'

'Why's he mad at them?'

'Jenna owes the college tuition for the past two semesters.'

'So? Does he have to pay it?'

'He won't, whether he should or not. On principle,' Becky said.

'What do you mean? He's against paying for college?'

'No. Not that. He didn't . . . Jenna was . . . Jenna is kind of arty.'

'You told me that,' Benny said, hoping he remembered correctly.

'Daddy didn't like what she was doing.'

Becky left it at that.

Benny wished he could tell her that he knew about the dinner table and the breast implants.

'I don't think the good deacon likes me,' Benny said.

'I don't think he likes anybody,' Becky replied. 'But you'll earn some points if you come to the hymn sing with me next week.'

'What kind of points?'

'Oh, I don't know. Maybe you'll get into heaven quicker.'

'Let me think about it,' Benny said.

And they did go back to Benny's house. And they did have sex. Unambitious, distracted sex. Benny kept seeing himself as a goat, hoofed and randy. And Becky, naked, seemed more grotesque, more animal-like than ever before. Jenna's before and after pictures, blood scars and all, flashed continually in Benny's mind. Becky, bruised from the incident at the fair, couldn't get comfortable. Both of them heard Doodle and the man who drove the white truck having their own kind of subdued sex on the other side of the wall. The next morning, after both Becky and the other man left, Benny listened to Doodle move furniture.

He took Squat out to pee.

'Hey, Benny Poteat,' Doodle said. Nothing else.

'Hey, Doodle.'

They were both a little embarrassed by the night before. Something akin to infidelity wedged itself between them.

'You going to Gnogg's picnic?' she asked.

'Yeah. You?'

'I think so.'

Gnogg's farm, owned and operated by the youngest Gnogg, Greg, only a few years older than Benny – remembered most for that one horrible incident at a high school football game – functioning more as a party spot than any kind of crop-producing farm (although the previous generations of Gnoggs peddled eggs, vegetables, and melons at a large roadside stand), lay in the thickets and kudzu draped pine copses where Alamance County slammed to a stop at the banks of the Little Toe River. Though fecund, able to bear and bear, those first Gnoggs were limited in vision and means, so the farm never amounted to more than a couple hundred poorly managed acres. But Gnogg's farm had a nice view of the river, and of Crowder's Mountain in the distance, and the lie of the land seemed particularly suited for parties, barn dances, corn shucks, bonfires, weddings, birthdays and holidays. Over time, folks started asking for permission to hold their special functions at Gnogg's Farm. Now, Greg leapt on every opportunity to host a bash.

One fenced pasture of several rolling acres was used for parking: $1 per vehicle. $5 got you an all-you-can-drink wristband for the cheap kegged beer. Food you generally paid for upon ordering. The July 4th menu included deer burgers, hot dogs, baked beans, coleslaw and the like. Only the music was free at Gnogg's parties.

'At'll be one dolla,' the man said when Benny rolled to a stop at the pasture gate. While it was clearly not the same man that made the same demands of Benny at the 4-H show, there were enough similarities to make Benny wonder whether they were related in some way, or even, if there wasn't perhaps an entire subspecies, or caste of persons filling these roles. The man was decked out in red, white and blue, with so many stripes going in so many directions that Benny, dizzied, had to look away.

'You ought to introduce him to Clyde,' Becky said, referring to Benny's neighbor who traditionally spent the July 4th holiday sitting on his porch in an Uncle Sam hat and beard, and had waved his flags enthusiastically at Benny and Becky when they left that morning.

'Clyde's got better taste,' Benny said.

They parked and headed for the festivities, but before they got too far, Jeeter, with quintessential Jeeter timing and flair, gave a quick double-rev and pulled his loud motorcycle to a stop beside Benny's van. And, even before Jeeter got the kickstand down, his passenger, not Angie from before, but some Angie-ish other woman, in short-shorts and a halter top, began pounding on Jeeter's back and on his helmet with her fists.

'Goddamnit! I told you to stop,' the woman screamed as she took off her helmet.

'What?' Jeeter yelled. 'What the fuck's the matter with you?'

'There's something wrong with this fucking motorcycle!' she yelled. By this time the woman had leapt off the bike and was prancing around, splay-legged, with one hand down the front of her pants and the fingers of the other holding the hem of the leg band out and away from her body.

'My goddamn pussy's blistered! Didn't you hear me telling you to stop?!'

Jeeter looked befuddled. Jeeter looked embarrassed. Jeeter looked mad.

'How the fuck was I supposed to know what you were yelling about? I thought you were enjoying the ride!'

When the woman threw her helmet on the ground and stormed off, Jeeter looked at Benny and shrugged.

'I need to go shoot something,' Jeeter said, joining Benny and Becky.

'Some *thing* or some *body*?' Benny asked.

'Whichever moves first.'

The crowd, already strong, was sure to grow steadily throughout the afternoon. Gnogg's parties historically ran clear into the next day. Benny and Becky, mostly Benny, had come early because of the music. Fat Mumford was playing. Fat belonged to several local bands, and played a number of instruments: guitar, banjo, mandolin sometimes. What he played best, though, was the fiddle, and Benny knew Fat would have his fiddle there that day.

Benny loved bluegrass and old time music. Nub and Honey used to take him to all the local fiddlers' conventions – regional music competitions, held in Spring, in school auditoriums, groups of all ages with little in the way of professional polish, competitions mostly about fun and the joy of singing and playing together – when he was a kid, and because everybody knew them and ate at the fishcamp, Benny always got to go backstage where the musicians practiced and warmed up in the classrooms. He never forgot the sights and sounds. Big and heavy, or lank and wizened, hardworking men, in their freshly washed overalls, perched in a circle on tiny kid chairs, making music, their tough hands gently coaxing high-pitched rhythm from their instruments. Bird-like women, their faces drawn tight, or solid fireplug-like matrons, singing in harmony so sweet Benny wanted to cry.

'Fat gonna be here?' Jeeter asked.

'Yep.'

'I'll get us some beer,' Jeeter said. 'You guys get the seats.'

As usual, Greg Gnogg had parked a flatbed trailer at the back of the largest barn where, fifteen feet out, the ground rose gently, forming a natural grass amphitheater. Off to the right of the barn, where the ground remained flat, the sounds of the horseshoe pit and a badminton game competed with the musicians playing on the trailer. Nobody seemed to mind. Benny and Becky picked a spot in the shade of an old mimosa tree. Their timing was perfect; just as they sat, Fat, fiddle case in hand, struggled up the steep riser at the trailer's end. Behind him, a skinny little man with a huge stand-up bass, a guitar player, and a banjo player, both of whom had their instruments slung around their necks.

The South in July is often a blast furnace. Some places, some times, even a breeze does more harm than good. But Gnogg's farm, situated just so, was often blessed with a cool breeze, such as the very breeze that meandered by at the exact moment when Fat Mumford sat his fiddle case across his wide lap, unclasped the three latches, and opened it up like a lopsided and sacred mouth. That sweet cleansing breeze, having recently tumbled down the slopes of the Blue Ridge mountains and over the foothills, trickled through the weeping willows that lined the Little Toe River and blew right across Fat Mumford's lap and the instrument he cradled there. Blew softly, but definitely, over the fiddle's belly and over the strings held taut by its carved bridge. And when that cool stir of air played across the catgut strings it pulled something, a silent and ancient something, out of the soundpost (that soul of the instrument), out of the f-holes; a plea, or sublime curse maybe, that it carried right off the farm, carried up the gravel road to where gravel became macadam, then along the crumbling potholed black path into town – or the scruffy edges of it anyway, where the weed-choked trash gullies gave way, reluctantly, to the houses on Mill Hill – wafting, in wind-like fashion, its quiet way up the front steps and onto the porch of the first house, belonging to a Mr Tick Freeze, where he sat with a glass of milk to soothe the ulcer his third wife had bestowed upon him, sat cursing the goddamn punks who kept running the stop sign on the corner, sat under the slit-eyed and wanting watch of an obese manx tomcat sprawled on the porch at his feet, one of a long long long lineage of felines, most of them feral and inbred, lop-eared, cross-eyed, kink-tailed and mangy. Tick Freeze, people would tell you, couldn't keep a wife because he stank. Tick Freeze stank of fish; partly by birthright, and partly by vocation.

Tick Freeze, and his daddy, and his daddy's daddy, and on back to when the Mill Hill was first built and all those farmers and folks came out of the mountains fooled into believing mill jobs with regular pay had to be better than depending on the earth and climate, all those Freezes supplemented their meager incomes by selling catfish caught in the river. Catfish eagerly purchased by churches for Friday night fish fries, or by tired women and hungry men. They were good, the Freezes, damn good at catching catfish, and before too long one of the Freezes had fashioned a murky pond in his back yard to raise the catfish. As good as they were at catching catfish, the Freezes were even better at cleaning them. Tick Freeze was the reigning Filet King; when his knife was sharp, and it was always sharp, Tick could skin and gut a catfish in thirty seconds. Put the filets, wrapped in newspaper, in your hand in forty-five.

But what do you do with the ropey wet guts and comb-like spines and the barbed heads – with their dimming fish-eyes – of all those catfish? The Freezes, generations of Freezes, gathered the innards in tin buckets, a day's worth at a time, and flung them, a red shower of viscera, into the gully behind their house. Catfish bark when you pull them out of the water. Guttural little yips of protest. Some say that if you walked past the gully behind Freeze's house at night, you'd hear the ghosts of the dead catfish, years and years of dead catfish swimming the dry banks, that you'd hear the guts and spines still barking. Crying out. That if you walk up to the edge of the gully, at night, you'd see all those catfish eyes looking up at you glinting in the milky moonlight.

It's true. There were things to hear and things to be seen by anyone who ventured past the unhallowed grounds, but those things were not piscine in nature or origin. Rather, they were feline. Wild cats, drawn to the gully by the stink of rotting guts and the promise of a feast. Beginning with the first tossed bucket of fish entrails, cats began to gather in the gully. Neighborhood cats. Alley cats. Barn cats. Cats with no regular residence. Even wampus cats. All coming to sup and grow fat and mean on the fishy carrion. And they stayed. Soon even the house cats stopped going home, back to their bowls of milk and their catnip sachets, back to their owners, doting or indifferent. Choosing instead to live with the growing pride. Dividing and subdividing into factions. Some liked only the fish heads. Others the gut or tiny fish hearts. A few, the meanest, would fight to the death for the eyeballs. Soon the Mill Hill teemed with cats, whiskers always slick and foul no matter how fastidious their grooming habits. And as cats are creatures of habit, the whole pack of them took to sleeping by day, and by night glutting themselves and yowling and fighting and fucking until dawn. Sleep, for anyone living near the gullies, was difficult. Years later the whole town seemed overrun. Children were afraid to go out at night. A friend of a friend of a friend actually lost a daughter to the cats. Look close at any photograph from the period; mill picnics, softball games, candid shots of the workday, even funerals; anyplace people gathered, you'll find a cat in the picture, hunched by a table leg, peering out from any available cranny. Look even closer and some of the cats become recognizable, showing up in picture after picture, year after year, with frightening longevity. People did look close, and recognized. And they named a few of those cats. Named them after the mill owners, for their tenacity, and other less-mentionable traits. A one-eyed manx, in particular, could be traced with photographic evidence at least one hundred years back. Outliving his contemporaries and most of the manx-ish cats he spawned. Surviving countless assassination attempts by the boys of the town who were paid one dollar for every dead cat they brought to the back door of city hall. Many a successful Buffalo Shoals entrepreneur got their start hunting cats, with .22-caliber rifles, for bounty. That old manx lost an eye to the bounty hunters, and was rumored to have been hit several more times. But he refused to die. He and his progeny tormented the town and county for years. The cat problem dominated many official discussions. And while it never occurred to anyone that perhaps the Freeze family could dispose of the fish guts in some other more sanitary way, the idea of poison came to Superintendent Brown in a dream one night, and all agreed on the plan. A handful of arsenic stirred into every bucket of fish remnants proved successful. Cats began to die all over. Every morning a fresh crop of feline carcasses littered the environs of Buffalo Shoals. Gape-mouthed and stiff on the seats and in the trunks of abandoned cars. Curled tight in the weedy ditches. Lumped in doorways. A few even had the audacity to die right in the middle of the sidewalk. So many dead cats. It didn't take long for the new problem to be identified. And not much longer for the bonfire solution, which also came to Superintendent Brown in a dream. Every Friday night, for an entire summer, at the back of the high school parking lot, the town maintenance crew stoked up a raging fire in the steel bed of the only municipal dump truck, and folks came from miles around with boxes, bags or handfuls of dead cats. For a while, it became a sort of social event, families coming with chairs and ham biscuits and gallons of tea. By wintertime, the cat population was decimated, and the stink of burning cat flesh which had permeated everything for months had begun to clear. The old one-eyed manx, still seen from time to time slinking along in the dusk or dawn, although slowed some by the loss of a back leg, continued to sow his seed. That winter was particularly hard and bitter. Not so much snow, but a cold snap so deep and persistent that it broke all records. As human nature goes, some folks began to pity the plight of the remaining cats, homeless and hungry as they were. Tick Freeze's mother was a woman of compassion. She knew of a new litter of kittens, curled and suckling at their sickly mother's teats in the dank black beneath the tool shed. She knew too that the old flannel shirt they lay on wasn't enough to stave off the cold. Having fretted all night with worry, Tick's mother went to bring them inside as soon as the sun came up. Went too late. The mother cat had hissed and run away. Tick's mother found all but one of the kittens dead. Stiff. She gave Tick the remaining kitten for his birthday.

And there it lay, years later, Tick's cat, named Cat, half asleep, languorous and heavy with history, waiting for Tick to finish the milk, knowing that the last few drops the old man would spill out on the porch floor for it to lap up. Lay there in torpid defiance of anything, except for the milk, that might compel it to move. Then came the breeze. The one that originated miles away, but had most recently played over the strings of a particular fiddle. Strings made of gut. Catgut, renowned for their stretchability and soft song. When that breeze crawled up the front steps of Tick Freeze's house, onto his front porch, along the flea-bitten leg of Cat and across its belly fur, that ancient something the breeze carried with it from the fiddle spoke to the animal. There was no way to know just what it said, but immediately the cat, pitched into a hissing and spitting frenzy, leapt up, charged into the street, where it was hit and killed by a car, one of them goddamn punks who'd just run the stop sign, thereby ending, as far as anyone could tell, the domesticated branch of a complicated, proud, and relatively historical feline lineage. Its death, piercing, coincided with the first note Fat Mumford played that day, a mile or more away, one long drawn out c-note to open up 'Soldier's Joy'. The note came out just a little flat, which puzzled and annoyed Fat Mumford, who'd just tuned the fiddle perfectly moments earlier.

'Can I get those for you?' somebody asked, walking by with a trash bag.

'Thanks, buddy,' Benny said, handing him the empty beer cups.

Flat note notwithstanding, everybody enjoyed the show.

'What's that he keeps putting on the bow?' Becky asked.

Fat paused between songs to take something out of his fiddle case and draw the bow across it.

'Rosin,' Benny said. 'It's a little cake of rosin.'

It's what allowed the horsehair bow to stutter out the sounds. Benny wished for a moment that he could put a cake of rosin under his tongue to help him say the things he struggled with.

'I gotta go find that girl,' Jeeter said. 'And make sure she's Ok.'

Jeeter came back a while later with the woman walking several paces behind.

'Will you give that girl a ride home?' Jeeter asked.

She didn't say a word to Benny or Becky the whole trip. Just sat in the back of the van, on the bed, with her legs spread.

Chapter 21

'Benny?' Becky called from the bedroom.

Benny sat at his kitchen table waiting for a cup of instant coffee to cool.

'Benny?' she said, a little louder.

Benny heard her call the first time, he just wasn't in the mood to answer.

'Didn't you hear me?' she asked coming into the room.

'Sorry,' he said. 'Guess I was daydreaming.'

'Have you seen my undies?'

'What?'

'My undies? I left them on the floor by the bed.'

'Look under the bed,' he said, not offering to help. 'Squat probably dragged them under the bed.'

'I did,' she said, clearly irritated. 'Can you help me look.'

Benny didn't move. Eventually, Becky sighed her discontent and looked for herself.

'If you find them,' she said. 'Will you please bring them when you come this afternoon?'

She refered to the hymn sing at Egg Rock Pentecostal Church, which Benny finally agreed to attend.

'Yep,' he said.

'It starts at four o'clock,' she said. 'Will you pick me up around three?'

'Yep.'

Bitch, he thought, when she left, then realized immediately that she'd done nothing to elicit the response. Benny wanted to watch Jenna's next tape. *Homemade Bible Stories. Fall 1999.* It's the main reason he was abrupt with Becky. The other reasons, he couldn't articulate anyway. Maybe he should just tell her that her stupid sister was dead. That she walked right into the Toe River, big new tits and all, and didn't come back up. Maybe he could explain the whole thing to Becky without her getting angry, or calling the police. What good would the police do now, anyway? Maybe he and Becky could watch the tapes again and she could explain things to Benny. Probably not, though. With Becky gone, he had a few hours to himself before the hymn sing. Benny put the tape into his VCR.

Dec. 11, 1999   • • • Rec
10:00 a.m.

The camera is mounted on the dashboard of a moving car. The scene jumps back and forth between forward- and rear-facing motion. By the sound of their voices, one Jenna's, and another male voice, two people are in the car, but it's unclear who drives and who is the passenger. Their conversation is limited.

'Here?'

'No.'

'Here?'

'No'

And on and on. They drive through the country, progressively hillier country, and come to a stop eventually . . .

'Here?'

'Yes.'

. . . in the middle of an orchard. An apple orchard. The scene jump-cuts and the camera has been moved outside the car, where it pans 360°; apple trees as far as the eye can see, split by a narrow road, the road itself flanked by barbwire fencing: three-strand. The camera fixes on the road, and in the distance, from no small distance, a walking figure appears. The day is blue. Blue. And the orchard is a great expanse of green, raked again and again by the gnarled gray branches, and stippled with the crimson red of apples.

The figure comes into focus. A woman, Jenna, wearing a short leather skirt and a tank top, walks without stopping up to and past the camera, which turns to follow as she walks to the fence. She climbs, with difficulty, over the top strand of wire and walks into the orchard where she stops at the first tree and picks an apple. Apple in hand, Jenna climbs back over the fence, faces away from the camera, lifts her skirt over her hips, hooks her thumbs in the waist of her white panties, pulls them off, hangs them between two of the barbs on the top strand of wire, making visible the circle and circle and circle bull's eye drawn over the front of the fabric, straightens her skirt, smoothes it over her buttocks, kneels, picks up the apple and nestles it into the crotch of the hanging undergarment where it sags low and distorts the circles.

The camera jump cuts, and Jenna stands in the middle of the road holding a gun at arm's length with both hands. She fires once into the air, once in the direction of the camera, then spins to fire the remaining shots at her underwear, hitting it twice, the apple exploding in a spray of white flesh from inside the fabric. Jenna stops, points the gun to her temple, smiles, clicks. Clicks. Clicks.

*   *   *

Stupid. Benny thought the whole damn thing was stupid. And the next segment, a thing with a loaf of bread and a can of sardines, stupid too. There were three other segments on the tape, but they were all boring as hell. Benny rewound the tape and tried jacking off to the scene where her butt showed, but no luck. Stupid.

Stupid, Benny thought, pulling up in the Employee of the Month spot at Claxton Looms. He'd rather be going anyplace than a hymn sing at Deacon Hinkey's church.

'Wait here, Squat,' Benny said. 'I'll be back in a minute.'

Squat lay still, in agreement. Benny brought him along because the old dog seemed a little out of sorts. Like he needed company or something. With a bowl of food and a bowl of water Squat would happily spend the afternoon in Benny's van.

'Hi, Squat,' Becky said.

Squat lay still as his greeting.

'He Ok?' she asked.

'Just old,' Benny said.

The Egg Rock Pentecostal Church parking lot teemed with Christians and Christian cars and trucks. While no uglier or more unattended to than most, Benny's van attracted attention when they drove in. Maybe because of all the unchristian, downright heathen, implications that go along with owning a conversion van, or maybe, probably even, because Deacon Hinkey's midget daughter sat up in the passenger's seat like nobody's business.

'You parked right beside daddy's car,' Becky said.

Moving was out of the question.

'Hey ya'll,' she said to any of the myriad of onlookers who watched her make the little jump out of Benny's van.

While it had been years, decades even, since Benny was last inside Egg Rock Pentecostal – the last time he remembered being the funeral of some withered friend or relative of Honey's – the hard, mean familiarity of its knotty pine interior pierced Benny's side; a stab of hot pain burrowed deep. Either that, or the tomato sandwich he'd eaten for lunch was coming back with a vengeance.

Benny followed Becky. He felt big, gargantuan, hideous and despicable; as if the months of lies and deceit seething and coursing through his veins had begun to fester and his bloated flesh and swollen muscles hung loose about his rancid bones, the whole damn mess ready to rupture at the slightest touch. They took their seats in the second pew from the front, where Becky's feet dangled a good six inches from the floor. Her mother sat, smiling, in the front. Lord have mercy. Despite the span of time, the dry pious smell of the old hymnbooks, the creaking and groaning of belabored pews, and the dizzying swirl of pine-knot patterns on the walls, all felt as if they'd been a daily part of Benny's existence. As did the hush that trickled, in two parts, over the congregation, first when the seven-hundred-year-old pianist tottered into view and unsteadily to her bench, then again when Deacon emerged from one of two narrow doors on either side of the pulpit.

If he saw Becky sitting there in the second pew, Deacon Hinkey gave no indication. If he saw Benny, monstrous or not, sitting close beside his dwarfish daughter, he gave less than no indication. When the good Deacon opened the service with a prayer for souls 'lost and wandering in sin,' Benny thought he detected a fleeting, pitiful, harangued spark of humanity.

The choir, in intent and purpose, strove to be choirly, robed, arranged according to some unknown criteria (pitch, or height, or age, or presence of unsightly hairs) behind the Deacon, and knuckling their hymnals. Becky had to elbow him in the side several times before Benny realized he was supposed to pick up his own hymnal and join the congregation as they struggled to catch up, then keep up, with the pianist's mad dash at 'Shall We Gather At The River', page 87. Then again through page 43, 'Rock of Salvation'. And again, and again. The manic quality of the hymns – the choppy, off-key piano, the cacophony of talentless but give-it-hell-anyway worshipers – never varied; Benny couldn't tell whether they were all charging towards heaven, or away from hell. Somewhere in the middle, Deacon Hinkey spoke about the virtues hard work, clean living, sobriety, and 'abstimoneousness', which elicited *amens* all around. After another hour of singing, the ordeal came to a close with a bitter prayer.

Every good Christian loves a dog. So when Benny went straight to his van after the hymn sing ended, to let Squat out to pee, Becky followed, and in the name of fellowship (and general nosiness) so did several others.

'At's a good dog,' someone offered when Benny opened the door to Squat lying on the van floor, looking no less forlorn than before. Benny had to help the old dog out of the van, and while Squat nosed around in the Johnson grass looking for, presumably, a place to urinate, Benny fielded questions about his age and breed and the various tricks he couldn't do.

Becky sat nervously on the footboard, knowing full well that there was a sizing-up element to the whole encounter. As if the congregation exercised some protective, familial rights on Becky. She sat nervously knowing full well that her father would be coming to his car any minute. Sure enough, coincidence, that sublime trickster, held sway.

'What you got in this thang?' a jowley, jovial Pentecostal asked, poking his head in the open door of Benny's van. Becky moved aside as Benny tried to deflect attention away from the bed. Nobody paid any attention to Squat. Nobody except a little boy named Punk, who called out, just as Deacon Hinkey walked up, 'They's something wrong with that dog!'

Everyone turned to Squat. Squat stood, heaving, on the grass. Rhythmic and violent spasms; his old dog back alternately arching, stomach sucked in, then relaxing.

'Probably just ate something,' Benny said, not too concerned. 'Probably ate some grass.'

Squat proved him wrong, though. The old dog hadn't eaten grass. Instead, what he ate, he chose to reveal the very instant Deacon Hinkey stepped into the small crowd.

'What's going on here?' he asked.

'Nothing,' Benny said.

'Nothing, Daddy,' Becky said.

'Something's wrong with that dog,' Punk said.

And Squat gave his last, most wrenching, heave, and there on the grass, swimming in a pool of yellow bile, lay the thing he'd eaten. Punk broke off a stick, and despite Benny's wish to the contrary, everyone gathered around to watch the little boy fish the thing from the dog puke.

'That's a damn panty!' somebody said. 'Your dog vomicked up a panty!'

And, in irrefutable fact, it was a panty – complete with the looping cursive *Sunday* stitched in thin red across the front panel – that hung by one chewed leg-hole from the stick held high in Punk's hand. Deacon Hinkey looked at Becky, then Benny, then Becky, then, finally, at Benny. Becky looked down, only down. Benny couldn't find a place to look. And everyone else took it all in with righteous relish. Everybody, except Punk, ignored the panty. Punk had begun to swing it around and around, the slow arc described by trails of thin yellow vomitus.

'Put that stick down, son!' the Deacon said. Punk obeyed the commandment immediately.

Eventually some merciful soul broke the spell of embarrassment. A friend of Becky's. Nadine.

'Hey, Becky,' Nadine said. 'A bunch of us are going to Plumb Bob's tonight for hot wings. Why don't ya'll come?'

Thus the crowd dispersed.

'I better ride home with mama,' Becky said. But Benny knew what she meant. With daddy.

Becky mouthed *call me later* from the back seat of Deacon Hinkey's car, with only her head visible over the car door. Benny picked up Squat and eased him into the van. The old dog seemed a little peppier after lightening his load.

'I'm sorry,' Becky said when Benny called her that afternoon.

'About what?' Benny asked.

'About this afternoon,' she said. 'Will you go to Plumb Bob's with me tonight?'

'Who's going to be there?'

'Nadine, the girl who asked me, and her boyfriend. Probably her sister, Nance, and Nance's fiancé too. I don't know who else.'

Benny hesitated.

'It'll be fun,' she encouraged.

Benny hesitated.

'They have really good wings. Hot.'

'I reckon,' Benny said. 'But I can't stay out too late.'

He had nothing to do, later or the next day, that might

prevent a late night. Benny just wanted to give himself an escape route.

'You know these folks well?' Benny asked before they got there.

'Pretty well. Nadine and Nance grew up in the church. The guys just sort of come and go.'

'Do you hang out with them a lot? I mean, I've never heard you mention them until today.'

'You think I didn't have a life before you, Benny Poteat?'

'No,' he said. 'I mean, yes. I didn't mean that at all. Sorry.'

Becky laughed, but it was a tiny pointy-faced little laugh.

Plumb Bob's, out on River Road, had a reputation, for several things. Fiery-hot chicken wings. One-dollar draft beers. Fooseball and karaoke. It used to be known for fights and trouble, especially on the weekends, but after a young tough was knifed and beaten, and bled nearly to death under a car in the parking lot, new owners came in and scrubbed the place up. Now the crowd seemed more wholesome. Or at least less prone to stabbing and shooting at each other.

'There's Nadine's car,' Becky said.

Once inside, the Egg Rock crowd was easy for Benny to spot. Half a dozen insipid Christians huddled around a table for four, laughing too often and too loud.

'This is Benny,' Becky announced to the table as they walked up, then named its occupants in counterclockwise order. 'Nadine. Raymond. Steve. Jinx. And Craig. Where's Nance?'

'She should've been here twenty minutes ago,' Craig said, turning his fist to scowl at the watch on his wrist. Benny recognized the man from somewhere. Not the church, although he may have been there.

'How's your dog?' Raymond asked.

'Ya'll order me some iced tea and some wings,' Becky said, pretending not to have heard the question. 'I'll be back in a jiff.'

Benny sat at a corner of the table, as far outside the ring of intimacy as he could get away with, watched Becky go into the bathroom. He, too, avoided the question about Squat. But Raymond pressed the issue.

'Wonder where he got a hold of those underwear?'

'Ya'll come here a lot?' Benny asked. 'What's good to eat?'

Nadine started to tell him about the chicken wings, but stopped mid-sentence when Craig spoke.

'They ever find that girl's sister?'

'No, Craig,' Nadine said. 'No one's heard from Jenna. *That girl's* name is Becky.'

Craig nudged Benny, who regretted sitting beside him.

'She tell you about that?' Craig asked.

The man brought something dangerous to the moment; Benny couldn't tell exactly what yet.

'About what?' Benny asked.

'Her spooky sister dropping off the face of the earth.'

Becky returned from the bathroom tailed by the waitress, before Craig could say anything else.

'Can I get you folks something to drink?'

Benny looked around the table. Craig had a beer, some kind of dark import. Raymond drank a cocktail that resembled iced tea. None of the other drinks were alcoholic.

'You got Coors on tap?' Benny asked.

'Nope. Bud. Bud light. And Yuengling.'

'Let me have a Budweiser.'

'Lemonade, please,' Becky said.

'How can you drink that piss-beer?' Craig asked.

'I know you from somewhere,' Benny said in response.

'I don't think so,' Craig said, dismissing the possibility. 'Unless you shop at my store.'

Craig puffed out his chest with that last statement.

'Contain your domain,' he said, repeating the slogan on his shirt in a way that let everyone know he said it often and meant it in every possible way.

'What?' Benny said.

'Contain your domain,' Craig said again, and nothing else.

'What the fuck does that mean?' Benny asked, and both he and Craig were surprised by the abruptness.

'He works at the Container Store out off the interstate,' Jinx, the other woman at the table, said from behind, and around, the fat straw in her mouth.

'I *manage* the Container Store,' Craig said, then sat back to pout a little. 'Where the hell is Nance!'

No doubt about it, Benny hated Plumb Bob's; dread crept like bile up the back of his throat, and when the already numbing din of table after table of yacking patrons was surpassed and ruptured by the pierce of microphone feedback, he knew things were only going to get worse.

'Karaoke,' Becky said, squeezing his thigh under the table. 'Want to try?'

Benny chose not to dignify the question. Many, in fact most, folks in the bar, including Becky and her friends, turned or positioned their chairs to better see the low stage tucked between the two bathroom doors. And they all seemed genuinely enthused when the first singer climbed drunkenly up to the mike. Singer didn't seem the right name for what the man did. He took an already bad song, something by Bob Seeger, and mashed it around in his liquored-up mouth until nothing made sense, but the meager audience roared and clapped their appreciation for the effort. Karaoke-er, karaoke-ist, karaokonist.

Benny looked at Craig, and looked closely. The man had turned to face the stage, but paid much more attention to the napkin he was shredding; tearing off little bits of paper, rolling them into tight balls between his thumb and forefinger, and piling them up on the table, beside the already peeled and shredded label from his beer bottle. Benny couldn't place Craig, but he knew they'd met before.

'Contain your domain.'

Craig said it to the waitress that time.

Two tables over, against a wall and beneath a poster of Miss Plumb Bob's 1997, and the autographed hardhat she wore in the picture – the hardhat that matched her bathing suit – a couple sat engaged in a conversation Benny wished he was privy to. It had to be more interesting than the Egg Rock claptrap. The woman at the other table cried. The man looked as if he wanted to, but couldn't. They would lean in, both of them, to speak or hear, then pull away to absorb and react. Benny wondered what made her cry. He tried reading lips, with no luck.

'Go for it, Becky,' Nadine said. 'Do it. Do the "Ache-y Break-y" Heart song.'

'Noooo,' Becky answered, but made it clear that she just wanted a little more encouragement.

'I'm going to call Nance!' Craig said, shoving his seat out from the table too quickly for the passing waitress to get out of its way. She spilled a tray of drinks. Apologized profusely. Craig offered nothing.

'Ok,' Becky said. 'I'm going.'

Benny watched Craig walk away. Watched Becky work to make the step onto the stage, the crowd hushing in anticipation. Then it hit him. No. Not *hit*. The realization rose, fog-like, around him. Memory eased lackadaisically into cognizance. He remembered where he'd seen Craig. Benny had never been into the Container Store out on the interstate, but he'd often looked down on it from high above, on the tower where he serviced the satellite dishes. He remembered the day the two men fought. He remembered the blow job. As Craig walked back to the table, looking less satisfied than when he left, certainty locked into place. Craig had won the fight that day.

'Nance tell any of you where she was going?' Craig asked.

'Nope.'

'Did she leave with Ja . . .'

'Shhh . . .' Jinx said.

'I told her the next . . .'

'Hush, Craig! Becky's singing,' Jinx said.

The others, grateful she spoke up, glared in solidarity.

And while the song itself grated on Benny's nerves, nipped and pinched at his own questionable sense of taste, what came out of Becky's mouth came out song-like. Her voice, rich and solid, overcame the ridiculous lyrics. Everyone else must've thought so, too; she got a huge round of applause and shouts of *One more*!

Becky chose, for her second number, another oddball, but at least one Benny liked. Nancy Sinatra's 'These Boots Are Made For Walking', and when Becky finished and walked, in her sturdy dwarf-shoes, off the stage, she got a helping hand from the next participant as she made the step down. Just as Becky was about to sit, Nance arrived.

'Hey, Nance,' everybody said. Everybody except Craig. Craig looked toward the wall. Craig looked toward the restrooms. Craig looked everywhere except at Nance, that is, until the others turned their attention back to Becky.

'You go, girl!'

'Rock on, mama!'

'Great job, Beck!'

Etcetera.

Benny smiled and nodded his quiet approval. And Becky basked, fairly wallowed in the moment.

Which is why she didn't see what happened. To Nance.

The woman pulled her chair in tight, close to Craig. Reached to pat his thigh. She smiled nervously at Benny; he was the only one looking her way. And when the next karaoke devotee started to bellow from the stage, everyone turned to watch. Except Benny. He rocked his chair back, balancing on the rear legs. Bored and wanting to go home. If not for the pause, the melodramatic second of silence in the song, Benny wouldn't have heard the faint snap. Had he not been watching Craig, and, over Craig's shoulder, Nance, he wouldn't have seen her face, that look of disbelief, that grimace that swept her face, and the shudder of realization. Craig broke her finger. He reached under the table, with both hands, to where her hand rested on his thigh, and snapped one of her fingers. Benny couldn't tell which, but he didn't doubt the fact.

Nance's face went flush, then pale. She tried not to cry. Everyone but Benny was turned away from her watching the performance. But she did cry. Benny watched the tears bead on the thin rim of her bottom lid, then spill over. Nance, because she was looking at Craig, was looking at Benny. She tried to smile, as if . . . But in that contorted gesture nothing smile-like emerged. Nevertheless, Benny couldn't believe her composure. No shriek. No apparent rage. No hitting. Only the forced smile through which she blew several sharp breaths. Nance didn't even bring her injured hand up to look at; rather she reached down under the table with her other hand and just sat there holding tight to her pain.

The crowd cheered – none louder than the Egg Rock table – and while they cheered the end of one karaoke song and the beginning of another, Benny couldn't help but think they were applauding Nance's performance, or Craig's.

Plumb Bob's reeked. Of fried chicken wings and onion bricks. Of bad beer. Of stupidity. Benny looked up in time to catch Craig glowering at him.

Fuck this, Benny thought. *This is not my business.*

'I have to go,' he said, standing.

'What?' Becky asked. Then again, not sure she heard. 'What? Why?'

'I forgot something. Are you coming with me or . . .'

He let the option hang in the air.

'I can give you a ride home, Beck,' Nadine said.

So Benny left, with the bare minimum of goodbyes.

He went home. He ate a shitty dinner. He went to bed.

'You seen the paper today?' Jeeter asked, when Benny picked up the phone.

'No.'

'Look at it.'

'I don't get the paper, Jeeter. What is it?'

'I ain't saying. You have to go get it.'

'Come on!' Benny said. 'Don't be an asshole.'

'It's what I do best,' Jeeter said. 'Hey, I got an idea for a new invention.'

'Against my better judgment, I'll ask, what is it?'

'A dick strap,' Jeeter said.

'A what?'

'A dick strap.'

'And what exactly do you do with a dick strap?'

'You ever wake up with a pee-boner?'

Benny could hear Jeeter's enthusiasm.

'Of course.'

'Ever wake up with it bent backwards or sideways and hurting?'

'Of course.'

'Well . . .'

Benny wasn't interested in the more technical details.

'What about your other invention? That dildo seat?'

'It's a vibrator, not a dildo. I'm still working out the kinks.'

After breakfast, Benny ventured out to the 7-11 for a *Buffalo Shoals Tribune*, and a stick of turkey jerky for Squat, which the old dog devoured unceremoniously on the floor of the van, in the parking lot, while Benny sat reading the paper.

'Son of a bitch!' he said, but got no response from Squat.

'Look at this,' he said, holding the paper down a little.

Truth was, Squat probably would've recognized Dink in the grainy black-and-white photograph on the front page of the community section, the one called Pasture Notes, except that Dink stood all but behind the real reason for the picture, which was a life-sized bust of Jesus made, no, crafted, solely out of dryer lint. Made, no, crafted by, who else, but Dink himself. Without the title indicating such, Squat probably wouldn't have been able to recognize Jesus, for a number of reasons. All in all, though, the form was vaguely familiar as both human and biblical.

'Son of a bitch,' Benny said again, with a little less emphasis.

According to the paper, Dink had been gathering dryer lint from all the lint traps at the Laundromat for years, working on the sly in the basement at his mother's house, with buckets of thin plaster, building the sculpture day by day. As it were, Jesus would've remained there, in that basement, for God knows how long if the repairman who'd come to change the filters and service the furnace before wintertime wasn't such a devout member of the newly formed, and still floundering, Baptist congregation that met in the vacant storefront between the Big Lots and Hammer's Gunshop in a strip mall just out of town. They were short on furnishings and accoutrements.

So moved was the repairman that he made several calls right away: his boss, who also happened to be the minister at the church, his wife (who suggested the next call) and the newspaper office.

Dink, said the paper, agreed to donate the bust to the church following a three-month public viewing at the Buffalo Shoals Public Library. The article closed with a few quotes.

'It's a miracle,' said the preacher's wife.

'Bless his heart,' said the repairman's wife.

'Smells find of funny,' said somebody's kid.

CHAPTER 22

BENNY CHUGGED FROM THE WATER BOTTLE STRAPPED to his belt, but up on the tower there was nothing to block the sun, nor any way to escape the August heat. Off in the distance, where Crowder's Mountain ought to be, a dense haze obliterated everything on the horizon. Benny finished all but the last couple inches in the bottle and poured the remaining water over his head. He hated this particular tower, mostly because of its proximity to the vinegar plant. Even on good days everything stank of vinegar, your eyes stung, and the taste settled in to the back of your throat and refused to leave.

Across the street, from the plant and the tower, a cemetery lay claim to a rectangle of earth the size of a football field. Shadeless, therefore parched, and cordoned off by a six-foot chain link fence, there was nothing remotely pastoral or restful about the lot, and Benny wondered why anybody would want to be buried, or allow a loved one to be buried there.

One family had recently made the choice. Near the far edge of the property a motley family – their connection evidenced by similarities in their mismatched ill-fitting clothes – made up of four little kids who clearly wanted to be somewhere else, half-a-dozen grownups no less eager to be there, and three old people who didn't seem to care one way or the other, formed a ragged circle around a humped mound of dirt, almost obscene in its redness.

Just as Benny tucked a wrench back into his belt, ready to begin the climb down, he heard the automatic sprinkler system come on. It would be hard to say who was more surprised, Benny or the mourners, as the perfectly spaced sprinkler heads rose from hiding out of the earth and began to spray crisscross patterns over the graveyard. Back and forth. Back and forth. And each sweep was timed so that the showers of water – there now, gone here – offered both opportunities for escape and drenching to the grieving family. So they ran, ant-like, between and around and from the sprays. And finally, in attack and retreat fashion, they placed their flowers and spoke their words, and to be sure, none escaped completely dry.

This was one of the silliest things Benny had ever seen. It left him so busy laughing that he couldn't remember if he'd actually checked that last bolt. But when Benny looked, from halfway down, straight back up to the top of the tower, a wave of vertigo so thoroughly swept his body that all he could do was cling to the hot and rigid steel frame, trembling, until the nausea and dizziness passed. It happened to him once before, and took several hours before he could actually make the climb down. Mercifully, it wasn't so bad this time. Benny took the last step down onto solid ground just before suppertime. He'd tell Becky about the whole experience that night.

After the incident at Plumb Bob's, the karaoke, the snapping finger, Benny had eased away, just a little, from Becky. But he missed companionship. Doodle spent most of her time with the guy in the white pickup truck. Jeeter dug ponds and cleaned fish tanks all day. And Dink, only tolerable in small doses during normal times, was even more obnoxious now that his dryer lint Jesus sat in the foyer of the public library.

Benny gave in. Succumbed to the oldest itch on the planet: desire. He'd called earlier that day to see if she wanted to get a beer or something. Maybe go to the softball game. When he picked her up that evening, they both decided that it was too hot to sit outside, so they went to Dairy Queen instead, where they met Jeeter and Dink, in the tiny but cool dining room, its air thick with the scent of sugar.

They sat licking their cones in silence. Until Dink spoke.

'Ya'll know how buzzards cool off on a hot day?'

'No, Dink,' Jeeter said. 'How do buzzards cool off on a hot day?'

'They screte on their legs!'

'What?!' Both Jeeter and Benny asked the question.

'Screte! They screte on they own damn legs!'

'You mean shit?' Benny asked.

'Fuckin-A I mean shit. They shit right down their own legs!'

'Doesn't everyone?' Jeeter said, without hesitation. 'I mean if it's a really hot day?'

The question baffled Dink into silence. For the duration of the stay.

Duplex. Later that night, Benny remembered the title of the next tape, by chronology, as *Duplex.* He'd be watching it now, except that he lost it. Or, better yet, the river took it. When he pulled the milk crate from beneath the bed, Benny noticed for the first time the warning stenciled on two of its four sides:

Unauthorized use of milk crates ILLEGAL.
Fine of $300 or up to 90 days imprisonment.
State Law, Act 37

He wondered how much of what he'd done constituted unauthorized use.

Benny folded back the NASCAR towel and plucked the tape entitled, simply, *March 3, 2000*, from the basket. With each successive tape he watched, the nearly ritualized act of getting ready then pushing *play* lost something, as did the attendant anxiety. He unceremoniously jammed the next tape into the slot and poked it home with his forefinger.

Immediately, Benny wished he'd taken more time. Prepared himself somehow. But time, no matter how much, wouldn't have been preparation for what he watched. Jenna, hospitalized. A series of artless scenes, devoid of style. Choppy, cold reportage. Jenna, hospitalized. Jenna talking to doctors. There had been an infection behind the implants. Behind the implants, the infection went undetected. Too long. Too late. Jenna needed emergency surgery. Too long, too late. More hospital rooms. More surgery. The infection, dogged in its mission, spread. Where were her emotions in all this? Jenna, like a trooper, kept up her poker face. Who recorded this horrible sequence of events? How in God's name was the camera allowed to watch? Amputations. Jenna lost two fingers on her right hand. Jenna lost her left leg just below the knee.

That's when Benny vomited. There, on the floor, beside his rocking chair. He stopped the tape, got some paper towels and spray cleaner, and just as he knelt to begin wiping up the mess, the phone rang.

'Hey, Benny.'

'Hi, Becky.'

'What're you doing?'

'Nothing.'

She wanted to come over.

Benny said Ok.

The next morning, Becky asked to borrow a tee shirt.

'Top drawer,' Benny said from where he sat drinking coffee at the kitchen table, then he left for work. Later that night, after half a day up in the air, Benny stood behind the heat lamp at Nub & Honey's, plating up a Captain's Platter – fried perch, clam strips, deviled crab, shrimp and scallops. When Becky walked through the back door, into the kitchen, he couldn't begin to guess why. But she looked upset.

Scotty, Jonette, and the others in the kitchen all tried to look as busy and uninterested as possible without leaving.

'Where'd you get this?' she asked, reaching high to drop the thing from her clenched fist onto the stainless steel shelf beneath the heat lamp. It rattled, then became still before Benny looked.

Becky had been crying. Cried still, just a little.

Hung like a horse. The button pin Benny found with the drowned girl's stuff, with Jenna's stuff, by the river that day so long ago. He'd kept it under the shirts and underwear in his drawer.

'What?' he asked. 'What is it?'

'It's yours Benny. You tell me what it is.'

Benny picked up the pin. Eyed it as if for the first time.

'Oh,' he said. 'I got this a long time ago. At the flea market. Why?'

'You don't know?'

'Becky, what the hell are you talking about?'

Everyone had stopped what they were doing to watch the exchange.

'Get the hell out of here!' Benny said to Scotty, but implied it to the rest.

He came around the counter to Becky, hands out, palms up. A sign of innocence.

'What's with the pin? I told you I got it at the flea market.'

'Jenna . . . Jenna had a pin like this,' Becky said, then fell against Benny and wept.

'Gosh,' Benny said.

'Do you think . . . ?' Benny started, never intending to finish the question.

'I don't know . . .'

Becky calmed down. Benny got her a glass of sweet tea and a little bowl of hushpuppies, and she sat on a low stepstool and gathered her wits while Benny filled the orders.

Benny thought everything was fine, crisis averted, until Becky got ready to leave.

'Benny?'

'Yep?'

'Tomorrow, will you take me to the flea market? Show me where you found this?'

So he did. He just picked a table near the entrance, told her he found it there. Of course, the seller had no idea what she was talking about. Didn't remember Benny. Didn't remember the pin. Didn't even remember being in that spot by the entrance so long ago. Finally, Benny pulled Becky away. They stopped at the library to see the dryer lint Jesus.

And so it went for months, the summer's heat collapsing in upon itself; thick and sticky air made movement, even breath, an effort. Friendships, relationships, work and play, everything slipped into a sort of automatic mode wherein the less done the better. Things slowed, grew static, then stopped. Things stagnated. Benny's secret lay dormant, beneath his bed and in his heart. Whatever emotion, triggered by the secret, that drew Benny Poteat and Rebecca Hinkey together and propelled them forward waned.

Stunned by the magnitude of what happened to Jenna Hinkey, by what he witnessed in the videotape he'd watched last, Benny couldn't bring himself to view the final one. He'd watched her movies, movies that chronicled years of her life. Watched her say and do and outrage with her saying and doing. Watched, finally, her loss. Her breasts. Her fingers. Her leg. Even Benny knew, blind and selfish as he was, that he couldn't begin to fathom the emotional and psychological toll those losses incurred. Had she any other recourse but to walk into the Toe River? Had Benny known what he took now as her motivation, would he have withheld the secret? Would he have entrenched himself so deeply into the dead girl's family?

Perhaps. Perhaps not. The questions were irrelevant.

Twice more, Benny accompanied Becky to Egg Rock Pentecostal Church, sans Squat. Each time there, and each of the few other times he'd seen the Deacon and Mrs Hinkey, she in particular looked worse and worse. The uncertainty, the not knowing, wreaked havoc. Benny possessed the answers, possessed the power to change that. And, to his credit, he toyed with the idea of coming clean.

'Let's bow our heads together now,' Deacon Hinkey said from the pulpit. 'And pray for the Lord's mercy . . . Lord God, we come to you, sinners all . . .'

And he went on for some time. Benny drifted in and out of attentiveness – he made a list of guns and calibers:

bolt action, pump shotgun, Colt .45, .44 magnum, .38 special, thirty nought six, muzzleloader, derringer, M-16, Glock 9 millimeter, breech-loader, twenty-two – coming round fully as the Deacon closed his prayer.

'We pray this day for Esther Hinkey, a lamb of God strayed from the flock. We pray for her safe delivery back into the church, your family, Heavenly Father, and if that is not your will, we pray that she be delivered into the loving arms of Jesus Christ our Savior.'

As far as Benny could tell, Jenna wasn't delivered anywhere. And things went as things tend to go when denied or left unattended: quietly to hell.

'Let's go pick out costumes,' Becky said.

August had mutated into September, which in turn kicked and spit its way right on into October. Hallowe'en was upon them in a week's time, and the requisite party at Gnogg's.

'Do you know what you want to be?' Benny asked, several answers occurring that he kept to himself.

'No,' she said. 'Not quite. Do you?'

'Yep . . .'

Benny let it hang, teasing.

'So . . . ?'

'Duct Tape Man.'

Becky laughed.

'You're kidding me, right?'

'Nope,' he said, then went into his bedroom and came back with three fat silver rolls of the tape.

'You're a certifiable nut,' she said.

'Can't we just make something for you?' Benny said, the idea of going into a costume store with Becky striking him as freakish.

'Come on, Benny,' she said. 'Don't be such a pooper.'

He conceded, but Becky had to drive. However, by the time she – in back and forth and back and forth fashion – parallel parked three blocks away from Cloak & Dagger, one block east of Independence Boulevard, near the old Coliseum, Benny wished he'd done the driving. Becky, had she realized that she'd parked directly in front of Buffalo Shoals Artificial Limb & Appliance Company, would've continued driving. In fact, she restarted the car and put it in drive before Benny stopped her.

'What are you doing?' he asked. 'The store's right down the street.'

'Can't we just park somewhere else?'

'For fuck's sake, why?'

'You don't have to curse, Benny.'

'Sorry,' he said. 'But what's wrong with this space?'

Becky turned, with exaggerated drama, and looked at the prosthesis store.

Benny got it. But he couldn't let her know.

'You have a bad experience with a wooden leg?' he said, trying to make a joke.

When Becky took a deep breath and held back a sob, Benny knew it was a bad joke.

'What's the matter, Becky?'

'My sister . . . ,' she started. 'Jenna . . . last year, Jenna got really sick.'

Then Becky told him the whole story about the staph infections that had settled in to Jenna's bloodstream after her breast implants, and had gone undetected until too much damage was done. She lost both breasts right away.

'They kept hoping . . . they kept trying to get it under control . . .'

Becky told Benny everything. Benny told Becky nothing.

'You guys still have no idea where she went?'

Becky didn't answer. Shook her head no.

'I bet she packed up and headed to California or some-thing.'

'Do you have a quarter?' Becky asked, climbing out of the car.

Benny fished in the pockets of his jeans until he found some coins; by the time he fed the meter, Becky stood half a block away, staring into the window of an abandoned storefront. Wing-wong's Chinese Market.

'Look!' she said, as Benny approached.

'Fuck.'

Flies. Hundreds, maybe thousands of flies, some living, many dead, clotted the wide sill and littered the smudged glass, fat black jewels basking in the sunlight.

'That's so disgusting,' Becky said, but watched and watched.

Beyond the window, empty shelves receded into dark-ness at the back of the store.

'Let's go if we're going,' Benny said, finally having to pull Becky away.

Mercifully, the costume shopping was painless and easy. Rebecca would go as Ronald Reagan. Nothing too ambitious. She bought only the mask, said she had a business suit at home.

'I'll make something for Squat,' she said. 'If you want to take him.'

'I'll drive,' Benny said, to which Becky agreed.

Independence Boulevard was infamous for its high traffic and frequent, often fatal, accidents. So far in town, though, the bumper-to-bumper, stop-and-go nature of the traffic flow made the trip more annoying than dangerous. Not two blocks from Cloak & Dagger, they pulled up at a stoplight behind a pickup truck. Powder blue, with Confederate flag decals at either end of a bumper that seemed much too chrome and much too big. A big tattooed man was behind the wheel. His passenger, a blonde woman, sat as far away from him as possible in the cab of the truck. Benny couldn't know that Becky didn't trust blonde women. She couldn't know that he didn't trust big men.

As the traffic crept from one light to the next, it became apparent that the man and woman in the truck were arguing. He'd speak, or she, and in their faces, the words so full of anger they were almost tangible. In very short order, things escalated. She moved closer to the driver, began emphasizing her words by jabbing a pointed finger into his shoulder. He pushed her hard against the passenger door just as they pulled to another stoplight.

'What do you think they're fighting about?' Benny asked.

'He pushed her,' Becky said.

They were both surprised when the woman got out of the truck, stood leaning into the open door screaming at the man.

'Fuck You! Fuck You! Fuck You!'

She slammed the door, turned and walked down the sidewalk. A worn denim purse hung low and bumped against her hip with each angry step.

'Good for her,' Becky said.

But then the man got out of the truck too.

'You've got to help her, Benny.'

'*What?*'

The street was busy, and the line of cars grew behind them. By that time the light had turned green and people started in with their horns. They watched it happen, sort of like a bad movie, one you're compelled to watch simply because you can't believe someone would make a movie so bad. At that point things took on a surreal patina for Benny. The sky suddenly got clearer, more watery. The grass, deadened by the approach of winter, seemed to green, to stand up a little straighter. The cars all got shinier, more round and more edgy at the same time. Every sound was isolated, its own moment in time. In that instant Benny knew that whatever happened between that man and woman would have ramifications, size unknown, in his life. Becky would see to it.

The man caught his companion easily; she wasn't running. He grabbed her wrist and began pulling her toward the truck. Benny couldn't tell if he was talking or not, but she definitely was.

'No! No! Goddamnit, let me go, Derek! I'm tired of this shit!'

"Do something, Benny!' Becky yelled, then at the man, 'Stop that! You let her go!'

She tried to put down the window, but Benny activated the childproof lock.

'Benny!'

'It's not our business, Becky.'

Then he hit her. Derek hit the woman. Benny couldn't believe it. He'd been in lots of fights in his life, even smacked a woman once because she was drunk and swinging wildly at him, but he'd never seen, in real life, a man hit a woman so hard. Closed fisted, and square on the mouth. The woman collapsed immediately into a frighteningly small pile at his feet. Benny thought of Saturday morning cartoons, the character shattering into hundreds of irregular pieces. His stomach lurched.

'You son of a bitch! You asshole! You son of a bitch!'

Becky tried to get out of the car. She reached across Benny to pound on the horn. The man picked the woman up in his arms, lay her with ridiculous care and tenderness in the bed of the truck.

'You chicken shit! You can't do that!'

Benny had never seen her so angry; didn't know she was capable of it.

After putting his unconscious companion in the truck bed, the man, much to Benny's horror, walked toward their car. Toward Benny in the driver's seat.

'This is not our business,' he said to himself, to Becky.

Benny put the car into reverse, backed at a sharp angle out of the line of traffic, into the opposite lane. He turned up over the sidewalk, through the parking lot of a 7-11, and away.

They drove in silence, until Benny tried to gauge the damage.

'That was fucking intense,' he said.

'Take me home.'

'What? Is something wrong?'

'Just take me home, Benny.'

'What did I do!?'

'Nothing, Benny. That's just it. You didn't do anything.'

Benny took Becky home, as requested, where she, presumably, seethed over Benny's inadequacies. Benny, too, acutely, spent the next few days bumping into, tripping over, and slogging through his shortcomings. But, in the end, Becky called, Hallowe'en morning.

'I made it,' she said.

'What?' Benny asked.

'Squat's costume.'

Benny had all but convinced himself that their date was off, that he'd go to the Halloween party alone, or maybe with Squat, going as Squat.

'What is it?' he asked, skeptically, not sure that he or Squat could bear the humiliation.

'Keep an open mind.'

'What is it?'

'Are you keeping an open mind?'

'What is it, Becky?'

Turns out, it wasn't so embarrassing after all. She'd made the old dog a horse costume: a little saddle, a mane and a tail.

'Will you come over and help me with mine?' he asked.

'You mean you can't transform yourself into Duct Tape Man alone!'

Things seemed Ok for the moment. They were playful. Excited about the party. The lurking dread was kept at bay, for the moment.

Becky came over after lunch. She showed Benny the horse costume, and Squat, apathetic as usual, allowed himself to be festooned.

'Oh,' Benny said. 'He looks pitiful.'

'Nooooo, he looks cute.'

Then, together, they wrapped Benny in the duct tape, a long-sleeved denim shirt and jeans providing the foundation for the superhero.

'Not too tight,' he said. 'It'll cut off my circulation.'

'Are you going to do anything with your face?'

'I don't know,' he said. 'I guess I could wear a ski cap. But that'll be hot.'

'How about face paint?'

They both decided that would work best. Benny spent

a little time trying to convince her to go as Reagan post-alzheimers, but Becky thought that was too crude.

Benny called Jeeter, to find out what time he planned on showing up at the party. He was a little surprised to get the answering machine.

'You've reached Rebel Yell Ponds and Aquarium Service, please leave a message. If this is an aqua-emergency please dial my pager number.'

'Pick up the phone, asshole,' Benny said. 'I know you're . . .'

'Hey, shithead,' Jeeter said. 'What's up?'

'You going tonight?'

The question struck Jeeter as absurd. They agreed to meet at Gnogg's at six o'clock.

'Hey,' Jeeter asked. 'Will you do me a favor?'

'Sure.'

'Swing by here and pick up a couple cases of homebrew. I'll leave it on the porch.'

'You riding your bike?' Benny asked.

'Yep. Looks like the weather'll be good.'

'So . . . how's the hot seat working?'

'We'll see tonight.'

'You didn't ask him what he was coming as,' Becky said.

'He wouldn't tell me. We never tell.'

They left Benny's house before dark, Benny tapping the horn to wave at Clyde. Hallowe'en was always a favorite holiday for Clyde. He gave out lots of candy. Chose his costume with love and care. That Hallowe'en, Clyde sat, as usual, in the rocking chair on his front porch. Beside him, close, another chair. In it, a full-size fake skeleton. Clyde had bound the left forearm of the skeleton to his own right forearm. Every time Clyde waved, the skeleton waved. Benny drove around the block just to see Clyde wave again.

In the back of the van, Squat grunted, most likely in discomfort. Or annoyance. Becky insisted on putting the dog's costume on before leaving. Benny had no doubt that the whole thing was going to embarrass him at the party. Becky wore her black business suit, tailored to fit her awkward frame. She'd put the mask on when they got to Gnogg's. Benny, his face and hands painted silver, sweltered inside his airless costume. He'd don dark glasses upon arrival.

'I'm going to pass out from the fucking heat,' he said. 'Will you crack your window?'

They picked up the beer. Jeeter had already left. By the time Benny and Becky and Squat got to Gnogg's, at six o'clock, the party was already in full swing.

'Something smells good,' Becky said, from the mouth hole of the Reagan mask.

'Didn't I tell you,' Benny said. 'Gnogg's Hallowe'en party is always a pig-picking.'

'Oooooo.'

Benny helped Squat out of the van. Not two steps and the poor old dog tripped on his stirrups.

'He looks ridiculous, Becky.'

In the time it took for the three of them to make their way to the kegs and the BBQ pit, enough people had laughed at poor Squat to make it clear that, to Benny anyway, the horse costume wasn't a good idea.

'Wow!' Becky said, as they stood in line with paper plates and plastic forks waiting for a man in a nurse's dress and shoes to serve them chunks of pork. 'Look at that pumpkin.'

A small pickup truck drove slowly by, headed towards the barn. In its bed, three, maybe four people sat holding the biggest damn pumpkin Benny had ever seen.

'How much does that thing weigh?' Benny asked.

''Bout eight hundred and fifty pounds.'

Low whistles all around. People, men in particular it seems, are impressed by overkill.

The lady standing in line in front of Benny and Becky turned and spoke to them.

'Ya'll know Shaw Bunchy?'

The jutting, misaligned, and blackened false teeth she wore made understanding her difficult, and the very realistic eyeball hanging convincingly from her cheek proved distracting in other ways.

'No,' Benny said. 'Why?'

'He growed that punkin,'' she said. 'They going to use a chainsaw and make a big old jack-o-lantern.'

'That so?' Benny said.

As if on her cue, Benny heard the chainsaw crank: two pulls then the high-pitched whining rev.

'Let's go watch,' Becky said.

'Let's wait for Jeeter first.'

She seemed disappointed.

'You can go if you want. I'll wait here, then when Jeeter comes we'll both come to the barn.'

Becky lacked the confidence to go alone, even as diminutive ex-president. Fortunately, they didn't have to wait long.

'What the fuck . . . ?' Benny said to Jeeter, who laughed for five full minutes at Squat before he could respond.

'Who the hell are you?'

'Duct Tape Man! And . . . what's all that shit hanging from you?'

'Well, clearly you are too functionally illiterate to get it. Becky?'

'Gosh,' she said. 'I don't know. Trash Dump Man?'

'Heathens! I'm Job. These are my plagues and boils and such.'

'Are you by yourself?' Benny asked.

'What do you think?' Jeeter asked, with exaggeration.

'Then where is she?'

'Fixing her costume,' Jeeter said, and winked at Benny.

The three of them stood waiting, periodically washed over by oily porcine smoke pouring from the two spits.

'Ya'll want a beer?' Becky asked. She left, then returned just as Jeeter's friend walked up.

'This is Crystal,' Jeeter said, nodding toward the woman dressed as a vampire who stood beside him. 'Crystal, Benny, Becky. Benny is the fool wrapped in duct tape.'

'Hey ya'll,' she said. 'Who's this cute little rascal?'

Crystal knelt to scratch at Squat's ears. Benny positioned himself to get a better look at her cleavage. Becky turned away. Shortly, they all meandered toward the barn to see the state of the pumpkin.

'Anybody seen Dink?' Benny asked. 'What's he coming as?'

'Nothing,' Jeeter said. 'He's not coming.'

'Why?'

'Got something bad mooching at Kroger's yesterday. He called this afternoon and said he'd been puking all day, and didn't feel like it was going to stop.'

'Reckon he's got enough sense to know if he needs to go to the doctor?'

'Well, I thought about that. But when he asked me if I'd ever seen a nekid lady puke, I figured he was going to be Ok.'

The party progressed, as large parties do. Random encounters, increasing drunkenness which leads to increasingly vapid, downright stupid exchanges with both strangers and acquaintances, seemingly epic shifts in perspective, moments of deep profundity, more moments of complete idiocy. And on and on, and there at Gnogg's Hallowe'en party, everything made more acute and heightened by the costumes. A group of three lunatics in particular seemed in random orbit around the party, stirring up little troubles each time they passed through. They were boys, drunken and stoned, and doubly dimwitted by the testosterone surging through their eighteen-year-old bodies.

'Look at those assholes,' Benny said, the first time he saw them taking turns caving in a pumpkin with their boots. The next time they wandered by, the boys spent several minutes harassing a man who'd passed out sitting against a hay bale. Dropping their cigarette butts into the beer bottle that the man still clutched in his hands was bad enough, but when they removed the man's boot and took turns urinating into it, several people told them to quit it. As if they'd listen.

Poor Becky, having had a more sheltered life than her companions, covered her eyes at least once every half hour. She and Crystal hit it off. They fell, easily, into conversation, Becky with her Reagan mask perched on top of her head. They'd all eaten. They'd all had enough beer to slow things down. They sat, with lots of other folks, on a covered patio between the barn and the house, where Gnogg had put out dozens of chairs. Folding chairs, and old ladder-back wooden chairs that always reminded Benny of family reunions.

'Where's Squat?' Becky asked.

'He'll be Ok,' Benny said.

'I haven't seen him for a while,' Becky said.

'He'll come back,' Benny said.

'What if he gets lost? Or somebody takes him?' Becky said.

'He won't, and they won't,' Benny said.

'Maybe we should go look for him,' Becky said.

'Becky,' Benny said. 'If you want to go look for the fucking dog, then go look for the fucking dog.'

Becky grew quiet, which didn't stop Benny.

'He's my goddamn dog. I'm not sure why you think you have a better idea of what's good for him than I do.'

Silence.

'I got to piss,' Crystal said, then patted Becky's leg. 'Come help me find the john.'

When they'd left, Jeeter reached into his costume robe for a small baggie of marijuana.

'What the fuck was that all about?' he asked.

'Nothing,' Benny said. 'She just went on too long about the fucking dog.'

Fact is, Benny may not have realized how over-the-top his response was. Nor, at that point in time, and in that state of mind, would he have been able to trace the gnawing and festering feeling that seemed to taint all his interactions of late back to the knocked-out lady in the bed of the truck. And as for naming it, well . . .

Throughout most of his life Benny had felt inadequate in many, and usually simultaneous, ways. But he'd never admit it.

Jeeter rolled several joints, lit the first and passed it to Benny, who took a hit, and in turn, passed it to Jack the Zipper, and down the line around the circle. After Jeeter's stash met its match, others brought forth. Jeeter and Benny were so engaged in a conversation about the relative beauty of koi fish that neither noticed the cowboy making his way around the circle. When the man stopped in front of them, all squint-eyed with his mouth drawn tight, Benny and Jeeter looked up at the same time. When the cowboy pulled the sawed-off shotgun from behind his back and held it at his waist, they both flinched at the same time. When he opened the breech and put his mouth up to the empty barrel, they both smiled at the same time. But when the warm stream of marijuana smoke begin to curl from the tip of gun barrel, Jeeter took the initiative and leaned forward to accept it.

'So,' Benny said. 'You get that girl all worked up on the way over here?'

'Just a tease,' Jeeter said. 'Not enough so that she'd figure it out. I kept turning it on and off. But tonight, on the way home . . .'

Before he could finish, Becky and Crystal returned.

'Where've ya'll been?' Benny asked, forgetting for the moment why they left in the first place.

Crystal answered.

'Partyin'. Ain't this a party?'

She came over, straddled Jeeter, and kissed him deeply.

'Hey,' Jeeter said. 'I heard something about a big pumpkin. Let's go find it.'

They did. They staggered and stumbled, to greater and lesser degrees, their ways around to the back of the barn just in time to see the last of what had been dozens of candles illuminating the monstrous orange vegetable, sputter out.

'Holy fucking shit,' Jeeter said.

'That's the biggest goddamn punkin' I ever seen,' Crystal said.

'Hmmm,' Benny said.

And Becky kept quiet. She'd pulled her Reagan mask back over her face, and stood presidentially stoic.

The mammoth pumpkin demanded attention. Maybe even respect. Propped with two-by-fours, it stood a good four-and-a-half feet high. Without the benefit of candle-light, the maniacal smile, upswept eyebrows, and jagged eyeholes glared pitch black at all who passed.

'They carved it with a chainsaw,' Benny said.

'I 'spect they had to,' Jeeter answered.

There were lots other jack-o-lanterns scattered around the grassy area behind Gnogg's barn, the place where the bands usually played, and among them even more inebriated partygoers. Gnogg had ringed the area with bales of hay, and when Jeeter sat down on one, Crystal, again, sat across him and made her intentions clear. Becky, still pouting and angry, strayed as far from Benny as she could. Benny went for more beer. When he returned, he returned with the young rowdies, mostly because they just happened to be walking the same direction.

It's funny, sometimes, other times disturbing, how one reacts to hurt and anger. How feeling helpless, or inadequate, turns inside of a man. Becomes something fueled by desperation. Benny didn't mean to suggest anything, any course of action, to the three drunken assholes. He just asked a simple question as they walked up together.

'I wonder if President Reagan there would fit in that big pumpkin?'

And that's all it took.

Becky sat alone, unaware and unprepared, and when two of them picked her up, she was too much in shock to protest right away. But, by the time she saw the third guy standing at the giant pumpkin, holding its cap by the massive stem, Becky realized what they had in mind. She began to kick, and scream. To no avail. The three boys shoved Becky inside the big pumpkin and put the cap back on. They held it in place while she fought and cursed from within the slimy orange cavern. Most of the people there thought it funny to see a diminutive president stuffed into a gigantic pumpkin, at least for a little while. Besides, things were loud all around. Benny could easily pretend he didn't see or hear the terrible thing that was happening to Becky. Job and the vampire had their tongues so deep in each other's mouths that it no doubt blocked their hearing too. But Benny was watching. And listening. He saw the big pumpkin rock unsteadily as Becky threw herself against its slick walls, and watched the rednecks hold it up and hold its cap down tight. Benny heard her screams and curses become wracking sobs. And he took note, too, of when the struggle stopped. When Rebecca Hinkey gave up.

That's when Crystal withdrew herself from Jeeter to see what all the racket was about.

'You motherfuckers!' she said, swinging as she went. 'Jeeter!'

Then, of course, Benny had to take action. Had to pretend to be as outraged as the rest. Crystal took the three troublemakers by surprise – Benny and Jeeter, too, for that matter – when she hit the biggest one, the one holding down the pumpkin's jagged cut cap, full-fisted in the back of the head. When they saw Jeeter and Benny coming behind her, the boys chose not to fight back. They could've easily hurt Crystal, but they ran away instead, laughing and laughing.

When they ran, the pumpkin tipped, and Crystal tried but couldn't keep it up alone. The orange behemoth fell forward, ruptured, and gave birth to a sticky dwarf in a Ronald Reagan mask. Becky wept. She sat up, hugged her knees and wept.

'Come on, honey,' Crystal said. 'Let's go get you cleaned up.'

'What a fucking trip that was,' Jeeter said.

Benny said nothing. Nothing was said to Benny.

When they returned, Becky had found a shirt somewhere; the pants they cleaned up as much as possible; the mask, absent.

'Take me home,' Becky said. She said it to Benny, but didn't call his name.

'Becky,' Benny said. 'I can't. I can't drive.'

'I want to go home.'

'Everybody here is completely wasted. There's no way.'

'I'm not drunk,' she said.

'But you can't drive my van. Not with . . .'

He didn't finish the statement.

'I'll walk,' she said, and turned to leave.

'Be . . . wait, Becky.'

Benny went to face her.

'Look, why don't we sleep in the van. In the morn . . .'

'I'm not sleeping anywhere with you, Benny!'

'Ok. Whatever. You stay in the van. I'll sleep in that lawn chair.'

Becky considered her options.

'I'm too mad to sleep. I'm too humiliated to sleep. I'm . . . ,'

'Come on. I'll take you to the van. Just try and get some sleep. Tomorrow morning everybody will be sober. And I'll take you home as soon as you want to go.'

'Here, Becky,' Crystal said. 'Here . . .'

She held out her hand, fist closed.

'Take these,' she said, and dropped two small blue pills into Becky's waiting hand.

'Oh,' Becky said. 'I don't . . . I mean I can't . . . are these *drugs*?' she finally asked.

'Just valium,' Crystal. 'I promise they'll just make you sleep. That's it.'

Becky, too tired and shocked to put up any fight, put the pills in her mouth and swallowed.

'Later, dude,' Jeeter said.

Poor Becky. Poor, poor Becky. She was staggering by the time Benny got her to the van.

Benny opened the door and before helping her inside, he tried to hug her.

'Nooo . . .' Becky slurred.

He moved out of the door and Becky crawled in, and crawling still, made her way back to the bed. Benny stood and watched. Within minutes, Becky, lying on her stomach, smelling of pumpkin and soap, lay breathing soundly asleep.

Fuck it, Benny thought. *This is my van.*

He climbed in, closed up the van, and lay down on the floor. The floor of the van stank, from years of dirt and years of Squat wallowing there. Benny, drunk and stoned, lay looking up at the spinning roof.

Fuck it, he thought. *This is my van.*

He shoved Becky over and lay down beside of her in the narrow bed. He lay still and tried hard to go to sleep, but his cloudy mind filled itself with images. Becky spilling out of that pumpkin, over and over again, all covered with pulp and crying. Soon enough, in his memory of the moment, she came naked out of the pumpkin, her flesh dotted with pumpkinseeds. Benny's hard on snuck up on him. And, almost as sneaky, his hand crept down and loosed it. Benny lay in the back of the van, his van, stroking himself beside the drugged sister of the drowned girl. This notion, logically, led Benny's mind to images of Jenna. Various naked images of Jenna. Ones he'd seen on the tapes, and ones he'd frequently imagined.

Benny stroked and pulled and imagined and remembered, but every time orgasm eased into sight, he lost focus. He needed a little more stimulus. Benny looked at Rebecca. He nudged her with his elbow. No response. He shook her more directly. No response. Benny rolled her over onto her back. No response. No response when he unbuttoned her blouse and put his hand into her bra. That was nice, but not enough; he still couldn't come. Benny undid her pants, and paused only for a moment before slipping his hand into her underwear. Just touching. That's all. Nothing serious. Nothing wrong. Benny yanked at his raw penis and stroked the folds of Becky's labia. Nothing. He brought his hand from between her legs, smelled it. She was dry. Unready. Benny licked his fingers and put the hand back to work. First the middle finger, then the index finger wiggling into her dry sex. Nothing wrong. He'd been there before, at her invitation. Nothing wrong. Benny fingered Becky and thought of Jenna and jacked his dick. Jenna naked on her knees. Jenna kneeling before him. Jenna posing for the artist. Jenna squatting for the artist. Jenna shitting for the artist. Why couldn't he come? Benny took his fingers out of Becky. *Pussy*, he thought, licking them. *Pussy*. Benny rose to his knees and pulled Becky's pants and underwear down to her ankles. Nothing wrong. Nothing bad. Just touching. He lay down again. He got up again, turned her onto her stomach. He lay down again, began to squeeze at the solid cheeks of her ass. He traced the cleft. Jenna naked. He circled her anus with a fingertip. Jenna doing all those terrible disgusting things. Jenna's scarred stump. Benny put his thumb to his mouth, got it wet with spit. Jenna kneeling and squatting. Jenna's near tit-less chest. He found the deep trench between her buttocks. Jenna on the low platform, under bright lights. He put his thumb tip at the closed bud. Jenna grunting with effort. He pushed his thumb quick and deep into her anus. Becky flinched, even in sedated sleep. Tried to pull away. Benny held her tight and shoved his thumb as deeply as it would go. And he came. And he came. And before he finished, before the disgrace set in, Benny yanked his thumb from her ass and put it quickly in his mouth. Shit. It tasted of shit. His nose filled with the scent of shit. He felt the pasty texture of shit on his tongue, smeared on his teeth.

Benny barely got the door of the van open before puking. Benny puked for a long time before he was able to get Becky's pants back up. He didn't bother buttoning them.

He lay, on the van's floor. Waves of nausea, waves of shame and disgust surging through him. Benny was horrified by what he'd just done. By the monster he'd become. And, even more horrific, as he played the scene over and over in his mind, Benny found, in the company of shame, however slight, a wicked undeniable satisfaction. Somewhere, at the edge of sleep, he heard Jeeter's motorcycle crank and rev. The familiar sound settled into his semi-consciousness and comforted him. Finally, Benny knew, in that moment, what he had to do. He had to tell Jeeter everything. About watching Jenna drown. About the tapes. About lying, to Rebecca, to him, to everybody. About the goats. He made a promise to himself; he'd tell Jeeter everything. Everything. He'd go out to Jeeter's house the next afternoon and tell him everything. And ask for his help.

Shortly after hearing Jeeter leave on the motorcycle, Benny slept.

Benny and Becky both woke, startled, to the sound of pounding. Someone pounding on the door of the van.

Pounding. And pounding.

'What!' Benny said.

'Hey, man,' someone answered. Benny didn't recognize the voice.

'What do you want?'

'You got a dog?'

Benny rose and opened the door. Becky watched groggily.

'Don't you have a dog? An old dachshund?'

'Why?' Benny said, worried.

'You better come here,' the man said, and walked off without waiting for an answer.

Benny followed, spitting and spitting on the ground, well into the walk before remembering to zip his pants.

The man led him around the buildings to the BBQ pit where the two pigs were cooked last night. When Benny walked up the man pointed at the pit.

'What?' Benny asked.

No answer. None needed. There in cool lifeless coals lay the body of his old dog Squat. Equally cool and lifeless. What had happened was plain to see. After smoldering all evening and into the night, the embers had died and gone cold sometime in the wee hours of the party. The pigs, delicious as they were, were too big to be eaten completely. They were picked at and gouged from until everyone had their fill, then abandoned on their spits. Everyone had their fill, except Squat. The good dog recognized an opportunity. Benny could almost imagine the valiant effort needed for him, and his stubby little arthritic legs to climb up into the carcass of that cooked pig. Benny could imagine the slick and oily sensation – no doubt heaven-like – of being surrounded by meat, slow-roasted meat. And Squat ate, all the way through, from one end of the pig to the other. Gorged. Glutted. And when the dog fell out the other end of that pig, greased up and sated, it must've been more joy than his tiny but mighty canine heart could stand. Squat died. Right there. In the gray ash and chunks of charcoal. Inches from where he'd exited the carcass of the barbecued pig.

Chapter 23

WHEN THE PHONE RANG, LATER THAT MORNING,
Benny figured it was Becky, calling to apologize for not
saying a goddamn word on the ride home from Gnogg's
place. When the phone rang, he figured that she'd been
freaked out by the presence of Squat's dead body lying in
the back on an old blanket. That's why she acted so damn
weird. When the phone rang, he expected to explain that
he'd have to go to Jeeter's that afternoon and build a casket
for his dog. When the phone rang, he picked it up, ready
to forgive.

'Yeah.'

'Benny?'

'Who's this?'

'Nub.'

'Hey, Nub.'

'Listen, I'm real sorry, son.'

'Well . . . he was a good old dog. Lived a long life.'

'What are you talking about, Benny?'

'Squat.'

'What about Squat?'

'Squat died. What are you talking about?'

'Jeeter.'

Benny took a deep breath. Jeeter. Jeeter died?

'Jeeter died?'

'You don't know?'

'Jeeter's dead?'

'No. No, Benny. Jeeter ain't dead. He ain't the same, but so far he's still alive.'

Benny sat back in his kitchen chair; it creaked and groaned under the burden.

'What happened?' Benny asked.

'He wrecked his motorcycle.'

Benny could hear Honey crying in the background.

'Where?' he asked. 'When?'

'Out on Plank. Sometime before daylight. Ran right off the road. And . . .'

'Yeah?' Benny said.

'They was a girl with him.'

'Is she . . . ?'

'Killed.'

'And Jeeter . . . ?'

Nub sucked air between his teeth.

'Just don't know yet, Benny. If he lives, he ain't likely to walk.'

Fuck.

'Do they know what happened?'

'No. Not really. It was a straight stretch of road.'

'Maybe he hit a deer or a possum or something.'

'No. No sign of that. Looks like he just drove off the pavement. The bike is a mess. Forks is caved in and the seat and tank are all burned up. They almost didn't find the girl. Tho'd her up into a bunch of pine trees.'

A lot of silence.

'He's at Mercy,' Nub finally said. 'Intensive Care.'

Benny dug the hole because the hole had to be dug. Even in the cool October air, Squat was drawing flies and beginning to stink, over and above the smells of cooked pig and old dog. As he worked the shovel into the soil, Benny thought about the vow he'd made the night before in the back of his van, his promise to tell Jeeter the secrets. Doubtful, now, the keeping. He dug it in the back corner of the lot at duplex. And because the rocky root-filled soil fought back so, Benny's hands bled by the time he'd finished.

No casket. No ceremony. Nothing, but the dead dog wrapped in a filthy blanket.

Two hours later, unwashed, Benny felt himself sucked into the antiseptic and fluorescent space of the Mercy Emergency Room. And when he made it as far as the nurse's station in the ICU, they turned him away.

'You can't come in here like that. Go home and clean up.'

Benny intended to go home. He did not, definitely did not intend to go to Claxton Looms. When he opened the door, he looked for Becky in the fish tank, as he'd seen her that first day. And not finding her there, skulked into the office. Becky, too, sent him home.

She refused to talk to him. Benny left without telling her about Jeeter or the girl.

Still, Benny did not want to go home. Not yet. He went, instead, to Jeeter's. To feed the fish. To look around. To cry, even, although that was unplanned, too. Benny wandered around Jeeter's compound, scaled back just a little since the storm hit in the summer, but still impressive in its scope. It took awhile before he got the nerve to go into the house. He planned to get Jeeter some things. A toothbrush, maybe. A few motorcycle magazines.

The shades were pulled and once inside, Benny stood

until his eyes adjusted to the dark. But, even in the dark, he knew the lay of Jeeter's home. The door of the narrow trailer, off center by several yards, opened in a space, more theoretical than real, between the kitchen and living room/dining room combo. To the immediate right, a crowded bathroom and laundry area all but blocked entry into a tiny bedroom anchoring that end of the trailer. The other way, left, led to a slightly larger bathroom, a room Jeeter used as an office cum den, and his bedroom. And his bedroom is where Benny stood opening and closing the dresser drawers when the police scanner barked from the nightstand, terrifying him.

Dispatch to Animal Control.

Benny's heart whipped itself into a frenzy.

Go ahead, Dispatch.

He'd forgotten about the scanner. Jeeter used to drive a tow truck; he'd listen for accidents then head to the scene.

Be advised, several chickens loose on the interstate, exit 7. The Cracker Barrel exit.

The radio scared him so bad, Benny forgot why he'd come. So he left, empty-handed. Almost. Benny pocketed the three dollar bills and handful of change that lay in a little fish-shaped bowl on Jeeter's dresser. Then, finally, Benny went home and showered.

Back at the hospital, the nurses were Ok with his level of hygiene, but almost refused to let Benny in to see Jeeter for a number of other reasons.

'He doesn't have any family,' Benny said. 'Can I just sit with him for a few minutes? Please?'

As unconscious as he was, Jeeter seemed in complete control of the high-tech vessel he lay perfectly still, and elevated slightly, in the center of. Benny could make no sense of the lights and sounds. And the smell . . .

He'd planned to stay all night, to sleep in the waiting room, but the sight of his friend, helpless, pale, stripped of all the fire and fervor that defined him, drove Benny away. Jeeter living, Jeeter dying. Which will it be? And who says? Jeeter, at the mercy of . . . what? So much nothing.

Past dinner time. Benny ought to be hungry, but wasn't. What day of the week was it? Maybe Friday. Maybe not. When he pulled into the Touch-less bay at Dinks Clean 'em Up, Benny's was the only vehicle on the property. Dink climbed into the passenger side, ready. And a valiant effort Dink made to do what was expected of him in the allotted time period. Three to five minutes had always been enough. But when the Drive Forward Slowly light glowed, Benny hadn't ejaculated yet. Not even close. He yanked Dink's head out of his lap just as the automatic door started its clanking rise.

'Get the fuck away from me!' Benny said.

Dink didn't answer. He'd dealt with rage before.

'Get out, Dink! Get the fuck out of my van now!'

He did, without complaint. Without payment.

As Benny squealed out of the parking lot, the van's rear end fishtailing, he saw another car pull into the bay, and behind it, still another lined up. Must be Friday night, he thought. Must be Friday night. Must be. Benny pulled to a stop at a payphone, one he could reach without getting out of the van. And he dialed 911.

'Buffalo Shoal Police. Is this an emergency?'

Benny, as if there were need, changed his voice. Pitched it way back in his throat.

'Hey, some retard just tried to give me a blowjob over at that carwash over on Pine Boulevard. Said he'd do it for five bucks.'

'What's your name, sir.'

'I seen some other cars there. I bet he's sucking away right now.'

Benny hung up. He drove away.

Nub and Honey sat, amid the flowers, all bunched to one side of Jeeter's hospital room. Benny knew the second he walked in the door that he'd never be able to tell Jeeter anything. Ever.

'Hey, Sugar,' Honey said. She'd been crying.

'Hey, Honey.'

'They said he come to a little bit last night,' Nub said.

'Ya'll been here long?' Benny asked.

'Not too long.'

Then, mostly, they just sat. Nurses came and went, attended to the machine of Jeeter's body and to the machines that, at the moment, allowed his machine to operate. The array of tubes and wires and pipes and bags, connected to, inserted in, or hanging near Jeeter's body – each giving or taking something – dizzied Benny.

'Ya'll hungry?' Benny asked. Asked in part because the sound of his traumatized friend's breathing – a grating shallow inhalation, and barely perceptible grunt each time he exhaled – became all but unbearable. Benny wanted out of the room.

'I could use a bite,' Nub said.

'Me too,' said Honey.

'I'll go down to the canteen and get us some sandwiches.'

'You sit right here, Benny,' Honey said. 'Me and Nub'll go. I need to stretch these old legs anyway.'

And their departure must've been some sort of subconscious cue for Jeeter to open his eyes.

'Jeeter?' Benny said softly, going to stand bedside. 'Hey, buddy.'

Clearly, there was little in the way of focus and recognition behind those eyes.

'How you doin'?' Benny asked.

In answer, Jeeter's eyes rolled back, showing swaths of the bloodshot whites, then his lids closed over them.

Benny stood by the bed a while longer. Stood there thinking. Was standing there thinking when he felt an arm ease around his waist.

'Hey, sexy. I got something to show you.'

'Hey, Doodle.'

Up to that point, Benny had mostly managed to contain his emotions. But when he turned into Doodle's hug, he could not hold back the single sob nor the tears that followed it. Doodle, always good at that sort of thing, held tight. Told him it was Ok. Then they sat, catching up, until Nub and Honey came in with the sandwiches. Nub, Honey and Benny each offered Doodle their sandwiches.

'No,' she said. 'Thank you anyway, but I've already ate.'

She stood to leave, patted Jeeter's very still leg, then kissed Benny on the cheek.

'You gonna be around this weekend?' she asked.

'Probably,' Benny said. 'Why?'

'Might have to ask you a favor.'

'You know where to find me.'

Benny, at home, and tired, found himself reaching beneath his bed for the milk crate containing the drowned girl's belongings. There was only one tape left to watch. *Untitled. April 3, 2001.* The tape that she'd left running in the camera. The tape of Jenna walking into the Toe River.

He sat in his rocker, feet propped on the ottoman. Benny hesitated for a split second before pushing play, trying to remember if he'd fed Squat. Then, he remembered he didn't have to feed Squat. Benny rewound the tape to its beginning.

April 3, 2001   • • • **Rec**
1:00 a.m.

Jenna, pale, tired, thin, sitting in her apartment at the kitchen table, looking at the camera.

'My name is Jenna. Jenna Hinkey.'

She pauses, too long, between each phrase.

'I am an artist. I make films.'

She drinks from a cup; her hands – bandages gone, a gape where her missing fingers ought to be – shake.

'I have made a mistake. I was confused. So confused.'

Jenna talks about her confusion, her various states of mind, as if they were visitors. Relatives who show up at her door unannounced, steamer trunks and duffle bags in tow, ready to catch up on all the family gossip.

'For a long time, I thought you made a self by adding to what you started with. I know, now, that subtraction is the only way to build a true self.'

April 3, 2001   • • • **Rec**
7:40 a.m.

The monologue continues.

'It's all about taking away. About not holding onto.'

Jenna, slurring and mumbling from time to time, talks and talks.

The Toe River rushes by, fills the picture frame. In the distance, the base of the Bard's Communication tower rises out of the field of vision. And off to one side, the blurry image of an orange van.

Benny paused the tape, not sure he was ready for what lay ahead. Where did the hours go? She'd been at her apartment in the morning, then nothing until the camera sat riverside. He needed more explanation. Did she make her plans then? How far in advance did she know what she had to do? Were there goodbyes? Reasons. Understanding. But he knew none would be forthcoming. He knew because he had seen.

Jenna steps into view. Strips naked. Her prosthetic leg a dull, lifeless tan. Stands for a brief moment, then, without looking back, she walks into the water. No hesitation. First she filled the camera's viewfinder, then she left it, empty. The surface of the water kept her secret, revealed nothing. Offered remarkably little sound. Revealed nothing about whether Jenna struggled or fought. Nothing about the murky water filling her mouth her nose her lungs her gut. Filling and filling. Nothing about fear or courage. Nothing about her body, the machine itself, and how it fought her resolve the moment consciousness left. Did she seizure? Did her mouth gape and close and gape and close? At what point did her automatic functions surrender?

Then, minutes and minutes of the river flowing by at flood stage. The camera watches, without judgment, all that passes. A suitcase; a road sign, its stenciled message bobbing – DO NOT DO NOT DO NOT – into and out of sight; detritus passing through the field of vision, almost as if staged by Jenna herself.

Benny stopped the tape again. Rewound it. Pushed play with the absurd hope that things would be different. Then again. And again, looking for clues, hoping for change, stopping each time the camera came to terms with her absence. Watched, over and over, the tiny speck of himself coming down from the tower, far off in the camera's view, and the van driving away. Finally he let it play on, and on, until Benny, unprepared in both places, watched himself appear on camera. Fearful then, fearful now, Benny felt the ligaments and tendons of time snap and ping inside himself. Benny watched himself walk to the river's edge, and for a moment wondered if he was going to walk right into the water after her.

'No!' Benny called out, there in his half of the duplex.

'Squat?' he called in that other world so long ago. 'Good dog.'

Then, Benny, too, disappeared from the camera's view. Moments later, the screen went black.

As soon as he'd put everything away, Benny called Becky's apartment, but when she answered, he hung up. Sleep came and went, fitfully; Benny dreamt of snakes, writhing masses of snakes. Benny dreamt himself in the pews of a church, and kneeling there amid the other congregants. The other congregants being fish: catfish and perch, crappie and sunfish, gar, snapping turtles, crawdads, all clicking their gills, their mouths, their claws in praise.

Jeeter, for the first time, seemed to recognize Benny. Jeeter, immediately, started to cry.

'Benny . . .' he whispered. 'What am I gonna do . . . ?'

Benny, working hard not to cry himself, took his friend's hand.

'You're gonna be Ok, man. You'll be out of here and good as new before you know it.'

Jeeter turned his face away from Benny, drifted into sleep.

Benny went out to his van, in the parking lot, climbed into the back and tried to nap. Mostly, though, he just looked out the rear windows. And mostly at the sign for Shinn's Market, which advertised a special deal on Vienna sausages, and bore this message on the marquee: Jesus Rules, Down You Beast.

On his way back into the hospital, Benny picked up a *Tribune* and, more out of boredom than genuine interest, a current *Creative Loafing*. He read while Jeeter moved in and out of consciousness. Moved in and out of despair.

'Jeeter,' Benny said, in a more cognizant moment. 'I could put a lift in my van. You know, a wheelchair lift.'

Jeeter closed his eyes and slept.

Fuck, Benny said aloud. There, in the *Buffalo Shoals Tribune* Police Blotter, Section A, page 13, the first entry reported the details of Dink's arrest for prostitution, and lewd and lascivious behavior. Fuck. Benny folded the paper carefully and dropped it in the wastebasket. Fuck.

Fuck. The word works perfectly in so many situations. Jeeter stirred, mumbled something through the drug haze, fell back into silence. Benny reached for the *Creative Loafing*. From time to time, Benny picked one up from the seemingly millions of boxes around the city, but the only thing he ever looked at with any attention were the Adult Services ads, and the personals. Women Seeking

Men. And he and Jeeter regularly found something to laugh at in the Other & Alternative listings.

'Hey, Jeeter,' Benny said, knowing full well he'd get no answer. 'How about this one?'

UNIQUE ATTRACTION. EDUCATED, articulate, not creepy MWM 41, wife lives out of state, ISO M/D/SWF amputee, 40 or younger, for dinners, outings, discreet, intimate fun. No strings. Love pleasing a woman, three or fewer limbs a must.

Benny thumbed through the paper, looking for distraction, and was about to toss it away with the *Tribune* when an article caught his eye. A photo, actually. A face he recognized. The headline, telling in and of itself: 'Art on the Razor's Edge'. And the photograph? Arrogance epitomized. Assholery made manifest. The artist MAX, self-serious and smug, glared at the camera. Benny read, and because the reading differed in tone and diction from most of the reading in his life, he struggled. Benny struggled, and as he struggled he became embarrassed. And as his embarrassment grew, Benny became angry.

Part interview, part bullshit manifesto, the article covered past scandals generated by Max's art. A two-part series called *Blood* caused some stir of late. One half of the series involved paintings, portraits mostly, of women, in blood. Menstrual blood. For the other half Max, always at the ready, took heavy paper to accident sights of all kinds, and pressed the paper into the spilled blood and body fluids.

'Accidents are all around us, waiting to be used. We just have to look.'

Bastard. Asshole. Fucker.

More disturbing was the reportage of Max's current

show at Firehouse Gallery. *Beautiful Women Shitting*.
Opening reception, the coming day, Friday.

'Becky,' he said. 'Are you there? Pick up the phone.'

She didn't, then, so he called back every fifteen minutes.

'What, Benny?'

'I'm sorry,' he said.

'For what?'

'Everything,' he said, hoping to cover all the bases. 'I want to go on a date.'

'What?'

'I want to take you out. We'll go eat. Then . . . I want to show you something.'

'What is it?' Becky asked, her hesitance plain.

'Can't tell you. It's a secret.'

'I don't know, Benny . . .'

Benny didn't want the opportunity to slip away.

'It'll be fun,' he said.

'I miss you,' he said, too emphatically, but such was Becky's need that she bought it all.

'Well . . .'

'I'll come get you tomorrow around five.'

'Where're we going?' Becky asked. 'I'm hungry.'

'I want show you something first,' Benny said. 'Before we eat.'

As it happened, the Firehouse Gallery stood less than a mile from Claxton Looms Luxury Apartments, in the heart of the gentrified neighborhood reclaimed by the au courant.

'What's this?' she asked, as they passed the crowd gathered in front of the building. They had to circle the block twice to find parking.

'An art thing.'

'What? What kind of art thing?'

'You know,' Benny said. 'An *opening*.'

Becky, clearly baffled by his choice, asked the logical questions.

'Do you know anything about art?'

'No,' Benny said. 'Not really.'

'I don't either. Do you . . . I mean do you care anything about art?'

'This I do,' he said. Benny didn't allow himself to think through what he was doing.

'Are you going to tell me what it's about?'

'You'll see.'

On approach, making their way down the sidewalk, it became clear that the crowd gathered in front of the Firehouse Gallery gathered there for a multitude of reasons. Not all came as art buffs. Certainly, the folks carrying signs reading things like The Body is the Temple of Christ, and Porn = Sin = Hell – each sign emblazoned with the acronym C.U.S.P. (Citizens United against Smut and Porn) – no doubt had agendas and goals that conflicted with the shorn, tattooed, boot-wearing, leather jacketed, braless, pierced, and surly group of womyn and their issues. And in fact each group took their stands on opposite sides of the doorway, and seemed to alternate directing their chants and rallies and dictums at the gallery and its contents and at, as it were, the opposing team.

'I can't go in there, Benny,' Becky said, stopping on the sidewalk.

'What do you mean you can't go in? You don't even know what the show is.'

'Well I know that some of those people are from Daddy's church. I can't go in there.'

Benny hadn't expected this.

'Look, we'll sneak in when nobody is looking.'

'Benny! People always look at me. I can't sneak anywhere.'

Giving up on patience and lobbying, Benny simply bent down, grabbed Becky's hand, and pulled her through the crowd. Force.

'No!!!' she said, but not wanting to attract anything beyond the normal gawking attention, said it more in whisper that anything else.

Benny led her right through the middle of the protesters, and into the open doors of the gallery. Once inside, the reason for all the hoopla outside became clear. These were the paintings – these and more – Benny had seen so long ago on the videotape in which Jenna had interviewed the artist.

'Benny,' Becky whispered with urgency driven by shame and embarrassment. 'What are we doing here?'

The canvases, big six-foot canvases, loomed on the walls. There was the woman squatting on the dining-room table. There, the woman shitting in the church. And there, and there, ten, maybe twelve larger than life, highly realistic paintings of women in the act of defecating. Standing before each of them, a pack of wine-swilling cheese-gumming aficionados, ooing and ahhing and gasping in exaggerated disbelief, and generally filling all the available air space with blah blah blah.

'I'm gonna be sick, Benny,' she said. 'I think I'm going to throw up.'

'No, you're not,' he said. 'Come on, I want to show you something.'

A complicated shame crept up from the pit of Benny's stomach. He squelched it.

Becky covered her eyes with her free hand, while Benny led her to the back of the gallery by the other.

Outside, on the walk, easily seen through the glass, the fundamentalists and the femi-nazis banged their pots.

'Please take me home, Benny. I want to go home now.'

And there it was. Bigger than some. The painting he knew would be there. Jenna. Benny didn't know how Max would do it, neither theme nor pose, but he had no doubt of the painting's existence. And there it was. Jenna, her limbs and fingers intact, squatting on a potters wheel. Squatting over a fat pile of a different kind of clay.

'Look,' he said to Becky. 'This is the one I wanted you to see.'

She refused.

'I don't want to see this stuff, Benny! It's obscene. It's nasty and disgusting. This isn't art . . . it's . . .'

'Just look, Becky! Open your fucking eyes and look at the picture.'

Benny spoke too loudly. People around them hushed, gave them some space, waited for the next move. Benny knew how horrible he was being. He lacked the power to stop himself.

'Why, Benny? Why am I looking at this?'

Benny leaned in toward the painting, with his index finger extended.

'Please don't touch the art sir.'

Benny stepped back a little. Pointed.

'Do you recognize something here, Becky? See something that looks familiar?'

He, of course, referred to the birthmark, the purplish one shaped something like a fish, on Jenna's buttock.

Her sister's buttock. There, on that taut buttock, on that mammoth painting, rendered in the same degree of perfection as the anus and its little ring of hairs, was the fish.

'Tha . . . Ben . . . do you . . . did . . .'

Becky seemed to have been fully infected by her mother's condition of incompletion. She couldn't say any whole thing.

'It can't . . . I mean . . . Benny!'

Then Becky broke down. She put her head into her hands and, there in front of all, sobbed and sobbed.

Again, as in the rear of his van not so long ago, a wave of shame washed through Benny. He forced it back into its dark hole, and in its absence *power* remained.

'Is everything Ok?' someone asked. Probably the gallery manager. 'Would you like to step outside?'

'How did you know this, Benny?' Becky demanded. 'Tell me how you knew about this. About my sister. About her birthmark.'

Benny, in lieu of answering, smirked ever so slightly.

Becky, barely able to catch her breath, stormed, to the degree that her little stubby legs would allow, out of the gallery and down the sidewalk. Her gait, monstrous. Careening. And when she walked right by Benny's van, he made no effort to stop her.

No effort. No effort to stop himself, on the way home, from pulling up to that very familiar pay phone, flipping through the phonebook, tracing a single fingertip down the column: Hesser, Hewitt, Hicks, Higgins, Hill, Hines, Hinkey . . .

Benny disguised his voice, practiced once, then again, and called.

'Hello,' Mrs Hinkey said. 'The Hinkey residence.'

'She's dead,' Benny said, although it may have come out like *sheep's head*.

'Excuse me?'

Benny paused, let the momentum carry him farther into meanness.

'Dead. Your stupid daughter is dead.'

'Uh . . . who . . .'

'The dumb bitch drowned herself. She's dead. Gone. Ain't coming back.'

Then he hung up, took three tries to fit the phone back into its cradle. Benny pulled away from the payphone without looking, pulled nearly into the path of a UPS truck, whose driver pounded the horn but kept his mouth shut. Benny drove home.

For the first time in months, despite the cool November air, Doodle sat on her front stoop reading a paperback book and drinking a beer.

'Hey, Benny Poteat,' she said. 'I got something to show you.'

'You waiting for me?'

'Maybe,' she said with that sweet tease he missed so.

'Where's Mr White Truck man?' Benny asked.

He sat down beside Doodle.

'Working,' she said. 'Hey, I heard about Squat. Sorry.'

'He was a good old dog.'

'Yeah. He was.'

They just sat a while then, Benny trying to calm himself down, or at least to seem calm. Doodle, just being Doodle.

'I got a favor to ask,' she said.

'What is it?' Benny answered, and reached for her beer.

'I need to go somewhere. I need you to take me somewhere.'

'Ok. But where?'

'St Augustine. Florida.'

'What the hell you want to go to St Augustine Florida for?'

'Can't tell you yet, Benny.'

'When do you want to go?' he asked.

'Tomorrow. Next day at the latest.'

'Let's go right now,' Benny said.

'What?'

'Now. Let's leave tonight.'

'Really?' Doodle asked, and in spite of herself scooted a little closer to Benny.

'I just need to get some stuff,' he said. 'I can be ready in fifteen minutes.'

'Can you give me half an hour?' Doodle asked. 'I need to sponge off.'

And while the water ran in Doodle's bathroom Benny secreted the milk crate of Jenna's belongings into the van, where he stashed it under the bed. He forgot to pack anything else.

'Want me to call Honey for you?' Doodle asked from her window.

'No,' Benny lied. 'I already did.'

A little over four hundred miles. Eight, maybe nine hours with stops.

'We can take turns driving,' Doodle said.

'I don't mind driving,' Benny said. 'We need to get a map though.'

'No,' Doodle said. 'I can get us there. There's Clyde, blow the horn.'

And so, in faith, Benny pulled out of the driveway,

swerved into November as if he hadn't a care in the world. As he drove, as he put more and more distance between himself and Buffalo Shoals, as he got farther away from the messy life he led there, leaving behind his damaged friends, Becky and her drowned sister and his hard secret, Benny felt like he got closer and closer to a way of thinking and being he'd almost forgotten. He felt like he was returning to himself.

He and Doodle talked. Small talk. Chitchat. For the first couple hours anyway. They reminisced about their time together at Nub & Honey's restaurant. They passed a sign for The Cyclorama at Columbia, and despite Benny's insistence on stopping, Doodle held sway.

'Honey used to make Nub take her there at least once every summer,' Benny said.

'Maybe we'll stop on the way back.'

'You still haven't told me why we're going to Florida,' Benny said.

'I know,' Doodle answered.

Benny, eventually, asked the question.

'So, who's your boyfriend?'

'Joe. His name is Joe.'

Benny told her a story about camping with Nub as a boy. They had an old pup tent out in the back yard.

'I was little,' Benny said. 'And I went to sleep right before it got dark. Next thing I know, Nub was shaking me awake . . . he'd gone out and caught a whole bunch of lightning bugs, must've been hundreds of them, and let them loose in the tent. I woke up and it was like magic . . .'

Doodle told him a story.

'The last time I made this trip . . . was fifteen years ago. With my ex-husband.'

'Doodle! You were married?'

'He wouldn't stop. Only to get gas. Nothing else. He peed in a milk jug. He wouldn't stop for me to feed our son.'

Doodle played out the revelations slowly.

'Whoa . . . married and a kid.'

'David, our boy . . . he was only four months old. Too little for such a long ride in the car. And that asshole wouldn't stop the car for anything. I had to change David's diapers going down the road. He wouldn't take a bottle yet, so I had to flop over his car seat with my tit hanging out of my shirt every couple hours.'

'Nice guy,' Benny said.

Three hours into the trip, they stopped at a Mobil station for gas, to pee, and to get some snacks.

'Pork rinds,' Benny said, as Doodle headed for the door. 'And will you get me two ice cream sandwiches?'

Benny pumped the gas, and paid little attention to the old man who pulled up at the next pump in a rusted out Plymouth Valiant, yellow. Benny paid little attention, until the man spoke anyway.

'I had me one of them one time,' the man said. Said while digging a thick fingertip into his ear.

Benny didn't answer at first, but the man kept talking.

'One of them Dodges. Used to be my son's. I got it when he died. Out there in California.'

Benny nodded, hoping that would be enough. The man didn't look particularly crazy, looked benign even standing there in a green and ill-fitting short sleeved dress shirt and tan slacks pulled high over his paunchy gut, but these days it paid to be careful.

'Wouldn't hardly run with all that ee-missions bullshit on it.'

'What are you talking about?' Benny finally asked.

'That damn Dodge. Wouldn't hardly run. It was that catalytic eunuch kept it from getting any gas. Know what I did? I busted it out with a horseshoe stob. Then it run like a damn top. Never did like that thing though. You like yours? What kind of mileage it get? Where ya'll headed? Hell fire, this my stomping ground; I was borned and raised not two mile from here. Ain't a bad place 'cept for the ticks and mosquitoes. That's a purty lady you traveling with. My name's Floyd, by the way. What's yours?'

And the man never slowed down long enough for Benny to answer; which didn't seem to bother the man who, by god only knows what logic, became convinced that Benny's name was Floyd, too.

'Ain't it funny we got the same name? I meet so many fellas named Floyd. A whole blessed army of us. Hell fire, ya'll ought to come over to the house for dinner one night. I'll get the old woman to barbecue up some goat. Ever eat any goat meat? God-a-mighty, talk about good eatin'. Bring your wife. Bring your girlfriend for all I care. Ya'll ever play canasta? Takes two decks.'

He was still talking when Doodle returned. She shifted the bag of food from one hand to the other so that she could open the van's door.

'Who's that?'

'Where've you been?'

They spoke at the same time.

'That's Floyd,' Benny said.

'I had to pee,' Doodle said. 'They couldn't find the key to the toilet.'

Floyd talked even as they drove away.

'Damn good to meet you, Floyd, and your fine woman, too. Ya'll drop in when you pass through again. We'll roast us a goat. And watch out for them ticks. And them mosquitoes too. Shit fire, I . . .'

Doodle, being a woman, and women being generally more curious than men in certain areas, after a tactful period of time, broached a subject she'd no doubt been stewing over for a while.

'So, do you like that girl, Benny?'

'What girl?' Benny asked, playing the dumb game. 'You mean Becky?'

'Who else? Do you?'

'Do I what?'

'Do you like her?'

Benny thought about the question. Was it possible to like someone and do the things he did to her? Is it possible to do the things he did to her without liking her?

'I don't know, Doodle. Why?'

She let it drop, for the moment anyway.

'Look,' Doodle said, pointing out the window at the car traveling beside them on the interstate. 'That car has a flat tire.'

Benny craned to look out her window, and in the clear moonlit night saw that in fact the left rear tire on the big red sedan was airless. The driver, his bouffanted wife, and the two kids sleeping in the back seat seemed oblivious.

'Reckon they don't know?' Doodle asked.

'They wouldn't keep that speed if they knew,' Benny said. 'Maybe you ought to tell them.'

Doodle thought about it for a minute. It was dark enough that the driver might not be able to read her lips, even if she gestured at the tire.

'I'll make a sign,' she said. 'Got something to write with?'

Benny remembered a laundry marker in the dash, left by Dink no doubt. Doodle scrounged around for a sheet of paper, then wrote in big block letters: YOUR TIRE IS FLAT, LEFT REAR. Benny pulled alongside the sedan and blew the horn while Doodle held the sign pressed to her window. Within a minute, the car pulled off on the shoulder, the driver waving and mouthing his gratitude.

'You've earned your girl scout points for the day,' Benny said. And when Doodle was just about to wad the sign up and toss it away he had an idea.

'Wait,' he said. 'Keep it.'

'Why?'

'Let's see how many cars we can get to pull over.'

For the next forty-five minutes, they played their silly joke on every fifth car that they passed, and all but one pulled over, nodding and waving and thankful. Then they tried different signs. SOMETHING HANGING FROM CAR. WHEEL FALLING OFF. YOUR CAR IS ON FIRE. Eventually moving into more suspect territory. JESUS LOVES YOU. They did this for miles and hours. Eventually, the gullibility of people pissed Benny off.

'People are stupid,' he said. 'They'll believe anything.'

Not that he could articulate the reasons for his feeling, but anger found its own way into articulation.

'Make another sign,' he said to Doodle.

'Ok,' she said. 'What?'

YOUR MOTHER JUST DIED

'No, Benny! I can't do that.'

'Just write the sign Doodle. I'll hold it up.'

She did as told, reluctantly. Did so even when Benny got meaner. YOUR HUSBAND IS SLEEPING WITH YOUR DAUGHTER. And, in response to political bumper stickers like *Charlton Heston is my President*, or *In Case of*

Rapture This Car Will be Abandoned, a sign reading simply FUCK YOU!

'This is too mean, Benny,' Doodle finally said. 'I'm not doing any more signs.'

Benny, his anger dulled by use, didn't argue.

By and by, the road eventually led them through the night. By and by, that same road led them to St Augustine.

'I'm hungry,' Benny said.

'Let's get some breakfast.'

Egg Harbor's neon *Open* sign blinked and blinked and beckoned them to stop, so they did. More shack than anything, and on a sand lot carved out of the mangroves, the restaurant made up for the absence of harbor, or any other water in sight, through an abundance of beachy décor.

'Can I get you folks some coffee?' the sole waitress asked of the sole customers.

'Yep.'

When she brought the coffee back, Doodle asked a question that surprised Benny.

'Excuse me, ma'am, would you happen to know where the courthouse is?'

She didn't, but she was sure Buster the cook would.

A minute later, she returned with cream, sugar and the information.

'Wonder when they open?' Doodle mused, more to herself than anyone else.

'Ten o'clock,' Buster said, from the serving window, his face framed perfectly there. Then he went about making their eggs and bacon.

Benny waited as long as his patience held out, then asked.

'You gonna' tell me why we're here?'

Doodle thought for a while.

'David,' she finally said. 'My ex is taking full custody of David. And I need to sign some papers.'

Benny didn't press the issue any further. They ate. Drank coffee. Killed some time.

'We still have an hour before the courthouse opens,' Benny said.

'Let's drive around a little bit.'

'Ya'll come back,' Buster called.

They both preferred back roads. So Benny just turned off the highway at the first opportunity, and they meandered through the neighborhoods of St Augustine proper, criss-crossing the main streets where Ripley's Believe It or Not, and The Fountain of Youth vied for their confidence and their money.

The first time Benny drove past The Tragedy in US History Museum, he would've missed it as a point of interest completely if Doodle hadn't pointed it out.

'Look at that,' she said. 'Go around the block.'

The next time around, Benny paid closer attention to the two-story stucco house. And did find something intriguing about the hand-painted sign out front that promised a wealth of experiences inside: Bonnie & Clyde's Bullet-Riddled Getaway Car, Original Human Bill of Sale, Old Spanish Jail With Real Human Skeletons Inside, The Car Jayne Mansfield (famous movie star) Lost Her Life In, Antique Torture Equipment – Headstock, Neckbreaker & Whippingpost, and Much More.

The third time past, Benny pulled up in one of the three dirt parking spaces beneath a moss-draped oak in front of the museum. Benny looked up in time to see someone pull a curtain aside in one of the open upstairs windows.

In the large glass-front window, by the entrance, in life-size diorama, a department store mannequin in Army fatigues with an ancient rifle balanced between his rigid arms, stood amid stacks of rotting cardboard boxes, each with the word BOOKS scrawled childlike on all sides. A sign nailed near the low ceiling read, Reenactment Of Oswald Killing President John F. Kennedy. Admission: $3.50.

Doodle rang the bell; they heard a door slam upstairs and the sound of someone coming down steps.

'Two adults, please,' Benny said to the woman who raised the shade of the ticket booth and smiled at them. Late thirties, probably, wearing a faded maroon smock with *Curator* stitched over the breast pocket, unbuttoned to reveal a mismatched tee shirt and what were either big panties or very small shorts. She had the look of someone interrupted, glad for the business, but distracted.

'That'll be seven dollars ya'll can just go on in it's the first floor of the house and the property out back enjoy the sights now and thank you for stopping.' Then she disappeared from the booth and they heard her run back up the steps.

Benny and Doodle entered through a narrow turnstile and wandered aimlessly, silently around the three tiny rooms. The exhibits were pathetic. Benny rarely visited museums, but even he recognized that fact. Lots of framed, illegible letters, faded newspaper articles, and yellowed photographs. As they stood against the red velvet ropes separating them from what was supposed to be The Car Oswald Used To Transport The Murder Weapon To The Texas Book Depository, muted laughter came from overhead. For a second Benny thought they were laughing at him and Doodle – another pair of dupes – but then the laughter gave way to a slow, rhythmic squeaking. Bed springs. As the pace quickened, each squeak squeak

squeak followed by a thump thump thump.

'Reckon we'll be charged extra for that?' Doodle asked, raising her eyebrows to acknowledge the noise.

A woman, a woman's voice, presumably the Curator's, began to 'ummph!' in the fraction of sound space between the squeaks and the thumps. Another voice, some lucky docent maybe, countering with his own 'ooosh!' And all this took place just above The Famous Zapruder Film Showing Each Bullet As It Struck The President, stretching frame by frame along the narrow hallway.

'That may be the greatest tragedy of all,' Doodle said.

'What? The dinky quality of this whole mess? Seven dollars to hear two strangers screwing above the dumbest museum in the world?'

'All of the above,' Doodle said.

Make no mistake, Benny was a voyeur in his heart, capable of morbid fascination with every element of that kind of experience. And his life, of late, and historically, reeked of voyeurism, mostly accidental. But there are some things you just don't want to imagine, naked or otherwise. Those two strangers rutting noisily overhead, just on the other side of a low, thin ceiling, and that documented and photographed mishmash of human decline, overwhelmed him. The tiny alcoves closed in.

'I've got to get out of here,' he said, pulling Doodle through the door. But there was no escape in the fenced back yard. Weeds, rust, and decay. Years of exposure to the hot Florida weather had taken its toll on the outdoor displays. And worse, the open windows on the second floor made the sounds of them doing *it* even clearer than inside.

'Kind of like group sex, huh?' Doodle said.

They couldn't find all of the Antique Torture Equipment. There was a huge iron cage, probably the Old Spanish Jail, and a dugout place the size of a small grave covered with thick glass, but the condensation was so dense on the glass that they couldn't see the Real Human Skeletons. Benny took it on faith that they were there. About the most interesting things were some laminated photographs hanging by the Bullet-Riddled Getaway Car. Pictures of the dead Bonnie and Clyde, both naked and bloody. Lots of obvious bullet holes.

'She was pretty,' Benny said. 'Even dead.'

'Nice breasts,' Doodle added. And they were.

'I would've paid more if they advertised this.'

'See The Tits Of Bonnie Parker Postmortem.'

The couple upstairs orgasmed as Doodle and Benny peered into the Mansfield car. They came loudly and apparently together. Within seconds, from the window, Benny and Doodle heard somebody urinating, then the toilet flush.

'I could've lived my life to the end having never heard all that, and been satisfied,' Doodle said.

'It's about ten, Doodle. You want to go to the court-house?'

Back in the van Benny turned the ignition.

'Maybe we should. But . . .'

'But what?'

'I'm tired all of a sudden,' she said. 'It's going to be hard signing those papers, and I'd like to take a nap before I have to do it.'

'Well,' Benny said, an idea hitting home like never before. 'We could get us a room?'

Doodle smiled. An easy, understanding smile.

'I don't think so, Benny.'

She must've seen the hurt, however subtle, cross his face.

'You know, it's got nothing to do with wanting to.'

'Maybe we can find someplace to sleep on the beach,' Benny said.

So they drove out of town, looking for such a place. And would've easily found one, except that Benny got distracted. Distracted. Distracted and determined. In the distance, somewhere off to the right, and knowing full well that the beach and its accompanying ocean lay to the left, Benny spotted a tower. A big, tall, skinny radio tower hurling itself a thousand or more feet into the hot Florida sky. And at its top, a flashing red beacon.

'Let's go this way for a second,' he said. 'I want to show you something.'

Doodle, trusting, agreed.

Before long, the mangroves gave way to acres and acres of orange trees. And as they drove, it became clear to Benny that the tower stood somewhere deep in the orange grove. Through part intuition and part visual tracking, he made his way left and right, through a grid work, a labyrinth of dirt roads until, sure enough, after one last turn, the tower's base, ringed in six-foot chain-link fencing, loomed before them.

'Where're we going, Benny?'

'We're here,' he said.

'Here?'

'Yep.'

'Why?' Doodle asked.

'You'll see,' Benny said, stopping the van right next to the fence, so close that the passenger doors wouldn't open. 'Sit tight.'

Benny got out, climbed onto the roof of the van, and jumped over the fence into trespass. Then, quickly, up the tower. Too quickly for safety's sake. Fifteen minutes later Benny was back at the bottom and scrambling over the fence.

'What in God's name are you doing?' Doodle asked, more amused than concerned.

Benny, out of breath from the climb, opened the van's door, reached into his shirt, and pulled out the red light bulb from the top of the tower. He held it out to Doodle; she leaned over the seat and accepted the gift.

'Ooo,' she said. 'It's still warm.'

'I've been a son of a bitch to you, Doodle.'

'No, Benny. No. You've been a good friend.'

'I've been mean. And I've lied to you. And I don't want to do that anymore.'

Benny climbed into the van, sat sideways in the seat, facing Doodle.

'It's Ok, Benny,' she said. 'I forgive you for whatever you think you did wrong.'

But, clearly, Benny had more than forgiveness in mind.

'I've been thinking,' he said. 'About all the things you've said to me.'

'What things?'

Doodle turned in her seat so that her knees wouldn't be so close to his. Not sure what else to do with her hands, she held tight to the red bulb.

'What things are you talking about Benny?'

'I don't remember exactly what you said Doodle, but I do know that you've been coming on to me since the day you moved into the duplex. And I've been turning you away for just as long.'

'Oh, Benny . . . most of that was just play, honey . . .'

'I've decided not to turn you away any more. I've decided I want whatever it is you've got to show me.'

'Benny, I can't. It's . . .'

Benny leaned into the narrow space between the seats; with the van parked so close to the fence on her side, she had nowhere to go.

'Let me kiss you one time, just one time before you say anything.'

And when he pushed closer into her, Doodle just went ahead and kissed him. It was a thing she'd done before. No big deal. But Benny's kiss got a little more intimate than she'd expected. When his guilty tongue wormed its way between her teeth, Doodle protested.

'Benny!' she said, dropping the bulb to the floor of the van. 'Stop it, Benny!'

And when he reached his hand into her shirt, Doodle swung at him.

'Goddamn it, Benny!'

Benny fell back into the driver's seat.

'What the fuck's the matter, Doodle?' he asked, in earnest. 'What have you been asking for the last seven years?'

'Benny,' she said. 'I'm getting married. Me and Joe are getting married next month. I'm signing divorce papers here, too.'

Benny thought over this new development. It never occurred to him that Doodle would reject him. Not even for the guy in the white truck.

'I want to show you something,' he said, and climbed between the front seats into the back of the van. When Benny knelt in the floor, and reached beneath the van's low bed – knowing that if he shared his secret with her, Doodle would have to, want to, choose him – he heard the van door open then slam shut.

'Doodle!'

By the time Benny got to the door himself, and missed and missed the handle twice until he got it open, then in his urgency, falling out onto the sand, before standing and squinting into the sun, Doodle had disappeared somewhere into the orange grove.

'Doooooodllllle! God damn you, Doodle! Come back here!'

But she didn't. Benny climbed onto the roof of the van, hoping to spot her moving in and out of the squatty trees. Those trees heavily laden with fruit, like a crop of new suns. Hoping to catch sight of her amid the globes. No such luck. Benny didn't know what to do. Where to turn. So he left.

And he drove. And he drove without sleep. Drove back towards home and all the misery there. Benny drove and drove and drove and drove straight through exhaustion. Drove beyond hunger. Drove through Waycross, Georgia, and up into Macon. And what drove Benny he didn't know, couldn't know, but even in the act of unknowing and in every thought that preceded unknowing there rested both history and potential. Benny drove through his past, from frost heave to equinox. Drove through desire, the hood-winked member dry as jute twine. Drove through memory right up the ass of dream, where potential sleeps its fitful sleep. Where history swings its brickbat. There is where it's found. It being both, past and present. Truth be known, future too. There, in consonance and in assonance. There, on shank's mare and in harm's way. There in the greasy circles of stains on paper plates left by the salmon patties she brought to jail that Sunday. There in his mother's averted eyes. Dead. Dead. In the rebuilt carburetor of a 1971 Ford Pinto: jet and bowl and float. In the thin blue wing of a pilot light beating itself senseless against a porcelain day. In the wet wheezing breath of the fat mailman who groped him twice on the porch that summer. Or, dressed in piss-yellow taffeta like the Dry Branch Pork Princess at the Alamance County Fair. In the pencil box and in the esophagus, in panties indiscreetly tossed to the floor, and in every stupid and pathetic and disgusting thing ever done in the name of loneliness. Find it in the bellies of all things living and dead. In the bellies and ears and eyes. And eyes. And one eye in particular. And here, come barreling out of history or potential, here comes Pig Eye, called Pig Eye on account of that mooneye that rolled around its socket according to its own gravity. Sometimes that Pig Eye spins around so that you look at his face and there sits the whole moon in place of his eyeball and up in the sky another moon, a screen door swings open and a woman stands there washing dishes except they ain't dishes she's washing really they're little babies all the drowned babies of the world she's washing the mud out of their eyes raking the sticks and twigs from their mouths rubbing their little blue limbs to give them some comfort except that it ain't comfort she brings them drowned babies who only want to lay still in their death suits and rot for all the years it takes them to get out of this godforsaken place place place of gutting knives it ain't nobody's mama standing there in the moon's kitchen which really if you take away the linoleum and the formica and the matching dishrags and the milk yellow light could be a tub and a spigot and a plank hear her schhhickk schhhhickk schhhickkk scraping not each of the dead drowned babies but rather little perch or sunfish yanked out of the pond that very morning or maybe catfish no scales but thick greeny skin and they bark little barks of pain of protest of fuck you you knife-wielding fucker until you nail their heads to the plank and with your sacred pliers all slick with purpose and under the tutelage of black ice learn the bootlick dance and peel back peel away skin hammer nail and blood and now their eyes purple crocuses praying up through wet loam a blackbird working against a headwind its epaulettes on fire and all their milk teeth spill pell-mell from the choked side ditches of their mouths like a murder of bleached crows refusing flight flight flood light flood fled flood floyd floyd who the fuck is screaming floyd and why and why?

'Floyd! Floyd! What you doing Floyd?'

Benny woke, a jarring shift.

'Floyd?'

Someone pounded on the window, the very window Benny's face lay pressed against.

'What are you doing, Floyd? Where's your wife?'

Benny, through the windshield, through the fog of exhaustion, saw a yellow car, a Plymouth Valiant, parked in front of him, and the interstate highway stretching out ahead through the Georgia landscape. He must've pulled over and fallen asleep.

'Floyd? It's me Floyd.'

Who the fuck was this lunatic? Then Benny remembered. It was that goddamn man with the stob and his catalytic eunuch.

'Where's your wife, Floyd? You Ok? You hungry?'

Benny cranked the van, jammed the shift lever into drive, and, turning sharp to miss the Plymouth, pulled away so quickly that he knocked Floyd to the ground.

Some people go their entire lives not knowing, or caring, or even wondering why they do the things they do. They simply do. They do things without the benefit of hindsight or foresight, and as a result, drift aimlessly – sometimes providentially, more often than not haplessly –

from birth to death without ever learning to see what lies ahead, and, more importantly, their role in that future. Who's to say whether Benny could've predicted his current predicament? And who could know whether, all those months ago, if he'd not clung so tightly to his secret, whether things would've turned out differently? Too, it would be impossible to judge whether or not, even with foresight, even knowing clearly all that would happen in his future if he chose to keep the secret, that Benny would've made a different decision. Who could know? Who's to say?

All those grand ideals have little bearing on the moment, in the moment. And most certainly, it's not what Benny thought about as he drove the length of a dirt road, a familiar dirt road, one he'd traveled once before, until it came to an end where the Big and Little Toe Rivers converged, and across the expanse of water the Bard's Communication tower jutted heavenward, and bore its full weight toward hell. Benny had no plan when he pulled the video camera, the tapes, the backpack, and the drowned girl's clothes from beneath the bed in the back of his pumpkin-colored van, lugged them out to the water's edge. And not until he had the video camera on its tripod – as close as he could remember to where he'd found it – and his eye to the viewfinder, looking across the water, looking for the tower, did he realize he was trying to find that tower.

Benny put all but one of the videotapes into the backpack. The final tape, the one in the camera when it last sat by the river all those months ago, Benny put back it into the camera and clicked it home. He lay the backpack beneath the legs of the tripod, fished the business card from his pocket, and lay it on the pack:

Claxton Looms Apartments
3 Shuttlecock Court
Rebecca Hinkey, Resident Manager

As for the drowned girl's clothes – the panties, the shirt, the shorts – Benny pressed each to his face, inhaled deeply, then tossed them to the ground. He put the milk crate back in the van, and returned to the camera, to fumble with the *on* button.

Nov 11, 2001   **● ● ● Rec**
3:37 p.m.

It clicked and whirred until he brought the tower into focus.

Redemption? Or retribution? What is it that Benny sought? No way of knowing. He stood there, by the water, and thought, without much in the way of clarity, about his options. The Toe Rivers offered little resistance, but kept their cold opinions to themselves. Benny knelt on the bank, painfully conscious of the camera's eye at his back. It seemed easy, on film anyway, the way the river welcomed Jenna. The way she allowed herself to be taken in. Benny stood. There, across the water, the familiar. The tower. Benny Poteat had seen a lot of things in his life. Most of those, the ones that he held to, and learned from, he'd seen from way up high.

When he stepped out of the camera's field of vision, it kept filming. With infinite patience, it captured, chronicled, without judgment, the life that passed before it: the flat rivers, peaceful now as they flowed toward winter, and in the distance, the hard vertical line made by the radio tower, and its angled guy wires barely visible. The camera, doubly masterful, held, too, the sounds that life offered it from moment to moment. The opening and closing of a door, the door of a vehicle, one would assume, the door of a pumpkin-colored van. The turn of an ignition, the revolution of a crankshaft, the corresponding up down slap of pistons. And the fading crunch of tires on gravel as the vehicle pulls out of sound. Benny drove away. The dirt road stretched a mile, maybe more. At its end, there would be two options. The camera would only acknowledge one. The camera only allowed for one. The camera . . . the camera . . .

BATTERY TOO LOW!
BATTERY TOO LOW!